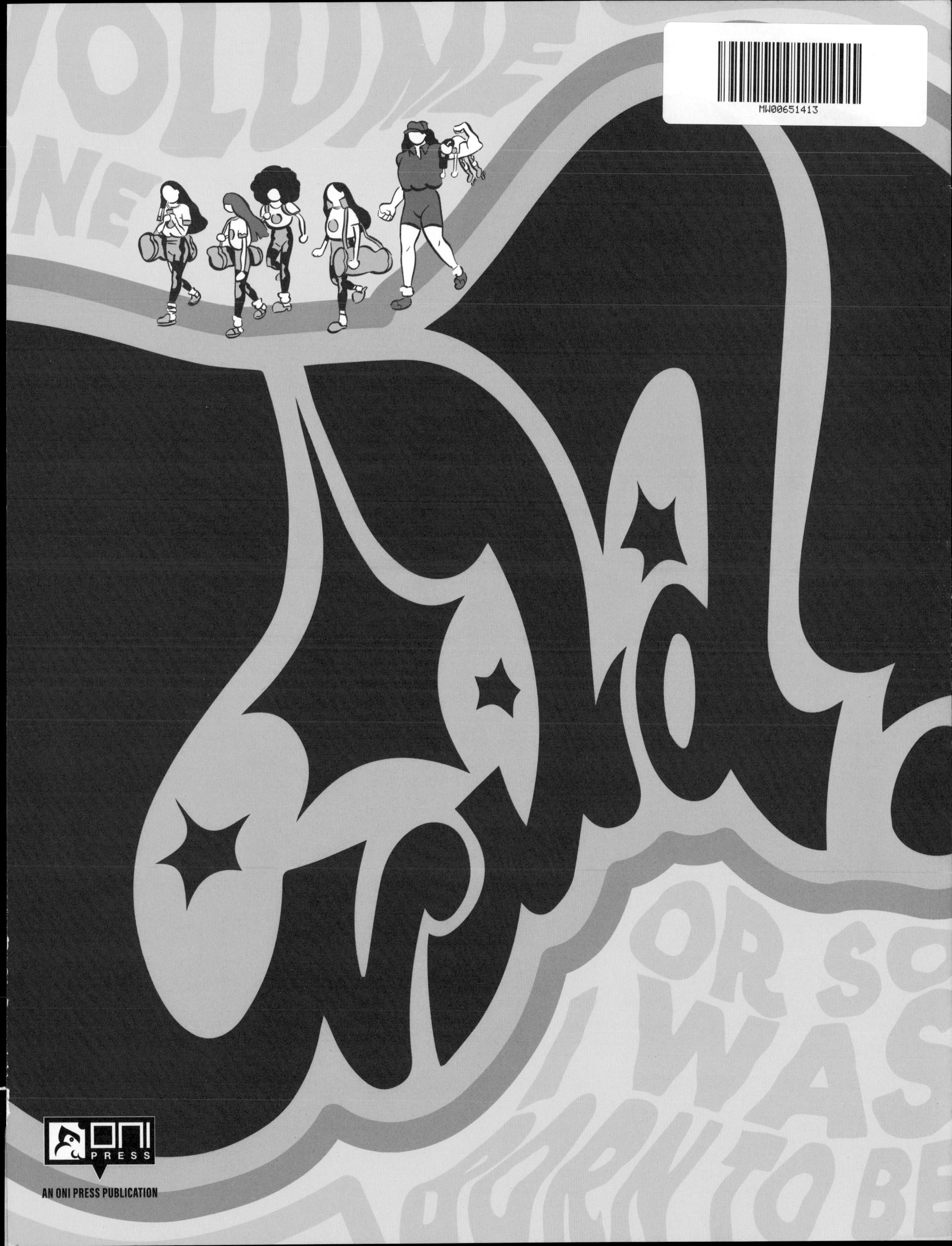

AN ONI PRESS PUBLICATION

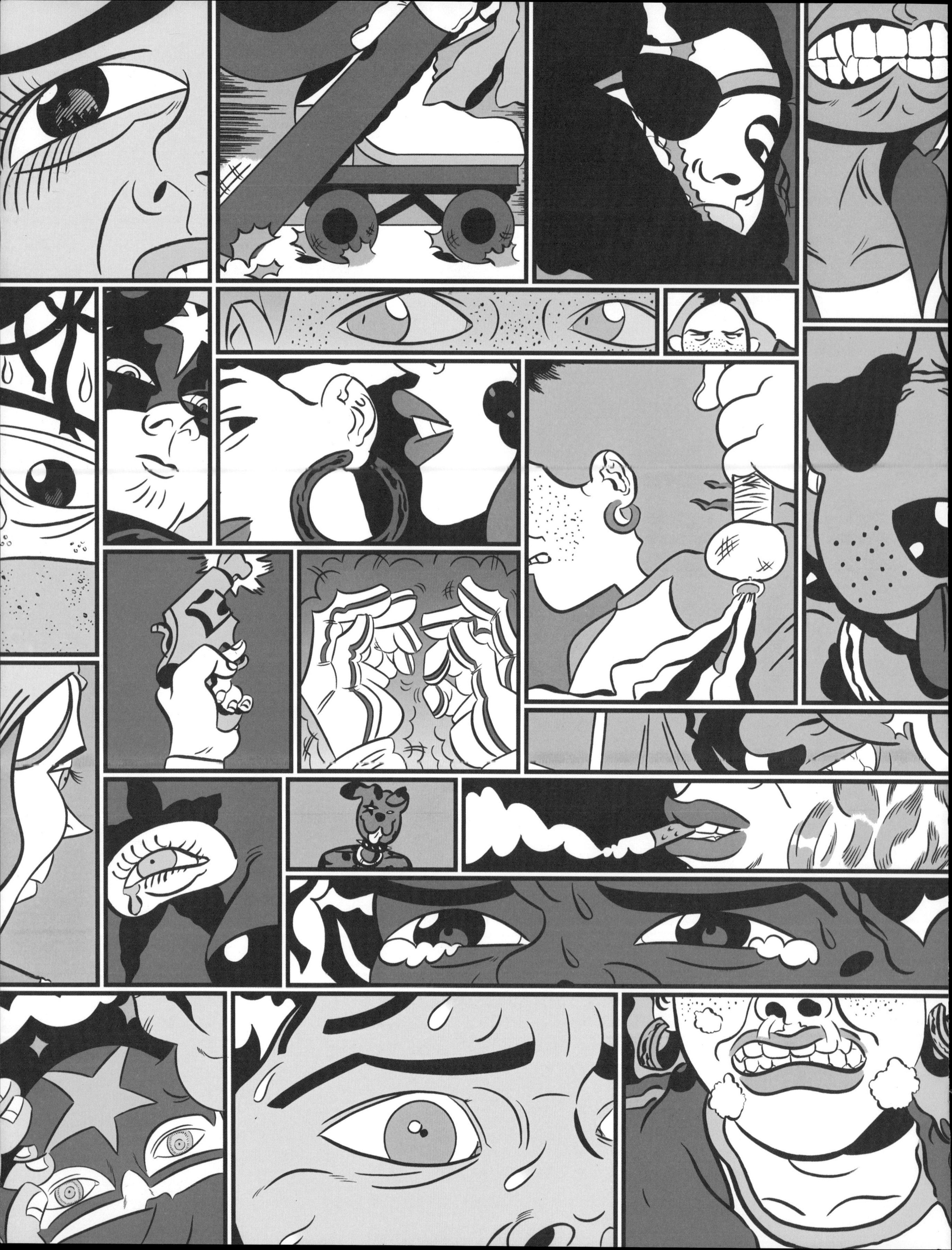

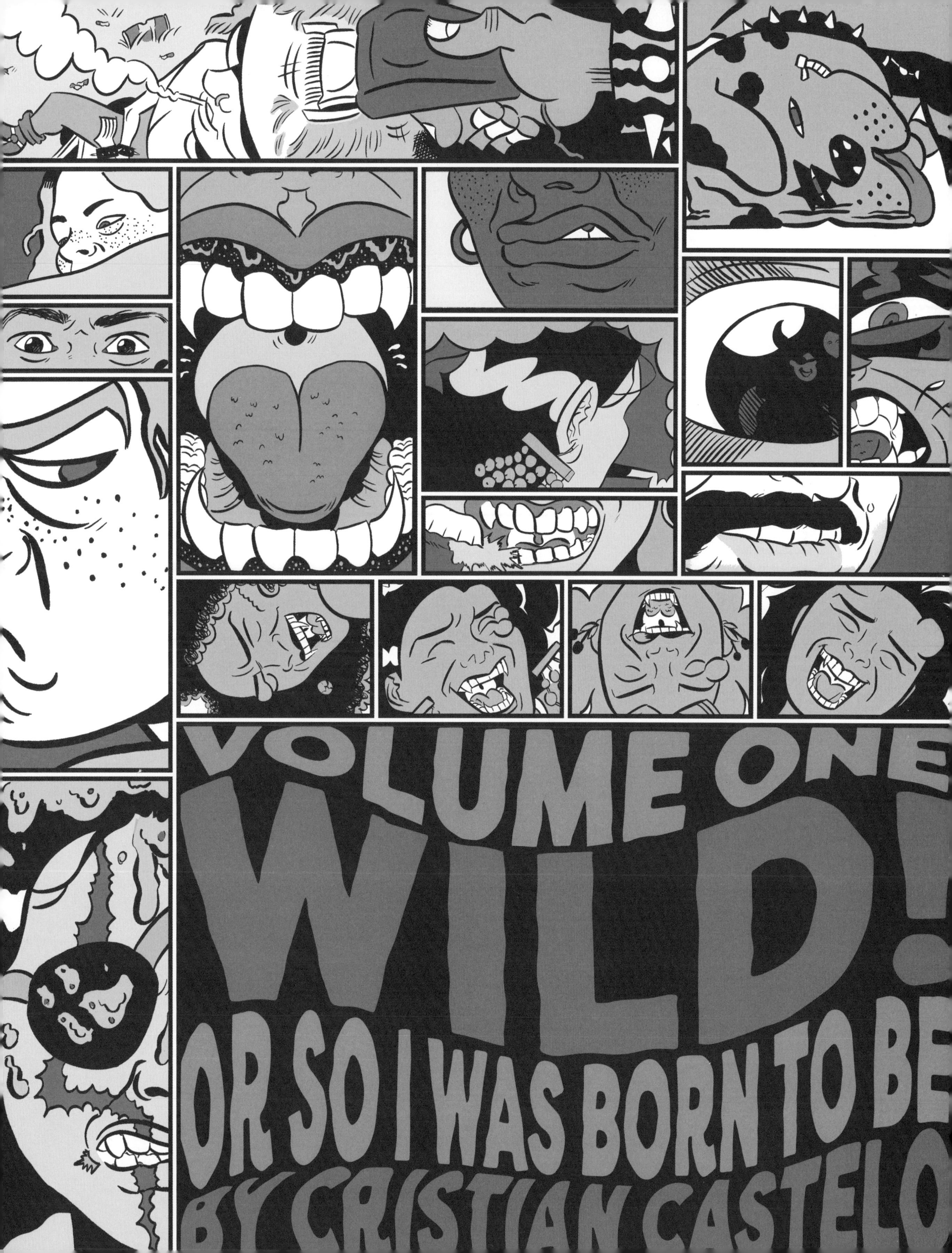
VOLUME ONE
WILD!
OR SO I WAS BORN TO BE
BY CRISTIAN CASTELO

EDITED BY **ZACK SOTO**
DESIGNED BY **CAREY HALL**
COVER DESIGN BY **CRISTIAN CASTELO**
LETTERING FONT CREATED BY **FRANÇOIS VIGNEAULT**

 Published by Oni-Lion Forge Publishing Group, LLC.
1319 SE Martin Luther King Jr. Blvd. Suite 240 Portland, OR 97214

JAMES LUCAS JONES president & publisher
CHARLIE CHU e.v.p. of creative & business dev.
STEVE ELLIS s.v.p. of games & operations
ALEX SEGURA s.v.p. of marketing & sales
MICHELLE NGUYEN associate publisher
BRAD ROOKS director of operations
KATIE SAINZ director of marketing
TARA LEHMANN publicity director
HENRY BARAJAS sales manager
HOLLY AITCHISON consumer marketing manager
LYDIA NGUYEN marketing intern
TROY LOOK director of design & production
ANGIE KNOWLES production manager
CAREY HALL graphic designer
SARAH ROCKWELL graphic designer
HILARY THOMPSON graphic designer
VINCENT KUKUA digital prepress technician
CHRIS CERASI managing editor
JASMINE AMIRI senior editor
AMANDA MEADOWS senior editor
BESS PALLARES editor
DESIREE RODRIGUEZ editor
GRACE SCHEIPETER editor
ZACK SOTO editor
GABRIEL GRANILLO editorial assistant
BEN EISNER game developer
SARA HARDING entertainment executive assistant
JUNG LEE logistics coordinator
KUIAN KELLUM warehouse assistant

JOE NOZEMACK publisher emeritus

onipress.com **f** facebook.com/onipress
y twitter.com/onipress **◙** instagram.com/onipress

FIRST EDITION NOVEMBER 2022 | **ISBN** 978-1-63715-093-1 | **EISBN** 978-1-63715-113-6
PRINTED IN CHINA | **LIBRARY OF CONGRESS CONTROL NUMBER** 2022933046
1 2 3 4 5 6 7 8 9 10

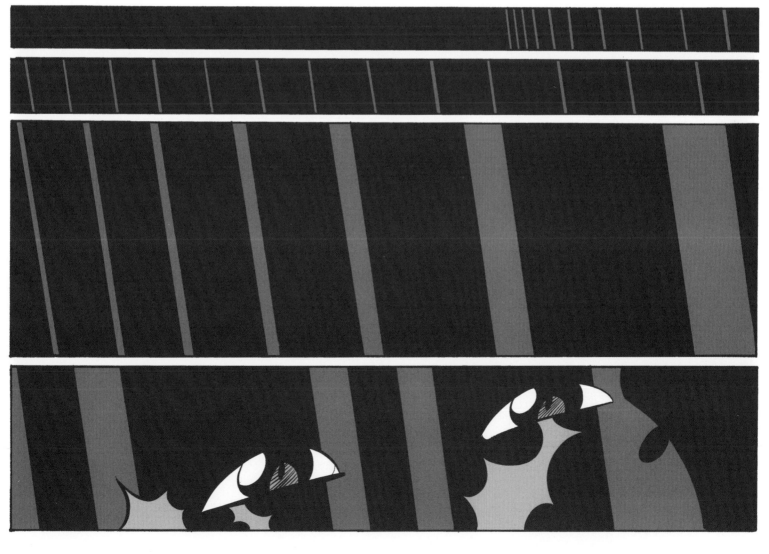

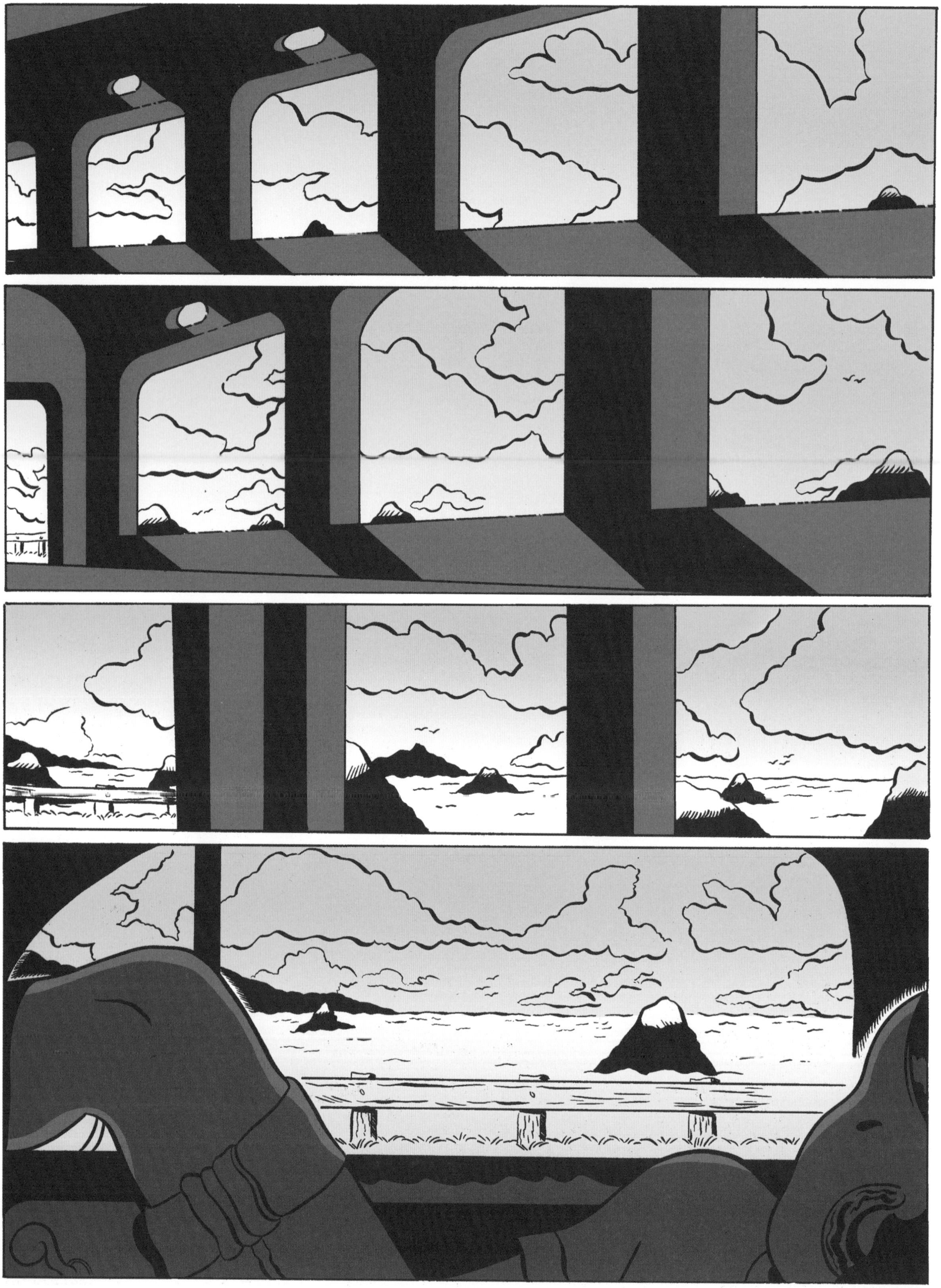

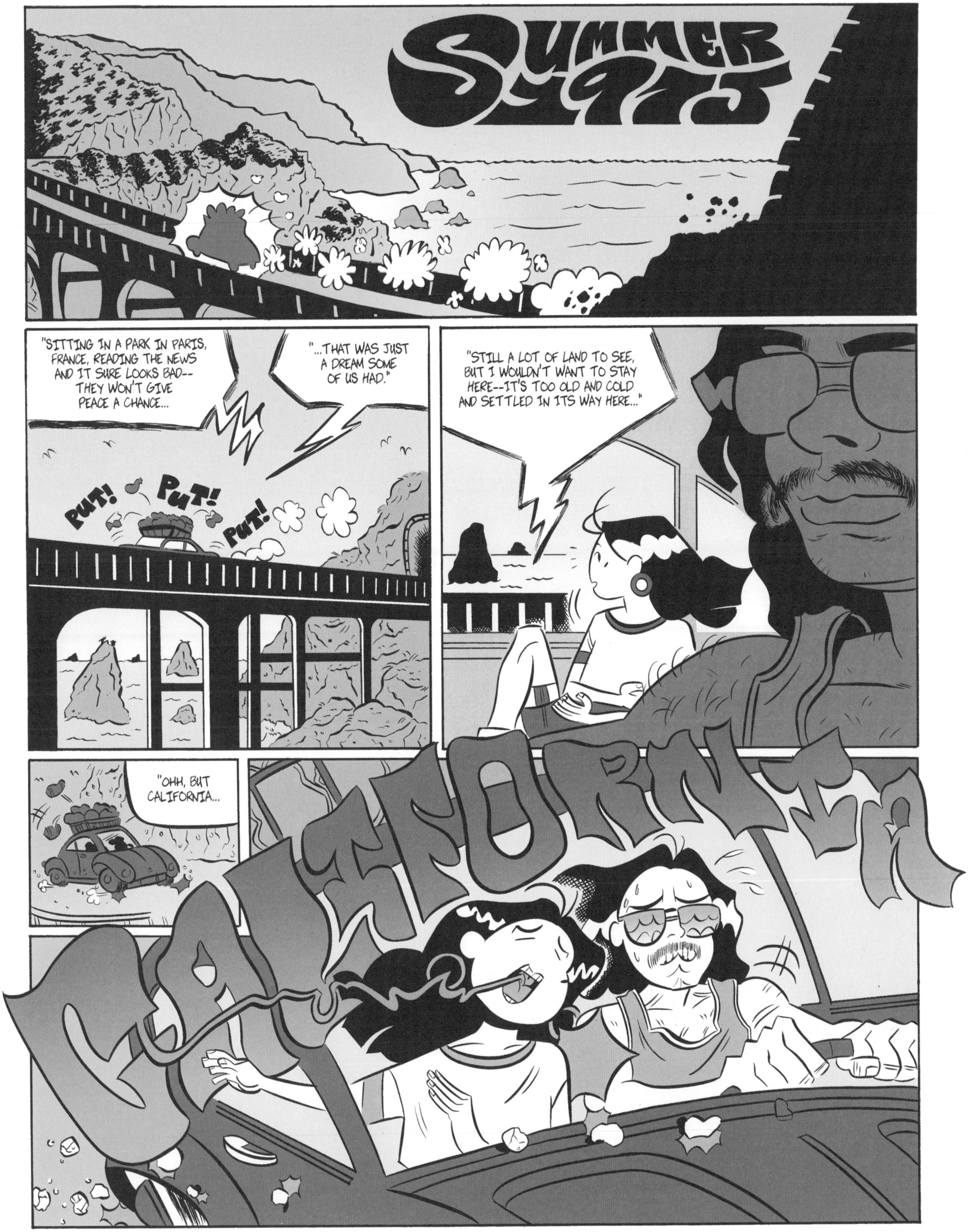
SUMMER 1975
"SITTING IN A PARK IN PARIS, FRANCE, READING THE NEWS AND IT SURE LOOKS BAD-- THEY WON'T GIVE PEACE A CHANCE...
"...THAT WAS JUST A DREAM SOME OF US HAD."
PUT! PUT! PUT!
"STILL A LOT OF LAND TO SEE, BUT I WOULDN'T WANT TO STAY HERE--IT'S TOO OLD AND COLD AND SETTLED IN ITS WAY HERE..."
"OHH, BUT CALIFORNIA...
CALIFORNIA

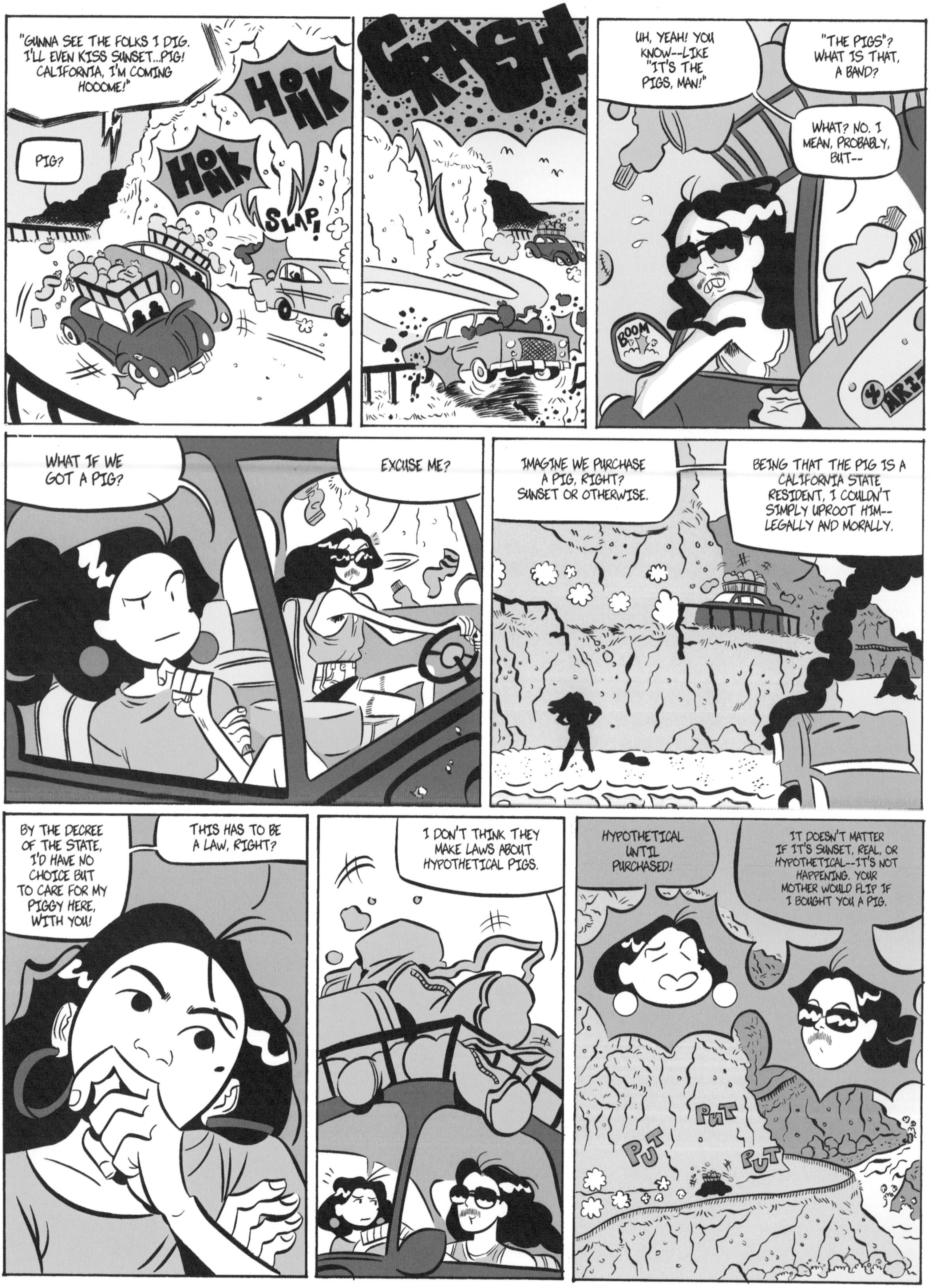
"GUNNA SEE THE FOLKS I DIG. I'LL EVEN KISS SUNSET...PIG! CALIFORNIA, I'M COMING HOOOME!"
PIG?
HONK
HONK
SLAP!
CRASH!
UH, YEAH! YOU KNOW--LIKE "IT'S THE PIGS, MAN!"
"THE PIGS"? WHAT IS THAT, A BAND?
WHAT? NO. I MEAN, PROBABLY, BUT--
BOOM
WHAT IF WE GOT A PIG?
EXCUSE ME?
IMAGINE WE PURCHASE A PIG, RIGHT? SUNSET OR OTHERWISE.
BEING THAT THE PIG IS A CALIFORNIA STATE RESIDENT, I COULDN'T SIMPLY UPROOT HIM--LEGALLY AND MORALLY.
BY THE DECREE OF THE STATE, I'D HAVE NO CHOICE BUT TO CARE FOR MY PIGGY HERE, WITH YOU!
THIS HAS TO BE A LAW, RIGHT?
I DON'T THINK THEY MAKE LAWS ABOUT HYPOTHETICAL PIGS.
HYPOTHETICAL UNTIL PURCHASED!
IT DOESN'T MATTER IF IT'S SUNSET, REAL, OR HYPOTHETICAL--IT'S NOT HAPPENING. YOUR MOTHER WOULD FLIP IF I BOUGHT YOU A PIG.
PUT
PUT
PUT

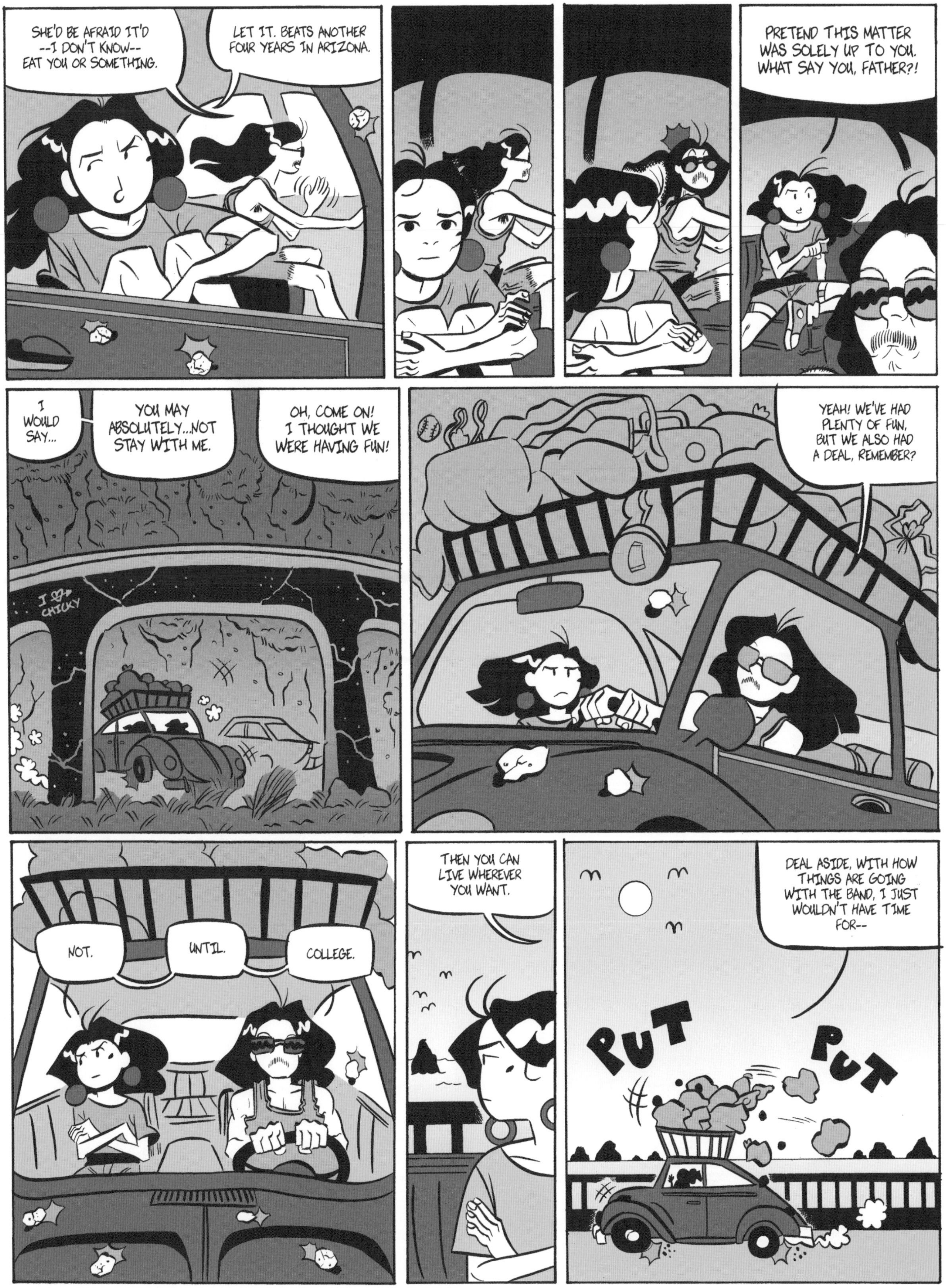
SHE'D BE AFRAID IT'D --I DON'T KNOW-- EAT YOU OR SOMETHING.
LET IT. BEATS ANOTHER FOUR YEARS IN ARIZONA.
PRETEND THIS MATTER WAS SOLELY UP TO YOU. WHAT SAY YOU, FATHER?!
I WOULD SAY...
YOU MAY ABSOLUTELY...NOT STAY WITH ME.
OH, COME ON! I THOUGHT WE WERE HAVING FUN!
I ♥ CHICKY
YEAH! WE'VE HAD PLENTY OF FUN, BUT WE ALSO HAD A DEAL, REMEMBER?
NOT.
UNTIL.
COLLEGE.
THEN YOU CAN LIVE WHEREVER YOU WANT.
DEAL ASIDE, WITH HOW THINGS ARE GOING WITH THE BAND, I JUST WOULDN'T HAVE TIME FOR--
PUT
PUT

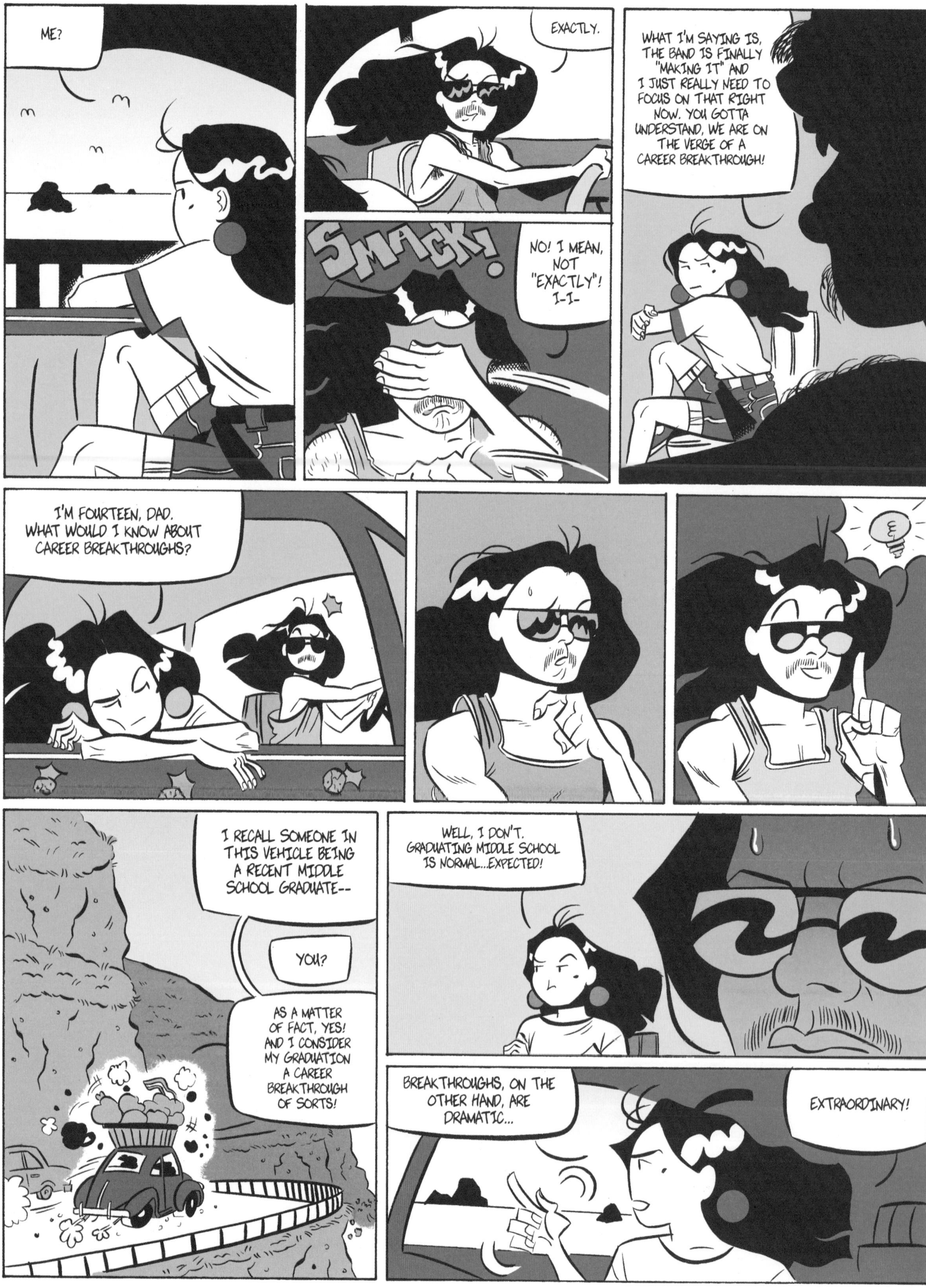
ME?
EXACTLY.
WHAT I'M SAYING IS, THE BAND IS FINALLY "MAKING IT" AND I JUST REALLY NEED TO FOCUS ON THAT RIGHT NOW. YOU GOTTA UNDERSTAND, WE ARE ON THE VERGE OF A CAREER BREAKTHROUGH!
SMACK!
NO! I MEAN, NOT "EXACTLY"! I-I-
I'M FOURTEEN, DAD. WHAT WOULD I KNOW ABOUT CAREER BREAKTHROUGHS?
I RECALL SOMEONE IN THIS VEHICLE BEING A RECENT MIDDLE SCHOOL GRADUATE--
YOU?
AS A MATTER OF FACT, YES! AND I CONSIDER MY GRADUATION A CAREER BREAKTHROUGH OF SORTS!
WELL, I DON'T. GRADUATING MIDDLE SCHOOL IS NORMAL...EXPECTED!
BREAKTHROUGHS, ON THE OTHER HAND, ARE DRAMATIC...
EXTRAORDINARY!

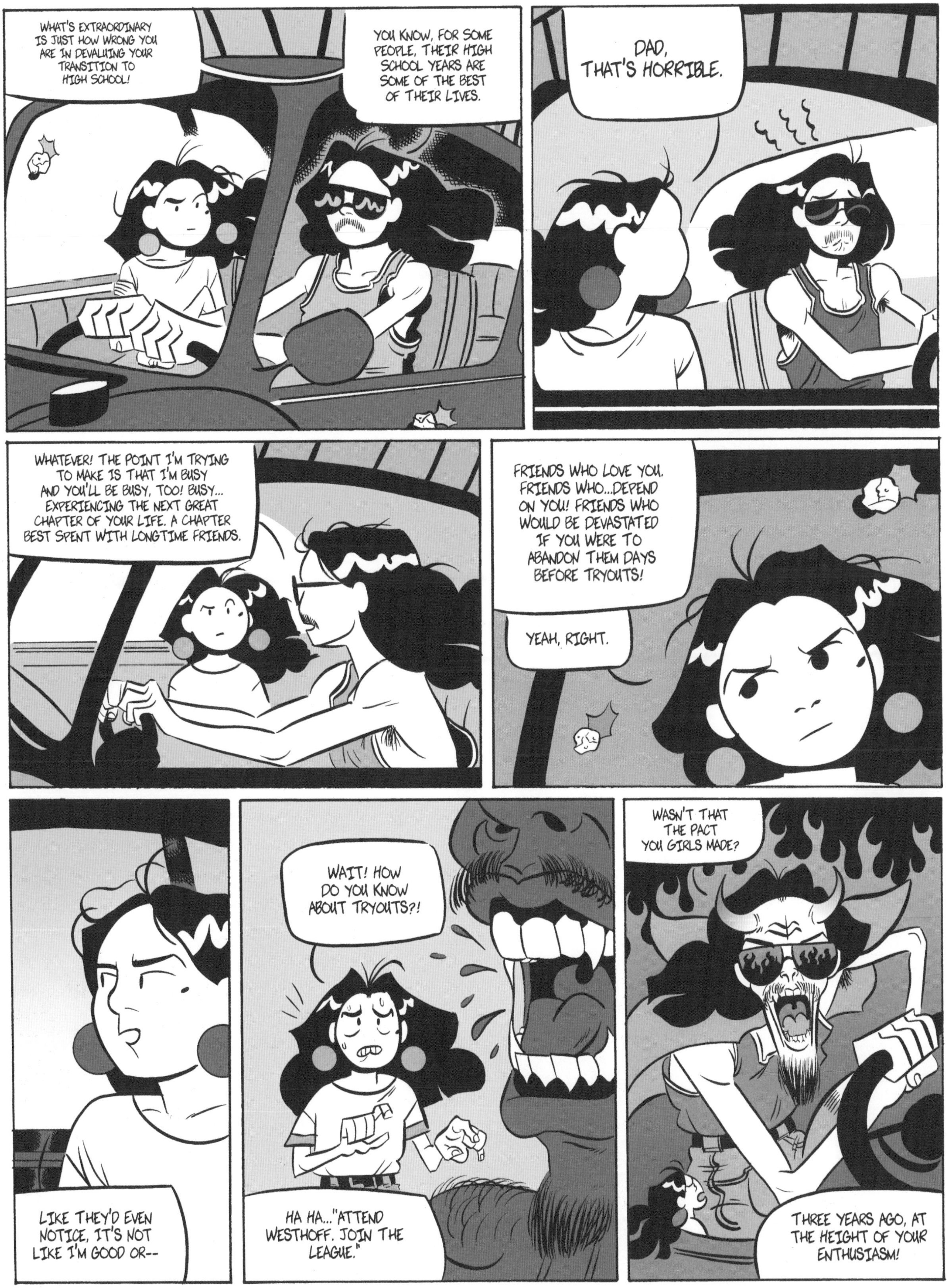
WHAT'S EXTRAORDINARY IS JUST HOW WRONG YOU ARE IN DEVALUING YOUR TRANSITION TO HIGH SCHOOL!
YOU KNOW, FOR SOME PEOPLE, THEIR HIGH SCHOOL YEARS ARE SOME OF THE BEST OF THEIR LIVES.
DAD, THAT'S HORRIBLE.
WHATEVER! THE POINT I'M TRYING TO MAKE IS THAT I'M BUSY AND YOU'LL BE BUSY, TOO! BUSY... EXPERIENCING THE NEXT GREAT CHAPTER OF YOUR LIFE. A CHAPTER BEST SPENT WITH LONGTIME FRIENDS.
FRIENDS WHO LOVE YOU. FRIENDS WHO...DEPEND ON YOU! FRIENDS WHO WOULD BE DEVASTATED IF YOU WERE TO ABANDON THEM DAYS BEFORE TRYOUTS!
YEAH, RIGHT.
LIKE THEY'D EVEN NOTICE, IT'S NOT LIKE I'M GOOD OR--
WAIT! HOW DO YOU KNOW ABOUT TRYOUTS?!
HA HA..."ATTEND WESTHOFF. JOIN THE LEAGUE."
WASN'T THAT THE PACT YOU GIRLS MADE?
THREE YEARS AGO, AT THE HEIGHT OF YOUR ENTHUSIASM!

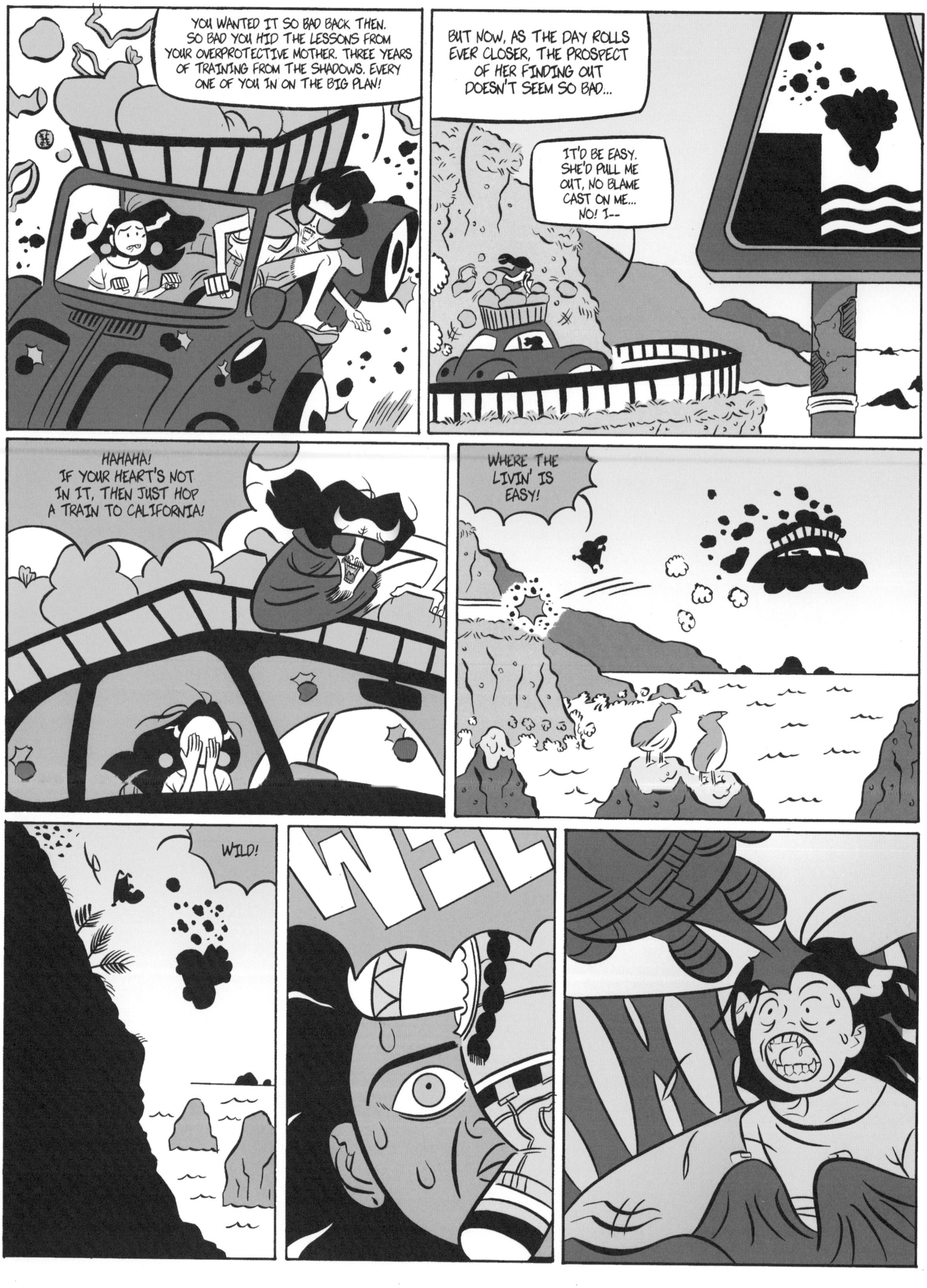
YOU WANTED IT SO BAD BACK THEN. SO BAD YOU HID THE LESSONS FROM YOUR OVERPROTECTIVE MOTHER. THREE YEARS OF TRAINING FROM THE SHADOWS. EVERY ONE OF YOU IN ON THE BIG PLAN!
BUT NOW, AS THE DAY ROLLS EVER CLOSER, THE PROSPECT OF HER FINDING OUT DOESN'T SEEM SO BAD...
IT'D BE EASY. SHE'D PULL ME OUT, NO BLAME CAST ON ME... NO! I--
HAHAHA! IF YOUR HEART'S NOT IN IT, THEN JUST HOP A TRAIN TO CALIFORNIA!
WHERE THE LIVIN' IS EASY!
WILD!

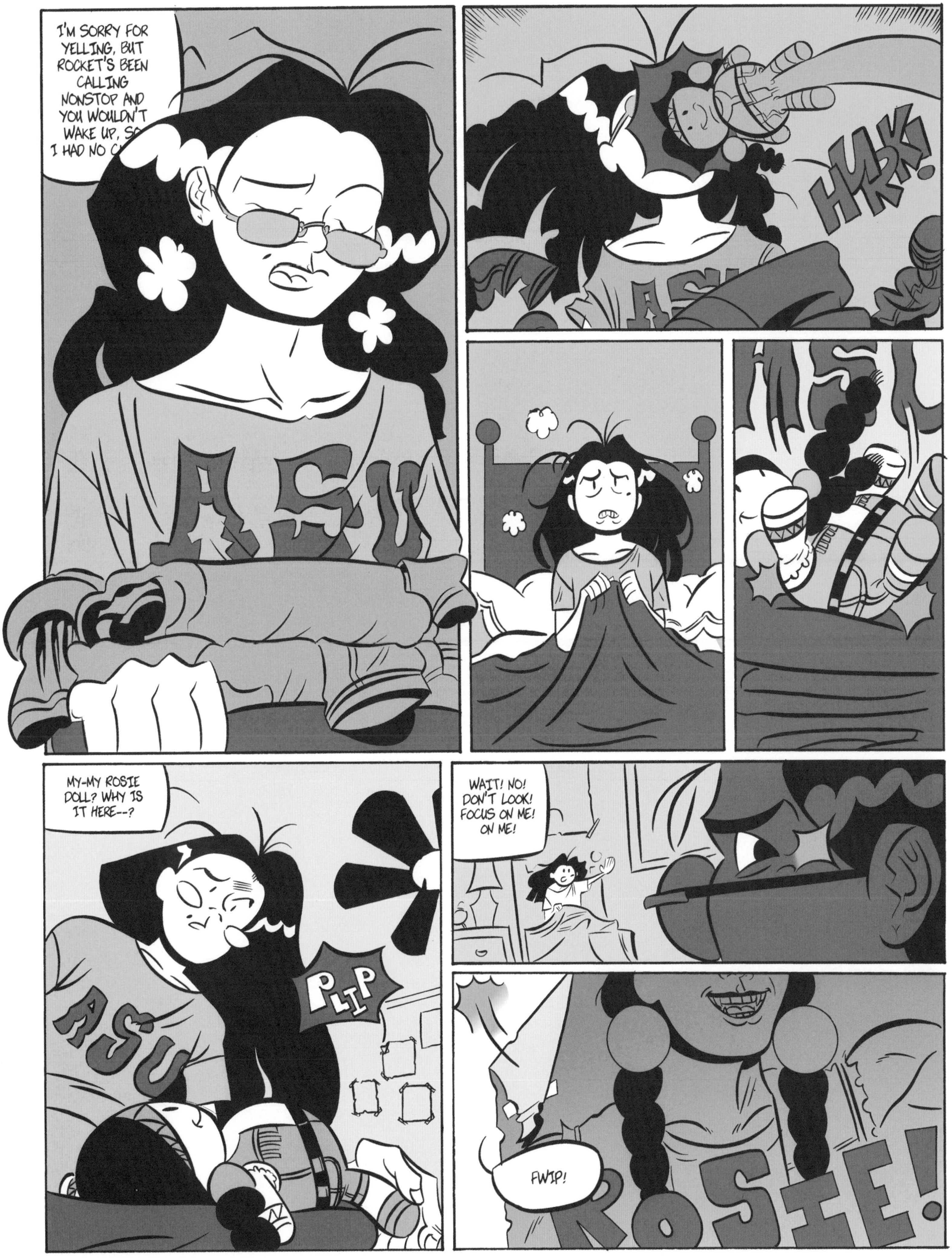
I'M SORRY FOR YELLING, BUT ROCKET'S BEEN CALLING NONSTOP AND YOU WOULDN'T WAKE UP, SO I HAD NO C...
ASU
HURK!
ASU
MY-MY ROSIE DOLL? WHY IS IT HERE--?
PLIP
ASU
WAIT! NO! DON'T LOOK! FOCUS ON ME! ON ME!
FWIP!
ROSIE!

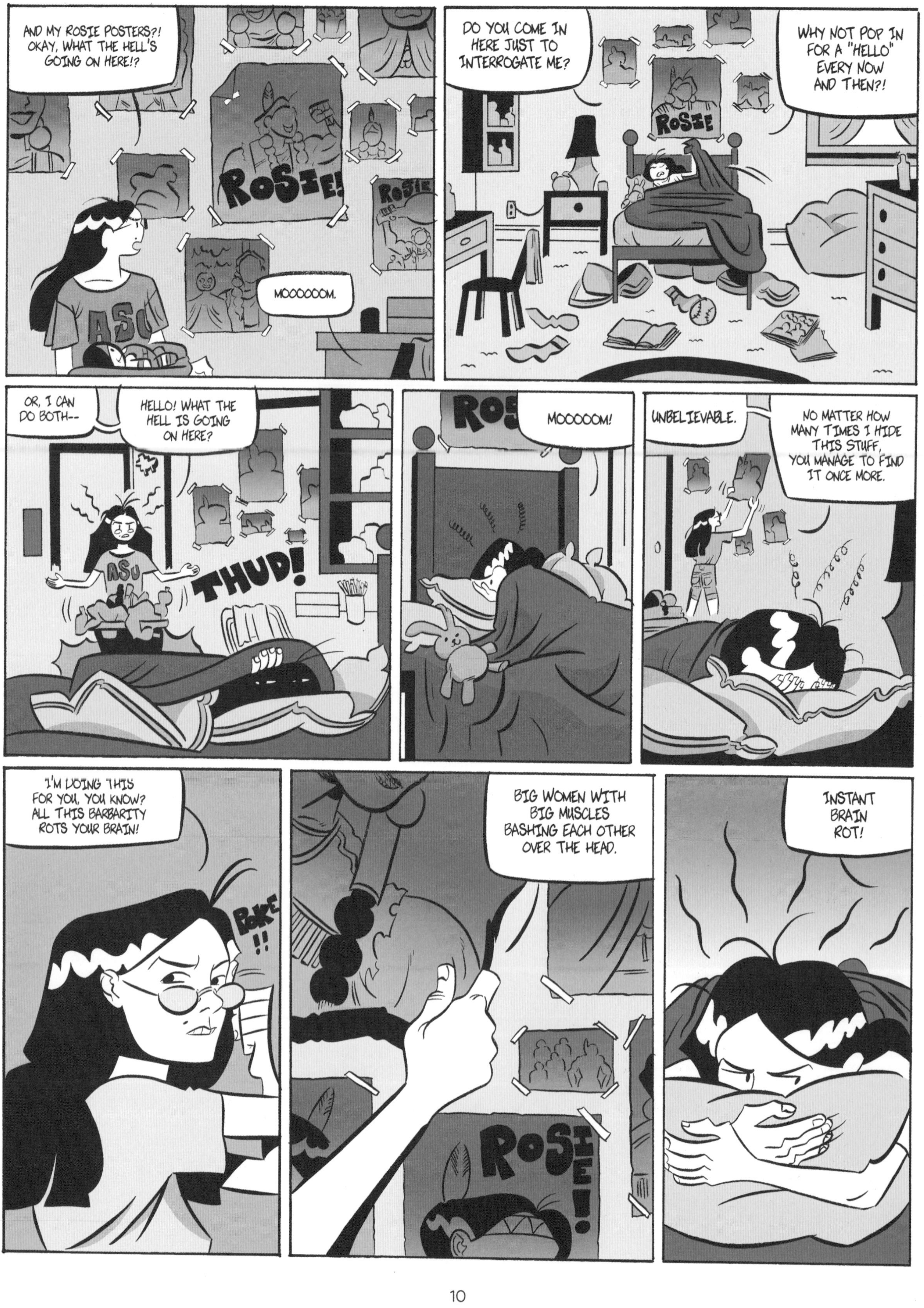
AND MY ROSIE POSTERS?! OKAY, WHAT THE HELL'S GOING ON HERE!?
ROSIE!
ROSIE
MOOOOOOM.
DO YOU COME IN HERE JUST TO INTERROGATE ME?
WHY NOT POP IN FOR A "HELLO" EVERY NOW AND THEN?!
ROSIE
OR, I CAN DO BOTH--
HELLO! WHAT THE HELL IS GOING ON HERE?
THUD!
MOOOOOM!
UNBELIEVABLE.
NO MATTER HOW MANY TIMES I HIDE THIS STUFF, YOU MANAGE TO FIND IT ONCE MORE.
I'M DOING THIS FOR YOU, YOU KNOW? ALL THIS BARBARITY ROTS YOUR BRAIN!
POKE !!
BIG WOMEN WITH BIG MUSCLES BASHING EACH OTHER OVER THE HEAD.
ROSIE!
INSTANT BRAIN ROT!

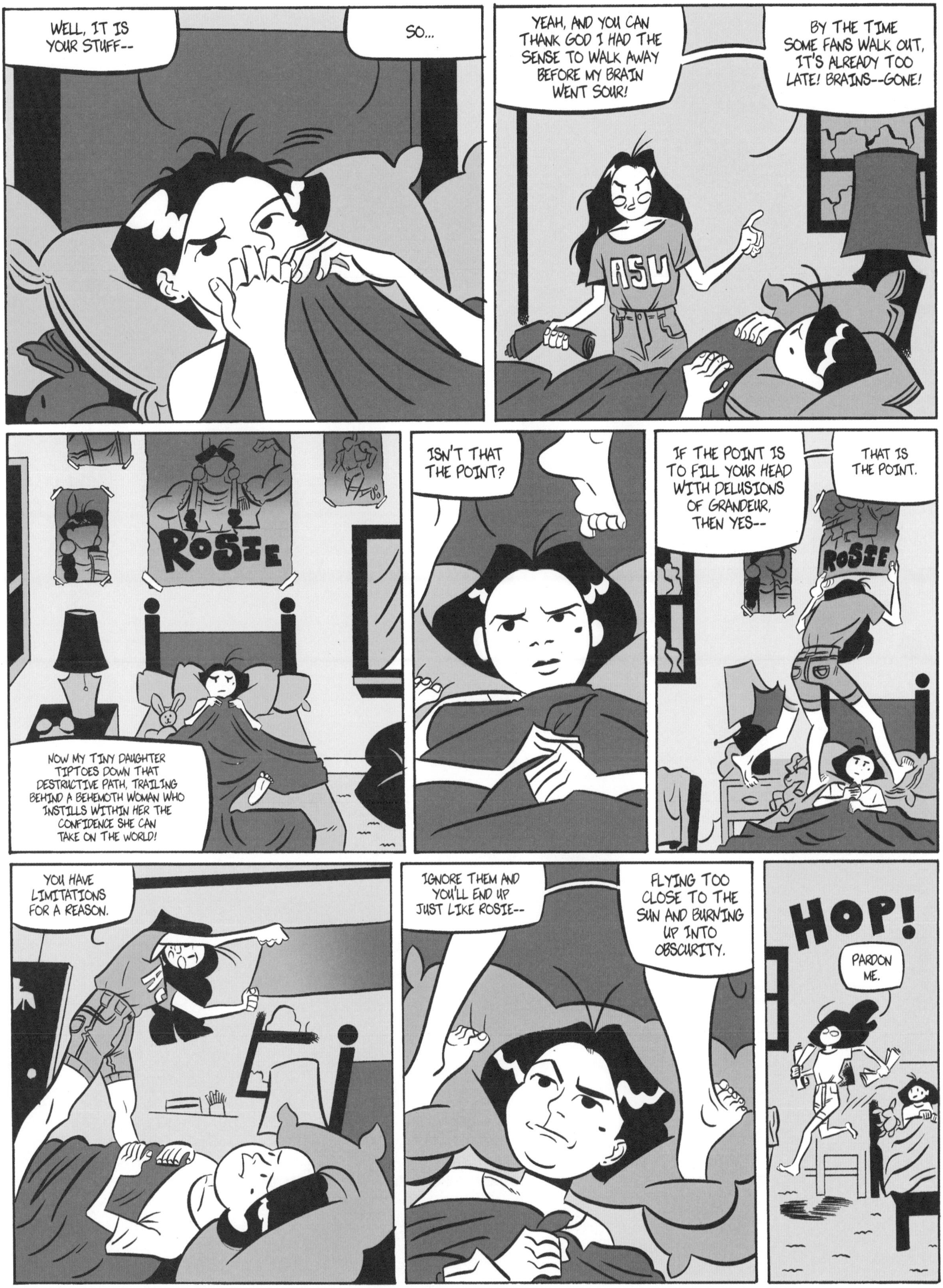

WELL, IT IS YOUR STUFF--
SO...
YEAH, AND YOU CAN THANK GOD I HAD THE SENSE TO WALK AWAY BEFORE MY BRAIN WENT SOUR!
BY THE TIME SOME FANS WALK OUT, IT'S ALREADY TOO LATE! BRAINS--GONE!
ASU
ROSIE
NOW MY TINY DAUGHTER TIPTOES DOWN THAT DESTRUCTIVE PATH, TRAILING BEHIND A BEHEMOTH WOMAN WHO INSTILLS WITHIN HER THE CONFIDENCE SHE CAN TAKE ON THE WORLD!
ISN'T THAT THE POINT?
IF THE POINT IS TO FILL YOUR HEAD WITH DELUSIONS OF GRANDEUR, THEN YES--
THAT IS THE POINT.
ROSIE
YOU HAVE LIMITATIONS FOR A REASON.
IGNORE THEM AND YOU'LL END UP JUST LIKE ROSIE--
FLYING TOO CLOSE TO THE SUN AND BURNING UP INTO OBSCURITY.
HOP!
PARDON ME.

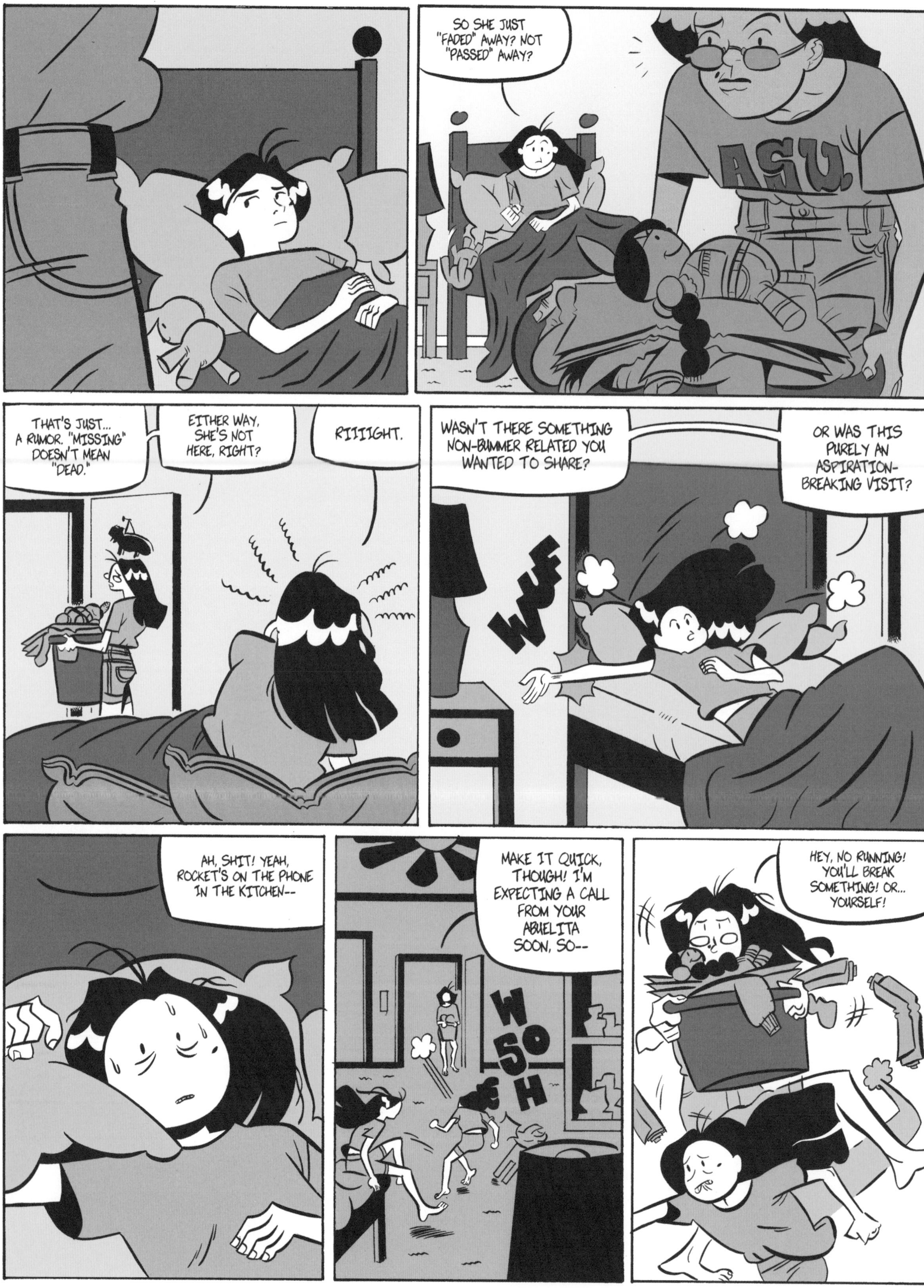
SO SHE JUST "FADED" AWAY? NOT "PASSED" AWAY?
ASU
THAT'S JUST... A RUMOR. "MISSING" DOESN'T MEAN "DEAD."
EITHER WAY, SHE'S NOT HERE, RIGHT?
RIIIIGHT.
WASN'T THERE SOMETHING NON-BUMMER RELATED YOU WANTED TO SHARE?
OR WAS THIS PURELY AN ASPIRATION-BREAKING VISIT?
WUF
AH, SHIT! YEAH, ROCKET'S ON THE PHONE IN THE KITCHEN--
MAKE IT QUICK, THOUGH! I'M EXPECTING A CALL FROM YOUR ABUELITA SOON, SO--
WOOSH
HEY, NO RUNNING! YOU'LL BREAK SOMETHING! OR... YOURSELF!

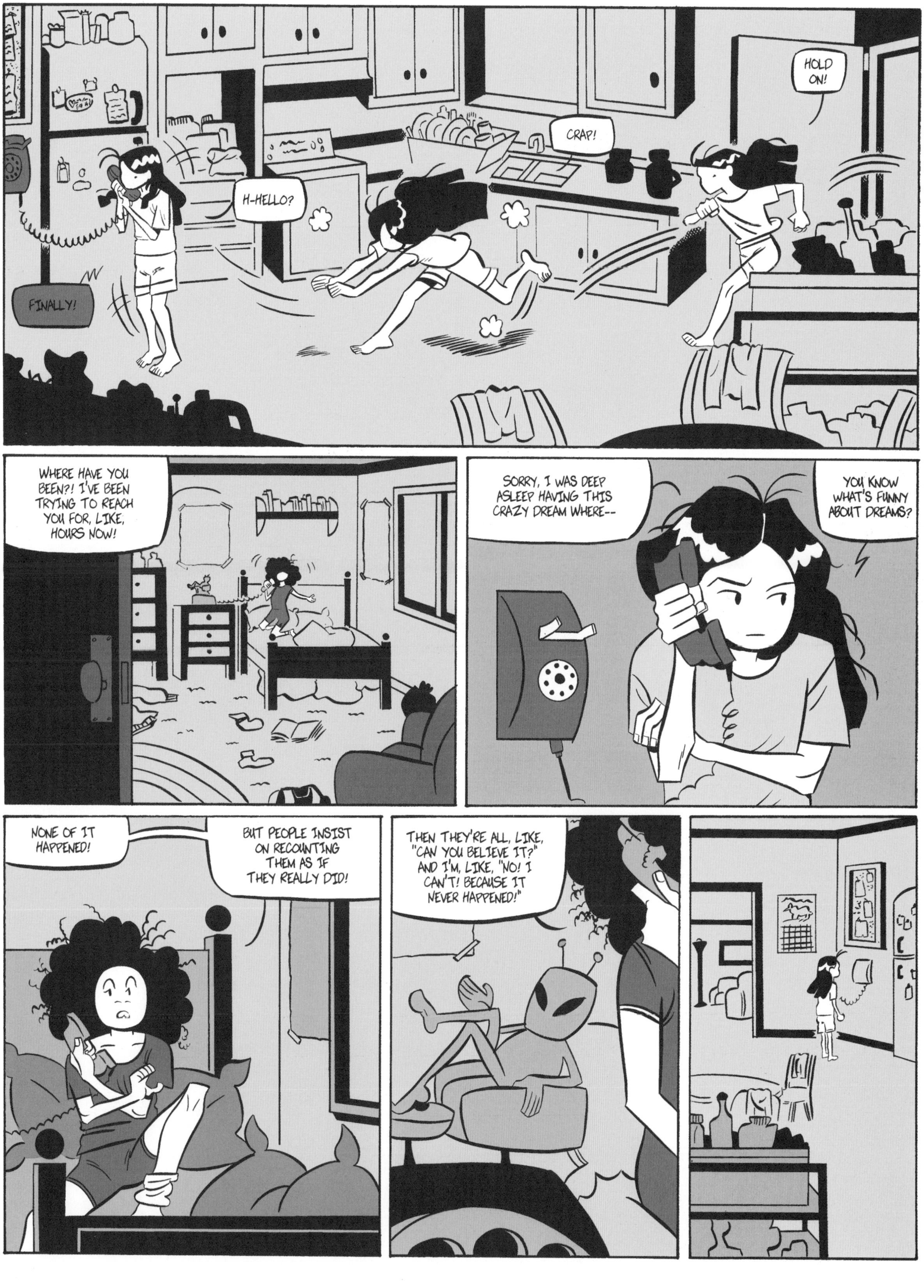
HOLD ON!
CRAP!
H-HELLO?
FINALLY!
WHERE HAVE YOU BEEN?! I'VE BEEN TRYING TO REACH YOU FOR, LIKE, HOURS NOW!
SORRY, I WAS DEEP ASLEEP HAVING THIS CRAZY DREAM WHERE--
YOU KNOW WHAT'S FUNNY ABOUT DREAMS?
NONE OF IT HAPPENED!
BUT PEOPLE INSIST ON RECOUNTING THEM AS IF THEY REALLY DID!
THEN THEY'RE ALL, LIKE, "CAN YOU BELIEVE IT?" AND I'M, LIKE, "NO! I CAN'T! BECAUSE IT NEVER HAPPENED!"

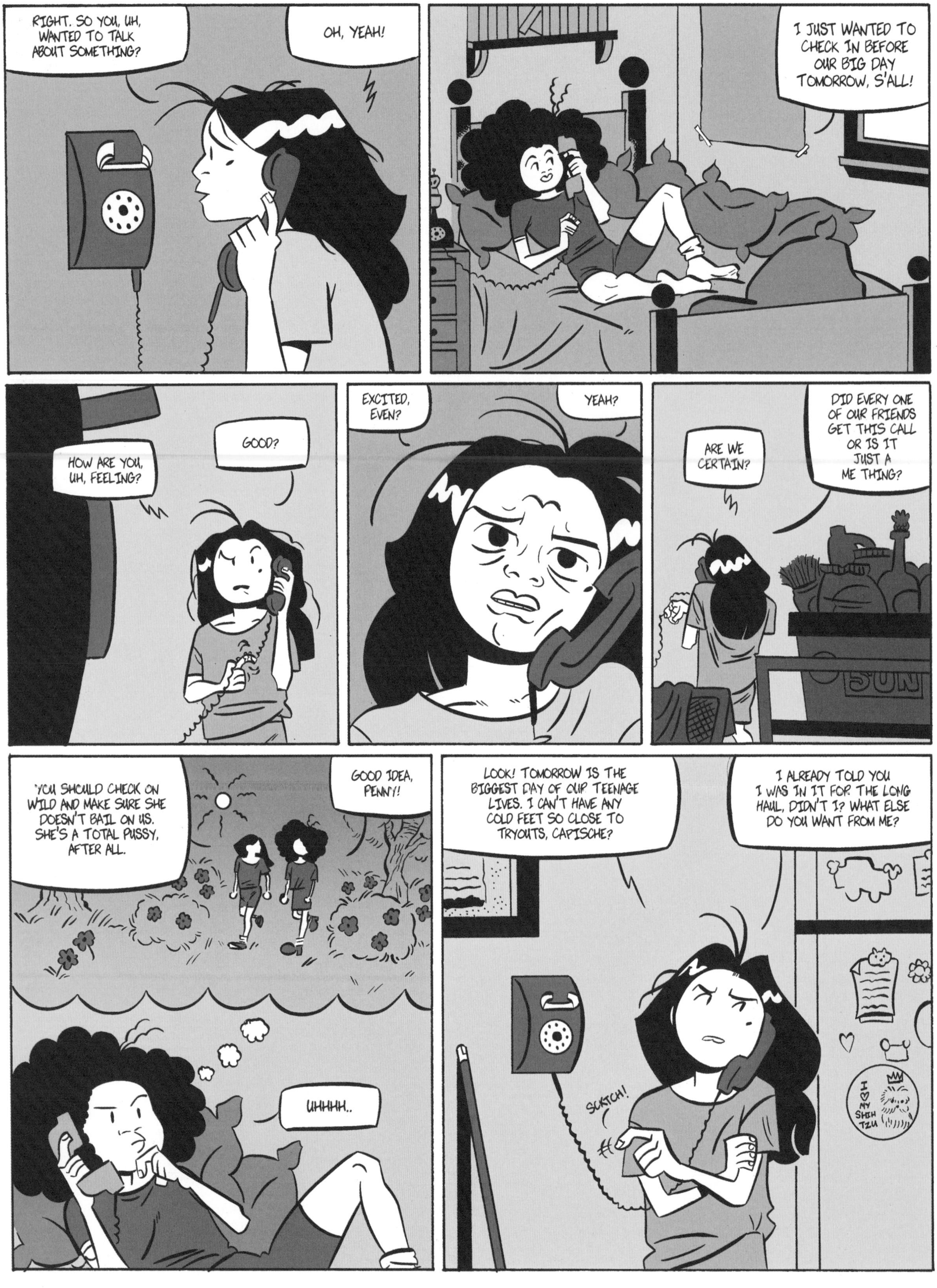

RIGHT. SO YOU, UH, WANTED TO TALK ABOUT SOMETHING?
OH, YEAH!
I JUST WANTED TO CHECK IN BEFORE OUR BIG DAY TOMORROW, S'ALL!
HOW ARE YOU, UH, FEELING?
GOOD?
EXCITED, EVEN?
YEAH?
ARE WE CERTAIN?
DID EVERY ONE OF OUR FRIENDS GET THIS CALL OR IS IT JUST A ME THING?
SUN
"YOU SHOULD CHECK ON WILD AND MAKE SURE SHE DOESN'T BAIL ON US. SHE'S A TOTAL PUSSY, AFTER ALL.
GOOD IDEA, PENNY!
UHHHH..
LOOK! TOMORROW IS THE BIGGEST DAY OF OUR TEENAGE LIVES. I CAN'T HAVE ANY COLD FEET SO CLOSE TO TRYOUTS, CAPISCHE?
I ALREADY TOLD YOU I WAS IN IT FOR THE LONG HAUL, DIDN'T I? WHAT ELSE DO YOU WANT FROM ME?
SCRTCH!
I ♡ MY SHIH TZU

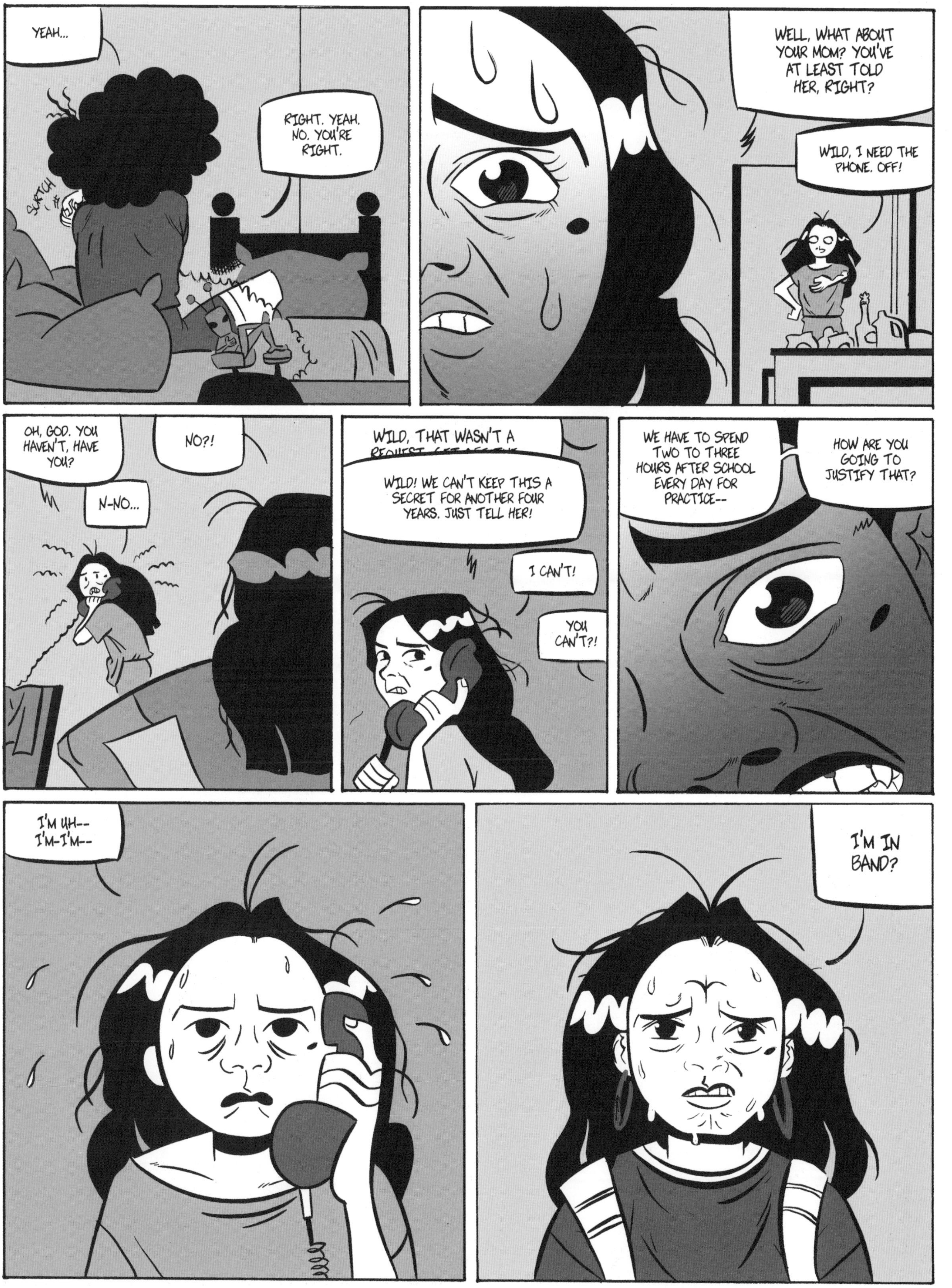
YEAH...
RIGHT. YEAH. NO. YOU'RE RIGHT.
WELL, WHAT ABOUT YOUR MOM? YOU'VE AT LEAST TOLD HER, RIGHT?
WILD, I NEED THE PHONE. OFF!
OH, GOD. YOU HAVEN'T, HAVE YOU?
NO?!
N-NO...
WILD, THAT WASN'T A
WILD! WE CAN'T KEEP THIS A SECRET FOR ANOTHER FOUR YEARS. JUST TELL HER!
I CAN'T!
YOU CAN'T?!
WE HAVE TO SPEND TWO TO THREE HOURS AFTER SCHOOL EVERY DAY FOR PRACTICE--
HOW ARE YOU GOING TO JUSTIFY THAT?
I'M UH-- I'M-I'M--
I'M IN BAND?

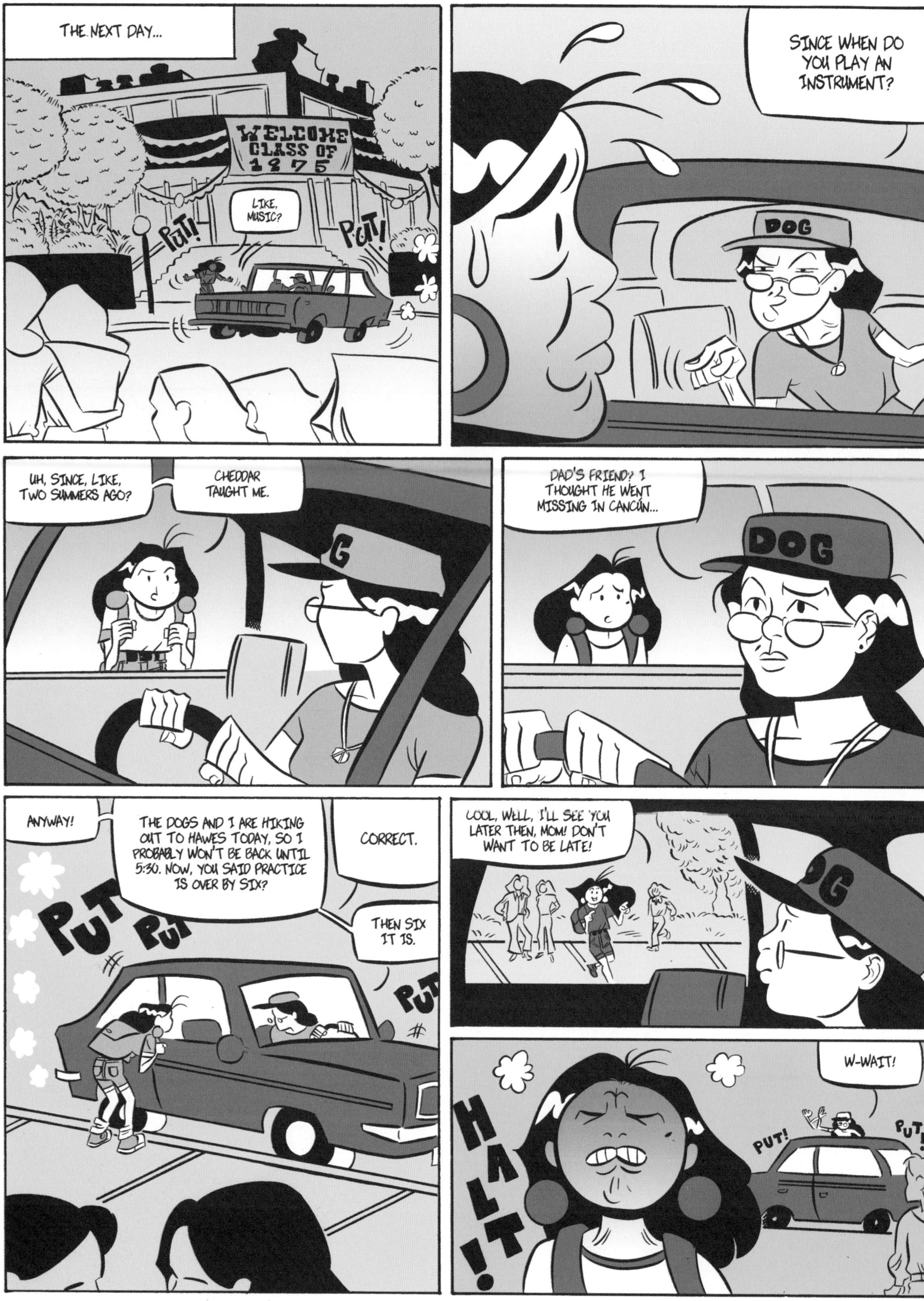

THE NEXT DAY...
WELCOME CLASS OF 1875
PUT!
LIKE, MUSIC?
PUT!
SINCE WHEN DO YOU PLAY AN INSTRUMENT?
DOG
UH, SINCE, LIKE, TWO SUMMERS AGO?
CHEDDAR TAUGHT ME.
DAD'S FRIEND? I THOUGHT HE WENT MISSING IN CANCÚN...
DOG
ANYWAY!
THE DOGS AND I ARE HIKING OUT TO HAWES TODAY, SO I PROBABLY WON'T BE BACK UNTIL 5:30. NOW, YOU SAID PRACTICE IS OVER BY SIX?
CORRECT.
THEN SIX IT IS.
PUT PUT
PUT
COOL, WELL, I'LL SEE YOU LATER THEN, MOM! DON'T WANT TO BE LATE!
W-WAIT!
HALT!
PUT!
PUT!

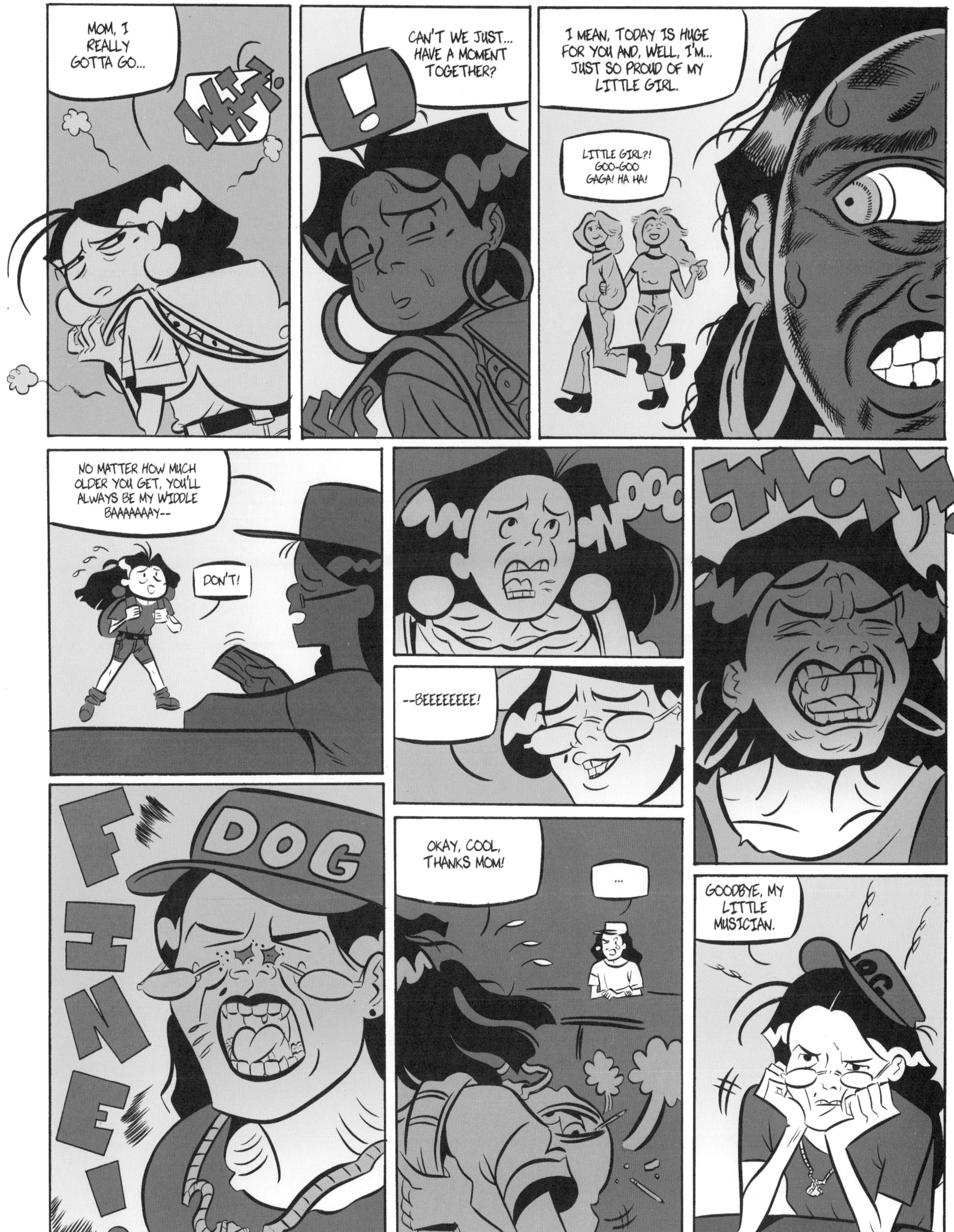
MOM, I REALLY GOTTA GO...
WAIT!
CAN'T WE JUST... HAVE A MOMENT TOGETHER?
!
I MEAN, TODAY IS HUGE FOR YOU AND, WELL, I'M... JUST SO PROUD OF MY LITTLE GIRL.
LITTLE GIRL?! GOO-GOO GAGA! HA HA!
NO MATTER HOW MUCH OLDER YOU GET, YOU'LL ALWAYS BE MY WIDDLE BAAAAAAAY--
DON'T!
NOOO
--BEEEEEEEE!
MOM!
FINE!
DOG
OKAY, COOL, THANKS MOM!
...
GOODBYE, MY LITTLE MUSICIAN.

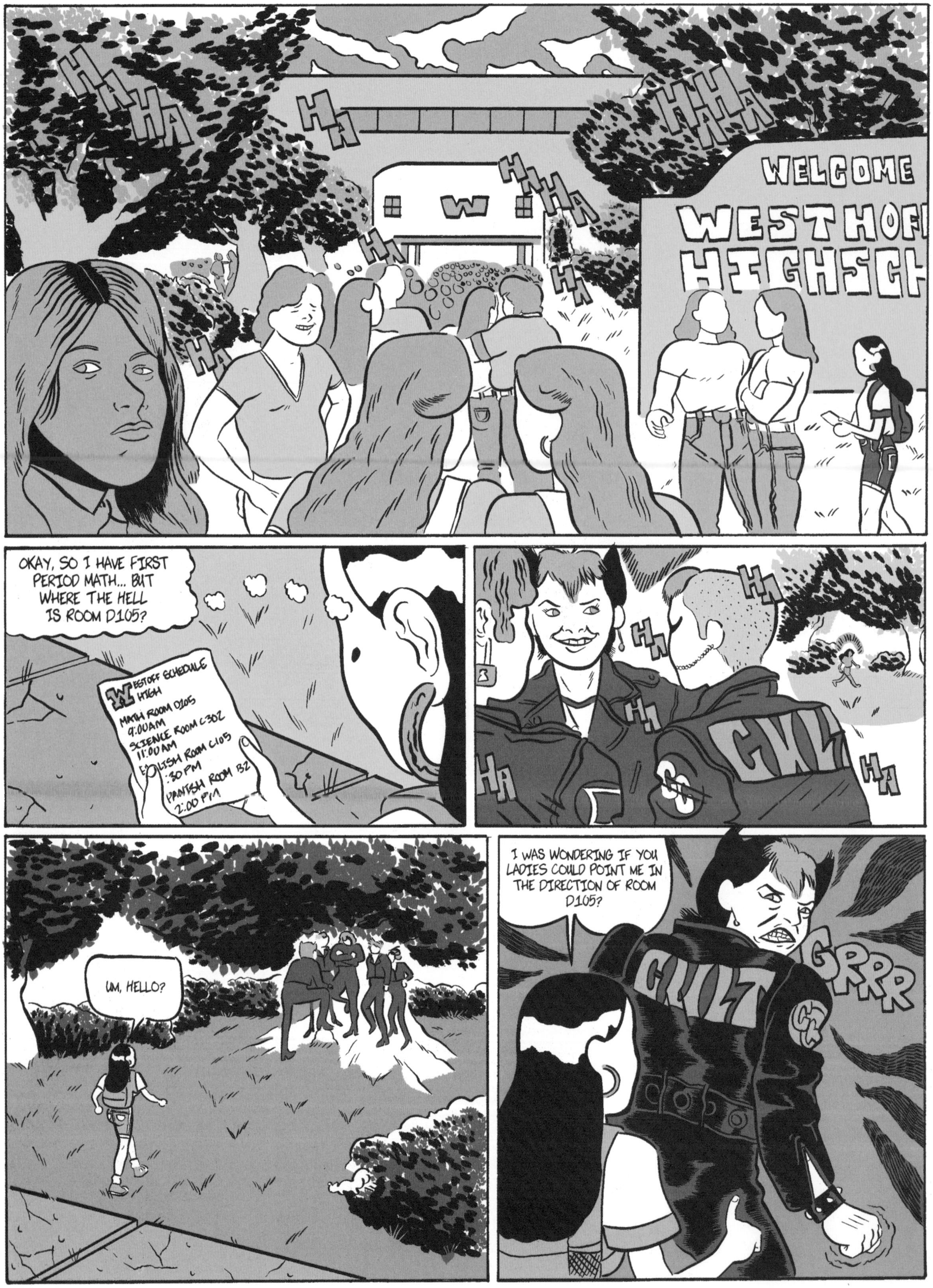
HA HA HA
WELCOME
OKAY, SO I HAVE FIRST PERIOD MATH... BUT WHERE THE HELL IS ROOM D105?
WESTOFF SCHEDULE HIGH
MATH ROOM D105
9:00AM
SCIENCE ROOM C302
11:00AM
2:00 PM
HA HA
UM, HELLO?
I WAS WONDERING IF YOU LADIES COULD POINT ME IN THE DIRECTION OF ROOM D105?
GRRR

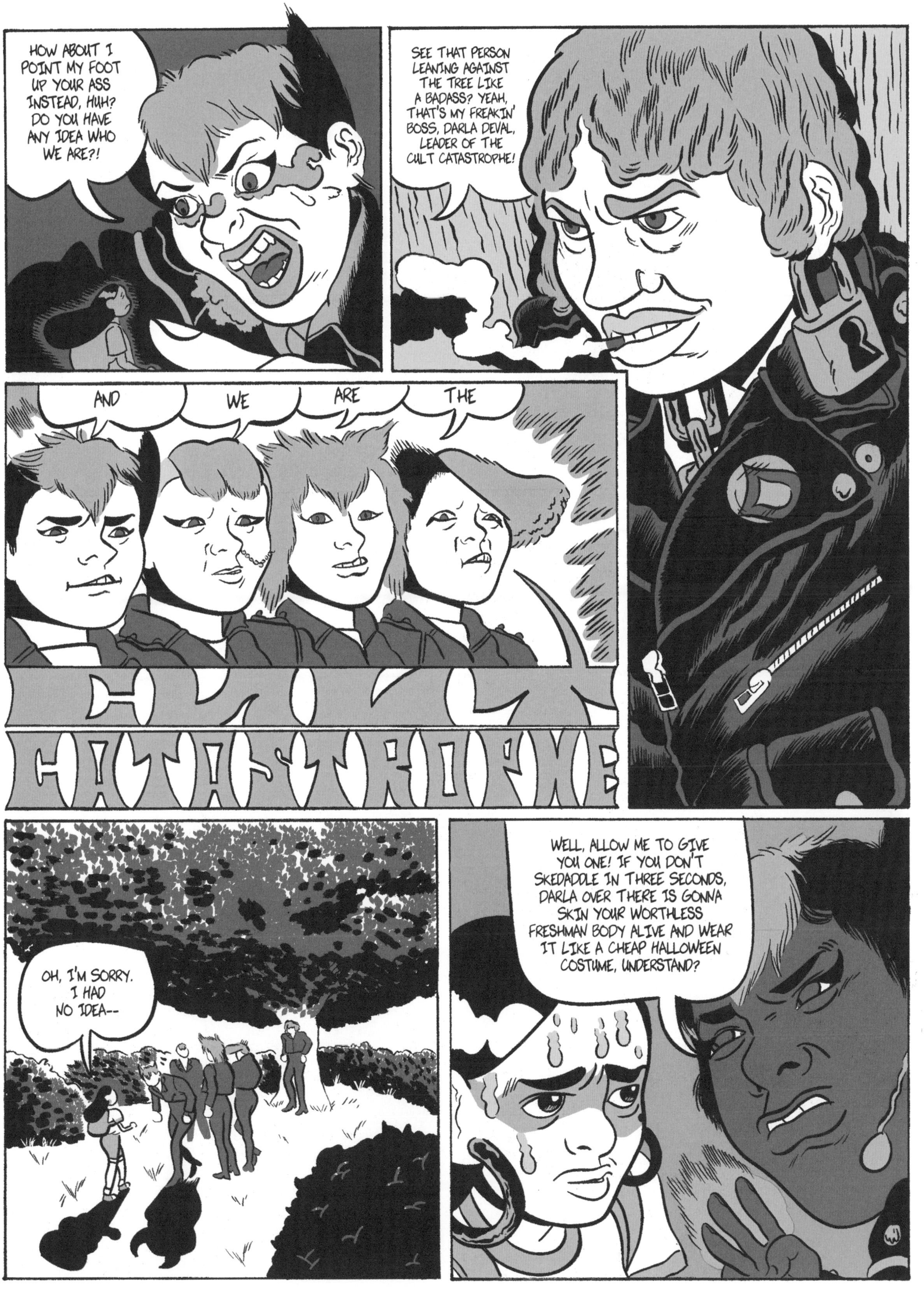
HOW ABOUT I POINT MY FOOT UP YOUR ASS INSTEAD, HUH? DO YOU HAVE ANY IDEA WHO WE ARE?!
SEE THAT PERSON LEANING AGAINST THE TREE LIKE A BADASS? YEAH, THAT'S MY FREAKIN' BOSS, DARLA DEVAL, LEADER OF THE CULT CATASTROPHE!
AND
WE
ARE
THE
CULT
CATASTROPHE
OH, I'M SORRY. I HAD NO IDEA--
WELL, ALLOW ME TO GIVE YOU ONE! IF YOU DON'T SKEDADDLE IN THREE SECONDS, DARLA OVER THERE IS GONNA SKIN YOUR WORTHLESS FRESHMAN BODY ALIVE AND WEAR IT LIKE A CHEAP HALLOWEEN COSTUME, UNDERSTAND?

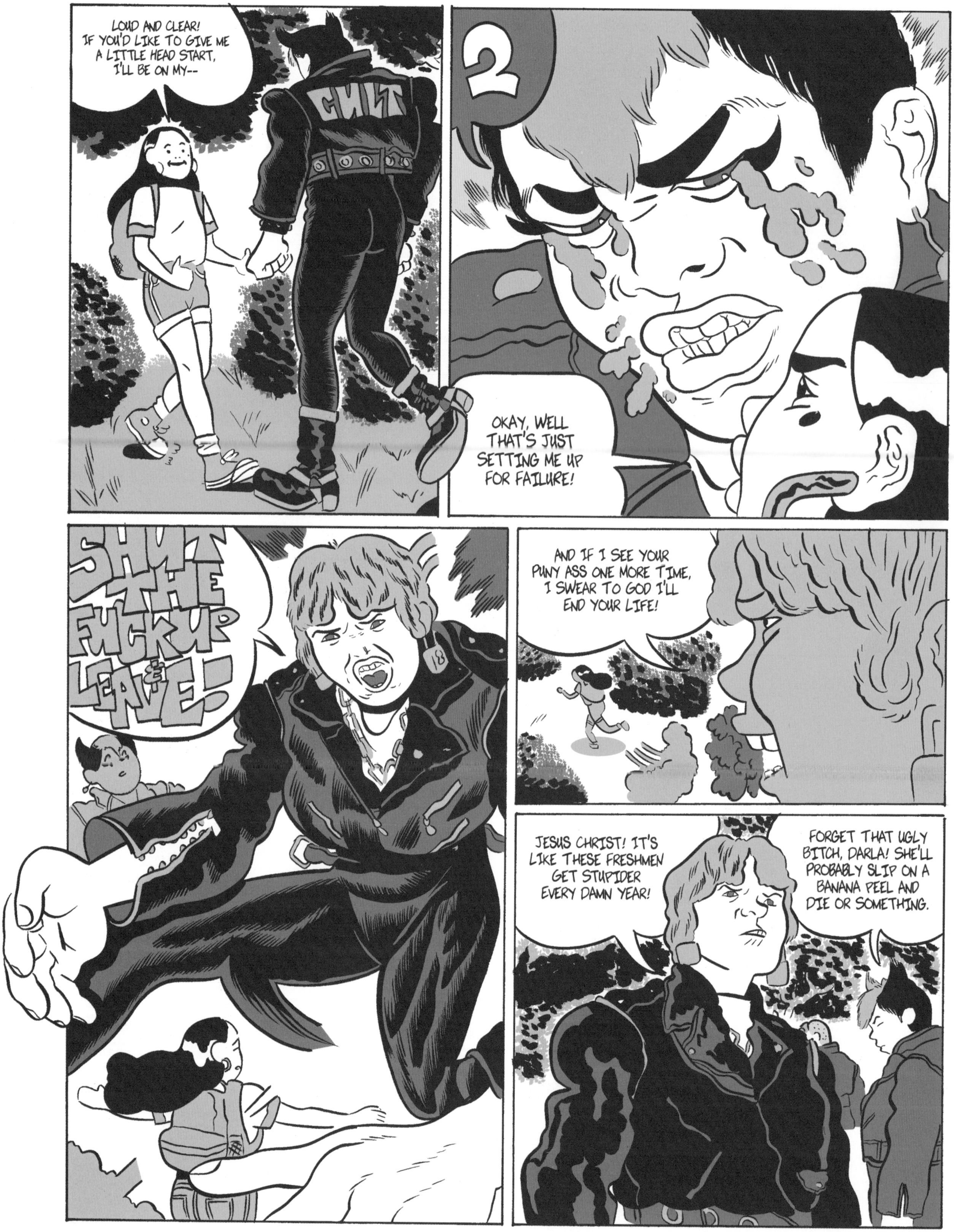
LOUD AND CLEAR! IF YOU'D LIKE TO GIVE ME A LITTLE HEAD START, I'LL BE ON MY--
CULT
2
OKAY, WELL THAT'S JUST SETTING ME UP FOR FAILURE!
SHUT THE FUCK UP & LEAVE!
AND IF I SEE YOUR PUNY ASS ONE MORE TIME, I SWEAR TO GOD I'LL END YOUR LIFE!
JESUS CHRIST! IT'S LIKE THESE FRESHMEN GET STUPIDER EVERY DAMN YEAR!
FORGET THAT UGLY BITCH, DARLA! SHE'LL PROBABLY SLIP ON A BANANA PEEL AND DIE OR SOMETHING.

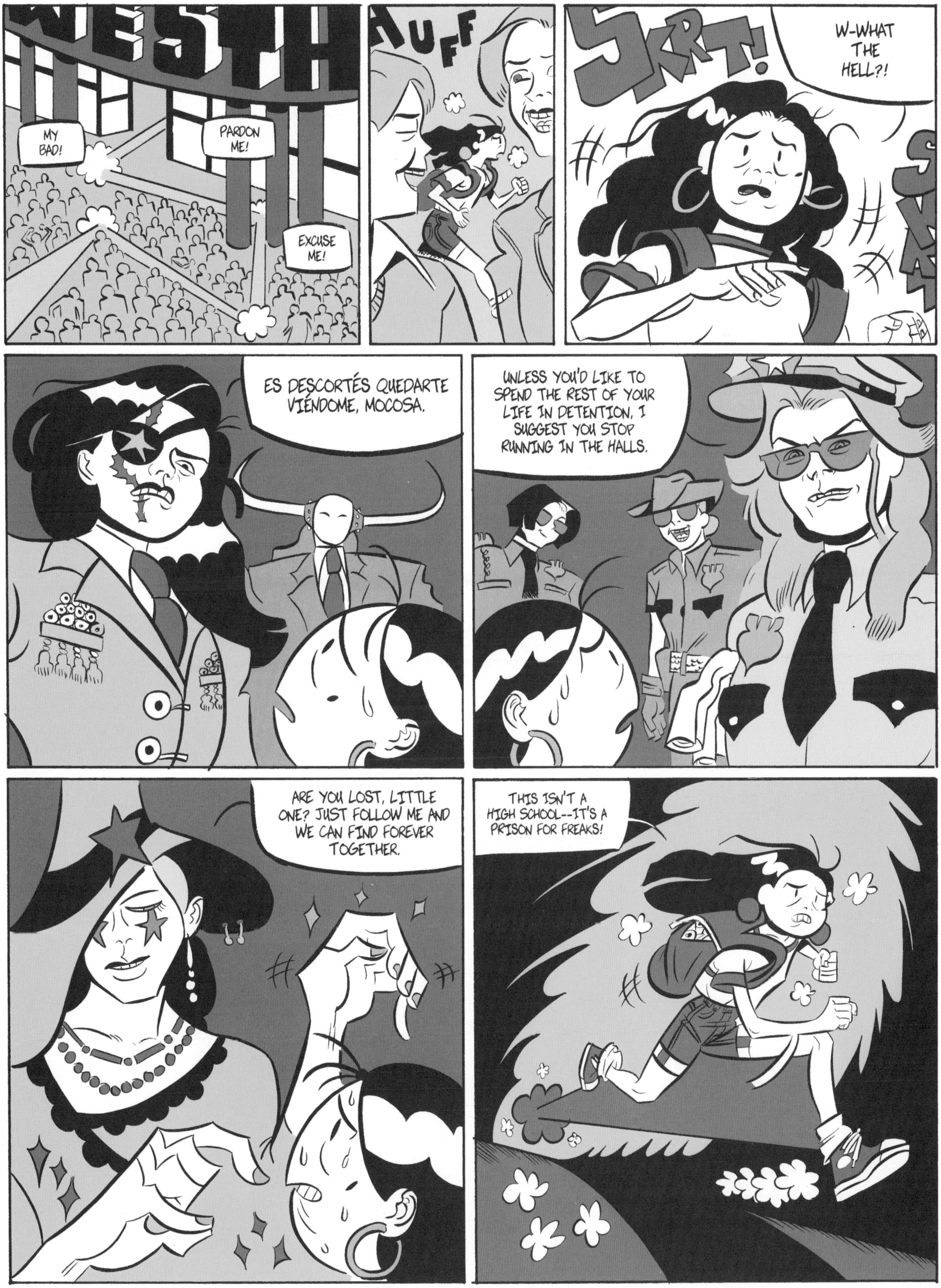
MY BAD!
PARDON ME!
EXCUSE ME!
AUFF
SKRT!
W-WHAT THE HELL?!
ES DESCORTÉS QUEDARTE VIÉNDOME, MOCOSA.
UNLESS YOU'D LIKE TO SPEND THE REST OF YOUR LIFE IN DETENTION, I SUGGEST YOU STOP RUNNING IN THE HALLS.
ARE YOU LOST, LITTLE ONE? JUST FOLLOW ME AND WE CAN FIND FOREVER TOGETHER.
THIS ISN'T A HIGH SCHOOL--IT'S A PRISON FOR FREAKS!

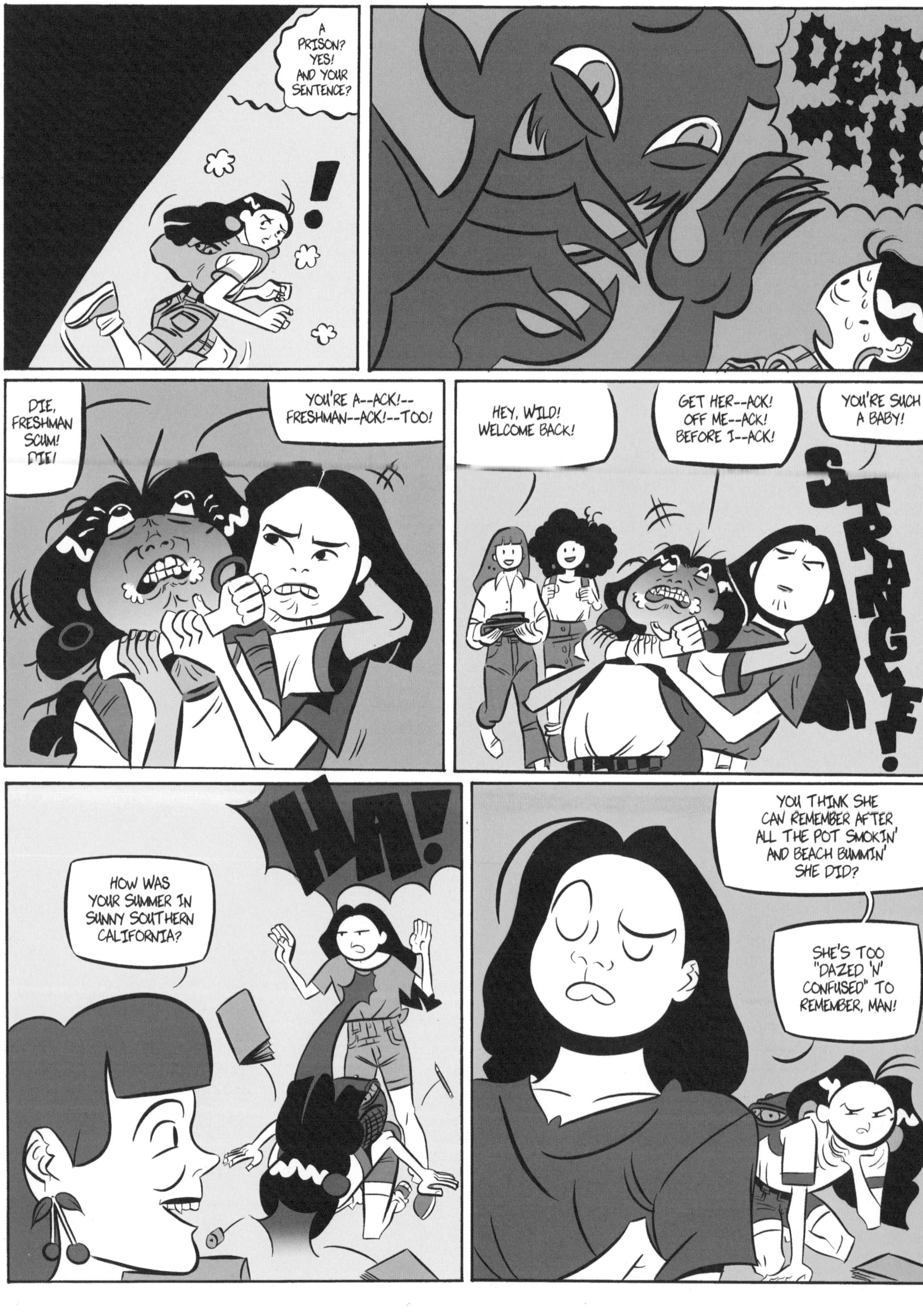
A PRISON? YES! AND YOUR SENTENCE?
!
DEATH
DIE, FRESHMAN SCUM! DIE!
YOU'RE A--ACK!--FRESHMAN--ACK!--TOO!
HEY, WILD! WELCOME BACK!
GET HER--ACK! OFF ME--ACK! BEFORE I--ACK!
YOU'RE SUCH A BABY!
STRANGLE!
HA!
HOW WAS YOUR SUMMER IN SUNNY SOUTHERN CALIFORNIA?
YOU THINK SHE CAN REMEMBER AFTER ALL THE POT SMOKIN' AND BEACH BUMMIN' SHE DID?
SHE'S TOO "DAZED 'N' CONFUSED" TO REMEMBER, MAN!

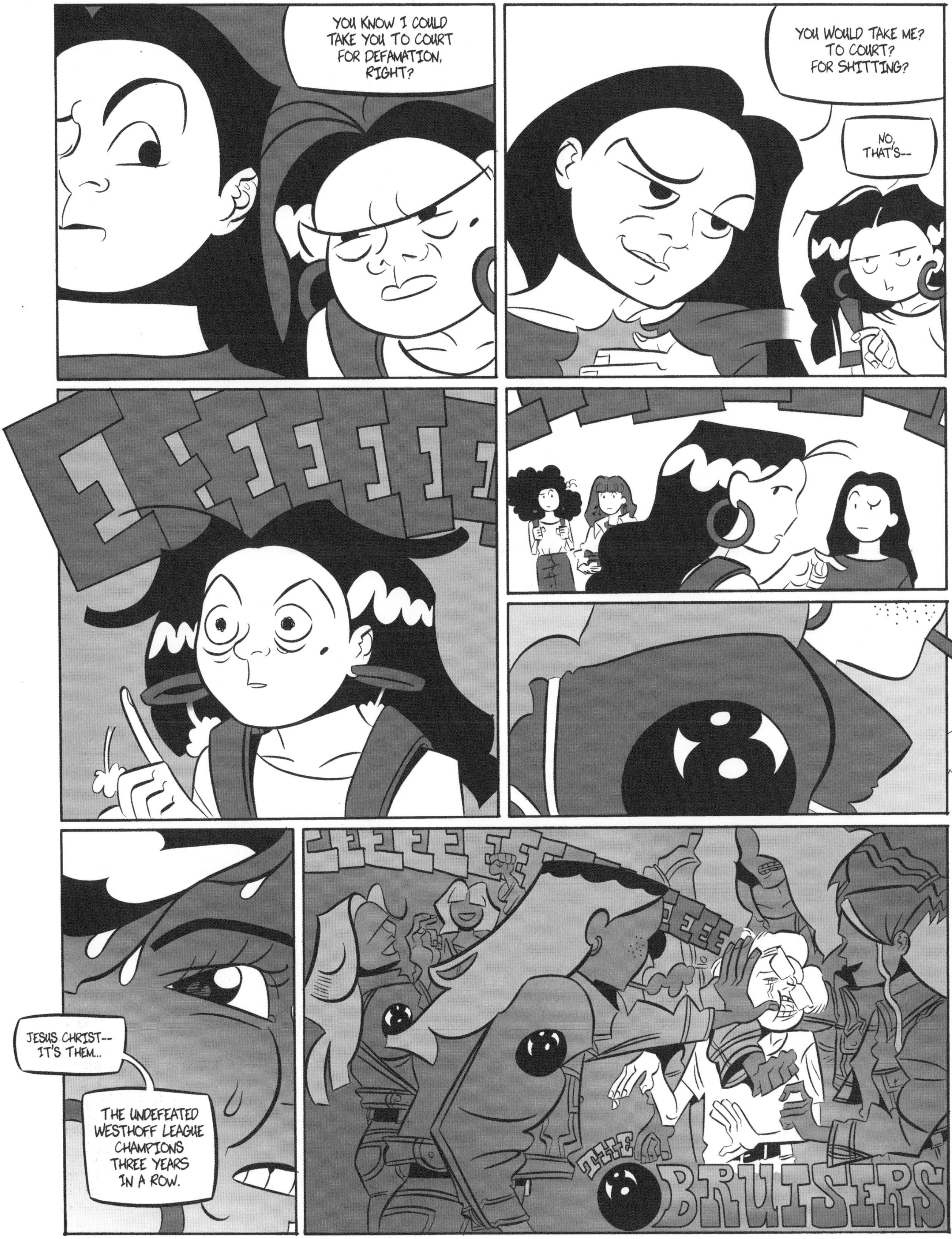
YOU KNOW I COULD TAKE YOU TO COURT FOR DEFAMATION, RIGHT?
YOU WOULD TAKE ME? TO COURT? FOR SHITTING?
NO, THAT'S--
JESUS CHRIST-- IT'S THEM...
THE UNDEFEATED WESTHOFF LEAGUE CHAMPIONS THREE YEARS IN A ROW.
THE BRUISERS

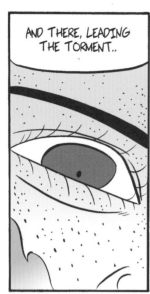

AND THERE, LEADING THE TORMENT..

Dixie Belle

...THE MYSTERIOUS TEXAS TRANSPLANT. RUMOR HAS IT SHE'S NEVER BROKEN A SWEAT SINCE ARRIVING IN ARIZONA.

EEEEEEE!!

YOU SEEM TO HAVE QUITE THE AFFINITY FOR HER! I ALWAYS SAY A NEW YEAR IS A TIME FOR NEW FRIENDS. GO OVER AND INTRODUCE YOURSELF!

LET HER KNOW YOU'RE GUNNING FOR HER SPOT AT THE TOP!

"HELLO, MISS BELLE. MY NAME IS WILD! I'M HOPING THAT ONE DAY WE COULD BECOME FRIENDS AND I COULD KICK THE SHIT OUT OF YOU." SOUND GOOD?

JUST LIKE THAT!

BEFORE WE CONSIDER WHOSE ASS WE'LL BE NEEDING TO KICK, WE SHOULD PROBABLY WORRY ABOUT MAKING THE TEAM!

CHERRY, IF YOU'D READ THE FLYER, PLEASE.

MY PLEASURE, BOSS!

SCING

"WOULD-BE ROCKET ROLLERS MUST ARRIVE AT THE SECOND GYM BLABLA...

NO LATER THAN.."

AHEM!

3:30. AND IT'S... WHAT NOW? FOUR? I THINK IT'S TIME WE ADMIT IT, LADIES. WE'VE BEEN HAD.

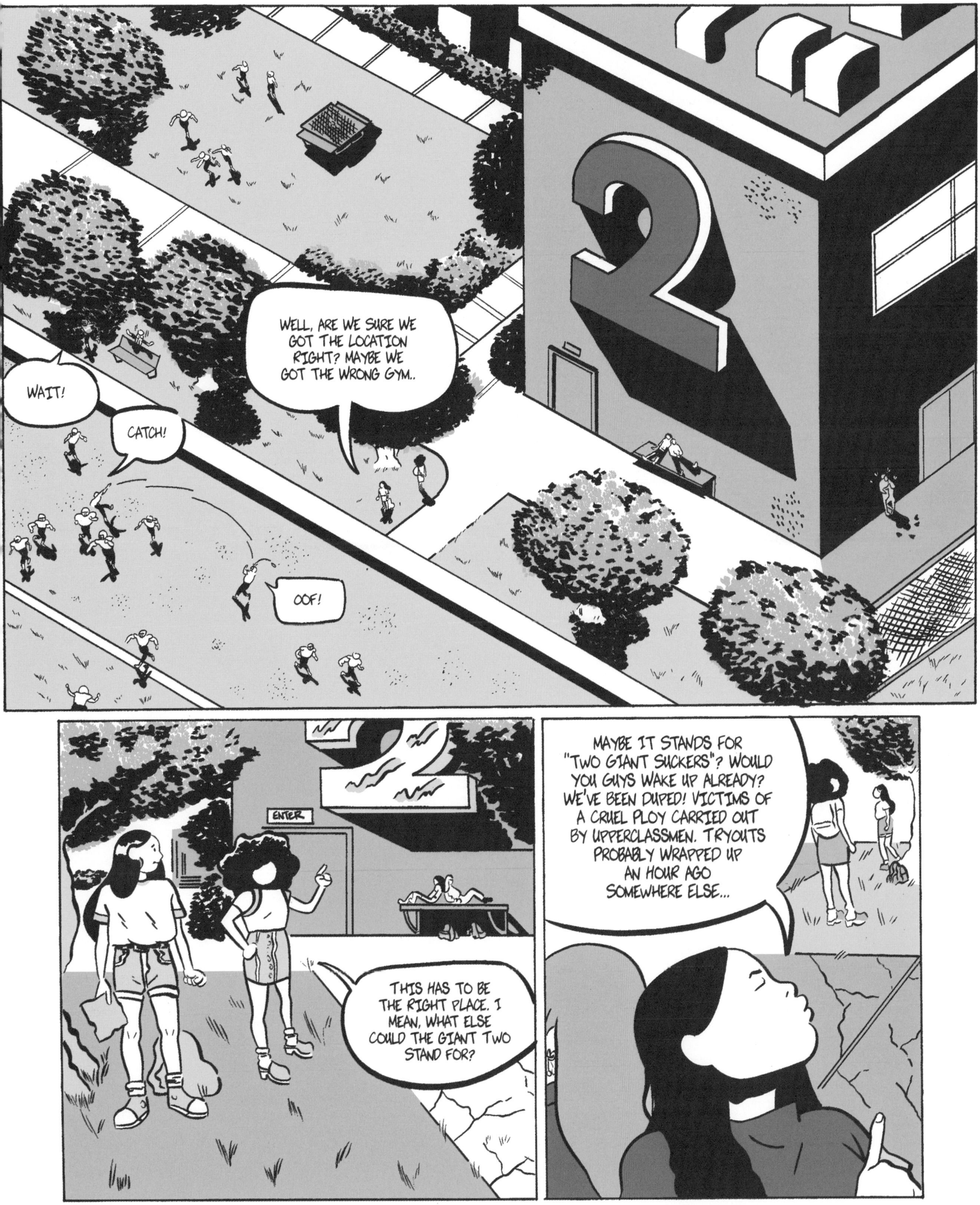

WELL, ARE WE SURE WE GOT THE LOCATION RIGHT? MAYBE WE GOT THE WRONG GYM..
WAIT!
CATCH!
OOF!
ENTER
THIS HAS TO BE THE RIGHT PLACE. I MEAN, WHAT ELSE COULD THE GIANT TWO STAND FOR?
MAYBE IT STANDS FOR "TWO GIANT SUCKERS"? WOULD YOU GUYS WAKE UP ALREADY? WE'VE BEEN DUPED! VICTIMS OF A CRUEL PLOY CARRIED OUT BY UPPERCLASSMEN. TRYOUTS PROBABLY WRAPPED UP AN HOUR AGO SOMEWHERE ELSE...

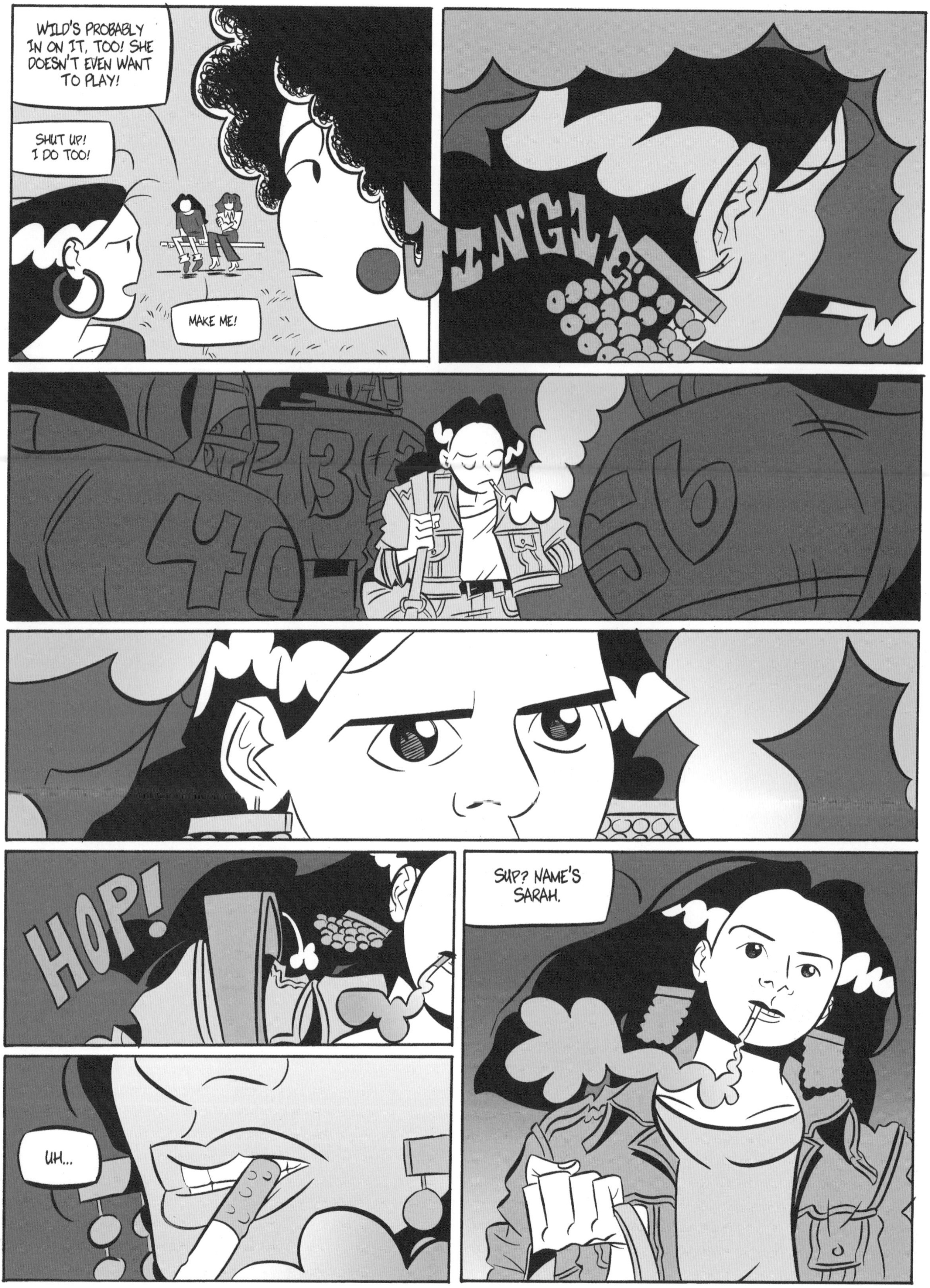
WILD'S PROBABLY IN ON IT, TOO! SHE DOESN'T EVEN WANT TO PLAY!
SHUT UP! I DO TOO!
MAKE ME!
JINGLE
HOP!
UH...
SUP? NAME'S SARAH.

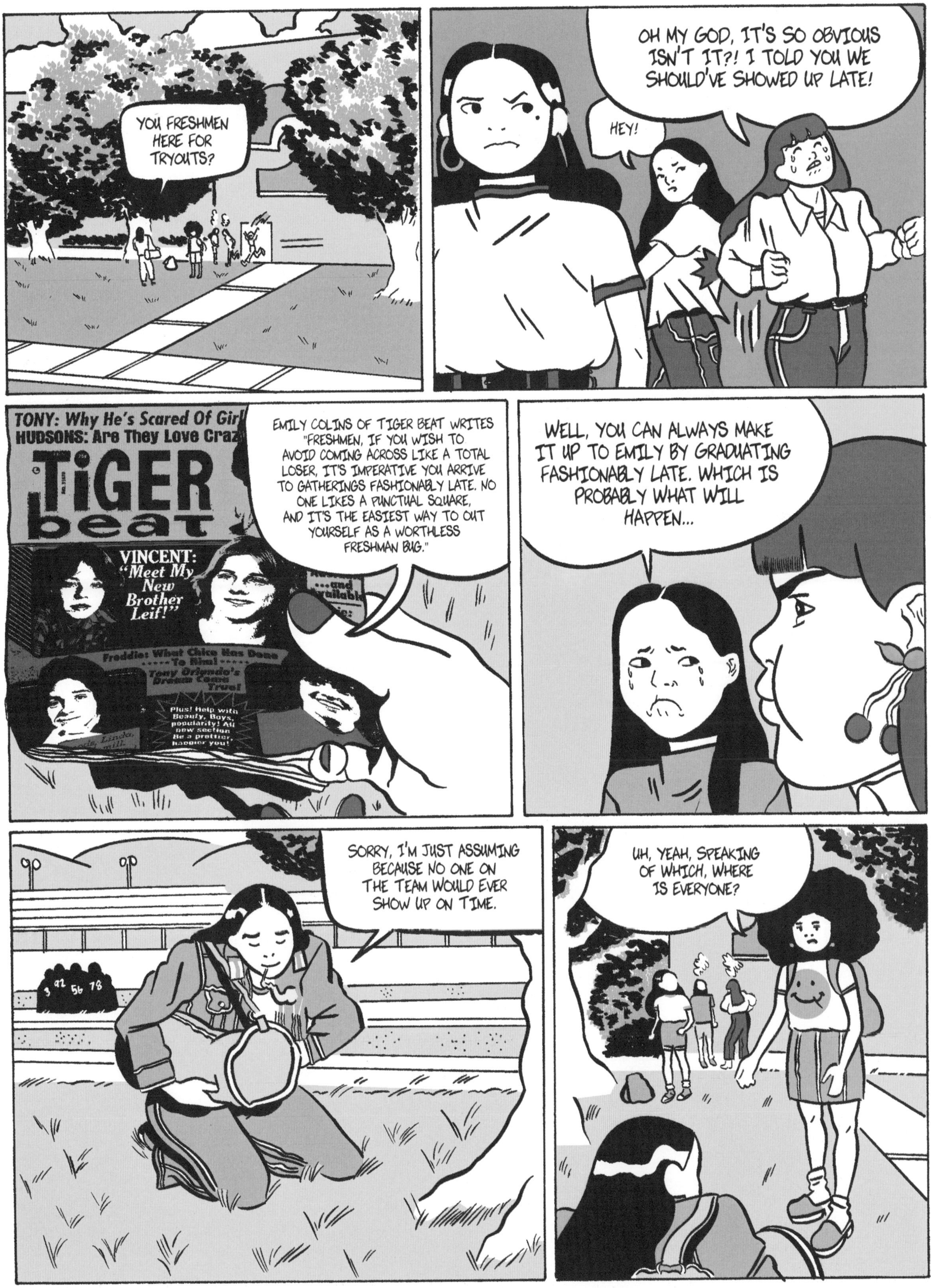

YOU FRESHMEN HERE FOR TRYOUTS?
OH MY GOD, IT'S SO OBVIOUS ISN'T IT?! I TOLD YOU WE SHOULD'VE SHOWED UP LATE!
HEY!
TONY: Why He's Scared Of Girl
HUDSONS: Are They Love Craz
TiGER beat
VINCENT: "Meet My New Brother Leif!"
Freddie: What Chico Has Done To Him!
Tony Orlando's Dream Come True!
Plus! Help with Beauty, Boys, popularity! All new section Be a prettier happier you!
EMILY COLINS OF TIGER BEAT WRITES "FRESHMEN, IF YOU WISH TO AVOID COMING ACROSS LIKE A TOTAL LOSER, IT'S IMPERATIVE YOU ARRIVE TO GATHERINGS FASHIONABLY LATE. NO ONE LIKES A PUNCTUAL SQUARE, AND IT'S THE EASIEST WAY TO OUT YOURSELF AS A WORTHLESS FRESHMAN BUG."
WELL, YOU CAN ALWAYS MAKE IT UP TO EMILY BY GRADUATING FASHIONABLY LATE. WHICH IS PROBABLY WHAT WILL HAPPEN...
SORRY, I'M JUST ASSUMING BECAUSE NO ONE ON THE TEAM WOULD EVER SHOW UP ON TIME.
UH, YEAH, SPEAKING OF WHICH, WHERE IS EVERYONE?

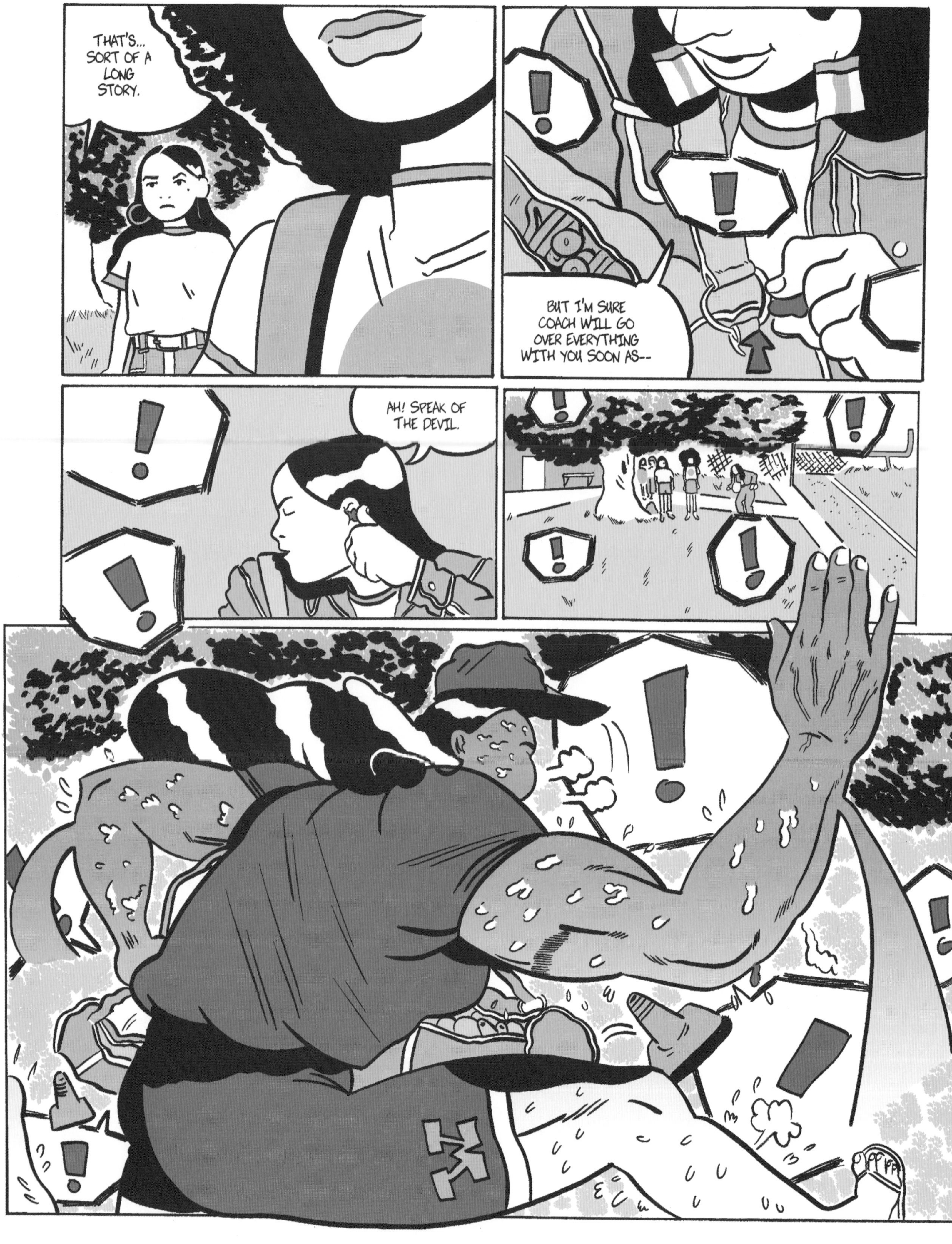
THAT'S... SORT OF A LONG STORY.
BUT I'M SURE COACH WILL GO OVER EVERYTHING WITH YOU SOON AS--
AH! SPEAK OF THE DEVIL.

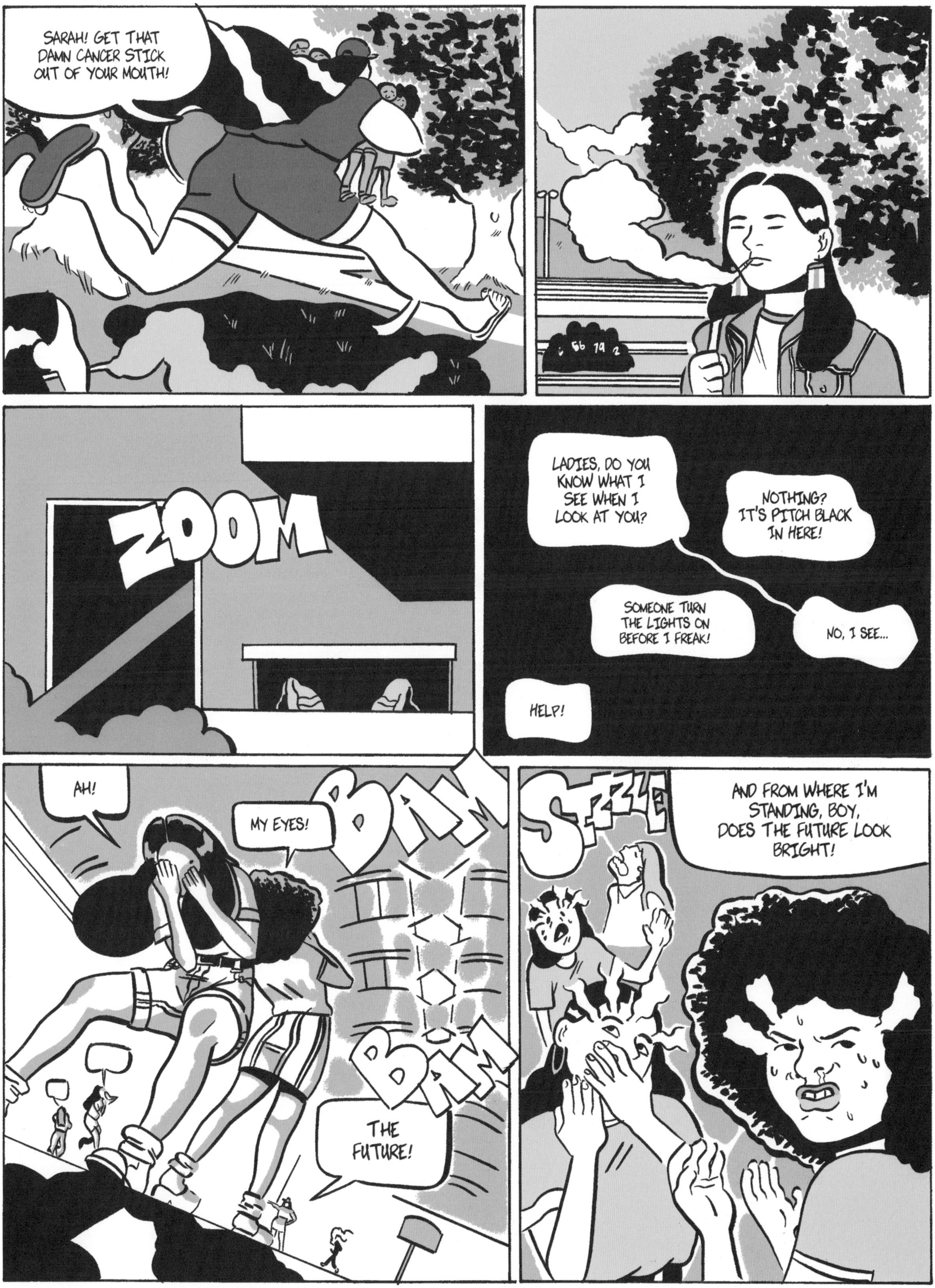
SARAH! GET THAT DAMN CANCER STICK OUT OF YOUR MOUTH!
ZOOM
LADIES, DO YOU KNOW WHAT I SEE WHEN I LOOK AT YOU?
NOTHING? IT'S PITCH BLACK IN HERE!
SOMEONE TURN THE LIGHTS ON BEFORE I FREAK!
NO, I SEE...
HELP!
AH!
MY EYES!
BAM
BAM
THE FUTURE!
SIZZLE
AND FROM WHERE I'M STANDING, BOY, DOES THE FUTURE LOOK BRIGHT!

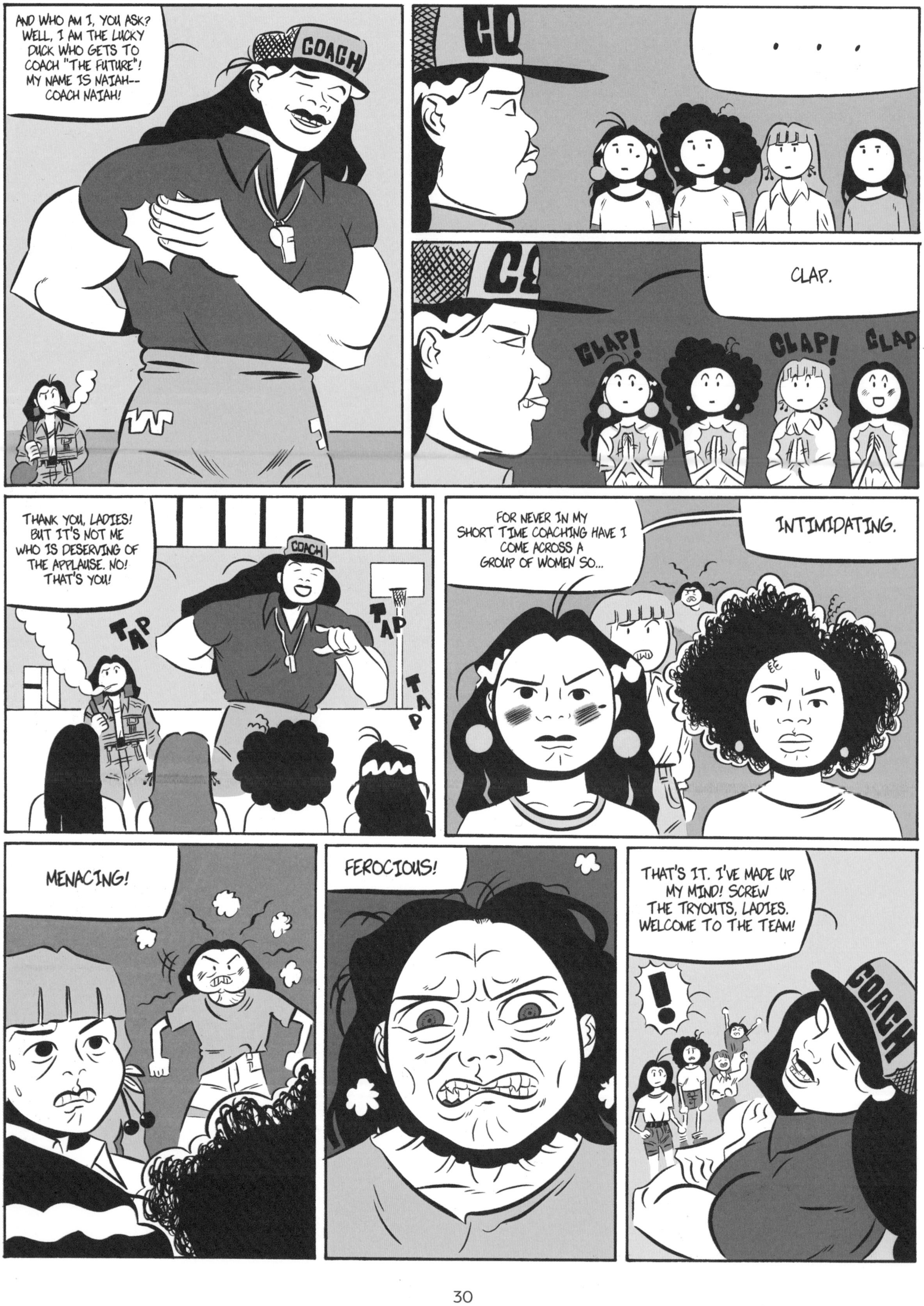
AND WHO AM I, YOU ASK? WELL, I AM THE LUCKY DUCK WHO GETS TO COACH "THE FUTURE"! MY NAME IS NAIAH-- COACH NAIAH!
COACH
. . .
CLAP.
CLAP!
CLAP!
CLAP
THANK YOU, LADIES! BUT IT'S NOT ME WHO IS DESERVING OF THE APPLAUSE. NO! THAT'S YOU!
COACH
TAP
TAP
TAP
FOR NEVER IN MY SHORT TIME COACHING HAVE I COME ACROSS A GROUP OF WOMEN SO...
INTIMIDATING.
MENACING!
FEROCIOUS!
THAT'S IT. I'VE MADE UP MY MIND! SCREW THE TRYOUTS, LADIES. WELCOME TO THE TEAM!
COACH

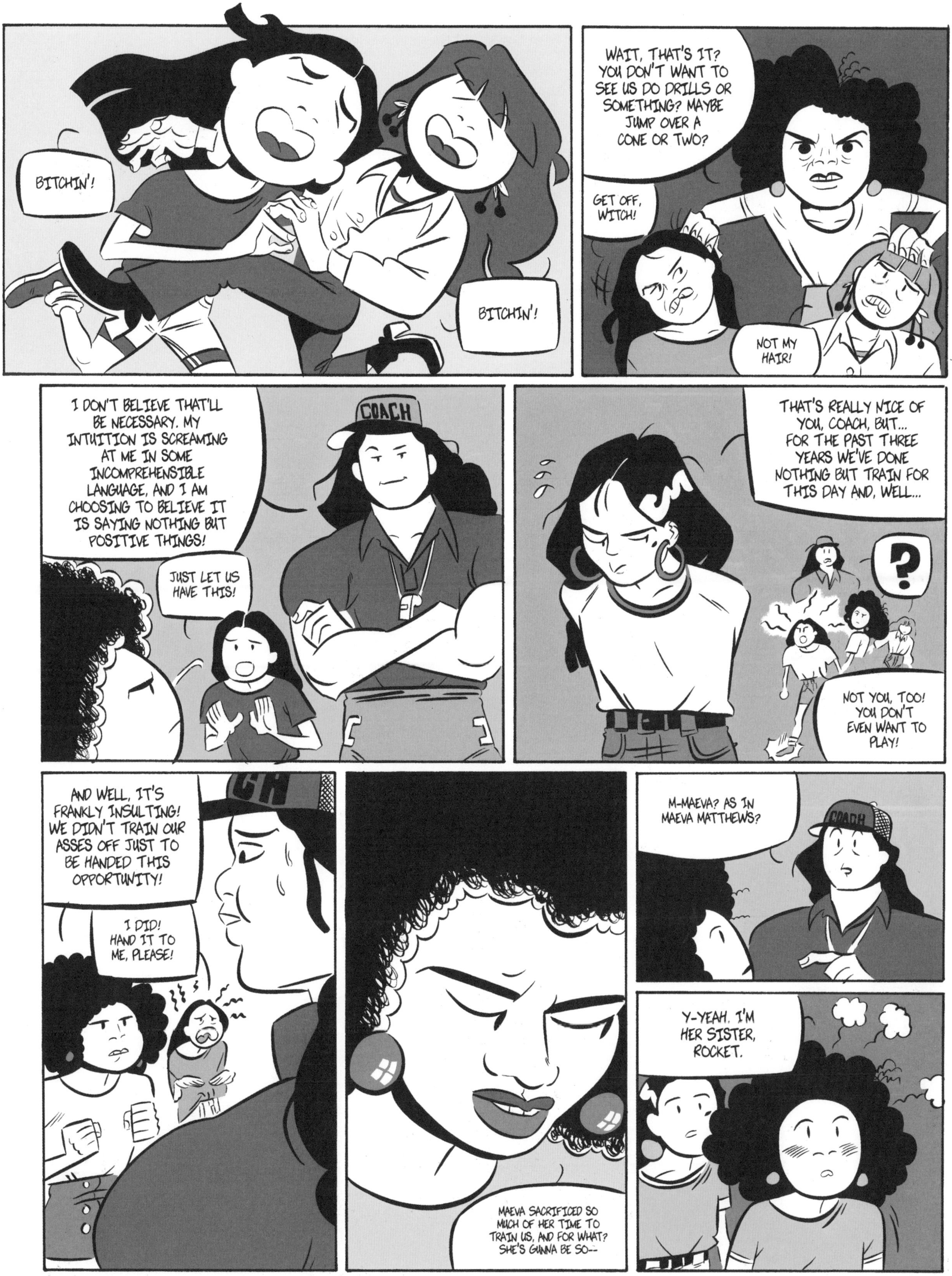
BITCHIN'!
BITCHIN'!
WAIT, THAT'S IT? YOU DON'T WANT TO SEE US DO DRILLS OR SOMETHING? MAYBE JUMP OVER A CONE OR TWO?
GET OFF, WITCH!
NOT MY HAIR!
COACH
I DON'T BELIEVE THAT'LL BE NECESSARY. MY INTUITION IS SCREAMING AT ME IN SOME INCOMPREHENSIBLE LANGUAGE, AND I AM CHOOSING TO BELIEVE IT IS SAYING NOTHING BUT POSITIVE THINGS!
JUST LET US HAVE THIS!
THAT'S REALLY NICE OF YOU, COACH, BUT... FOR THE PAST THREE YEARS WE'VE DONE NOTHING BUT TRAIN FOR THIS DAY AND, WELL...
?
NOT YOU, TOO! YOU DON'T EVEN WANT TO PLAY!
AND WELL, IT'S FRANKLY INSULTING! WE DIDN'T TRAIN OUR ASSES OFF JUST TO BE HANDED THIS OPPORTUNITY!
I DID! HAND IT TO ME, PLEASE!
MAEVA SACRIFICED SO MUCH OF HER TIME TO TRAIN US, AND FOR WHAT? SHE'S GUNNA BE SO--
M-MAEVA? AS IN MAEVA MATTHEWS?
COACH
Y-YEAH. I'M HER SISTER, ROCKET.

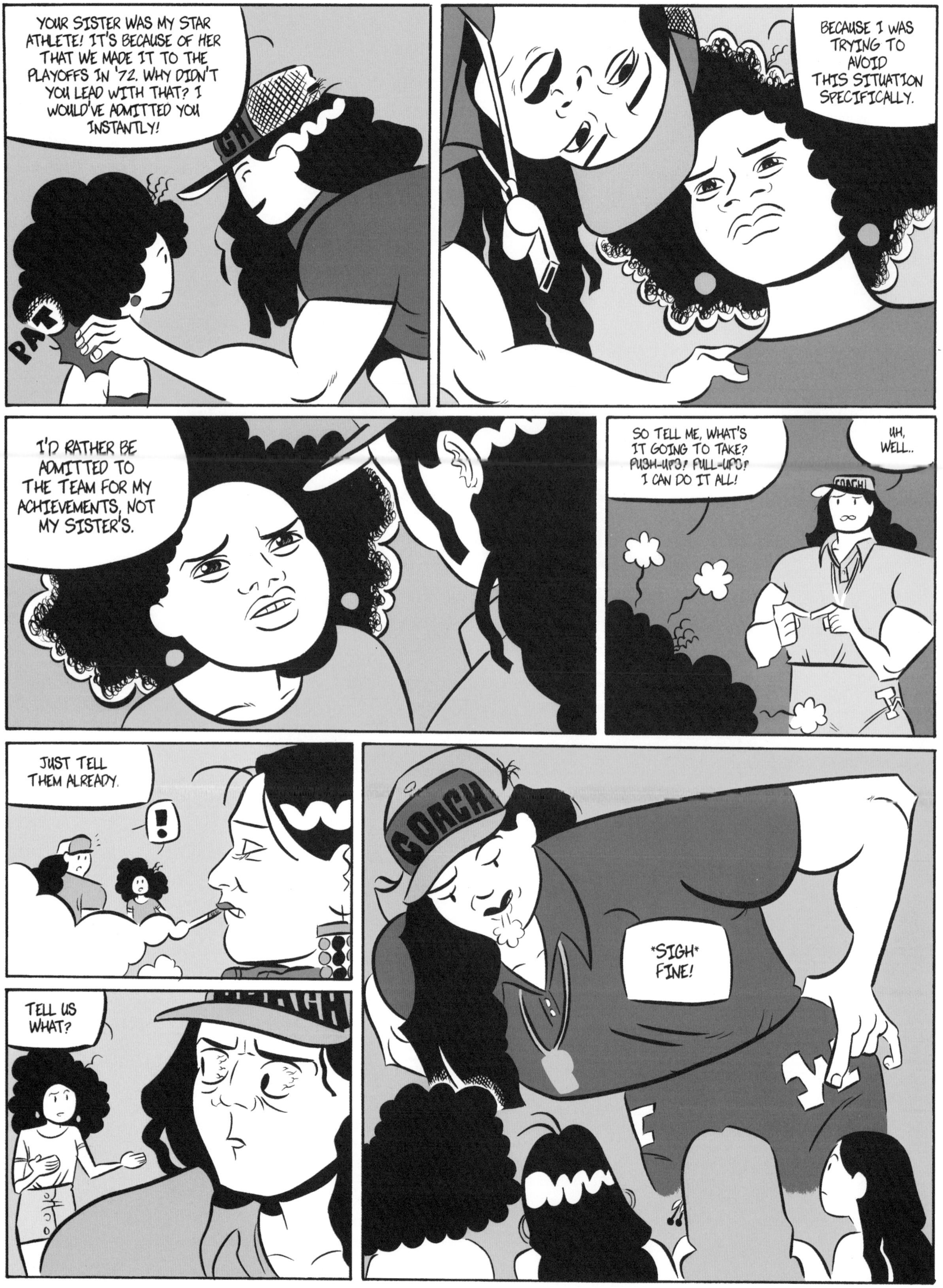
YOUR SISTER WAS MY STAR ATHLETE! IT'S BECAUSE OF HER THAT WE MADE IT TO THE PLAYOFFS IN '72. WHY DIDN'T YOU LEAD WITH THAT? I WOULD'VE ADMITTED YOU INSTANTLY!
PAT
BECAUSE I WAS TRYING TO AVOID THIS SITUATION SPECIFICALLY.
I'D RATHER BE ADMITTED TO THE TEAM FOR MY ACHIEVEMENTS, NOT MY SISTER'S.
SO TELL ME, WHAT'S IT GOING TO TAKE? PUSH-UPS? PULL-UPS? I CAN DO IT ALL!
UH, WELL..
COACH
JUST TELL THEM ALREADY.
!
TELL US WHAT?
COACH
SIGH FINE!

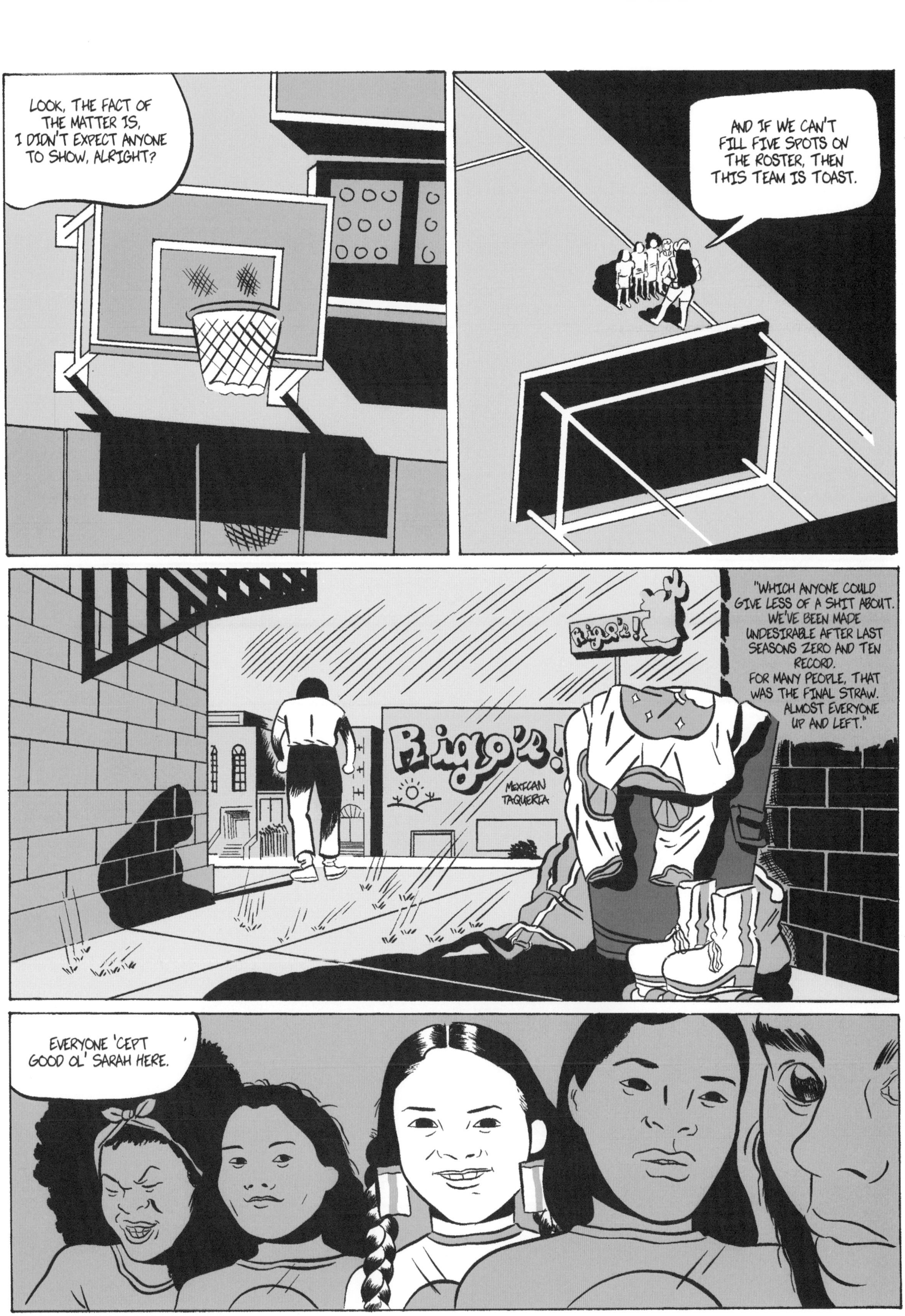
LOOK, THE FACT OF THE MATTER IS, I DIDN'T EXPECT ANYONE TO SHOW, ALRIGHT?
AND IF WE CAN'T FILL FIVE SPOTS ON THE ROSTER, THEN THIS TEAM IS TOAST.
"WHICH ANYONE COULD GIVE LESS OF A SHIT ABOUT. WE'VE BEEN MADE UNDESIRABLE AFTER LAST SEASONS ZERO AND TEN RECORD.
FOR MANY PEOPLE, THAT WAS THE FINAL STRAW. ALMOST EVERYONE UP AND LEFT."
Rigo's!
Rigo's!
MEXICAN TAQUERIA
EVERYONE 'CEPT GOOD OL' SARAH HERE.

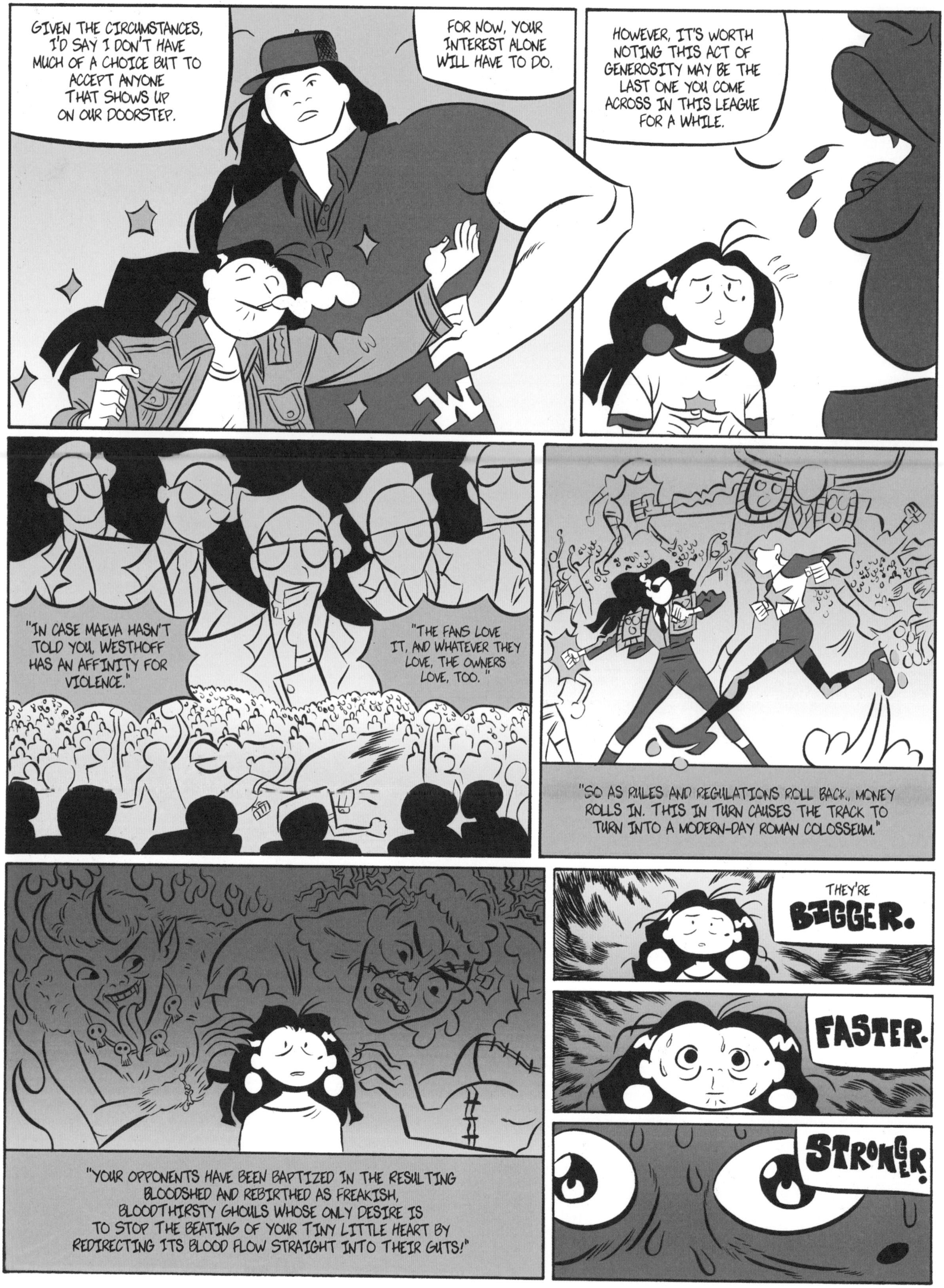
GIVEN THE CIRCUMSTANCES, I'D SAY I DON'T HAVE MUCH OF A CHOICE BUT TO ACCEPT ANYONE THAT SHOWS UP ON OUR DOORSTEP.
FOR NOW, YOUR INTEREST ALONE WILL HAVE TO DO.
HOWEVER, IT'S WORTH NOTING THIS ACT OF GENEROSITY MAY BE THE LAST ONE YOU COME ACROSS IN THIS LEAGUE FOR A WHILE.
"IN CASE MAEVA HASN'T TOLD YOU, WESTHOFF HAS AN AFFINITY FOR VIOLENCE."
"THE FANS LOVE IT, AND WHATEVER THEY LOVE, THE OWNERS LOVE, TOO."
"SO AS RULES AND REGULATIONS ROLL BACK, MONEY ROLLS IN. THIS IN TURN CAUSES THE TRACK TO TURN INTO A MODERN-DAY ROMAN COLOSSEUM."
"YOUR OPPONENTS HAVE BEEN BAPTIZED IN THE RESULTING BLOODSHED AND REBIRTHED AS FREAKISH, BLOODTHIRSTY GHOULS WHOSE ONLY DESIRE IS TO STOP THE BEATING OF YOUR TINY LITTLE HEART BY REDIRECTING ITS BLOOD FLOW STRAIGHT INTO THEIR GUTS!"
THEY'RE BIGGER.
FASTER.
STRONGER.

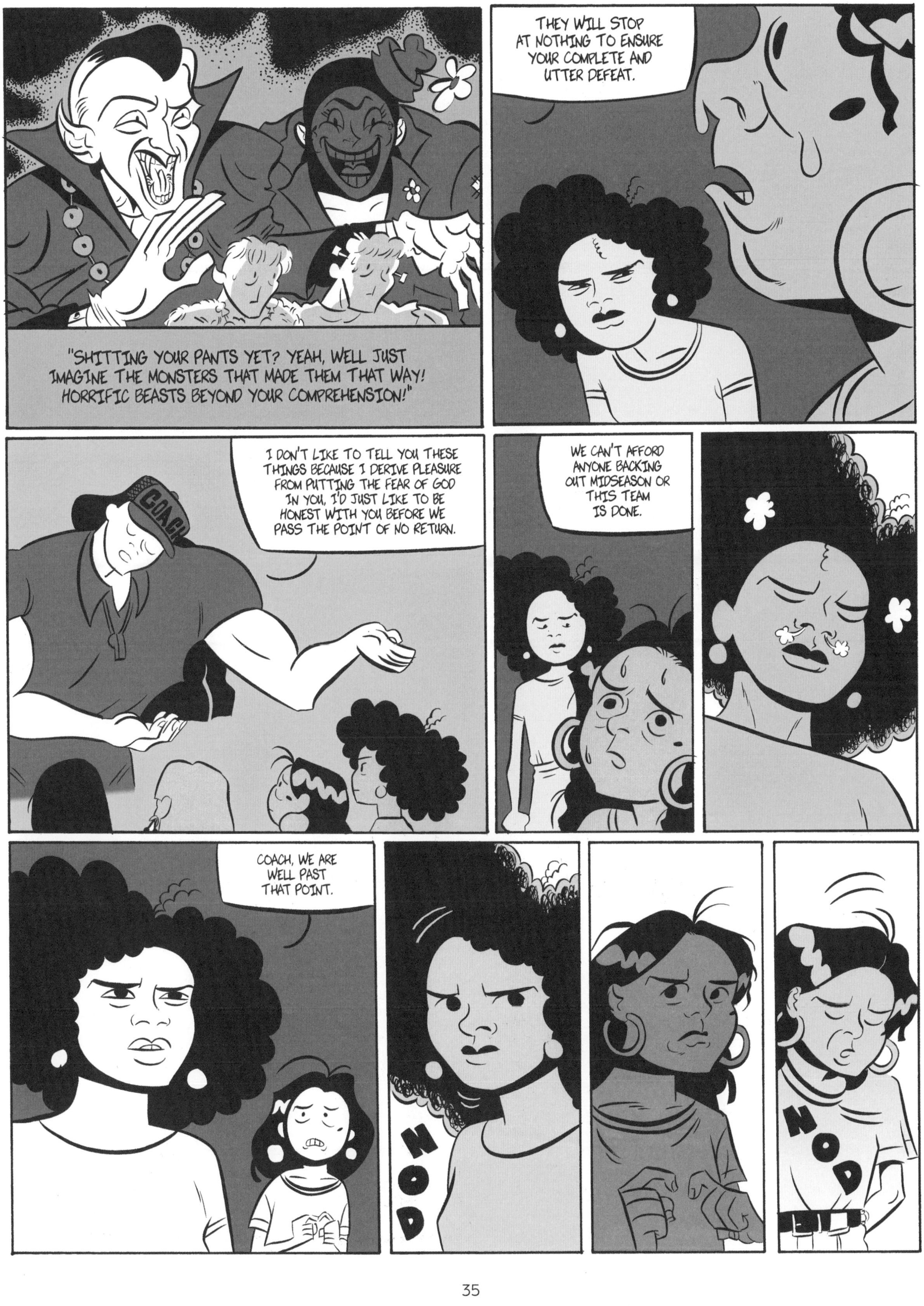
"SHITTING YOUR PANTS YET? YEAH, WELL JUST IMAGINE THE MONSTERS THAT MADE THEM THAT WAY! HORRIFIC BEASTS BEYOND YOUR COMPREHENSION!"
THEY WILL STOP AT NOTHING TO ENSURE YOUR COMPLETE AND UTTER DEFEAT.
COACH
I DON'T LIKE TO TELL YOU THESE THINGS BECAUSE I DERIVE PLEASURE FROM PUTTING THE FEAR OF GOD IN YOU, I'D JUST LIKE TO BE HONEST WITH YOU BEFORE WE PASS THE POINT OF NO RETURN.
WE CAN'T AFFORD ANYONE BACKING OUT MIDSEASON OR THIS TEAM IS DONE.
COACH, WE ARE WELL PAST THAT POINT.
NOD
NOD

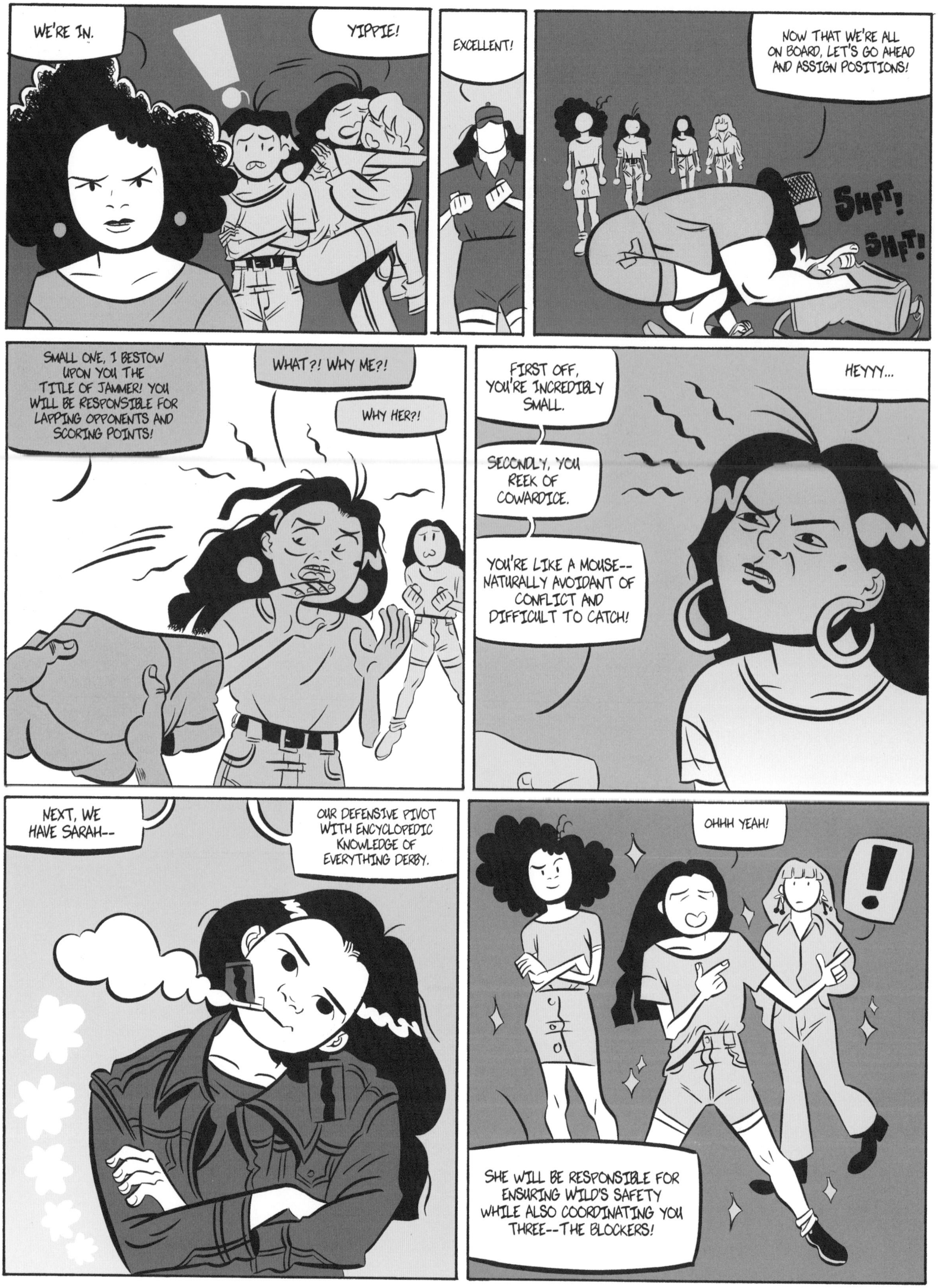
WE'RE IN.
YIPPIE!
EXCELLENT!
NOW THAT WE'RE ALL ON BOARD, LET'S GO AHEAD AND ASSIGN POSITIONS!
SHFT! SHFT!
SMALL ONE, I BESTOW UPON YOU THE TITLE OF JAMMER! YOU WILL BE RESPONSIBLE FOR LAPPING OPPONENTS AND SCORING POINTS!
WHAT?! WHY ME?!
WHY HER?!
FIRST OFF, YOU'RE INCREDIBLY SMALL.
HEYYY...
SECONDLY, YOU REEK OF COWARDICE.
YOU'RE LIKE A MOUSE-- NATURALLY AVOIDANT OF CONFLICT AND DIFFICULT TO CATCH!
NEXT, WE HAVE SARAH--
OUR DEFENSIVE PIVOT WITH ENCYCLOPEDIC KNOWLEDGE OF EVERYTHING DERBY.
OHHH YEAH!
SHE WILL BE RESPONSIBLE FOR ENSURING WILD'S SAFETY WHILE ALSO COORDINATING YOU THREE--THE BLOCKERS!

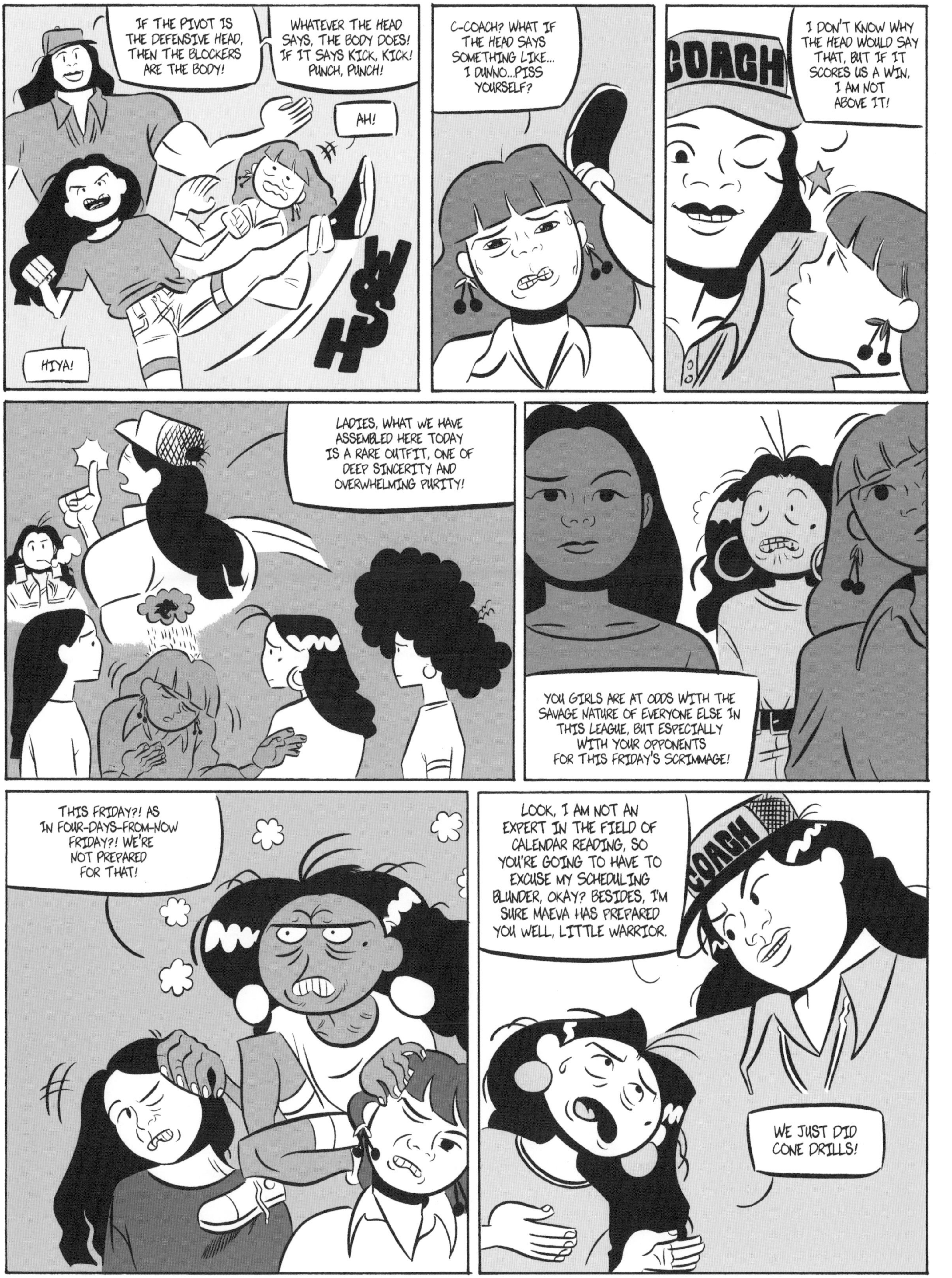

IF THE PIVOT IS THE DEFENSIVE HEAD, THEN THE BLOCKERS ARE THE BODY!
WHATEVER THE HEAD SAYS, THE BODY DOES! IF IT SAYS KICK, KICK! PUNCH, PUNCH!
AH!
WHOOSH
HIYA!
C-COACH? WHAT IF THE HEAD SAYS SOMETHING LIKE... I DUNNO...PISS YOURSELF?
COACH
I DON'T KNOW WHY THE HEAD WOULD SAY THAT, BUT IF IT SCORES US A WIN, I AM NOT ABOVE IT!
LADIES, WHAT WE HAVE ASSEMBLED HERE TODAY IS A RARE OUTFIT, ONE OF DEEP SINCERITY AND OVERWHELMING PURITY!
YOU GIRLS ARE AT ODDS WITH THE SAVAGE NATURE OF EVERYONE ELSE IN THIS LEAGUE, BUT ESPECIALLY WITH YOUR OPPONENTS FOR THIS FRIDAY'S SCRIMMAGE!
THIS FRIDAY?! AS IN FOUR-DAYS-FROM-NOW FRIDAY?! WE'RE NOT PREPARED FOR THAT!
LOOK, I AM NOT AN EXPERT IN THE FIELD OF CALENDAR READING, SO YOU'RE GOING TO HAVE TO EXCUSE MY SCHEDULING BLUNDER, OKAY? BESIDES, I'M SURE MAEVA HAS PREPARED YOU WELL, LITTLE WARRIOR.
COACH
WE JUST DID CONE DRILLS!

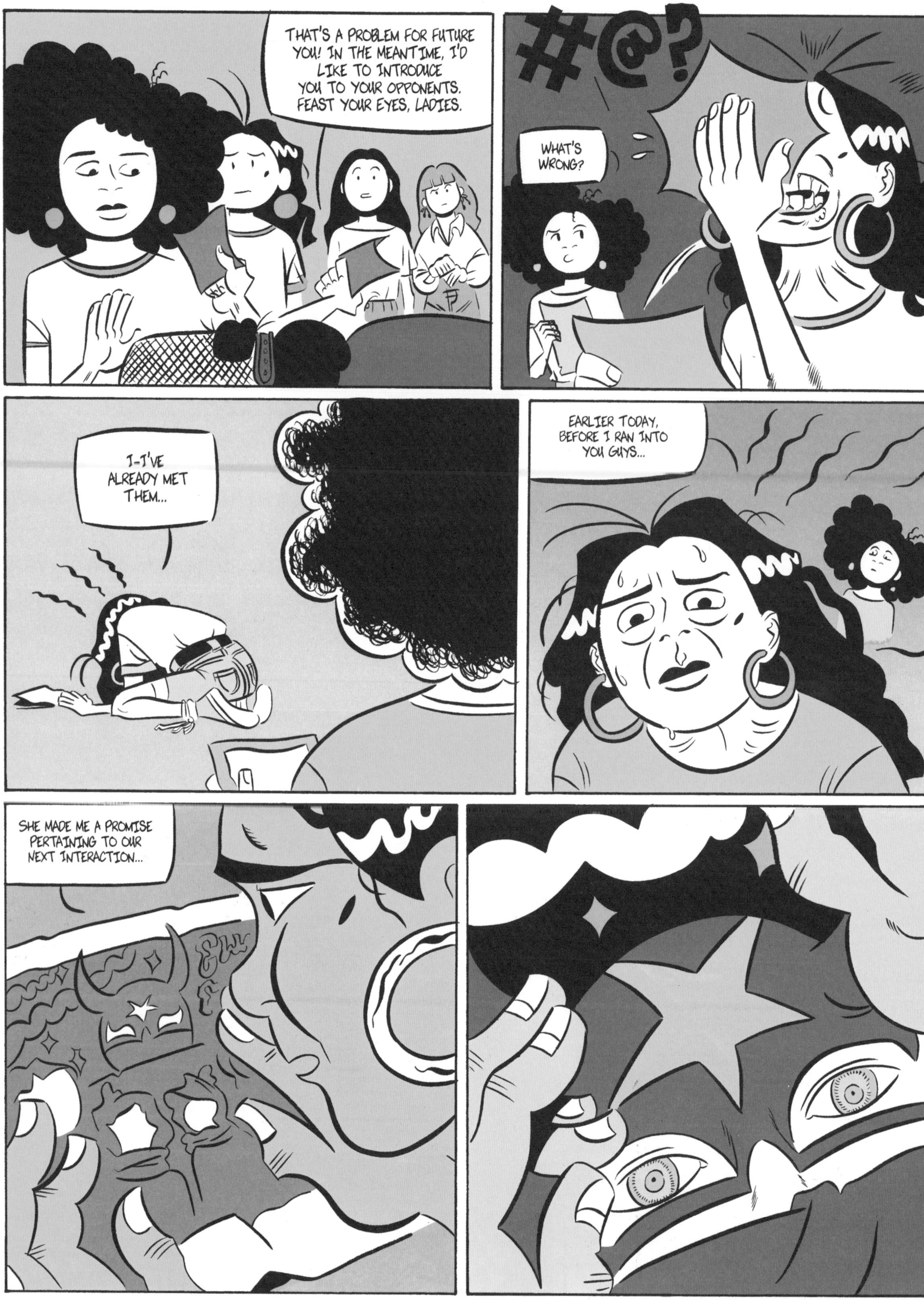
THAT'S A PROBLEM FOR FUTURE YOU! IN THE MEANTIME, I'D LIKE TO INTRODUCE YOU TO YOUR OPPONENTS. FEAST YOUR EYES, LADIES.
#@?
WHAT'S WRONG?
I-I'VE ALREADY MET THEM...
EARLIER TODAY, BEFORE I RAN INTO YOU GUYS...
SHE MADE ME A PROMISE PERTAINING TO OUR NEXT INTERACTION...

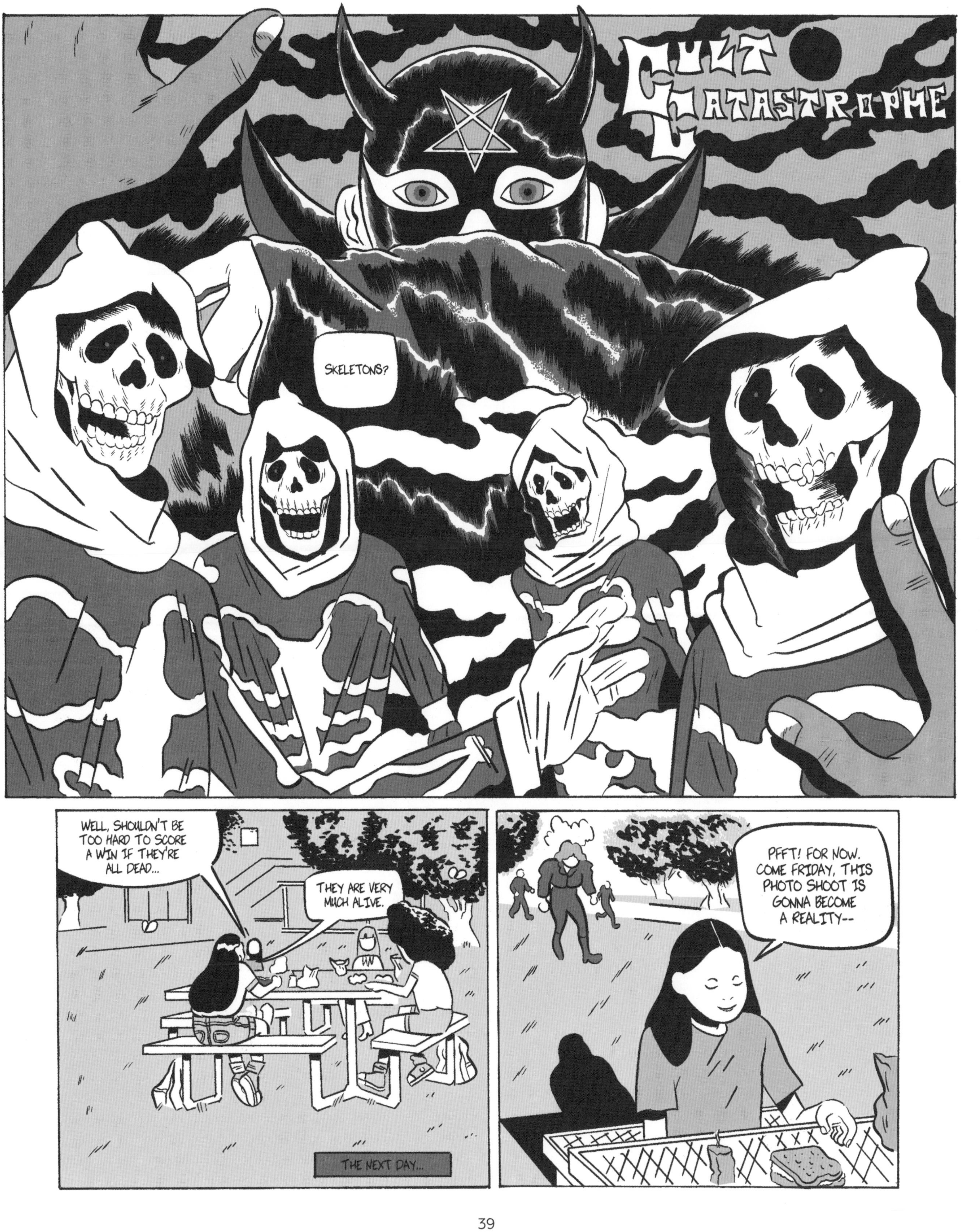
CULT CATASTROPHE
SKELETONS?
WELL, SHOULDN'T BE TOO HARD TO SCORE A WIN IF THEY'RE ALL DEAD...
THEY ARE VERY MUCH ALIVE.
THE NEXT DAY...
PFFT! FOR NOW. COME FRIDAY, THIS PHOTO SHOOT IS GONNA BECOME A REALITY--

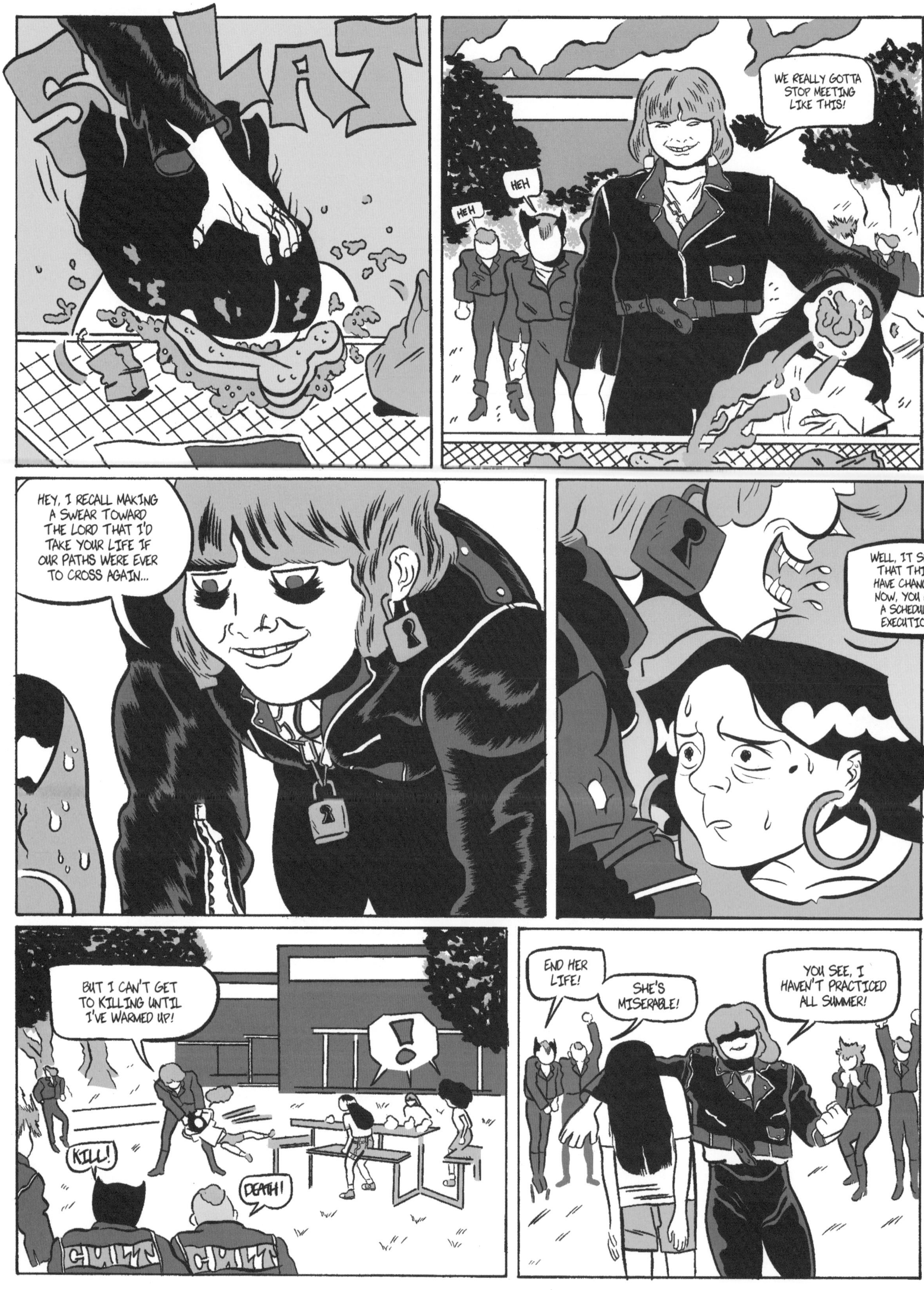
SPLAT
WE REALLY GOTTA STOP MEETING LIKE THIS!
HEH
HEH
HEY, I RECALL MAKING A SWEAR TOWARD THE LORD THAT I'D TAKE YOUR LIFE IF OUR PATHS WERE EVER TO CROSS AGAIN...
WELL, IT SEEMS THAT THINGS HAVE CHANGED! NOW, YOU HAVE A SCHEDULED EXECUTION.
BUT I CAN'T GET TO KILLING UNTIL I'VE WARMED UP!
!
KILL!
DEATH!
END HER LIFE!
SHE'S MISERABLE!
YOU SEE, I HAVEN'T PRACTICED ALL SUMMER!

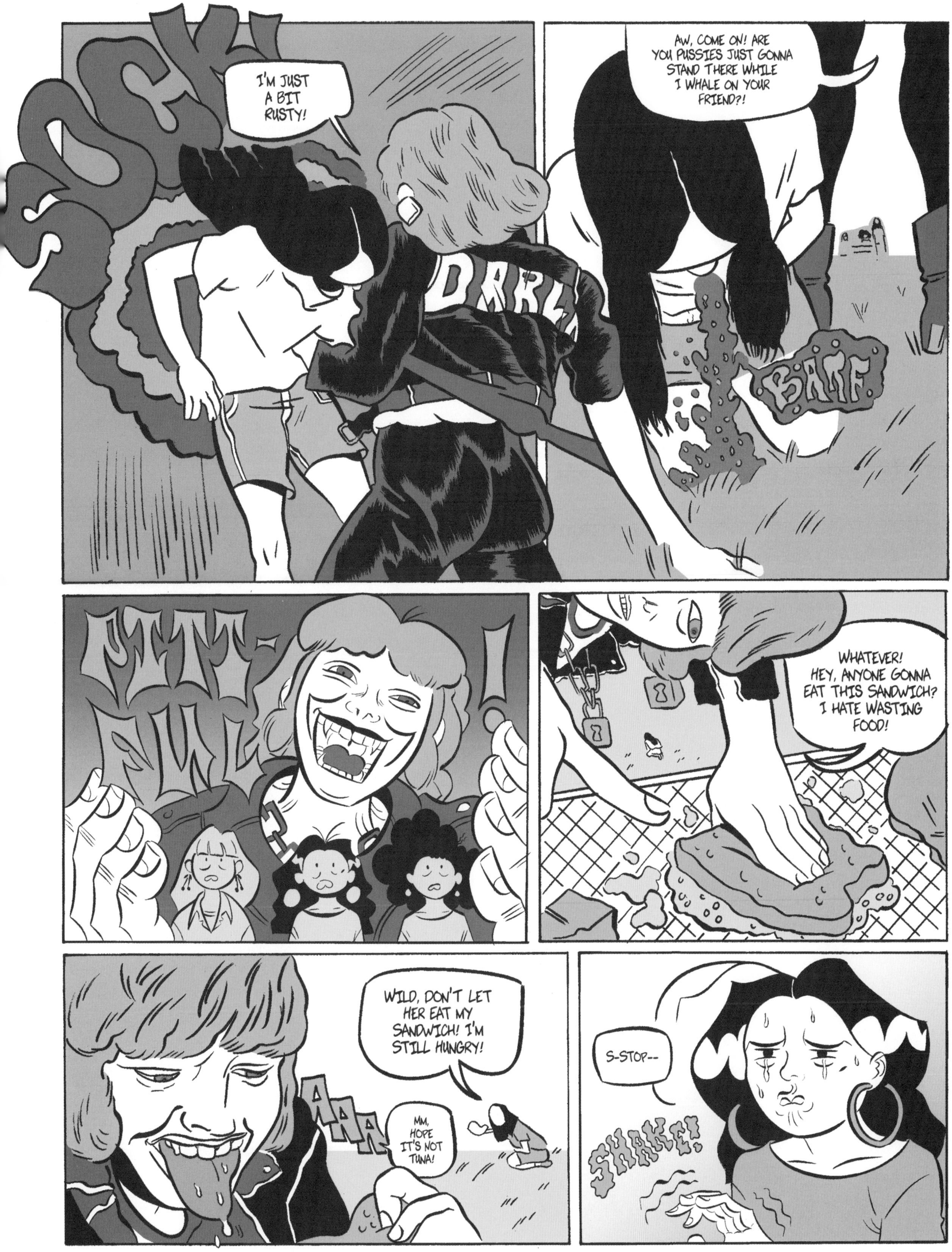
SOCK!
I'M JUST A BIT RUSTY!
DARLA
AW, COME ON! ARE YOU PUSSIES JUST GONNA STAND THERE WHILE I WHALE ON YOUR FRIEND?!
BARF
WHATEVER! HEY, ANYONE GONNA EAT THIS SANDWICH? I HATE WASTING FOOD!
WILD, DON'T LET HER EAT MY SANDWICH! I'M STILL HUNGRY!
AAAA
MM, HOPE IT'S NOT TUNA!
S-STOP--
SHAKE!

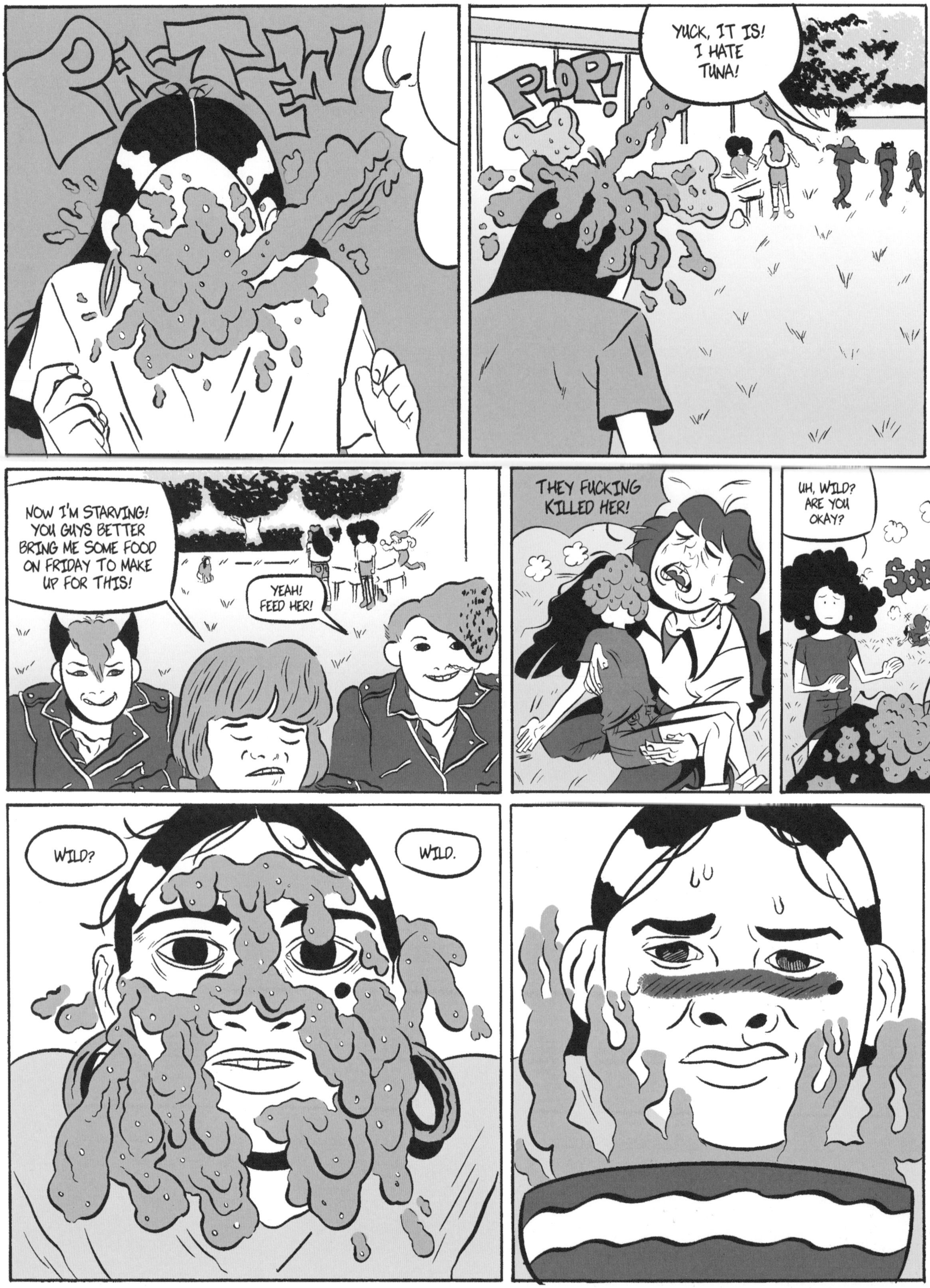
PLOP!
YUCK, IT IS! I HATE TUNA!
NOW I'M STARVING! YOU GUYS BETTER BRING ME SOME FOOD ON FRIDAY TO MAKE UP FOR THIS!
YEAH! FEED HER!
THEY FUCKING KILLED HER!
UH, WILD? ARE YOU OKAY?
SOB!
WILD?
WILD.

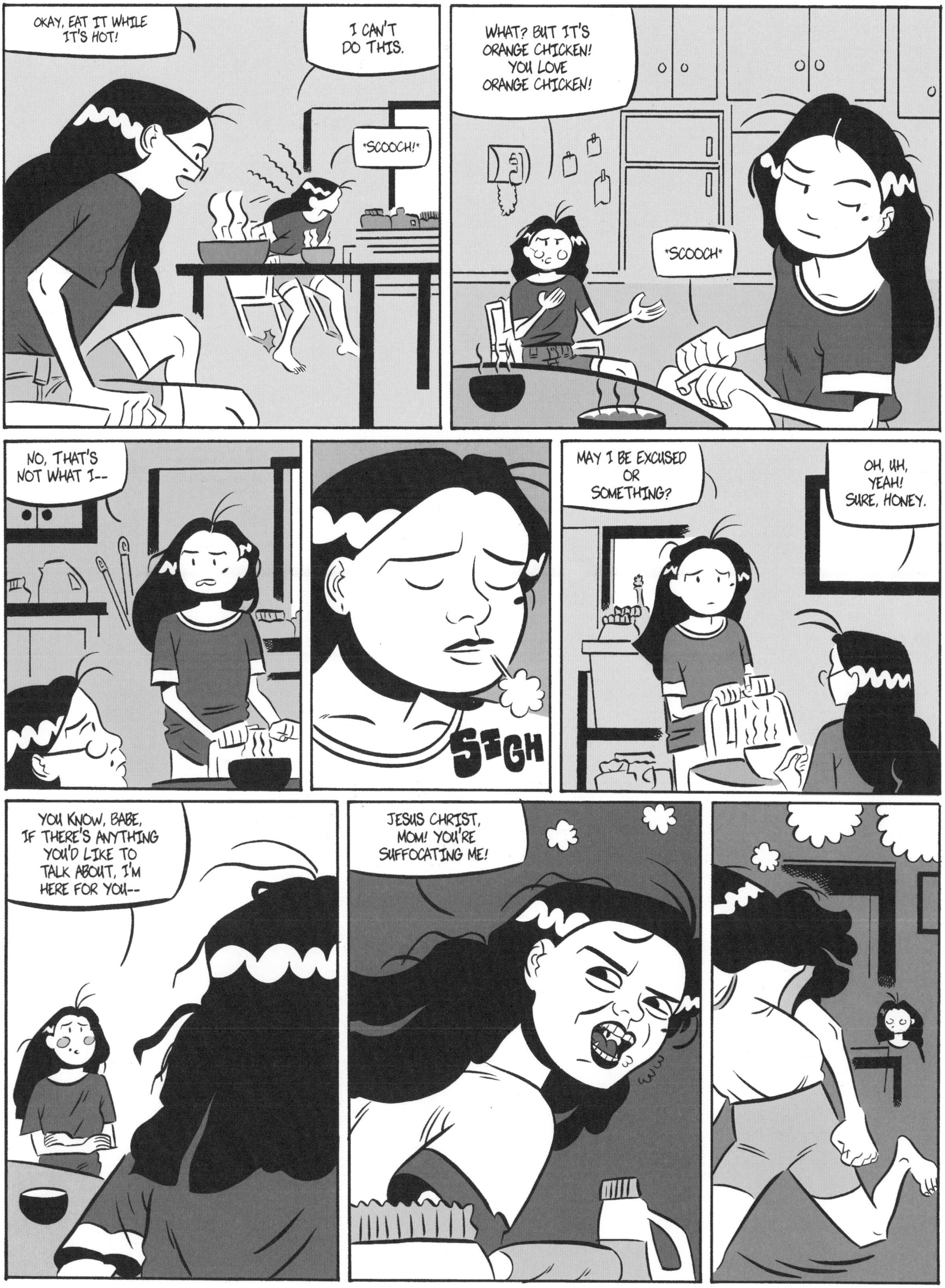
OKAY, EAT IT WHILE IT'S HOT!
I CAN'T DO THIS.
SCOOCH!
WHAT? BUT IT'S ORANGE CHICKEN! YOU LOVE ORANGE CHICKEN!
SCOOCH
NO, THAT'S NOT WHAT I--
SIGH
MAY I BE EXCUSED OR SOMETHING?
OH, UH, YEAH! SURE, HONEY.
YOU KNOW, BABE, IF THERE'S ANYTHING YOU'D LIKE TO TALK ABOUT, I'M HERE FOR YOU--
JESUS CHRIST, MOM! YOU'RE SUFFOCATING ME!

WOW! YOU HAVEN'T EVEN PLAYED FOR A SECOND AND YOU'RE ALREADY LETTING EVERYONE DOWN!

WHAT DO YOU THINK'S GONNA HAPPEN ON FRIDAY, HUH? THINK YOU'RE GONNA WALK ONTO THE TRACK AND JOIN A KUMBAYA CIRCLE?

GET A GRIP! YOU'RE OUT OF YOUR LEAGUE HERE, SQUIRT. YOU'RE NO ATHLETE! YOU'RE JUST AN OVERZEALOUS FAN!

AH!

WAIT!

C'MON, C'MON...

TA-DA!

ONLY ME AND THE TOOTH FAIRY KNOW ABOUT YOU, BABY.

ROLLER READER

OCTOBER 1960

TIME FOR A LITTLE MOTIVATIONAL READ!

AHEM!

"IN JUST UNDER TWO YEARS, ROSIE ROZENE HAS MANAGED TO GARNER A FOLLOWING THE LIKES OF WHICH NO ATHLETE IN THE WORLD ROLLER DERBY FEDERATION HAS EVER CULTIVATED BEFORE! NOW, HAVING SECURED HER PLACE IN THE '60 FINALS AGAINST MARY MANHATTAN, ROSIE WILL SURELY ONLY INCREASE IN POPULARITY AMONGST FANS NEW AND OLD!"

YAWN!

I FORGOT THERE WERE SO MANY WORDS.

"PREVIOUS FAN FAVORITES SUZANNE SPIT AND MARY MANHATTAN HAVE BEEN TOSSED TO THE WAYSIDE IN FAVOR OF A BIGGER AND BETTER ATHLETE. THOUGH THEY MAINTAIN CONTINUED SUPPORT FROM A DEDICATED FEW, THEIR POPULARITY NOW PALES IN COMPARISON TO THAT OF ROSIE ROZENE AND HER DESERT ROSES."

"IMMEDIATELY FOLLOWING HER SEMIFINAL VICTORY OVER SUZANNE SPIT AND THE LOVE BUGS --"

YAWN!

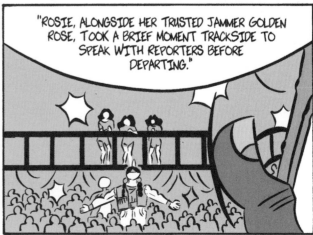

"ROSIE, ALONGSIDE HER TRUSTED JAMMER GOLDEN ROSE, TOOK A BRIEF MOMENT TRACKSIDE TO SPEAK WITH REPORTERS BEFORE DEPARTING."

45

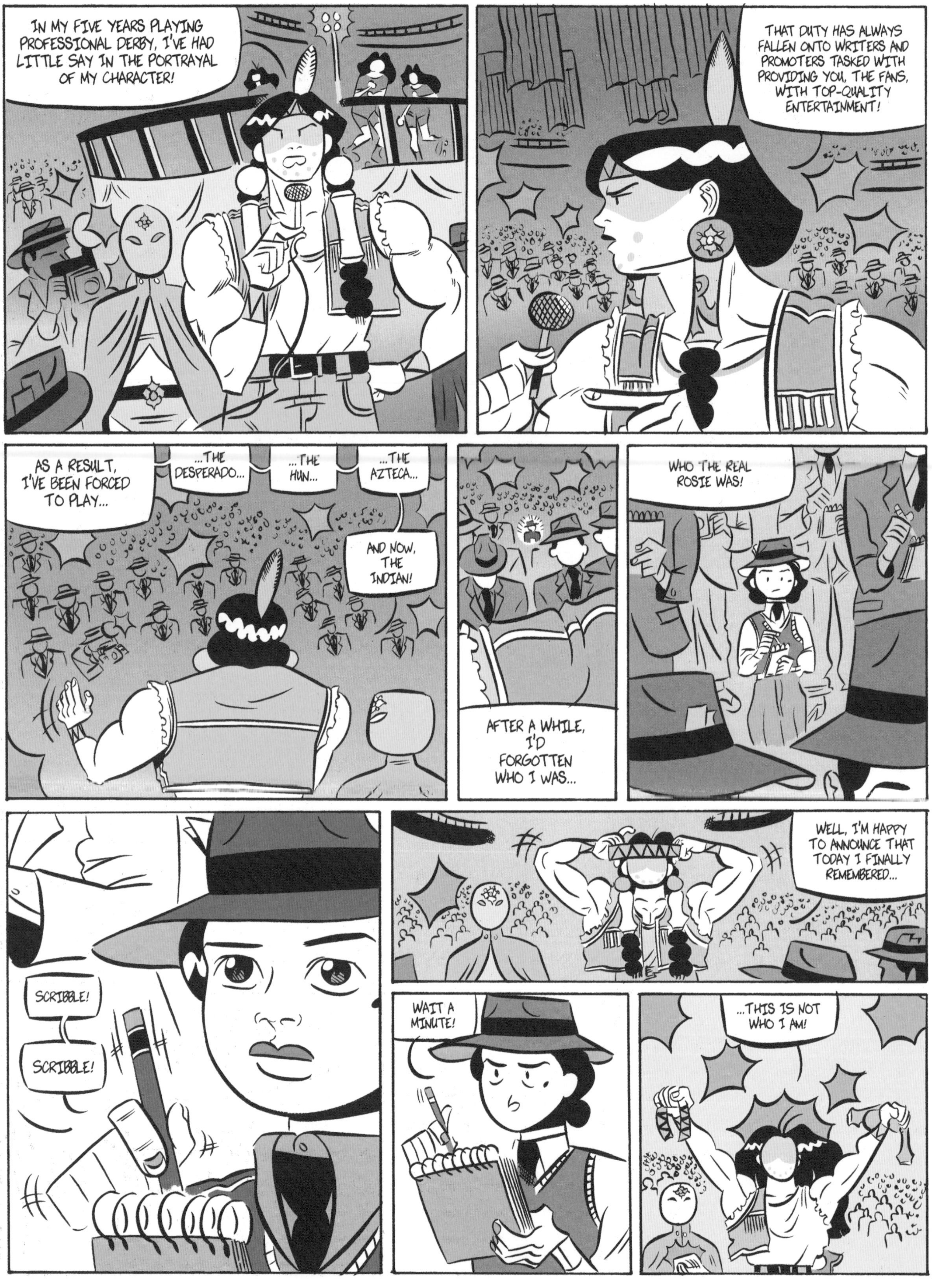

IN MY FIVE YEARS PLAYING PROFESSIONAL DERBY, I'VE HAD LITTLE SAY IN THE PORTRAYAL OF MY CHARACTER!
THAT DUTY HAS ALWAYS FALLEN ONTO WRITERS AND PROMOTERS TASKED WITH PROVIDING YOU, THE FANS, WITH TOP-QUALITY ENTERTAINMENT!
AS A RESULT, I'VE BEEN FORCED TO PLAY...
...THE DESPERADO...
...THE HUN...
...THE AZTECA...
AND NOW, THE INDIAN!
AFTER A WHILE, I'D FORGOTTEN WHO I WAS...
WHO THE REAL ROSIE WAS!
SCRIBBLE!
SCRIBBLE!
WELL, I'M HAPPY TO ANNOUNCE THAT TODAY I FINALLY REMEMBERED...
WAIT A MINUTE!
...THIS IS NOT WHO I AM!

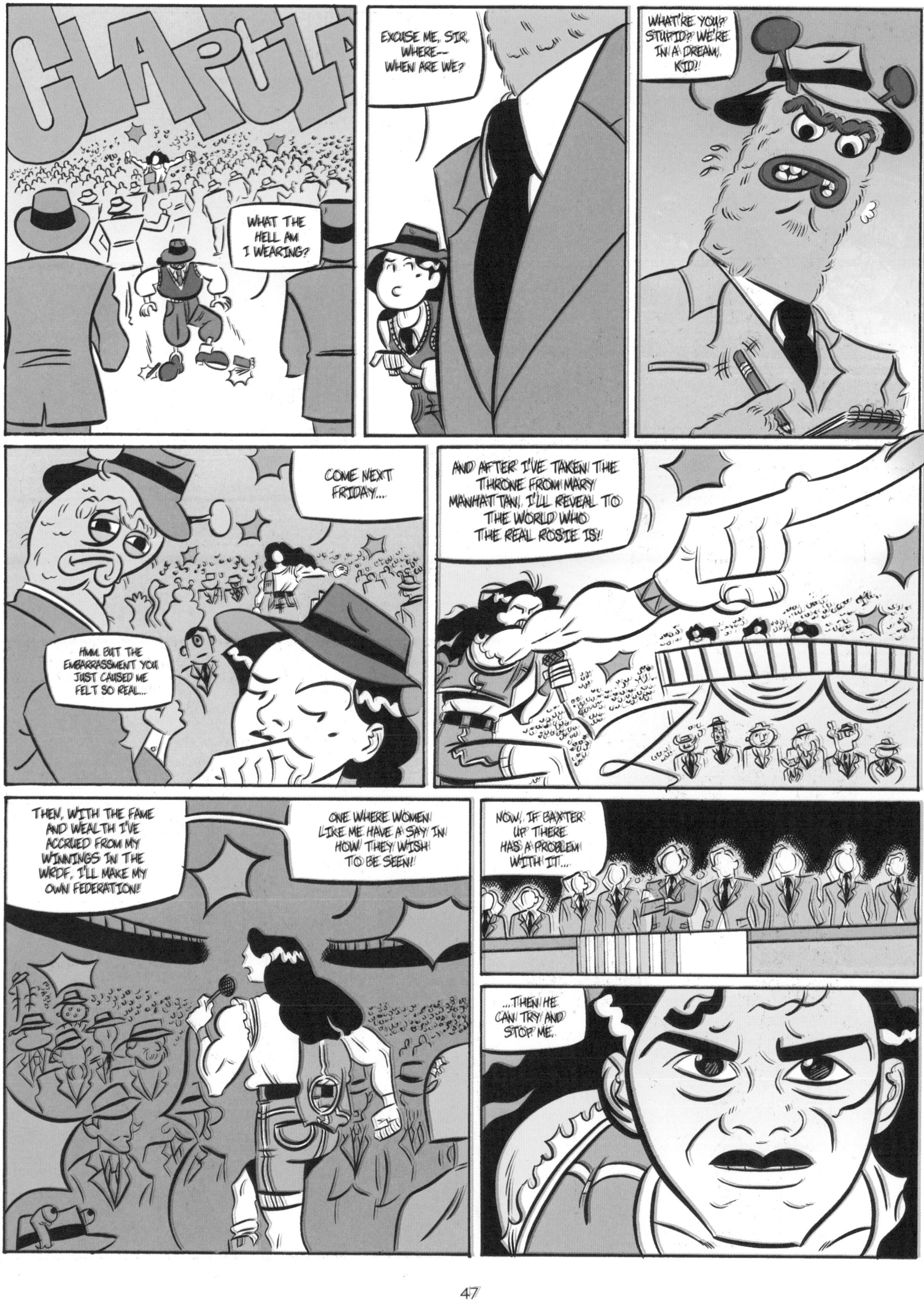
CLAP CLAP
WHAT THE HELL AM I WEARING?
EXCUSE ME, SIR, WHERE-- WHEN ARE WE?
WHAT'RE YOU? STUPID? WE'RE IN A DREAM, KID!
COME NEXT FRIDAY...
HMM. BUT THE EMBARRASSMENT YOU JUST CAUSED ME FELT SO REAL...
AND AFTER I'VE TAKEN THE THRONE FROM MARY MANHATTAN, I'LL REVEAL TO THE WORLD WHO THE REAL ROSIE IS!
THEN, WITH THE FAME AND WEALTH I'VE ACCRUED FROM MY WINNINGS IN THE WRDF, I'LL MAKE MY OWN FEDERATION!
ONE WHERE WOMEN LIKE ME HAVE A SAY IN HOW THEY WISH TO BE SEEN!
NOW, IF BAXTER UP THERE HAS A PROBLEM WITH IT...
...THEN HE CAN TRY AND STOP ME.

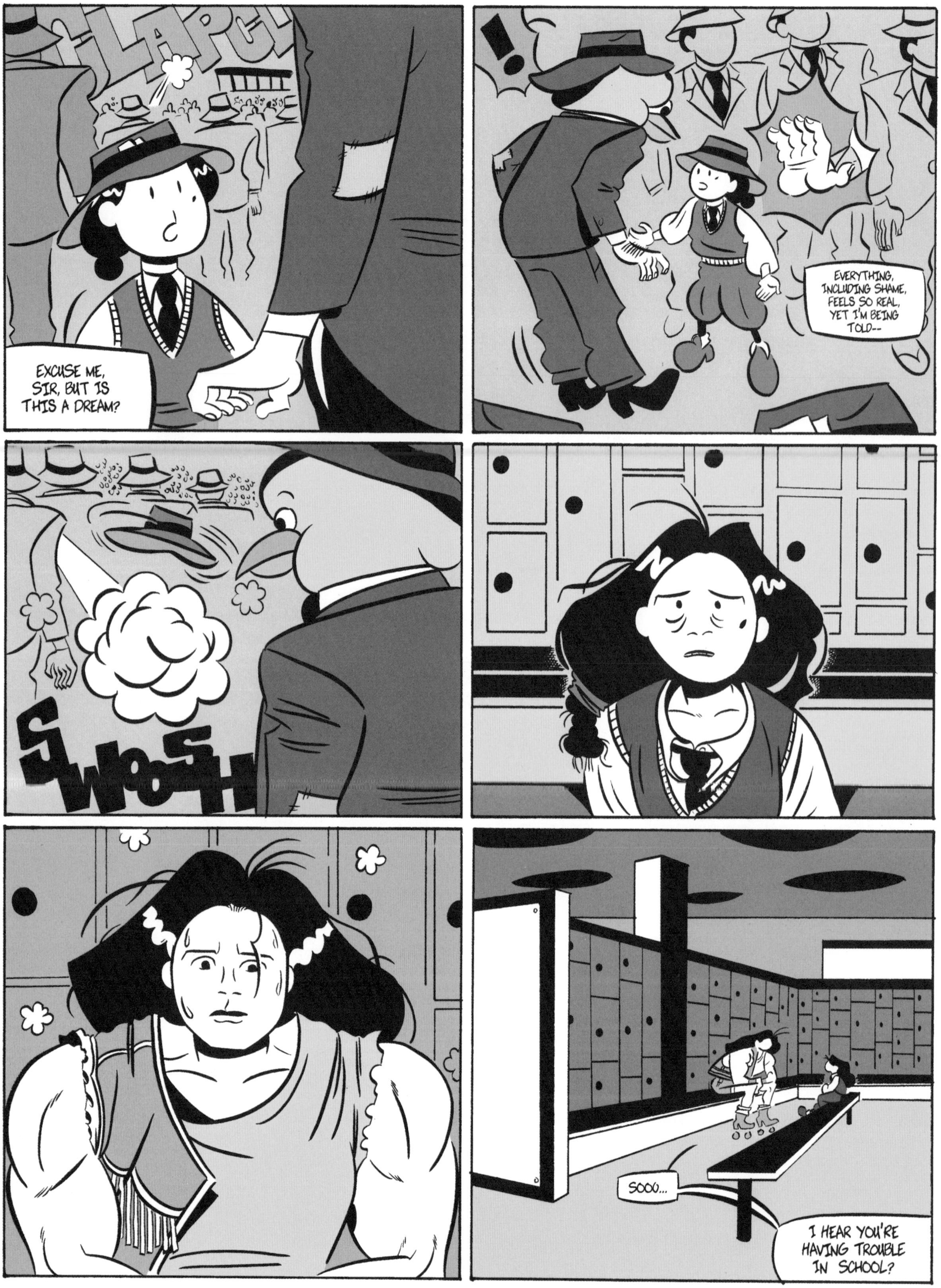
FLAPCH
EXCUSE ME, SIR, BUT IS THIS A DREAM?
!
EVERYTHING, INCLUDING SHAME, FEELS SO REAL, YET I'M BEING TOLD--
SWOOSH
SOOO...
I HEAR YOU'RE HAVING TROUBLE IN SCHOOL?

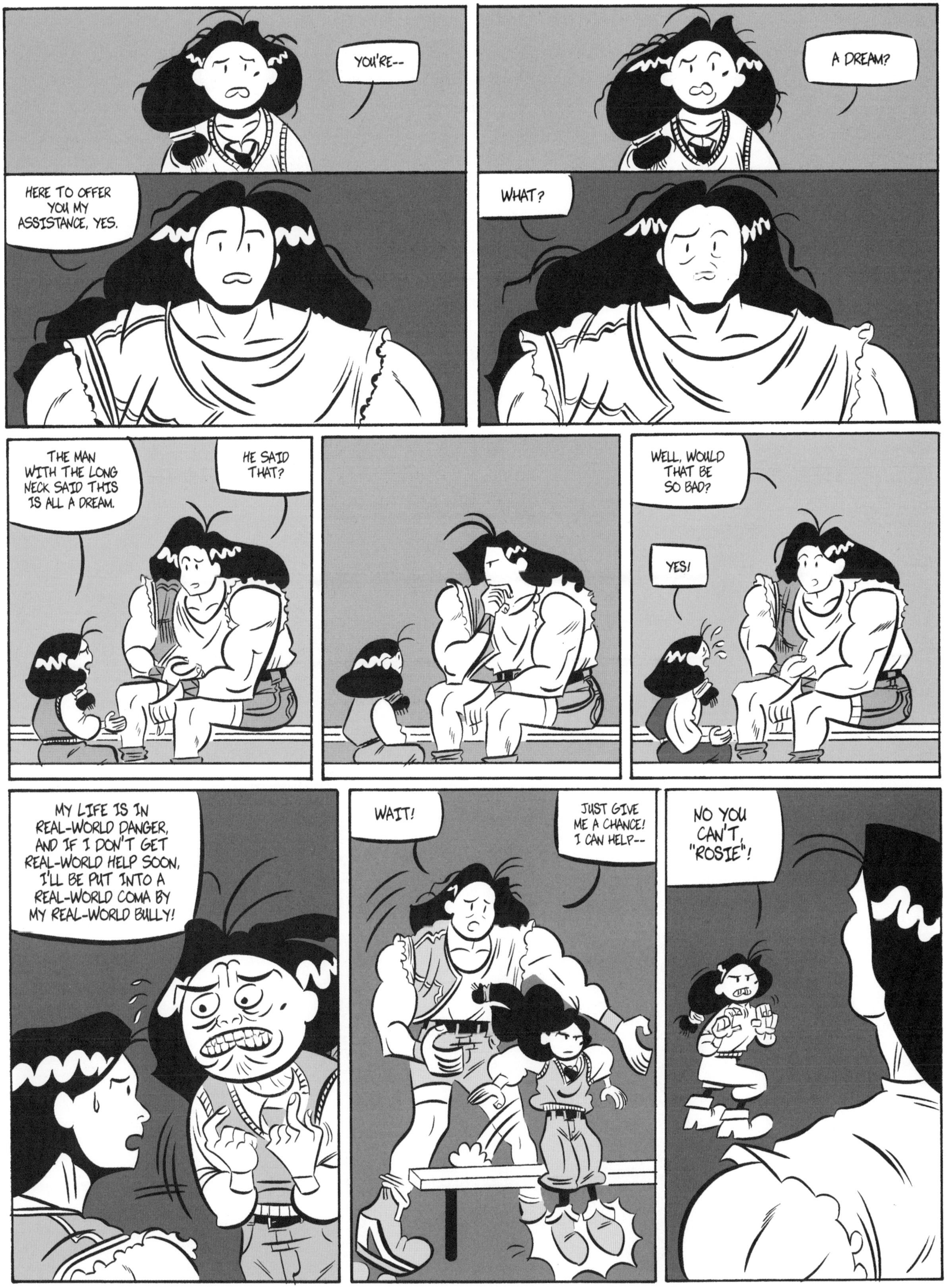
YOU'RE--
A DREAM?
HERE TO OFFER YOU MY ASSISTANCE, YES.
WHAT?
THE MAN WITH THE LONG NECK SAID THIS IS ALL A DREAM.
HE SAID THAT?
WELL, WOULD THAT BE SO BAD?
YES!
MY LIFE IS IN REAL-WORLD DANGER, AND IF I DON'T GET REAL-WORLD HELP SOON, I'LL BE PUT INTO A REAL-WORLD COMA BY MY REAL-WORLD BULLY!
WAIT!
JUST GIVE ME A CHANCE! I CAN HELP--
NO YOU CAN'T, "ROSIE"!

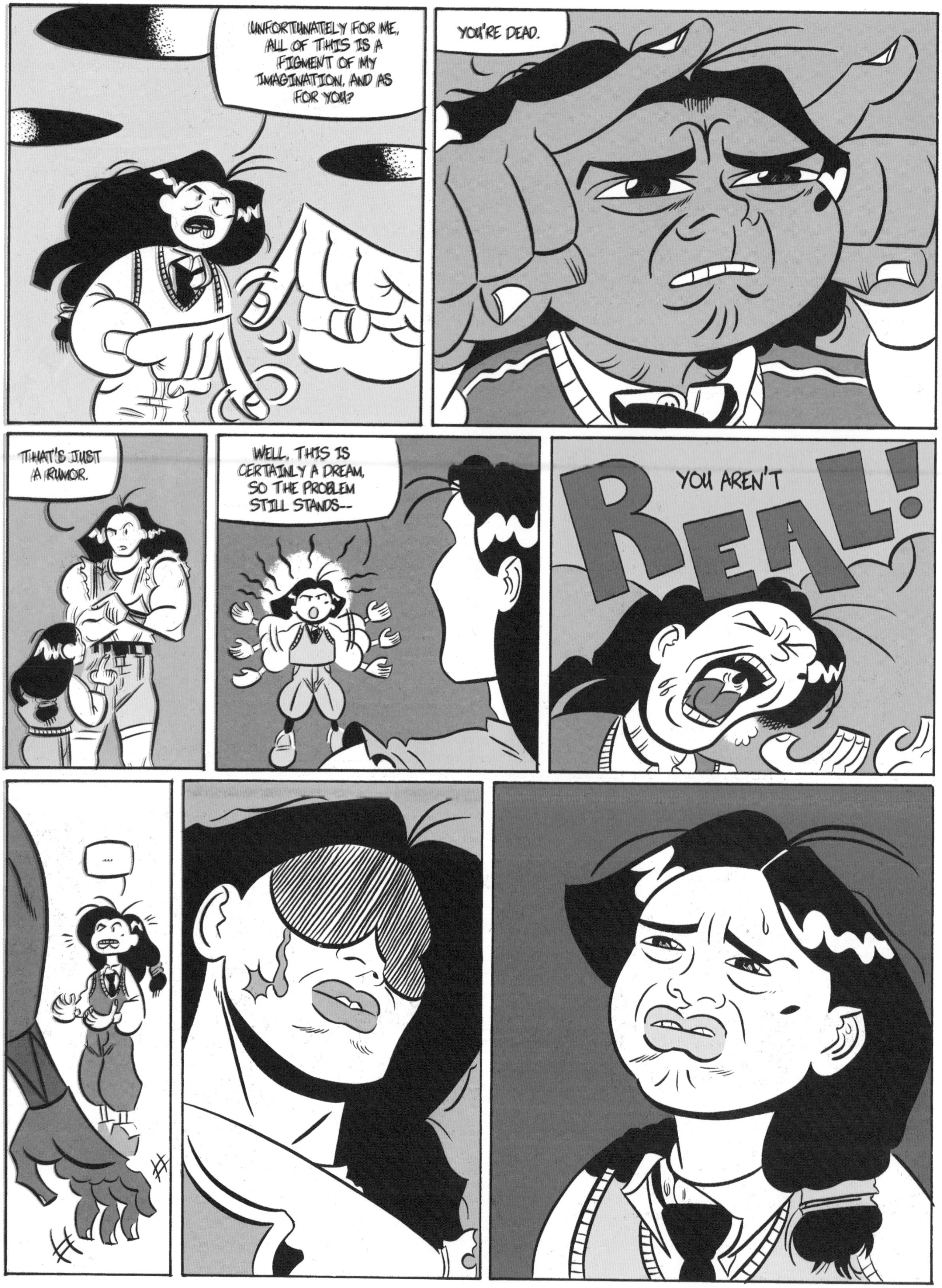
UNFORTUNATELY FOR ME, ALL OF THIS IS A FIGMENT OF MY IMAGINATION, AND AS FOR YOU?
YOU'RE DEAD.
THAT'S JUST A RUMOR.
WELL, THIS IS CERTAINLY A DREAM, SO THE PROBLEM STILL STANDS--
YOU AREN'T
REAL!
...

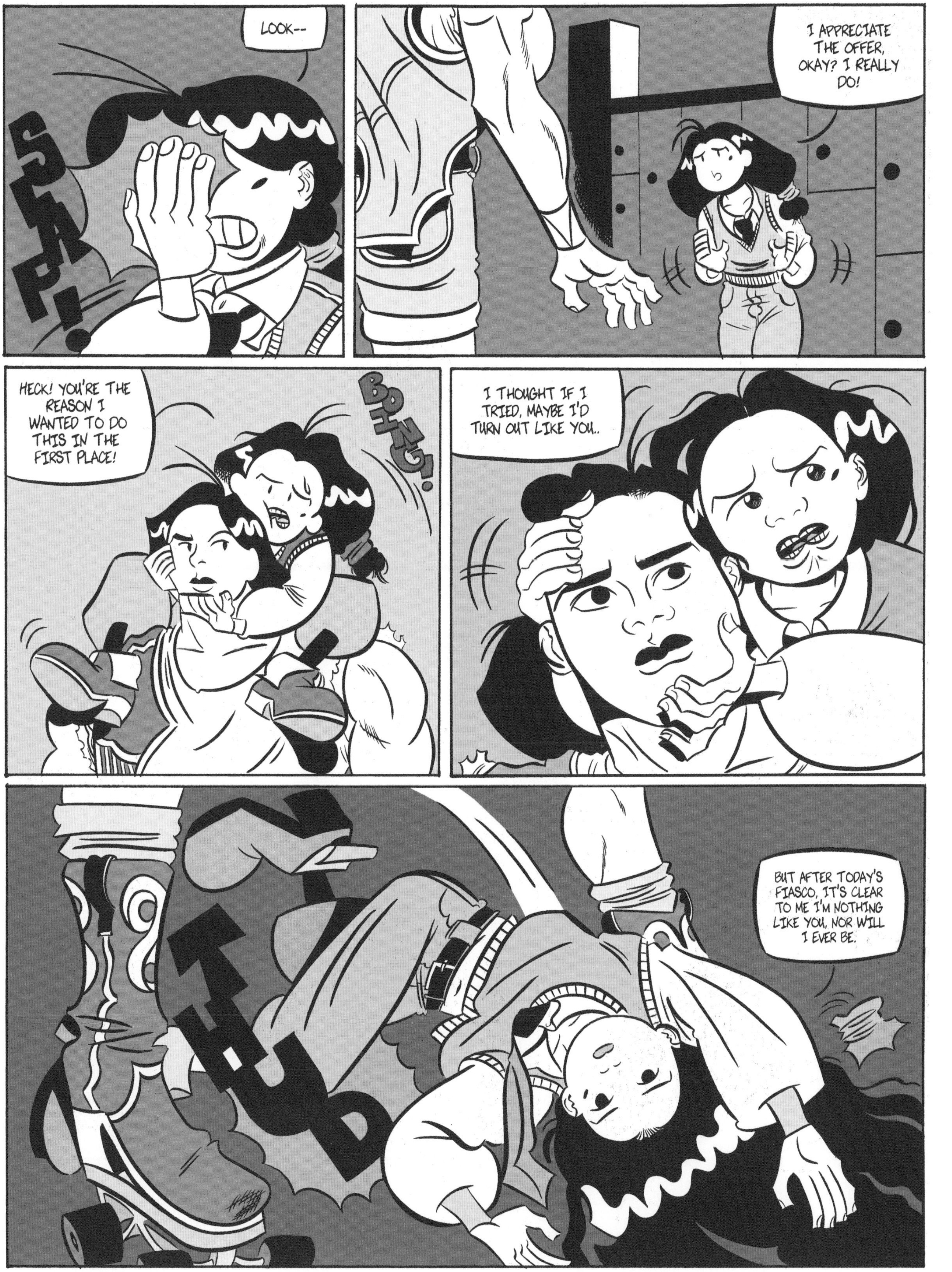
LOOK--
SLAP!
I APPRECIATE THE OFFER, OKAY? I REALLY DO!
HECK! YOU'RE THE REASON I WANTED TO DO THIS IN THE FIRST PLACE!
BOING!
I THOUGHT IF I TRIED, MAYBE I'D TURN OUT LIKE YOU..
THUD
BUT AFTER TODAY'S FIASCO, IT'S CLEAR TO ME I'M NOTHING LIKE YOU, NOR WILL I EVER BE.

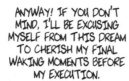

ANYWAY! IF YOU DON'T MIND, I'LL BE EXCUSING MYSELF FROM THIS DREAM TO CHERISH MY FINAL WAKING MOMENTS BEFORE MY EXECUTION.

PTT

NOW, SINCE THIS IS A DREAM...

...IT WOULD BE PERFECTLY LOGICAL...

...THAT THIS LOCKER WOULD BE AN EXIT!

NOW LET ME SEE HERE...!CLICK! JUST TURN IT....!KRK!...THEN ROTATE...!CRK!

OKAY, SO I MAY NEED YOUR ASSISTANCE AFTER ALL.

RIGHT! WELL, IT'S BEEN "REAL," BUT I'VE GOTTA RUN!

WAIT--BEFORE YOU GO...

I KNOW YOU HAVE DOUBTS, BUT MY OFFER STILL STANDS. JUST REACH OUT IF YOU NEED ME.

UH, THANK YOU, ROSIE.

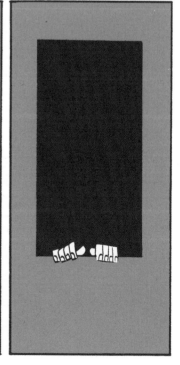

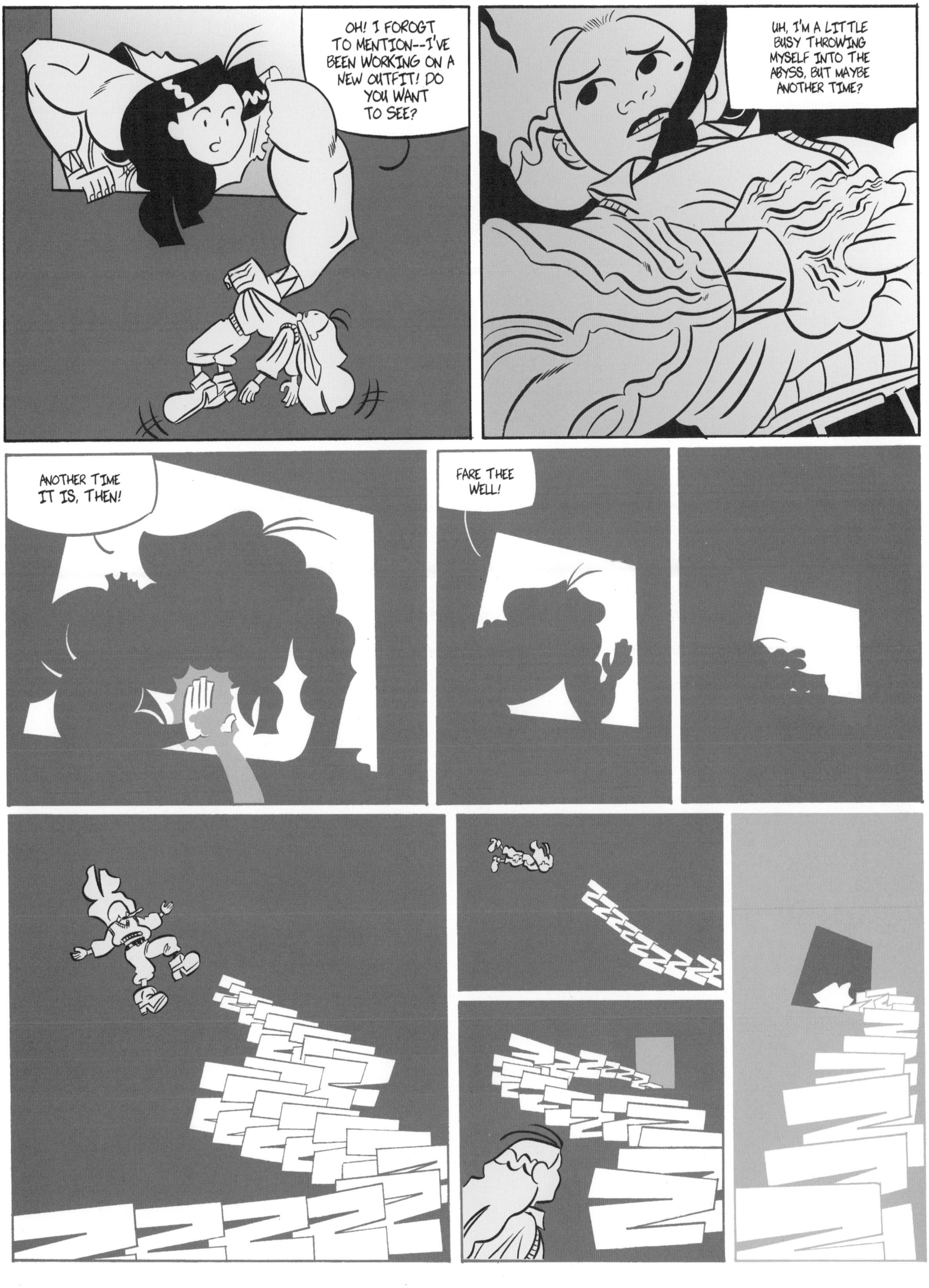
OH! I FOROGT TO MENTION--I'VE BEEN WORKING ON A NEW OUTFIT! DO YOU WANT TO SEE?
UH, I'M A LITTLE BUSY THROWING MYSELF INTO THE ABYSS, BUT MAYBE ANOTHER TIME?
ANOTHER TIME IT IS, THEN!
FARE THEE WELL!

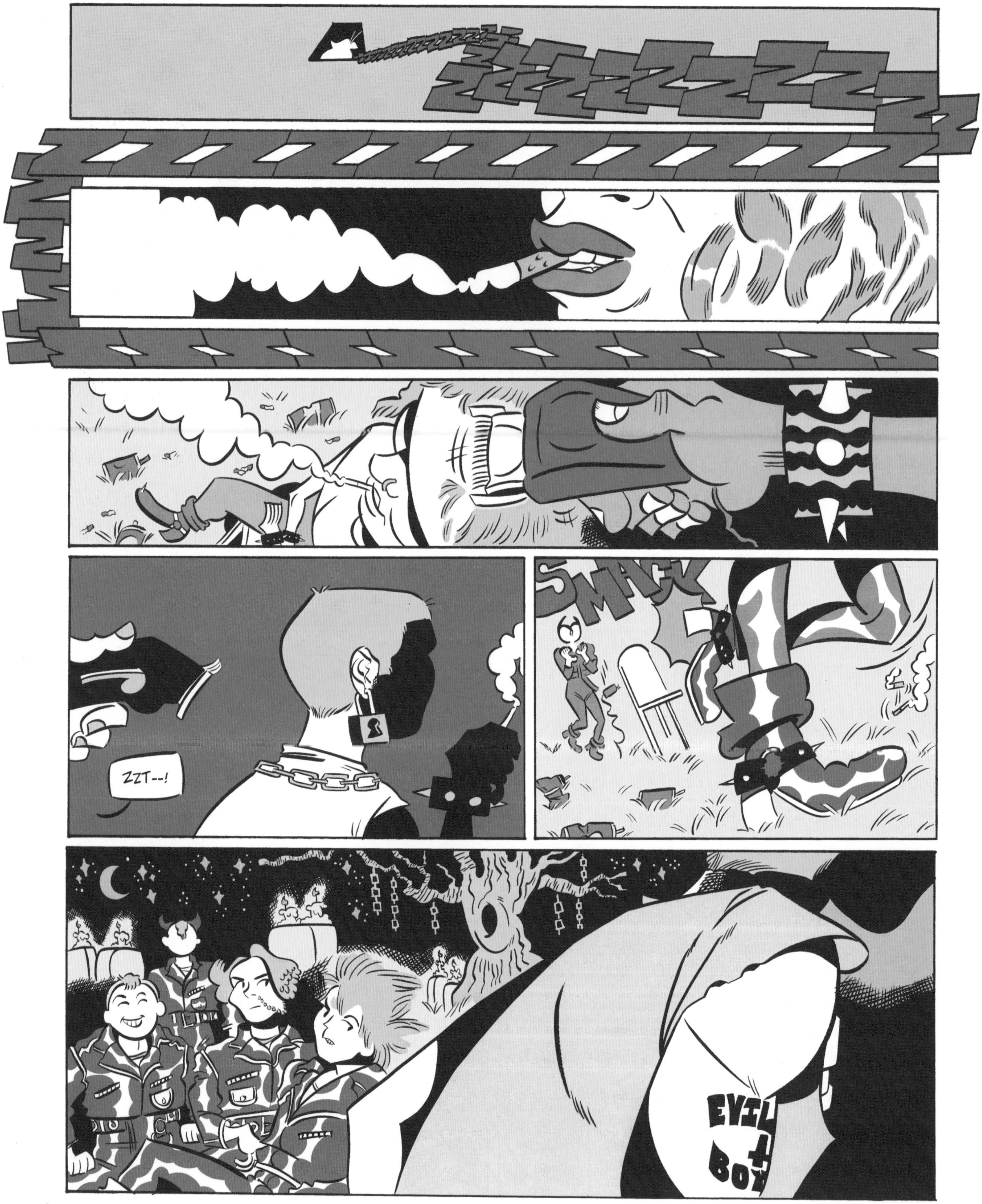
AZZZZZZZZZZZZZZZZZZZZZZZZZZZZZZZZZZZZZZZZZZZZZ
ZZT--!
SMACK
EVIL BOY

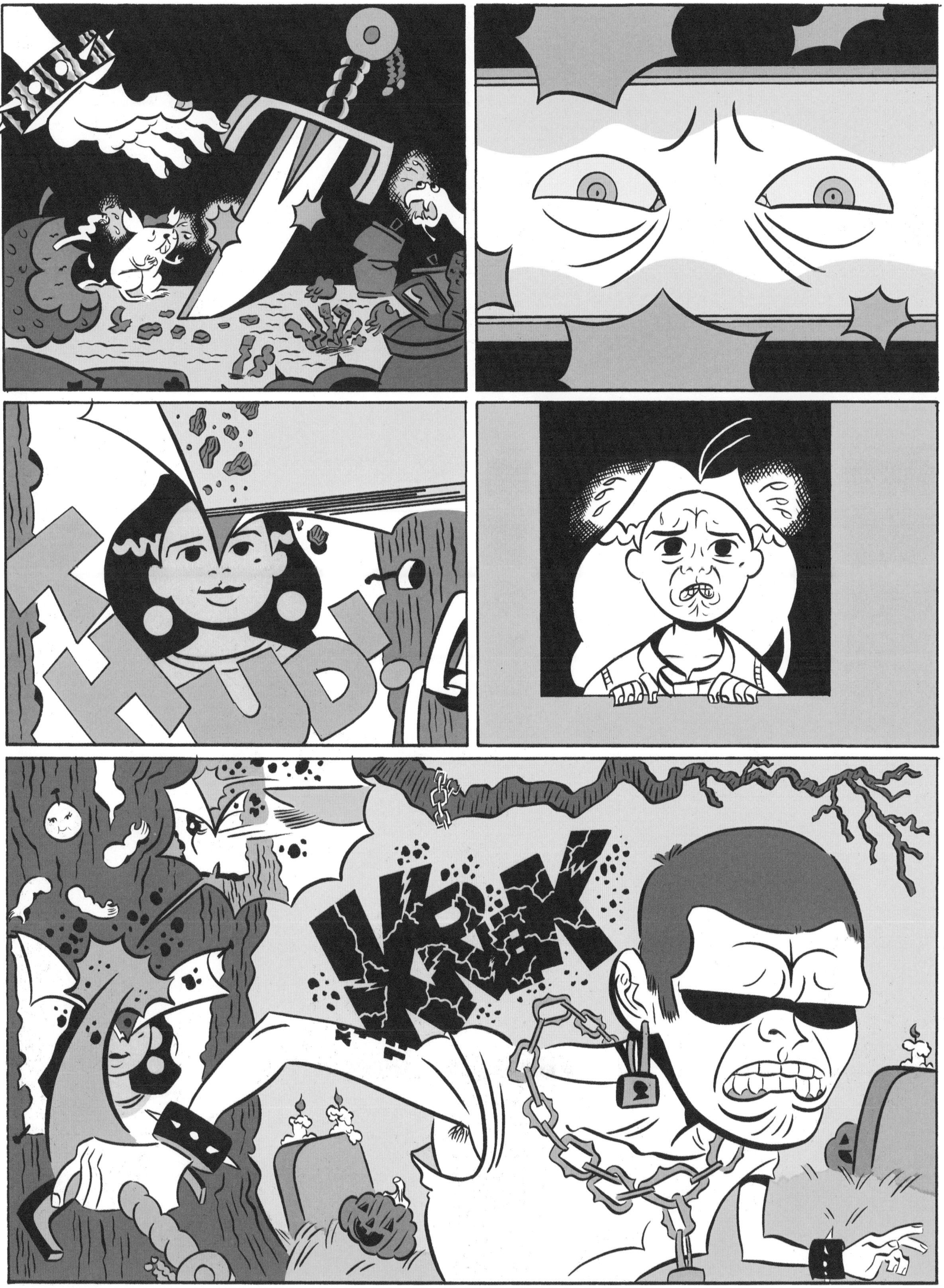
THUD!
KRAK

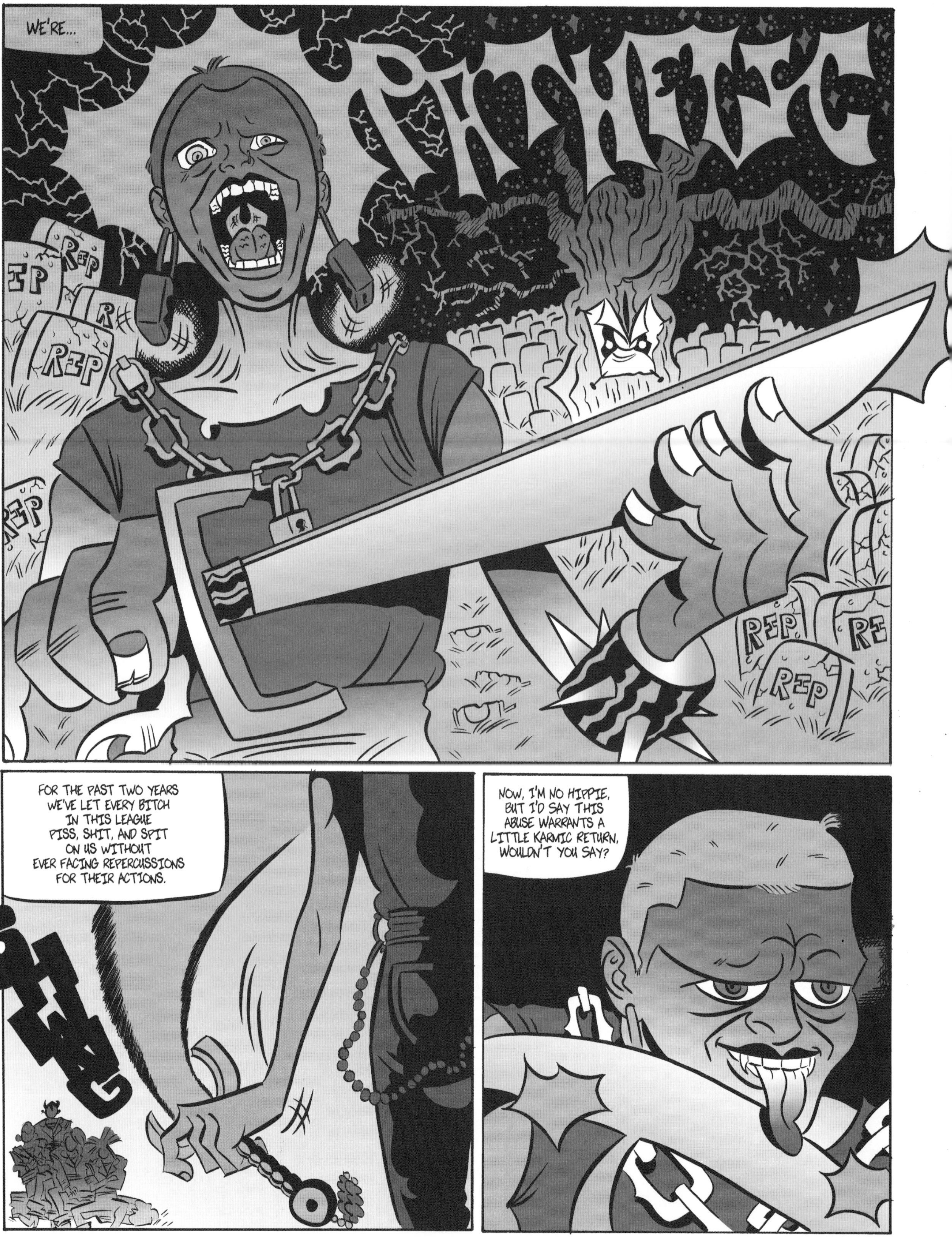
WE'RE...
PATHETIC
FOR THE PAST TWO YEARS WE'VE LET EVERY BITCH IN THIS LEAGUE PISS, SHIT, AND SPIT ON US WITHOUT EVER FACING REPERCUSSIONS FOR THEIR ACTIONS.
NOW, I'M NO HIPPIE, BUT I'D SAY THIS ABUSE WARRANTS A LITTLE KARMIC RETURN, WOULDN'T YOU SAY?

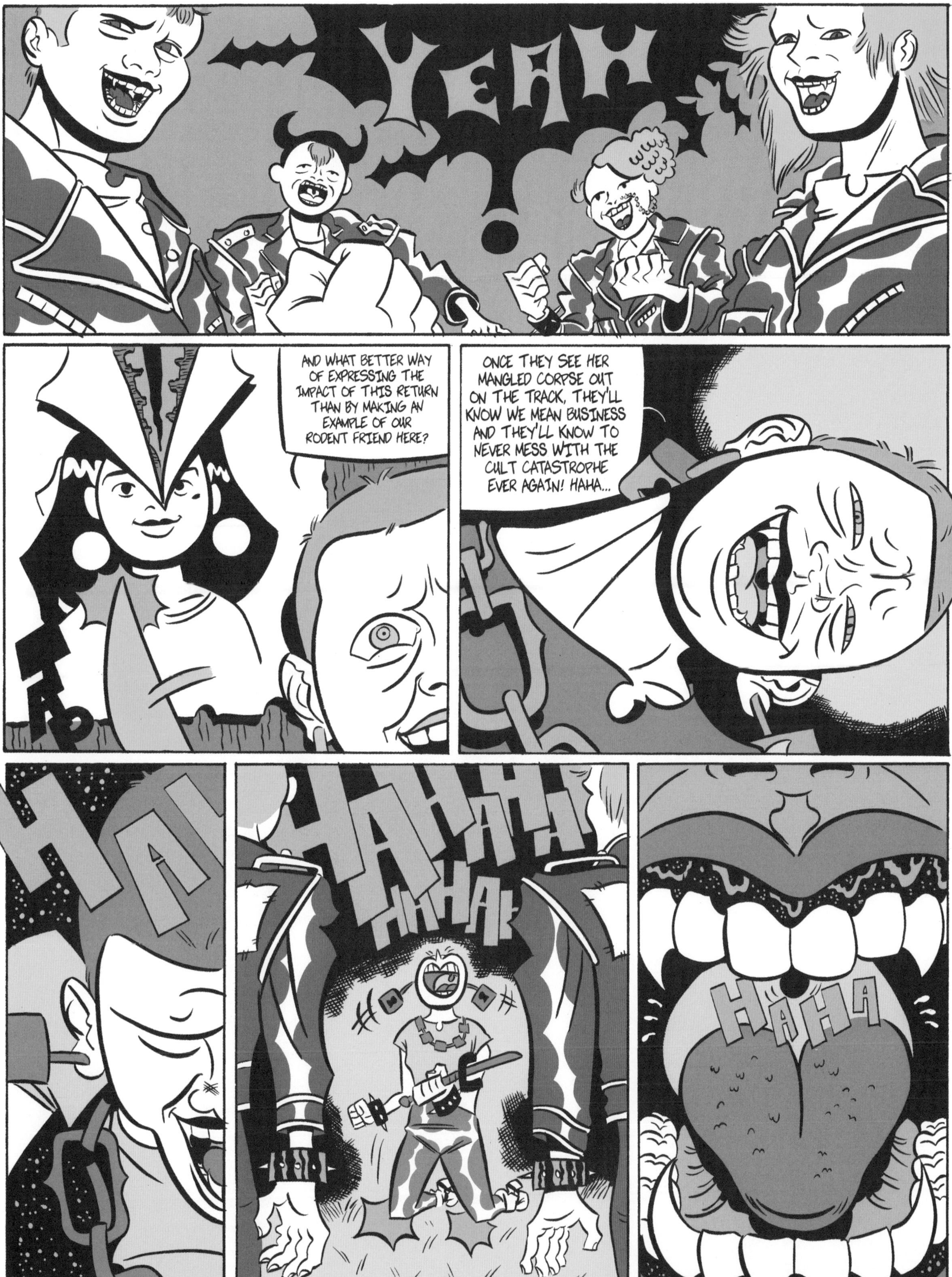
YEAH!
AND WHAT BETTER WAY OF EXPRESSING THE IMPACT OF THIS RETURN THAN BY MAKING AN EXAMPLE OF OUR RODENT FRIEND HERE?
ONCE THEY SEE HER MANGLED CORPSE OUT ON THE TRACK, THEY'LL KNOW WE MEAN BUSINESS AND THEY'LL KNOW TO NEVER MESS WITH THE CULT CATASTROPHE EVER AGAIN! HAHA...
HA!
HAHAHAHA
HAHA
HAHA

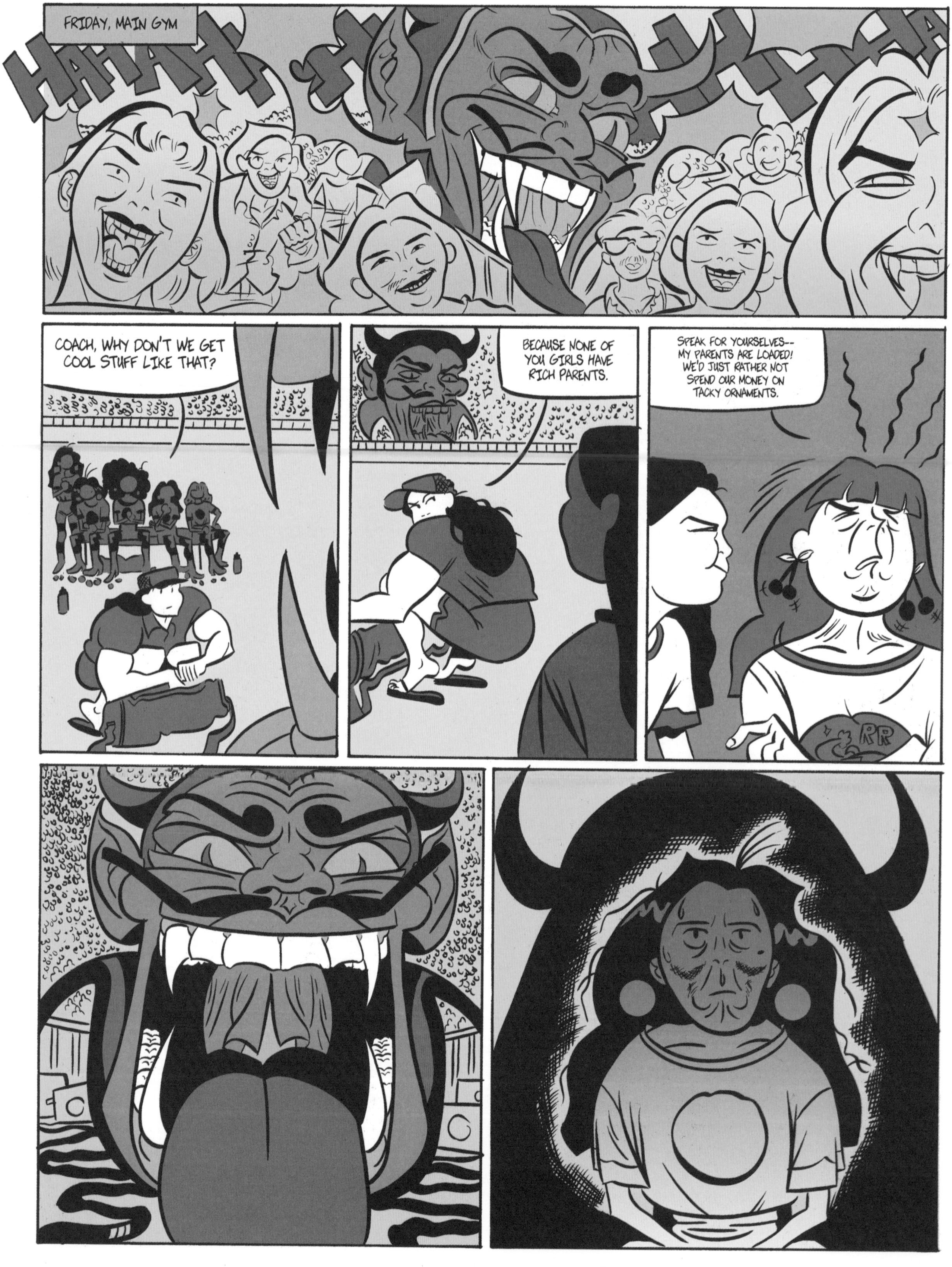
FRIDAY, MAIN GYM
HAHAHA
COACH, WHY DON'T WE GET COOL STUFF LIKE THAT?
BECAUSE NONE OF YOU GIRLS HAVE RICH PARENTS.
SPEAK FOR YOURSELVES-- MY PARENTS ARE LOADED! WE'D JUST RATHER NOT SPEND OUR MONEY ON TACKY ORNAMENTS.

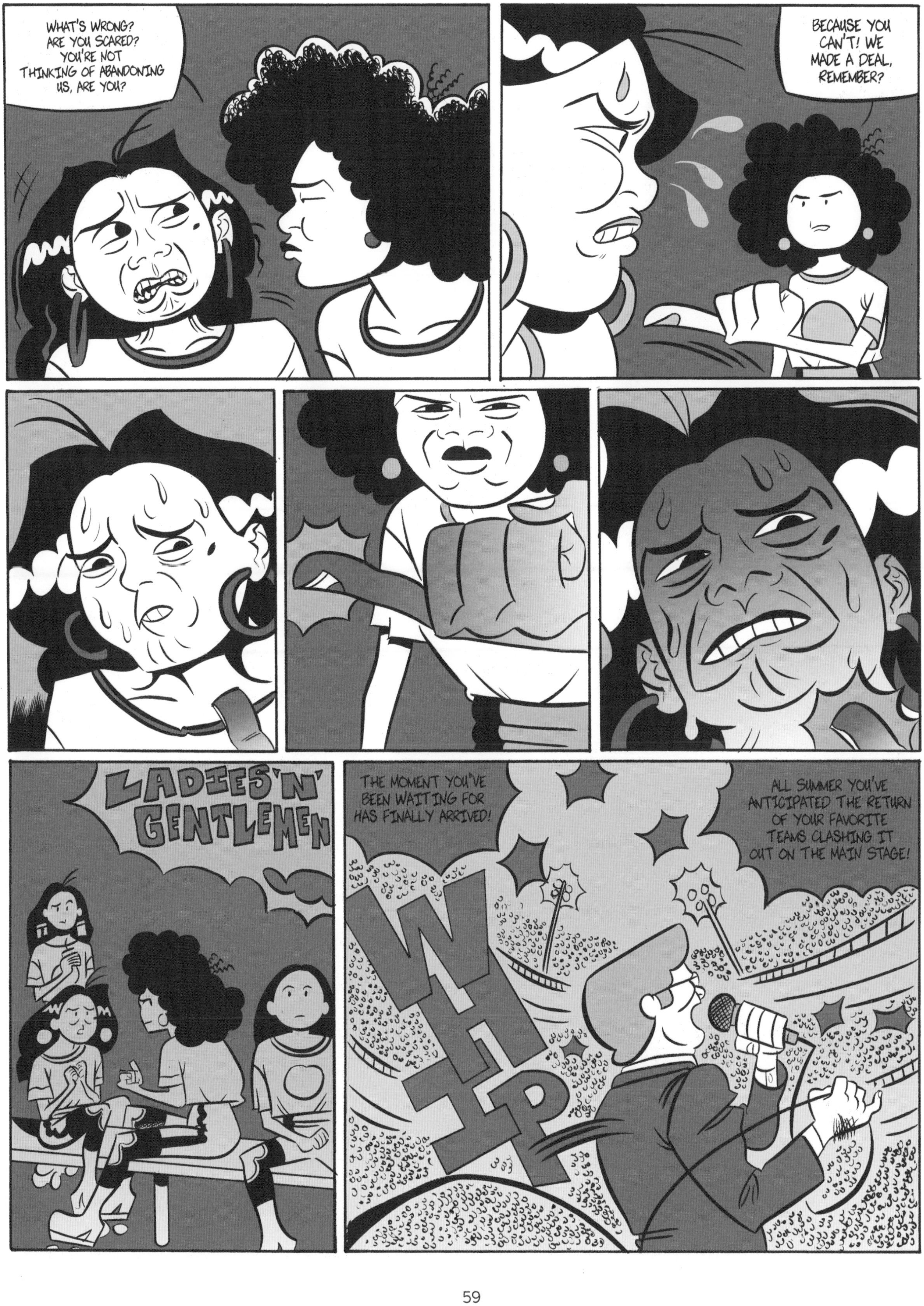
WHAT'S WRONG? ARE YOU SCARED? YOU'RE NOT THINKING OF ABANDONING US, ARE YOU?
BECAUSE YOU CAN'T! WE MADE A DEAL, REMEMBER?
LADIES 'N' GENTLEMEN
THE MOMENT YOU'VE BEEN WAITING FOR HAS FINALLY ARRIVED!
ALL SUMMER YOU'VE ANTICIPATED THE RETURN OF YOUR FAVORITE TEAMS CLASHING IT OUT ON THE MAIN STAGE!
WHIP

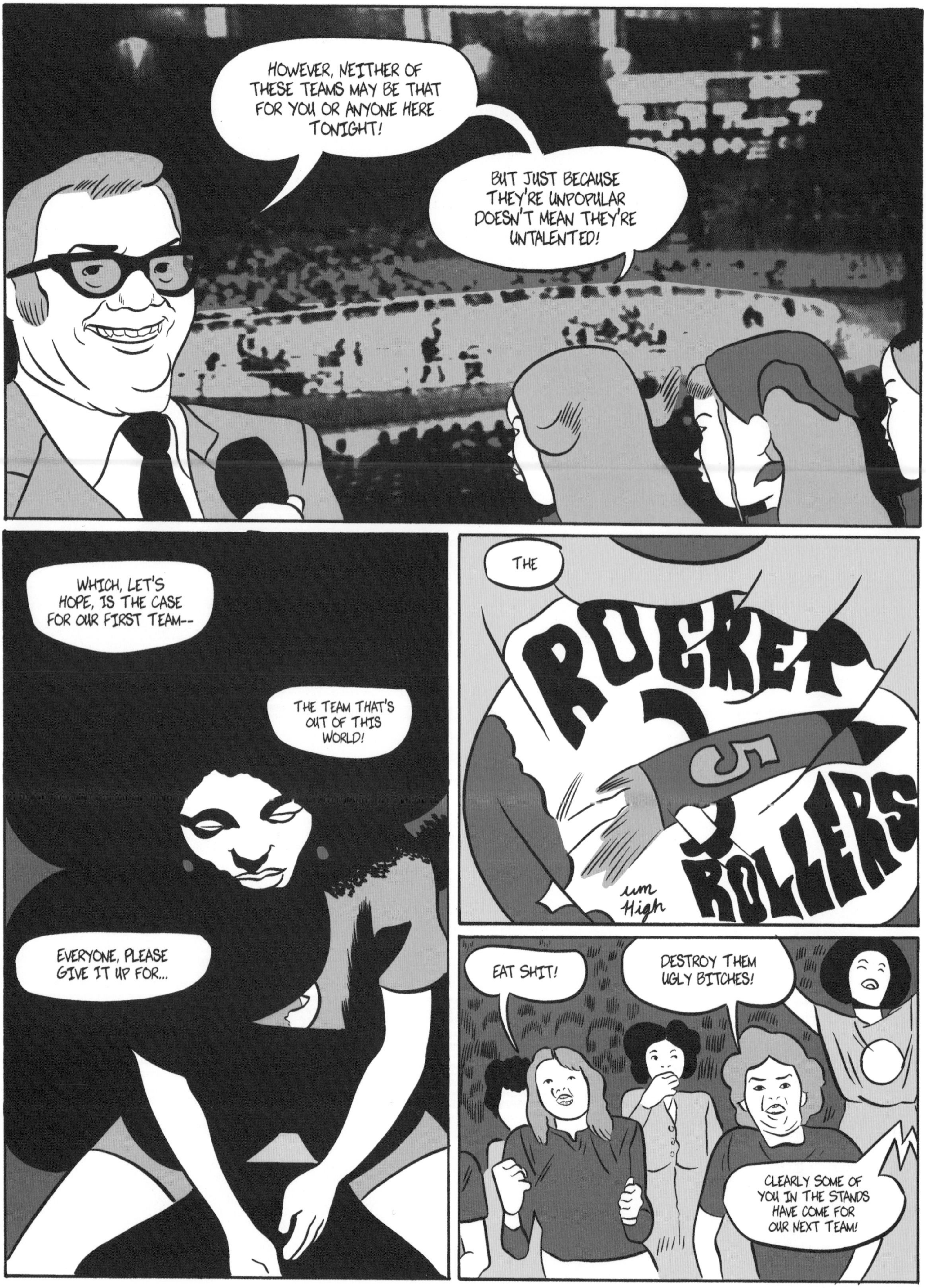
HOWEVER, NEITHER OF THESE TEAMS MAY BE THAT FOR YOU OR ANYONE HERE TONIGHT!
BUT JUST BECAUSE THEY'RE UNPOPULAR DOESN'T MEAN THEY'RE UNTALENTED!
WHICH, LET'S HOPE, IS THE CASE FOR OUR FIRST TEAM--
THE TEAM THAT'S OUT OF THIS WORLD!
EVERYONE, PLEASE GIVE IT UP FOR...
THE
ROCKET 5 ROLLERS
EAT SHIT!
DESTROY THEM UGLY BITCHES!
CLEARLY SOME OF YOU IN THE STANDS HAVE COME FOR OUR NEXT TEAM!

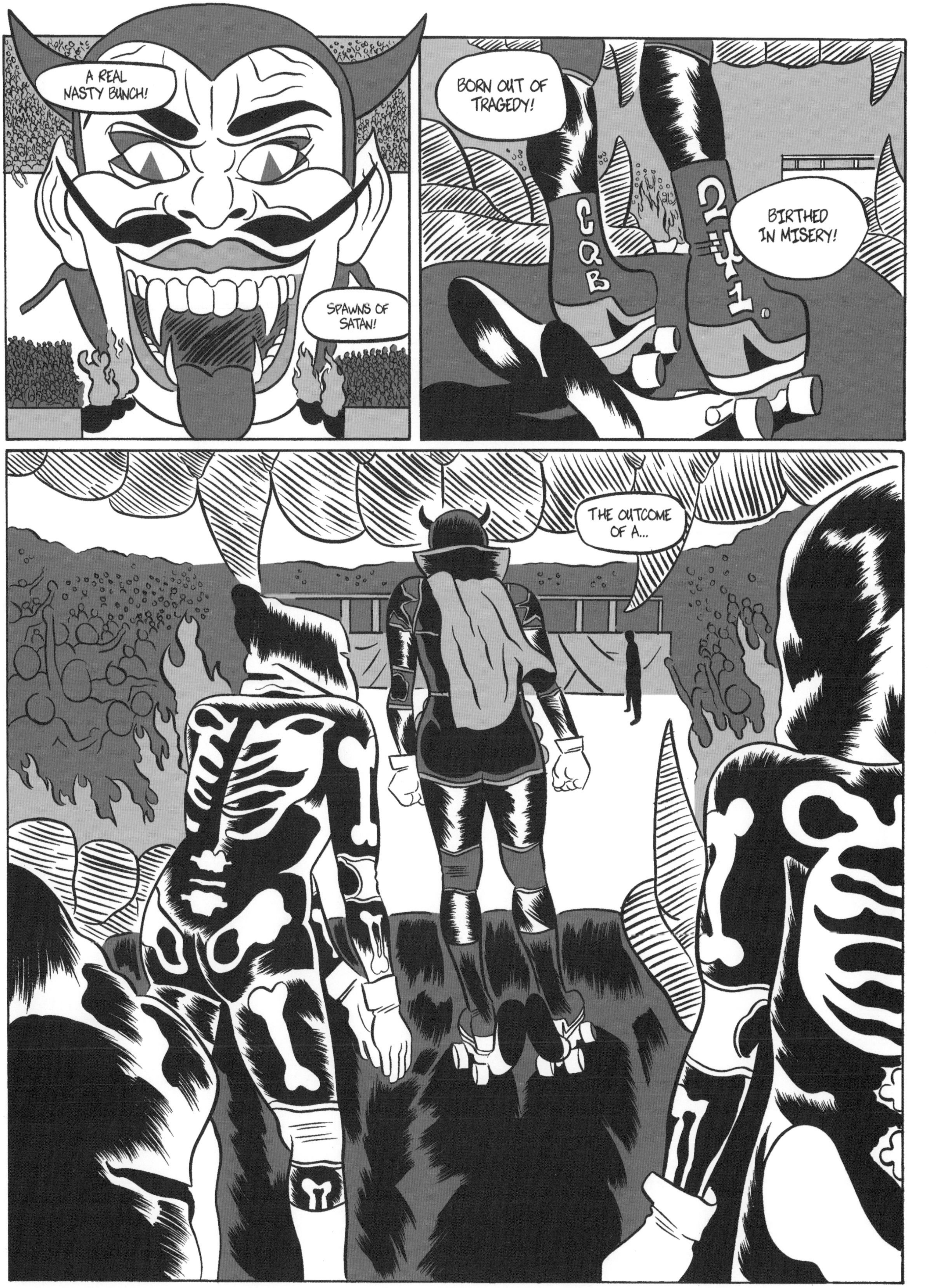
A REAL NASTY BUNCH!
SPAWNS OF SATAN!
BORN OUT OF TRAGEDY!
BIRTHED IN MISERY!
THE OUTCOME OF A...

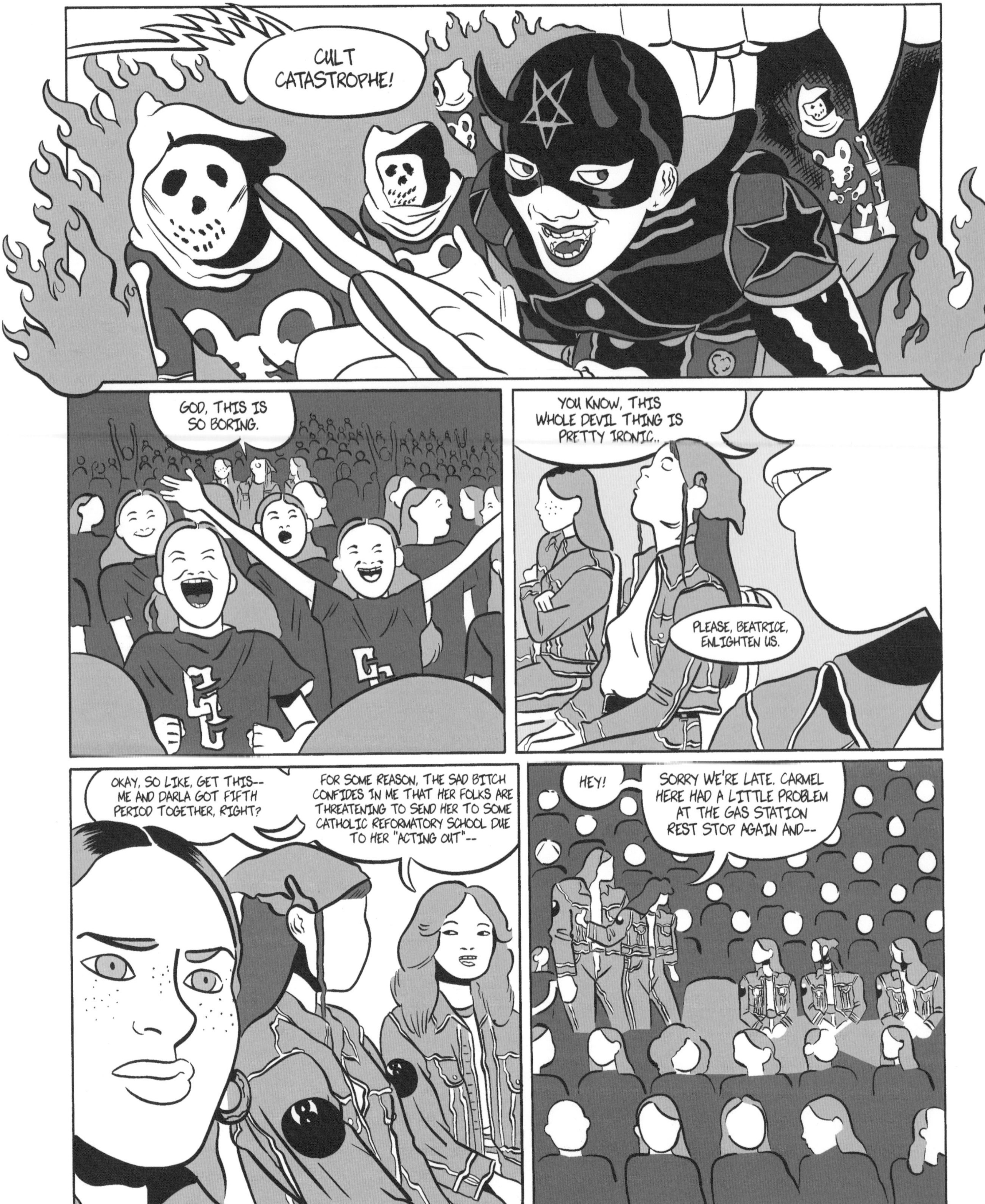
CULT CATASTROPHE!
GOD, THIS IS SO BORING.
YOU KNOW, THIS WHOLE DEVIL THING IS PRETTY IRONIC..
PLEASE, BEATRICE, ENLIGHTEN US.
OKAY, SO LIKE, GET THIS-- ME AND DARLA GOT FIFTH PERIOD TOGETHER, RIGHT?
FOR SOME REASON, THE SAD BITCH CONFIDES IN ME THAT HER FOLKS ARE THREATENING TO SEND HER TO SOME CATHOLIC REFORMATORY SCHOOL DUE TO HER "ACTING OUT"--
HEY!
SORRY WE'RE LATE. CARMEL HERE HAD A LITTLE PROBLEM AT THE GAS STATION REST STOP AGAIN AND--

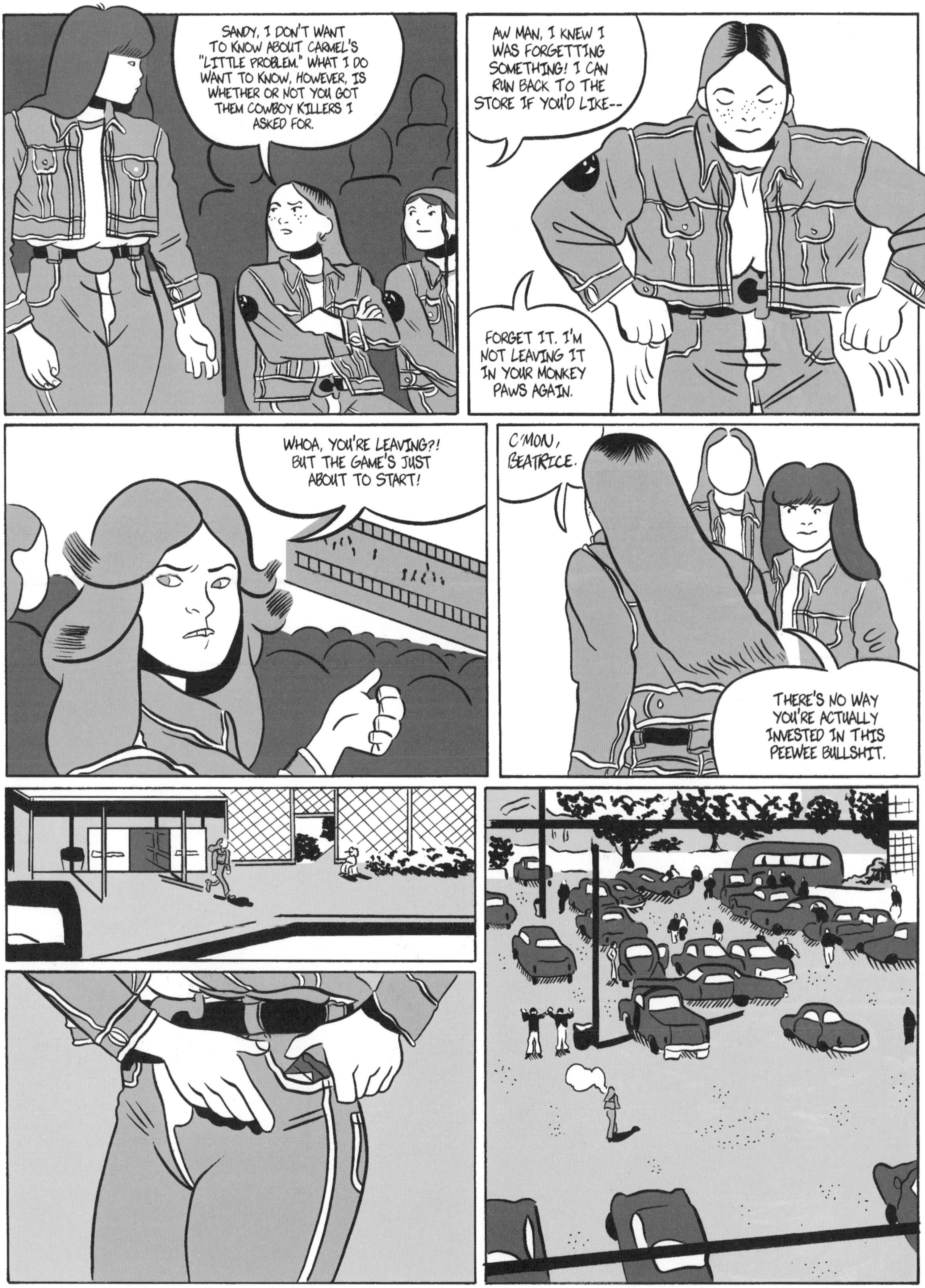
SANDY, I DON'T WANT TO KNOW ABOUT CARMEL'S "LITTLE PROBLEM." WHAT I DO WANT TO KNOW, HOWEVER, IS WHETHER OR NOT YOU GOT THEM COWBOY KILLERS I ASKED FOR.
AW MAN, I KNEW I WAS FORGETTING SOMETHING! I CAN RUN BACK TO THE STORE IF YOU'D LIKE--
FORGET IT. I'M NOT LEAVING IT IN YOUR MONKEY PAWS AGAIN.
WHOA, YOU'RE LEAVING?! BUT THE GAME'S JUST ABOUT TO START!
C'MON, BEATRICE.
THERE'S NO WAY YOU'RE ACTUALLY INVESTED IN THIS PEEWEE BULLSHIT.

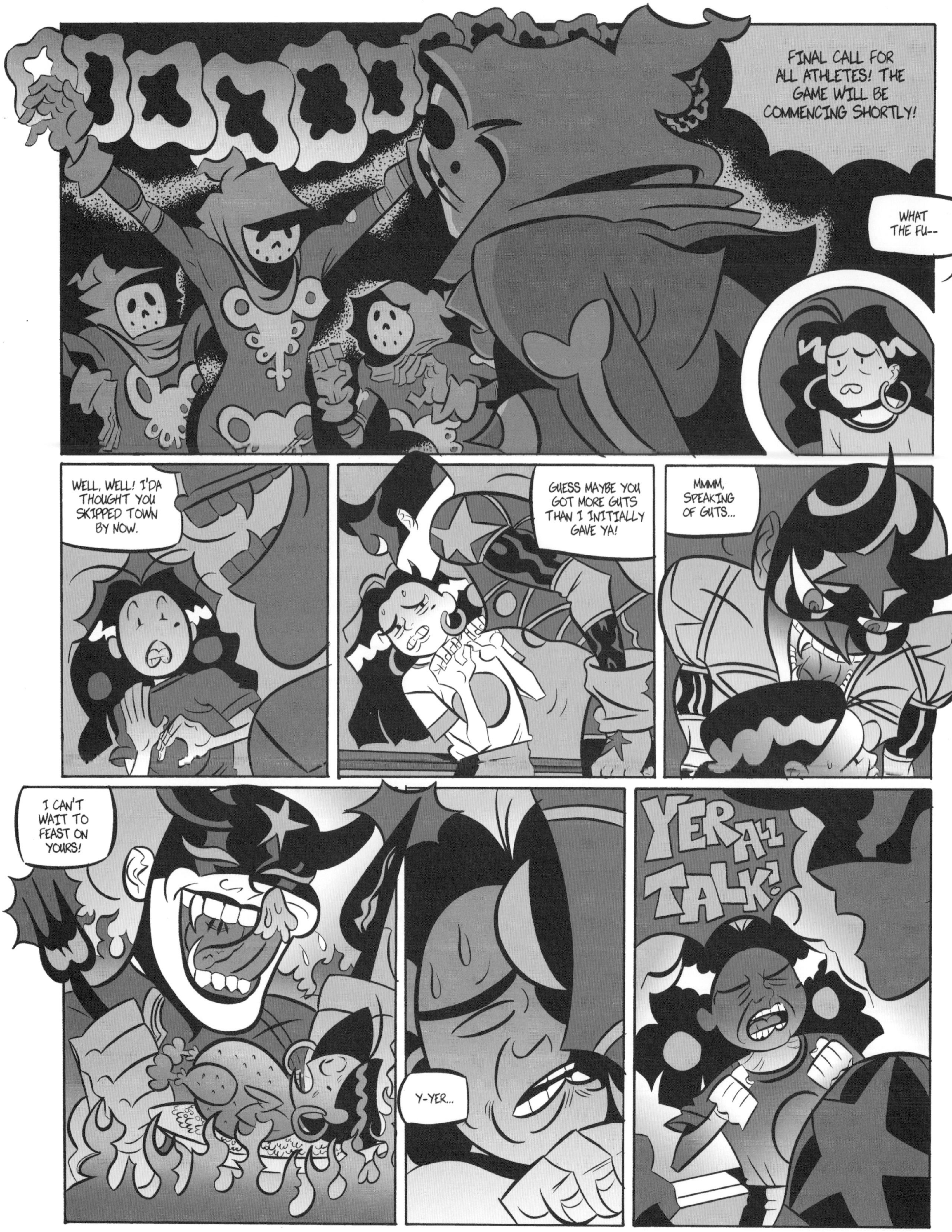
FINAL CALL FOR ALL ATHLETES! THE GAME WILL BE COMMENCING SHORTLY!
WHAT THE FU--
WELL, WELL! I'DA THOUGHT YOU SKIPPED TOWN BY NOW.
GUESS MAYBE YOU GOT MORE GUTS THAN I INITIALLY GAVE YA!
MMMM, SPEAKING OF GUTS...
I CAN'T WAIT TO FEAST ON YOURS!
Y-YER...
YER ALL TALK!

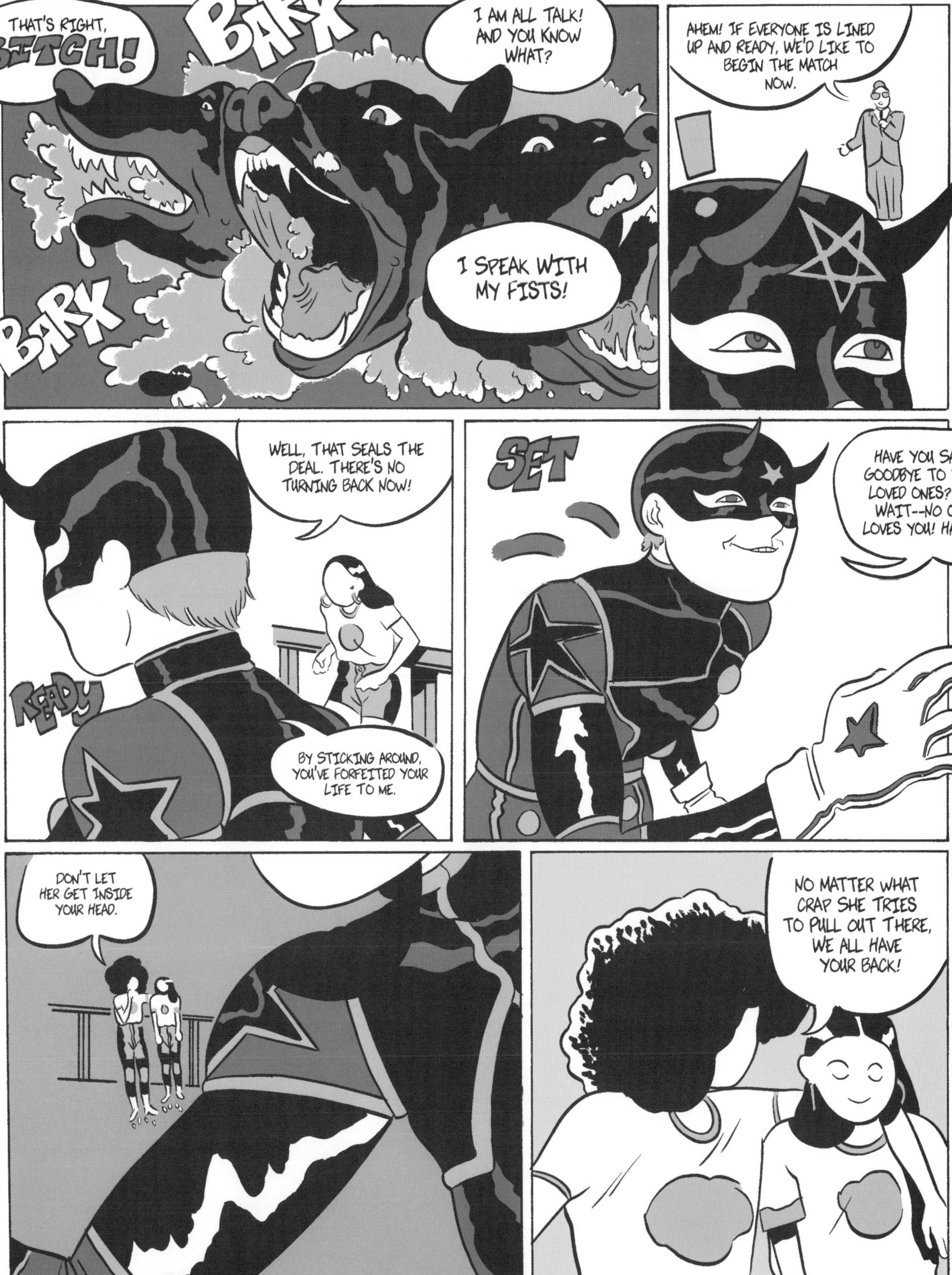
THAT'S RIGHT, BITCH!
BARK
I AM ALL TALK! AND YOU KNOW WHAT?
I SPEAK WITH MY FISTS!
BARK
AHEM! IF EVERYONE IS LINED UP AND READY, WE'D LIKE TO BEGIN THE MATCH NOW.
WELL, THAT SEALS THE DEAL. THERE'S NO TURNING BACK NOW!
READY
BY STICKING AROUND, YOU'VE FORFEITED YOUR LIFE TO ME.
SET
HAVE YOU SAID GOODBYE TO YOUR LOVED ONES? OH, WAIT--NO ONE LOVES YOU! HA HA!
DON'T LET HER GET INSIDE YOUR HEAD.
NO MATTER WHAT CRAP SHE TRIES TO PULL OUT THERE, WE ALL HAVE YOUR BACK!

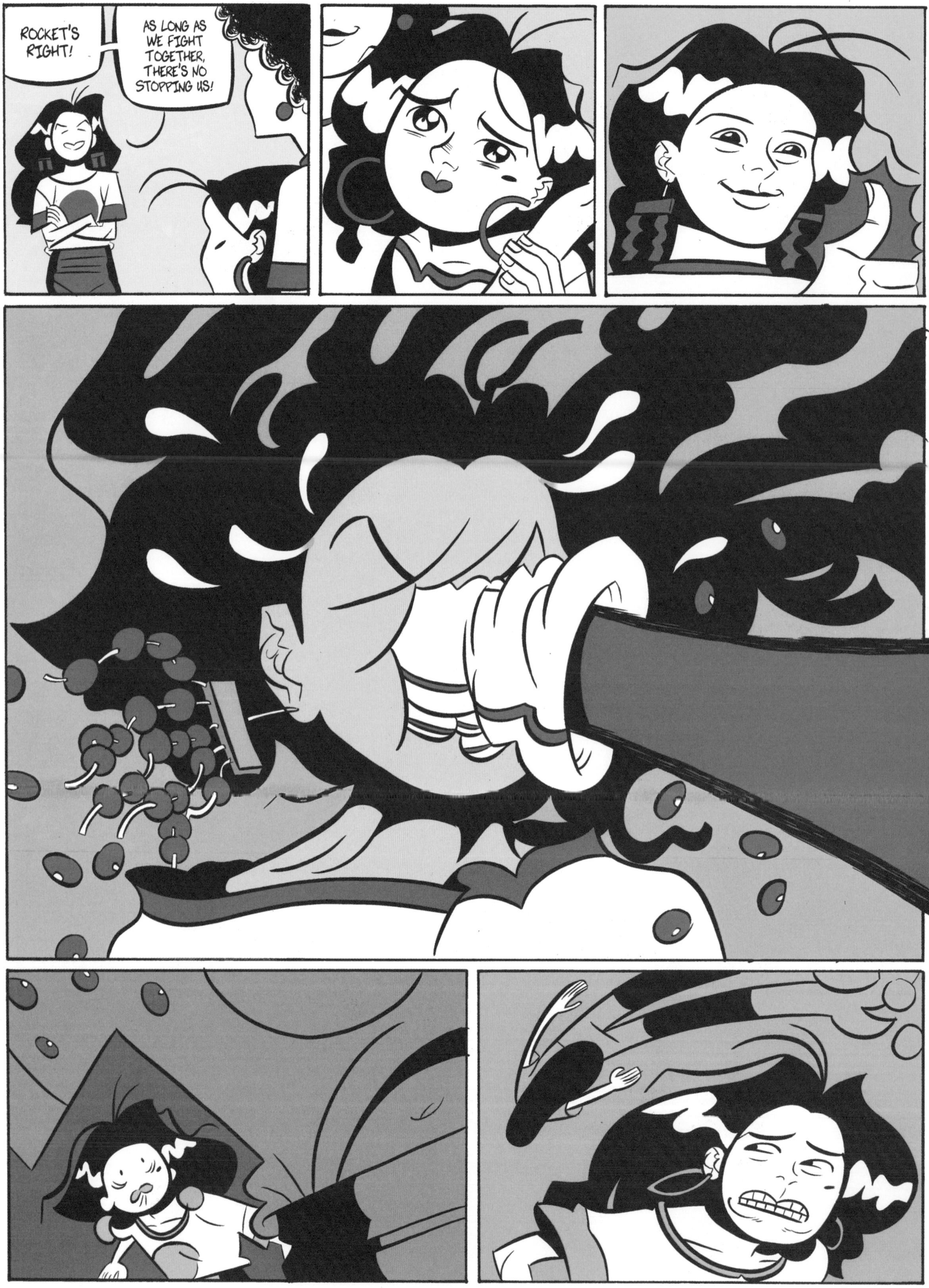
ROCKET'S RIGHT!
AS LONG AS WE FIGHT TOGETHER, THERE'S NO STOPPING US!

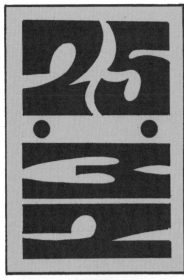

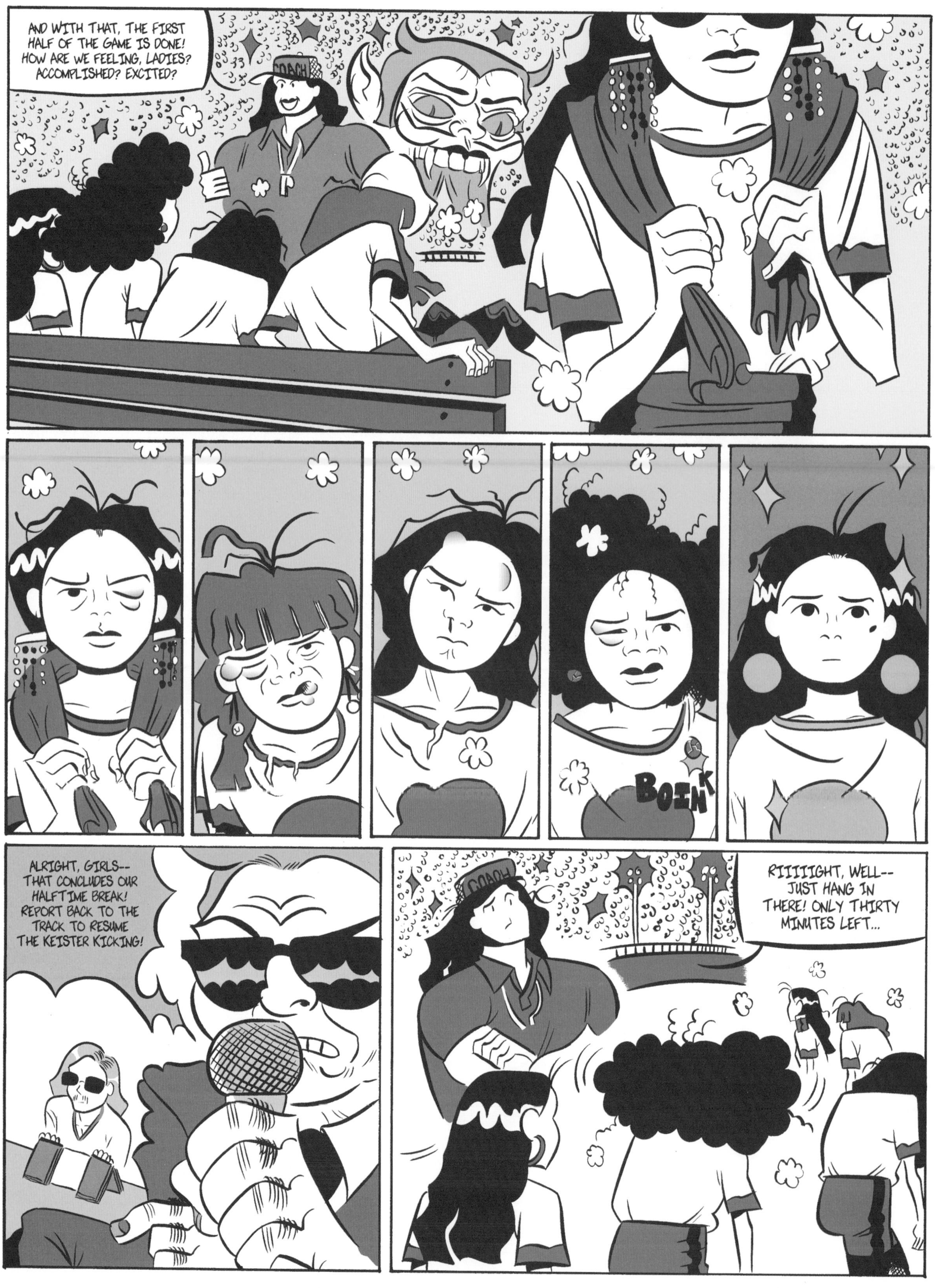
AND WITH THAT, THE FIRST HALF OF THE GAME IS DONE! HOW ARE WE FEELING, LADIES? ACCOMPLISHED? EXCITED?
COACH
BOINK
ALRIGHT, GIRLS-- THAT CONCLUDES OUR HALFTIME BREAK! REPORT BACK TO THE TRACK TO RESUME THE KEISTER KICKING!
COACH
RIIIIIGHT, WELL-- JUST HANG IN THERE! ONLY THIRTY MINUTES LEFT...

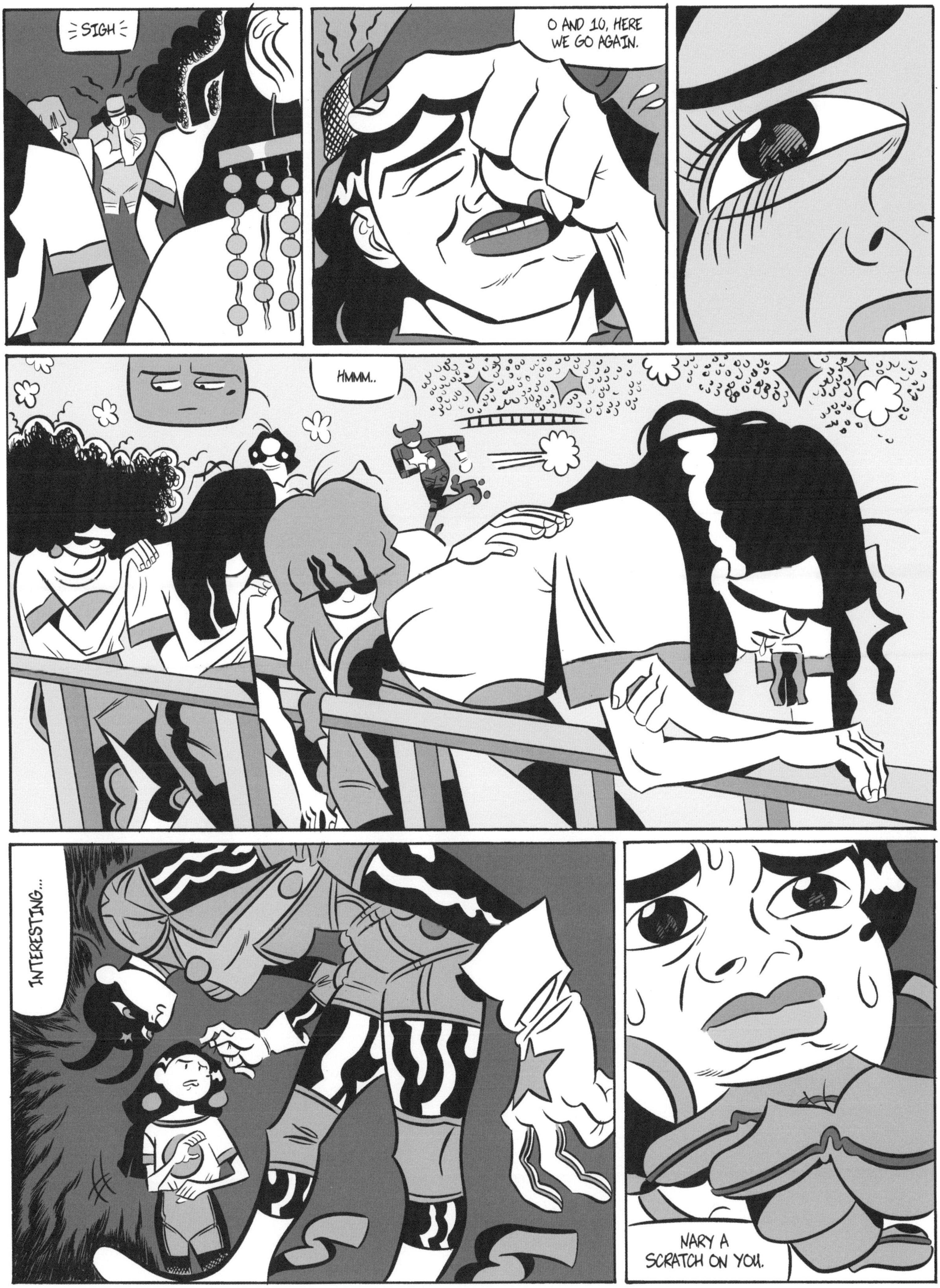
SIGH
0 AND 10, HERE WE GO AGAIN.
HMMM..
INTERESTING...
NARY A SCRATCH ON YOU.

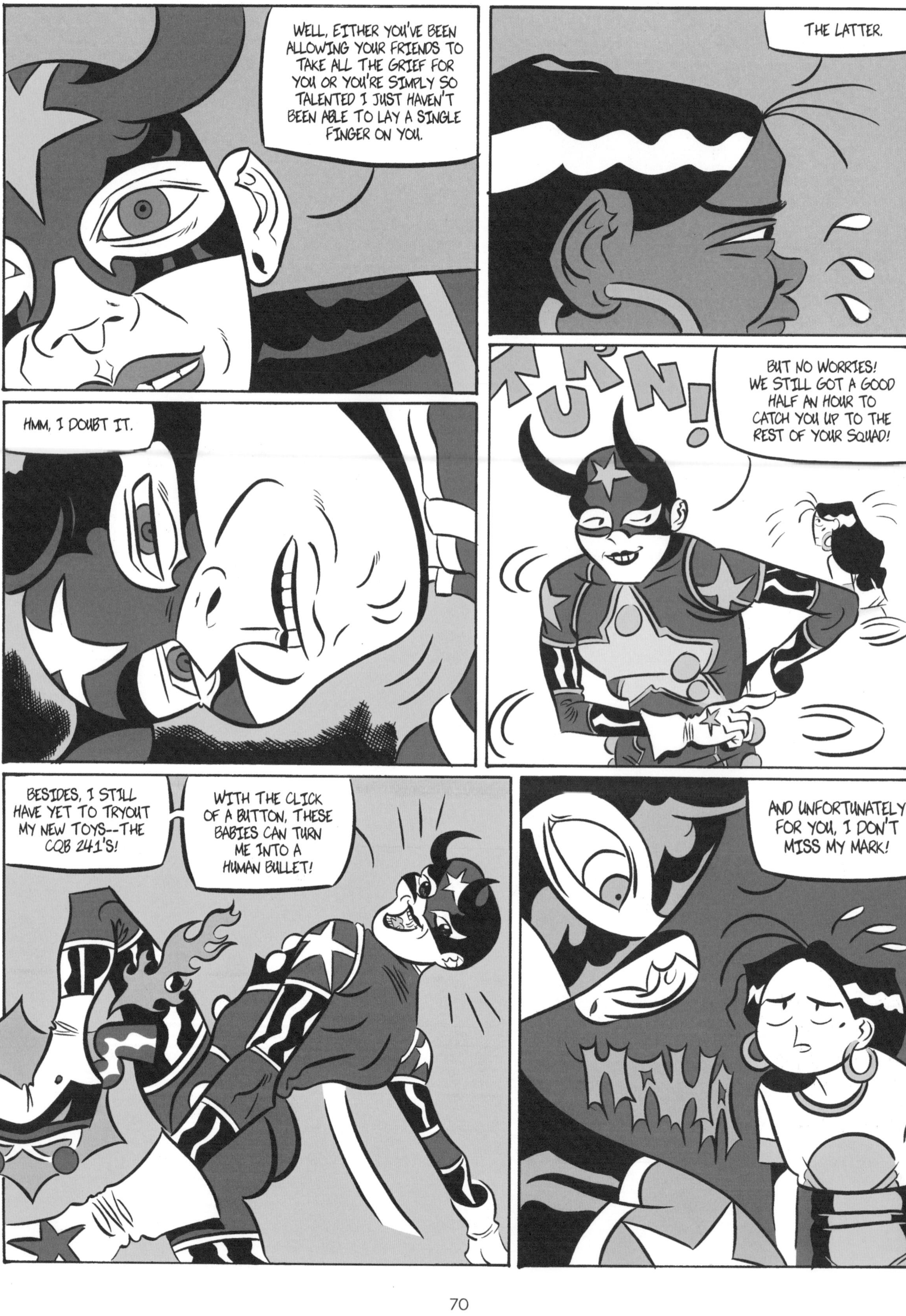
WELL, EITHER YOU'VE BEEN ALLOWING YOUR FRIENDS TO TAKE ALL THE GRIEF FOR YOU OR YOU'RE SIMPLY SO TALENTED I JUST HAVEN'T BEEN ABLE TO LAY A SINGLE FINGER ON YOU.
THE LATTER.
HMM, I DOUBT IT.
BUT NO WORRIES! WE STILL GOT A GOOD HALF AN HOUR TO CATCH YOU UP TO THE REST OF YOUR SQUAD!
BESIDES, I STILL HAVE YET TO TRYOUT MY NEW TOYS--THE CQB 241'S!
WITH THE CLICK OF A BUTTON, THESE BABIES CAN TURN ME INTO A HUMAN BULLET!
AND UNFORTUNATELY FOR YOU, I DON'T MISS MY MARK!

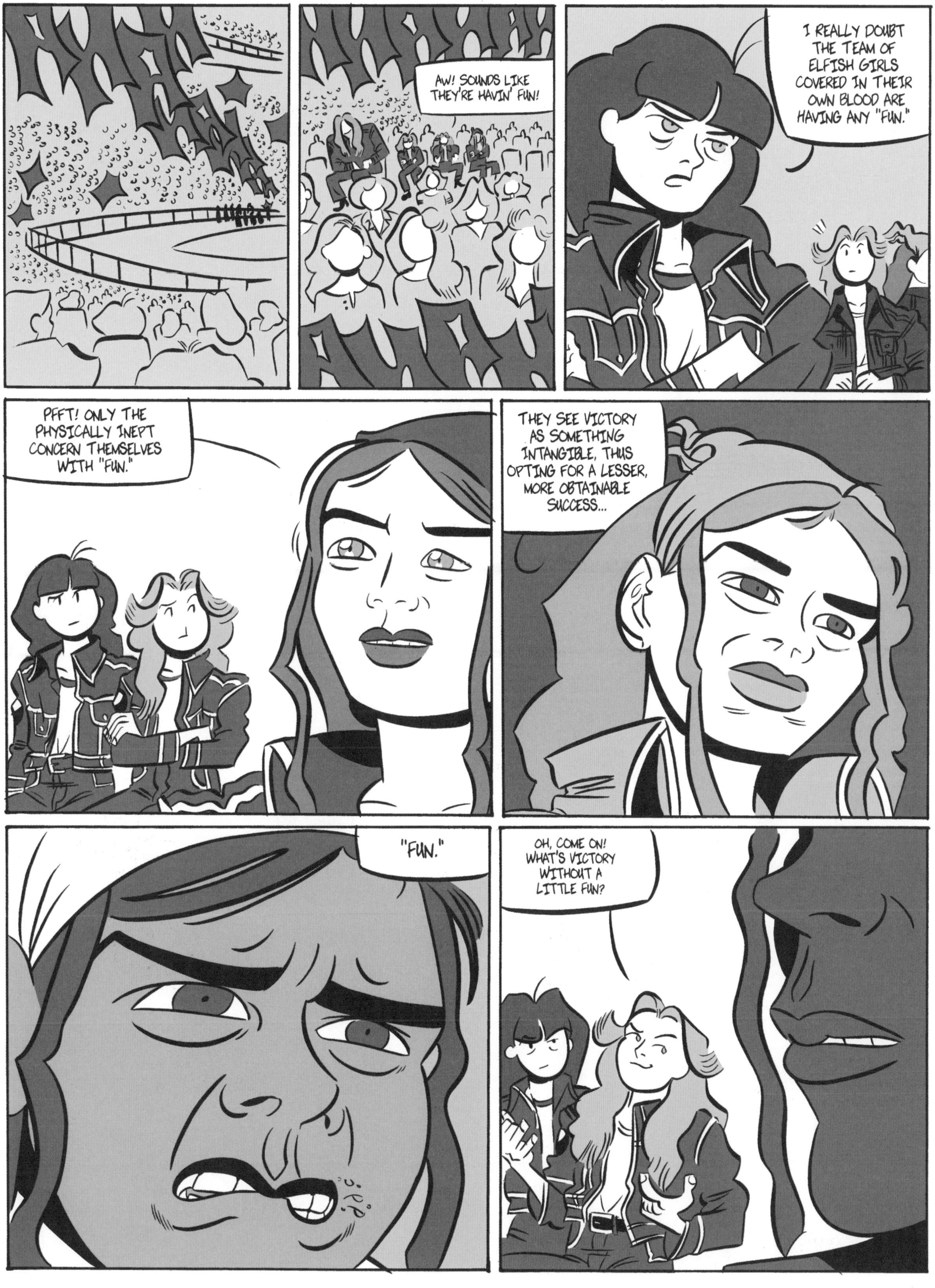
AW! SOUNDS LIKE THEY'RE HAVIN' FUN!
I REALLY DOUBT THE TEAM OF ELFISH GIRLS COVERED IN THEIR OWN BLOOD ARE HAVING ANY "FUN."
PFFT! ONLY THE PHYSICALLY INEPT CONCERN THEMSELVES WITH "FUN."
THEY SEE VICTORY AS SOMETHING INTANGIBLE, THUS OPTING FOR A LESSER, MORE OBTAINABLE SUCCESS...
"FUN."
OH, COME ON! WHAT'S VICTORY WITHOUT A LITTLE FUN?

REALITY.

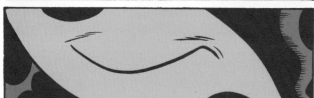

GRAH! A WHOLE HALF SPENT WITHOUT A LICK OF ACTION! I DON'T KNOW ABOUT YOU LADIES, BUT I'M BORED OUTTA MY MIND!

ME TOO!

YAWN!

BORING!

SOOO BORING!

I'M GLAD WE'RE ON THE SAME PAGE! WHAT SAY WE LIVEN THINGS UP A BIT, AY?

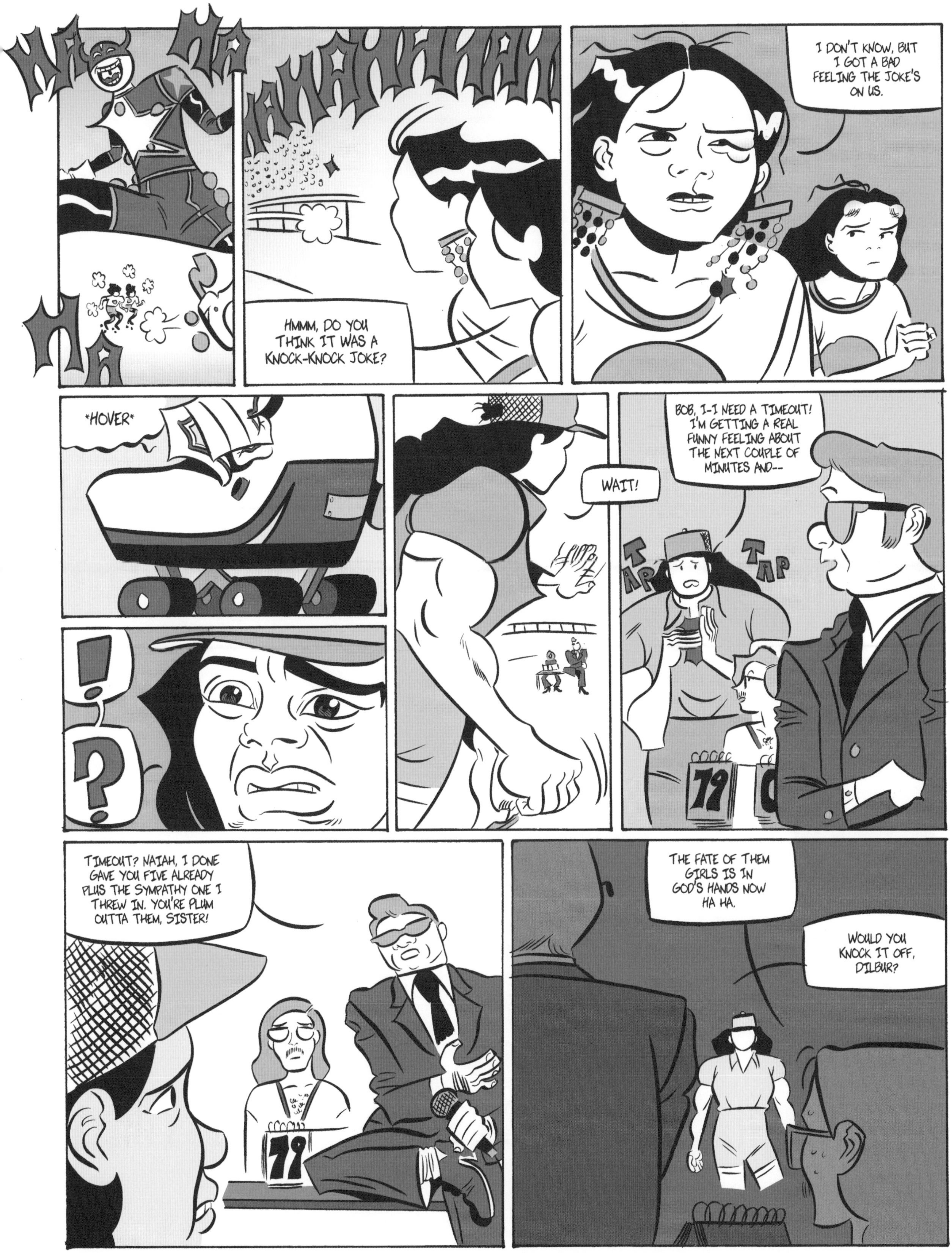
HA HA
HAHAHAHAHAHAH
HA HA
HMMM, DO YOU THINK IT WAS A KNOCK-KNOCK JOKE?
I DON'T KNOW, BUT I GOT A BAD FEELING THE JOKE'S ON US.
HOVER
WAIT!
BOB, I-I NEED A TIMEOUT! I'M GETTING A REAL FUNNY FEELING ABOUT THE NEXT COUPLE OF MINUTES AND--
TAP TAP
79
TIMEOUT? NAIAH, I DONE GAVE YOU FIVE ALREADY PLUS THE SYMPATHY ONE I THREW IN. YOU'RE PLUM OUTTA THEM, SISTER!
79
THE FATE OF THEM GIRLS IS IN GOD'S HANDS NOW HA HA.
WOULD YOU KNOCK IT OFF, DILBUR?
79

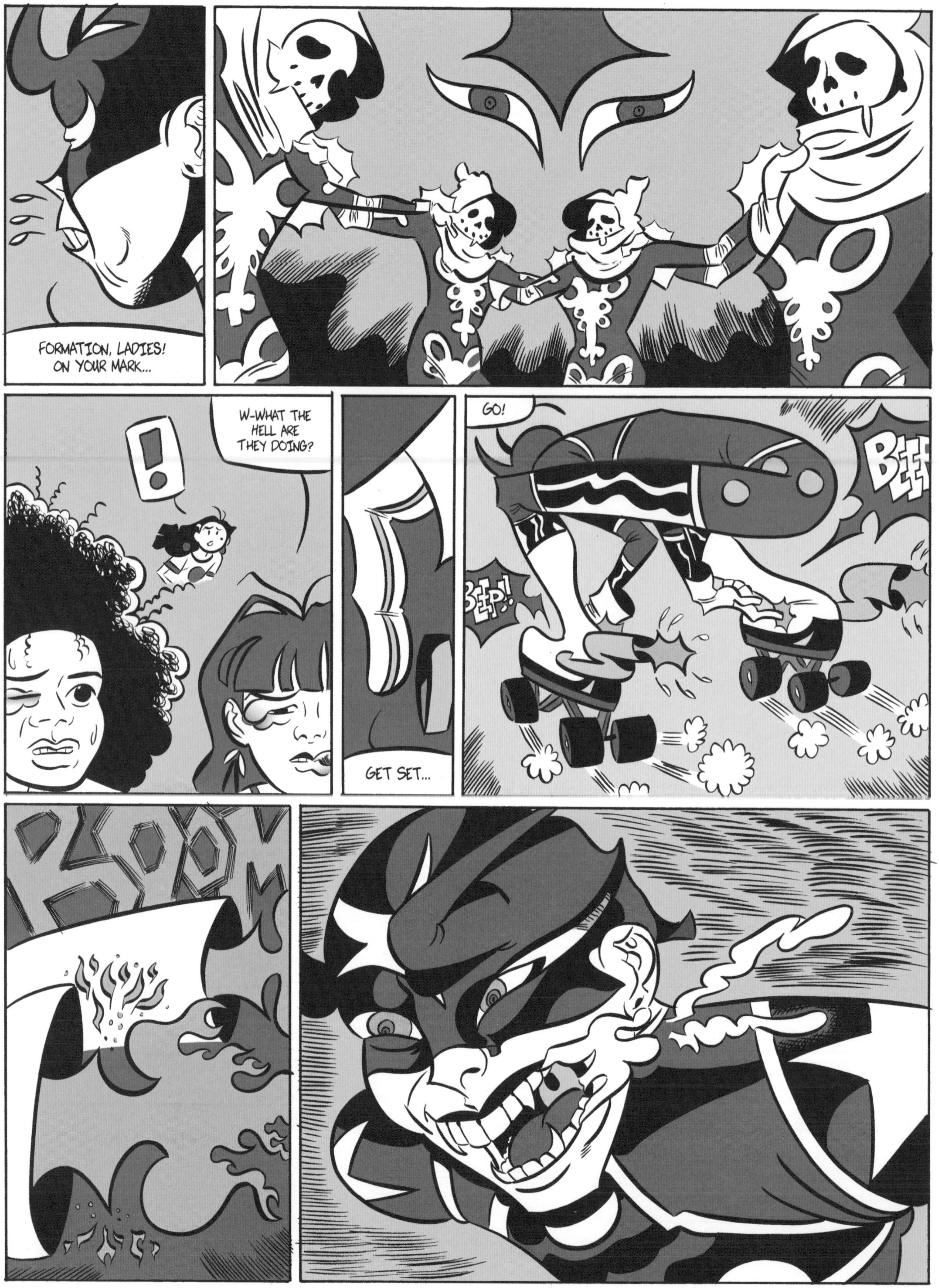
FORMATION, LADIES! ON YOUR MARK...
W-WHAT THE HELL ARE THEY DOING?
GET SET...
GO!
BEEP!

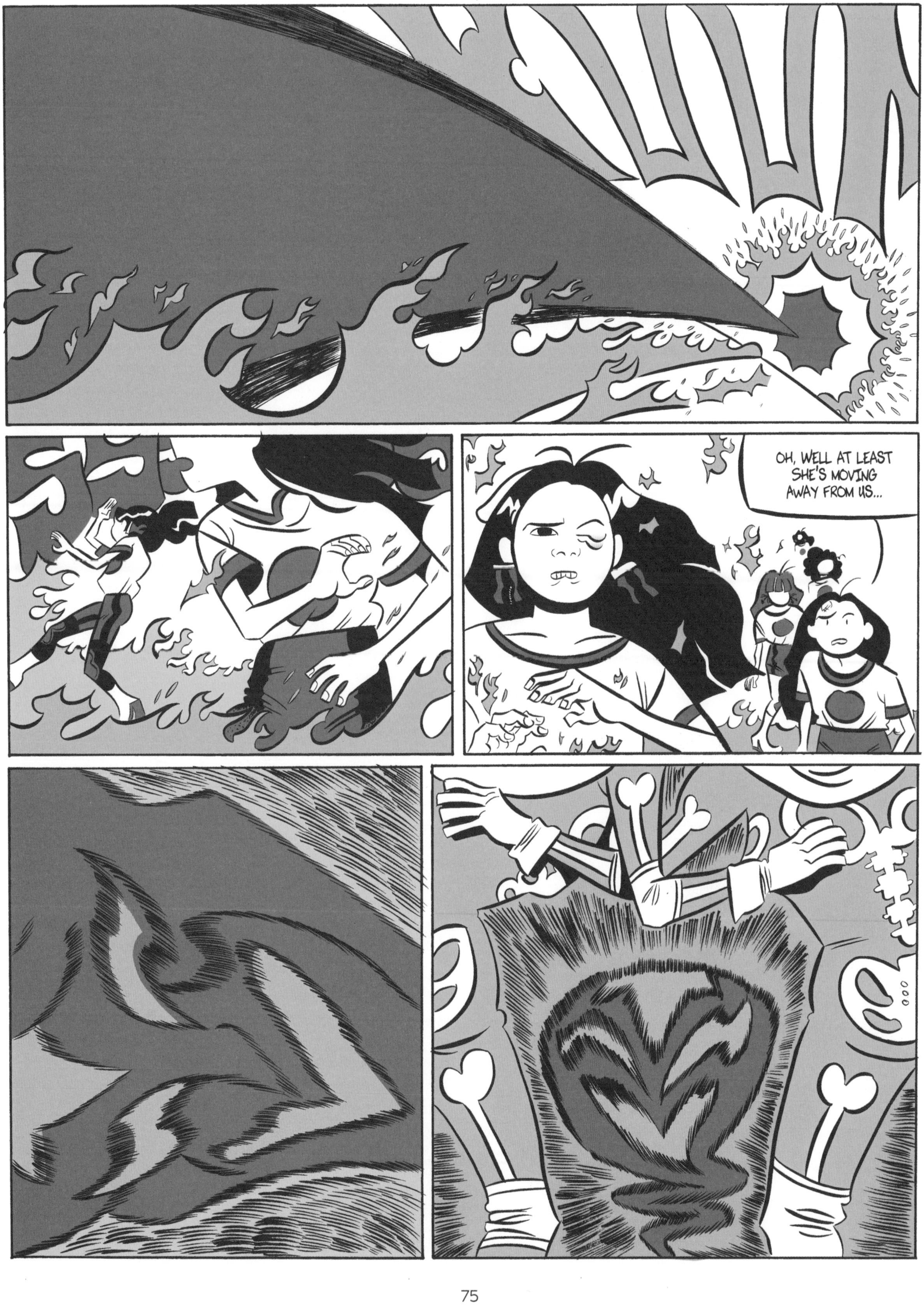
OH, WELL AT LEAST SHE'S MOVING AWAY FROM US...

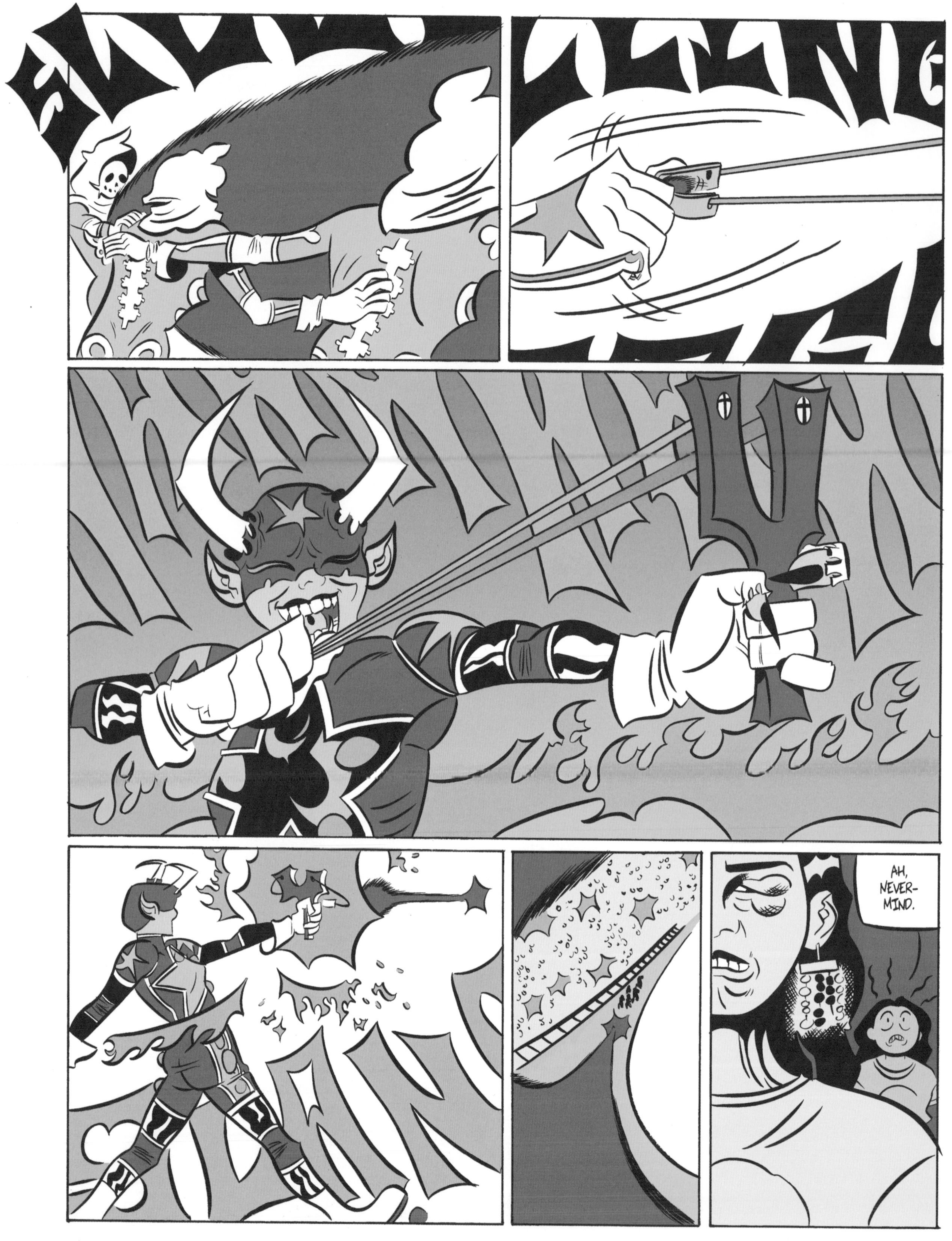
AH, NEVER-MIND.

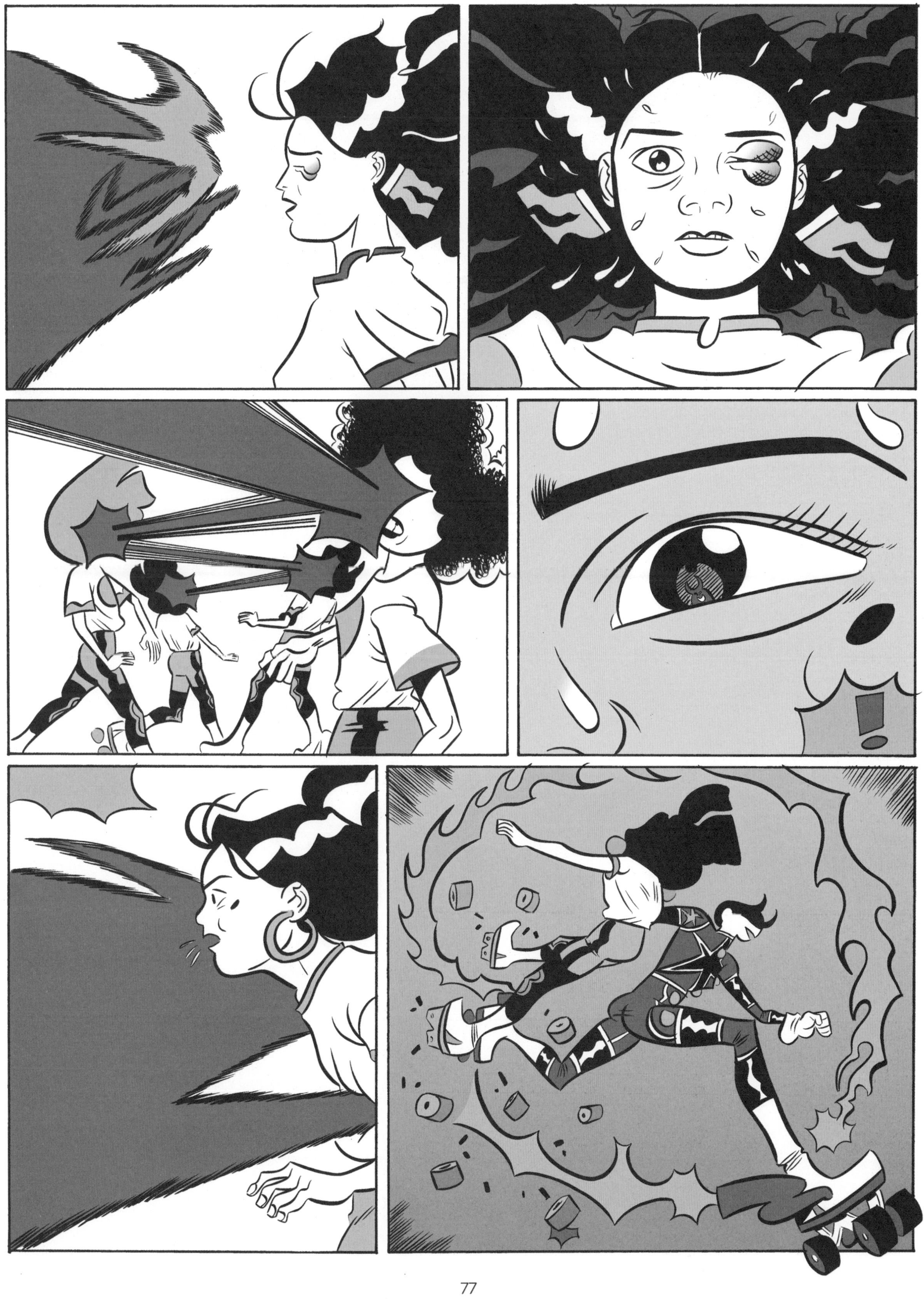
!

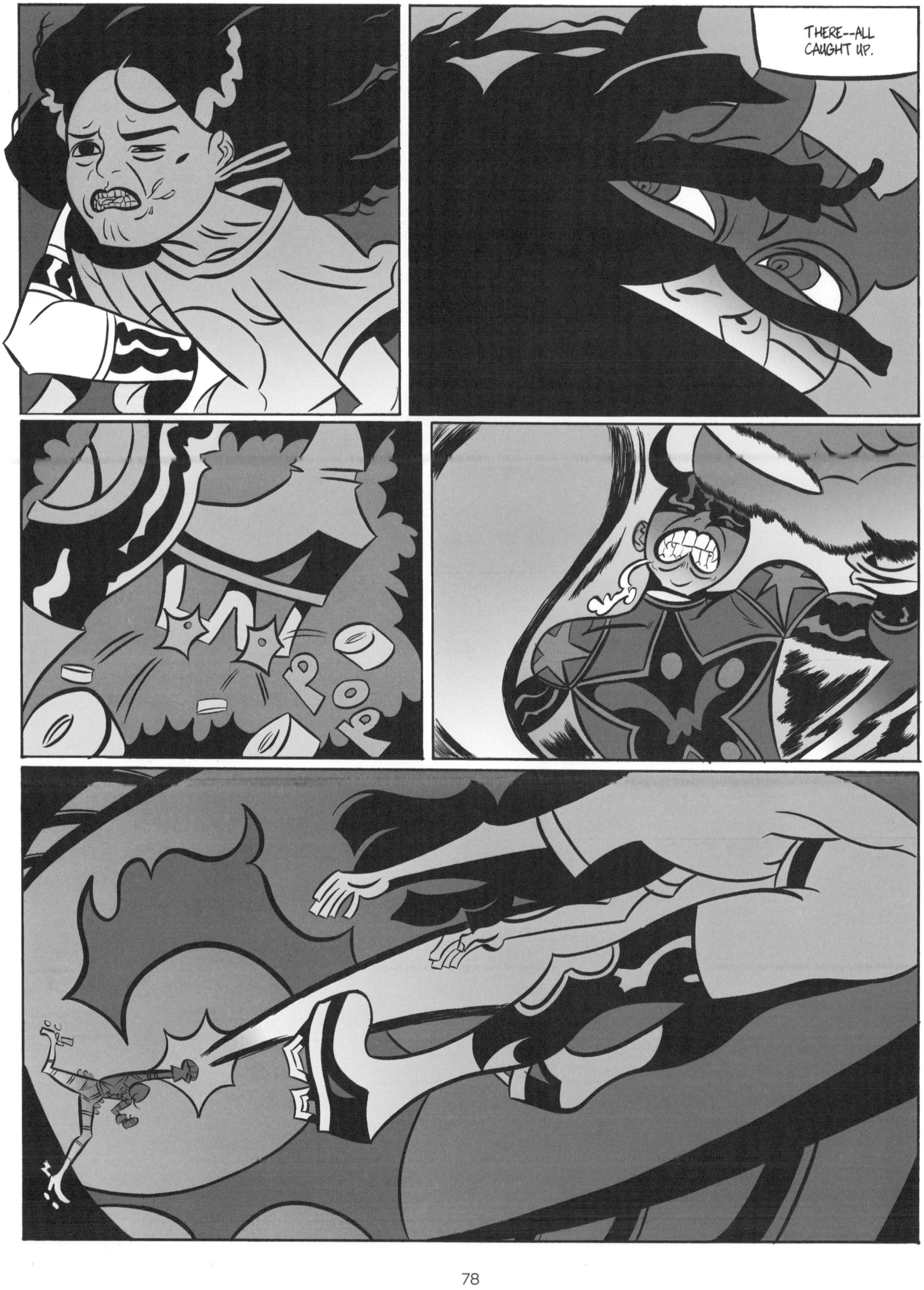
THERE--ALL CAUGHT UP.
POP

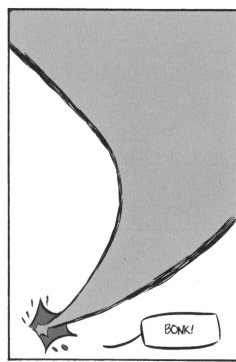

BONK!

SO BADASS, DARLA!

WASN'T IT?!

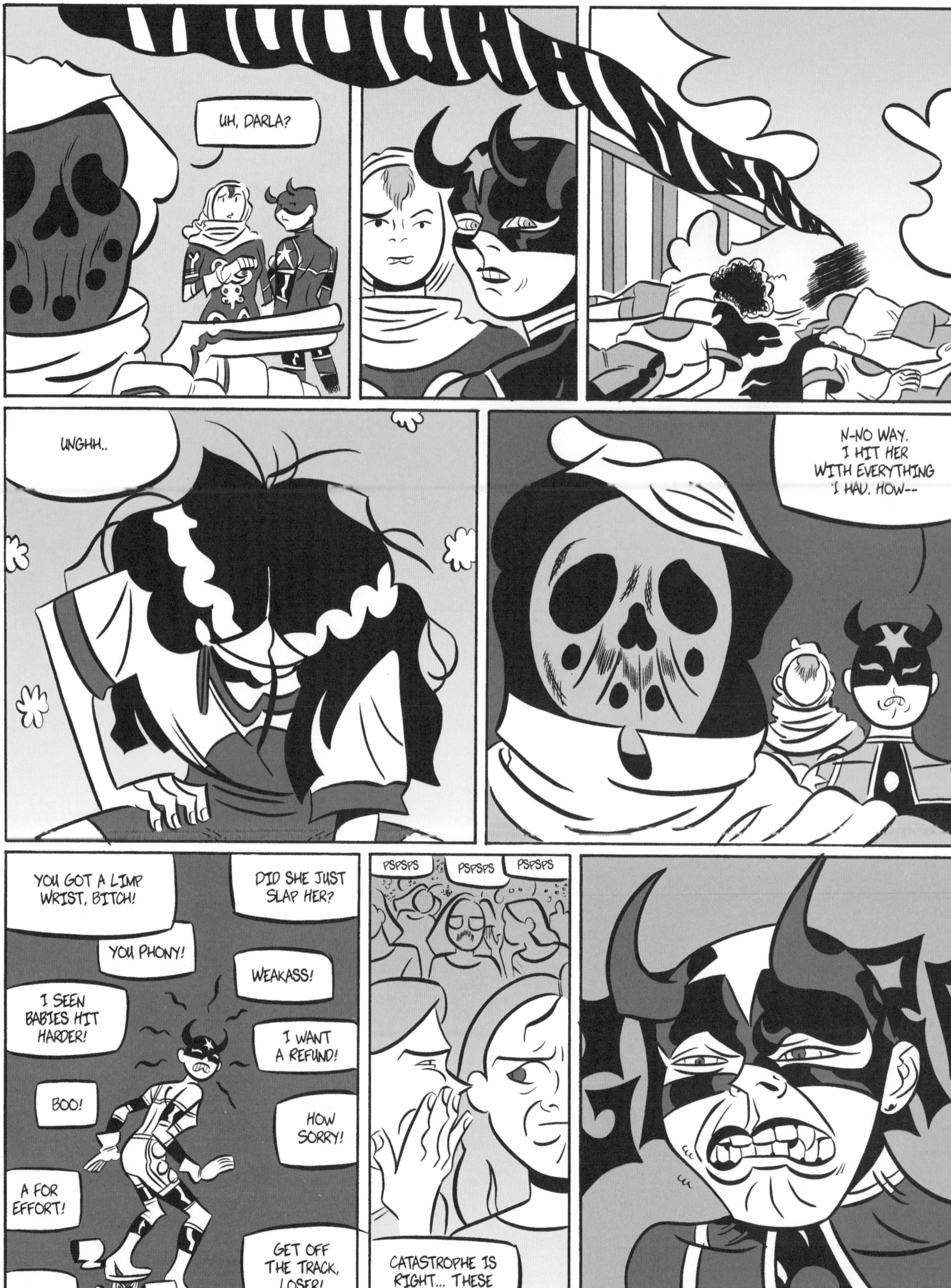
UH, DARLA?
UNGHH..
N-NO WAY. I HIT HER WITH EVERYTHING I HAD. HOW--
YOU GOT A LIMP WRIST, BITCH!
DID SHE JUST SLAP HER?
YOU PHONY!
WEAKASS!
I SEEN BABIES HIT HARDER!
I WANT A REFUND!
BOO!
HOW SORRY!
A FOR EFFORT!
GET OFF THE TRACK, LOSER!
BOO!
PSPSPS
PSPSPS
PSPSPS
CATASTROPHE IS RIGHT... THESE GIRLS BLOW!

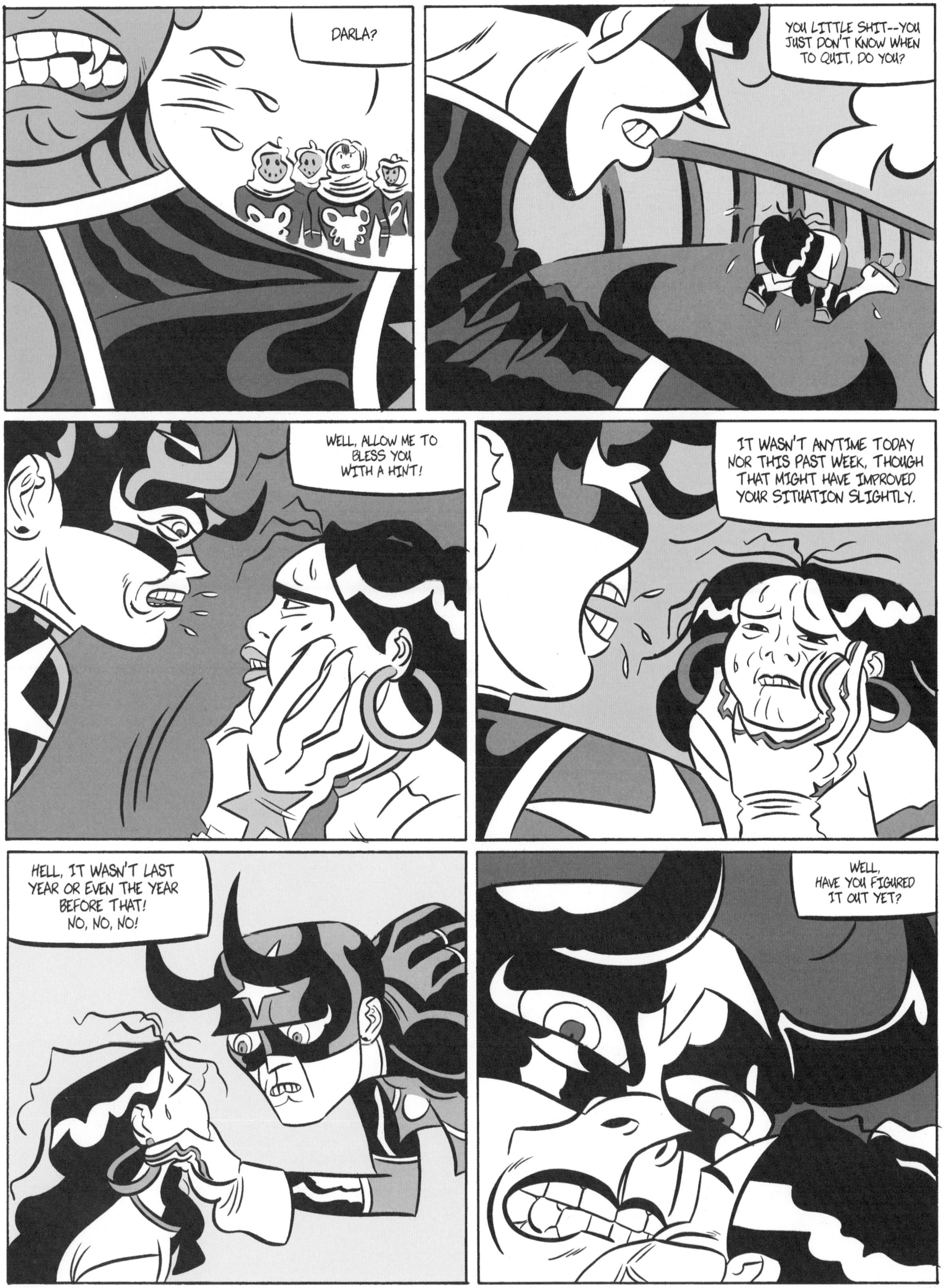

DARLA?
YOU LITTLE SHIT--YOU JUST DON'T KNOW WHEN TO QUIT, DO YOU?
WELL, ALLOW ME TO BLESS YOU WITH A HINT!
IT WASN'T ANYTIME TODAY NOR THIS PAST WEEK, THOUGH THAT MIGHT HAVE IMPROVED YOUR SITUATION SLIGHTLY.
HELL, IT WASN'T LAST YEAR OR EVEN THE YEAR BEFORE THAT! NO, NO, NO!
WELL, HAVE YOU FIGURED IT OUT YET?

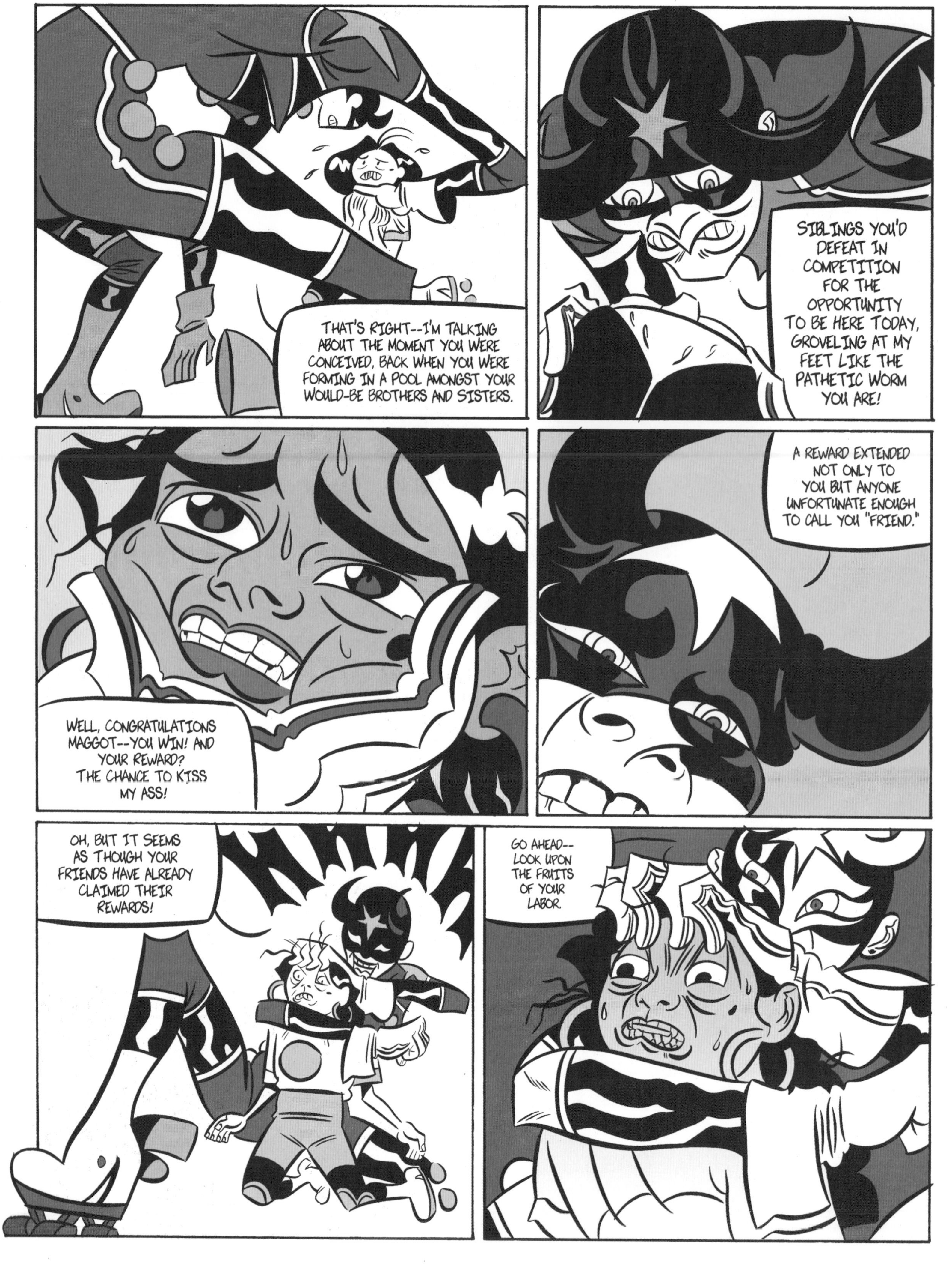
THAT'S RIGHT--I'M TALKING ABOUT THE MOMENT YOU WERE CONCEIVED, BACK WHEN YOU WERE FORMING IN A POOL AMONGST YOUR WOULD-BE BROTHERS AND SISTERS.
SIBLINGS YOU'D DEFEAT IN COMPETITION FOR THE OPPORTUNITY TO BE HERE TODAY, GROVELING AT MY FEET LIKE THE PATHETIC WORM YOU ARE!
WELL, CONGRATULATIONS MAGGOT--YOU WIN! AND YOUR REWARD? THE CHANCE TO KISS MY ASS!
A REWARD EXTENDED NOT ONLY TO YOU BUT ANYONE UNFORTUNATE ENOUGH TO CALL YOU "FRIEND."
OH, BUT IT SEEMS AS THOUGH YOUR FRIENDS HAVE ALREADY CLAIMED THEIR REWARDS!
GO AHEAD--LOOK UPON THE FRUITS OF YOUR LABOR.

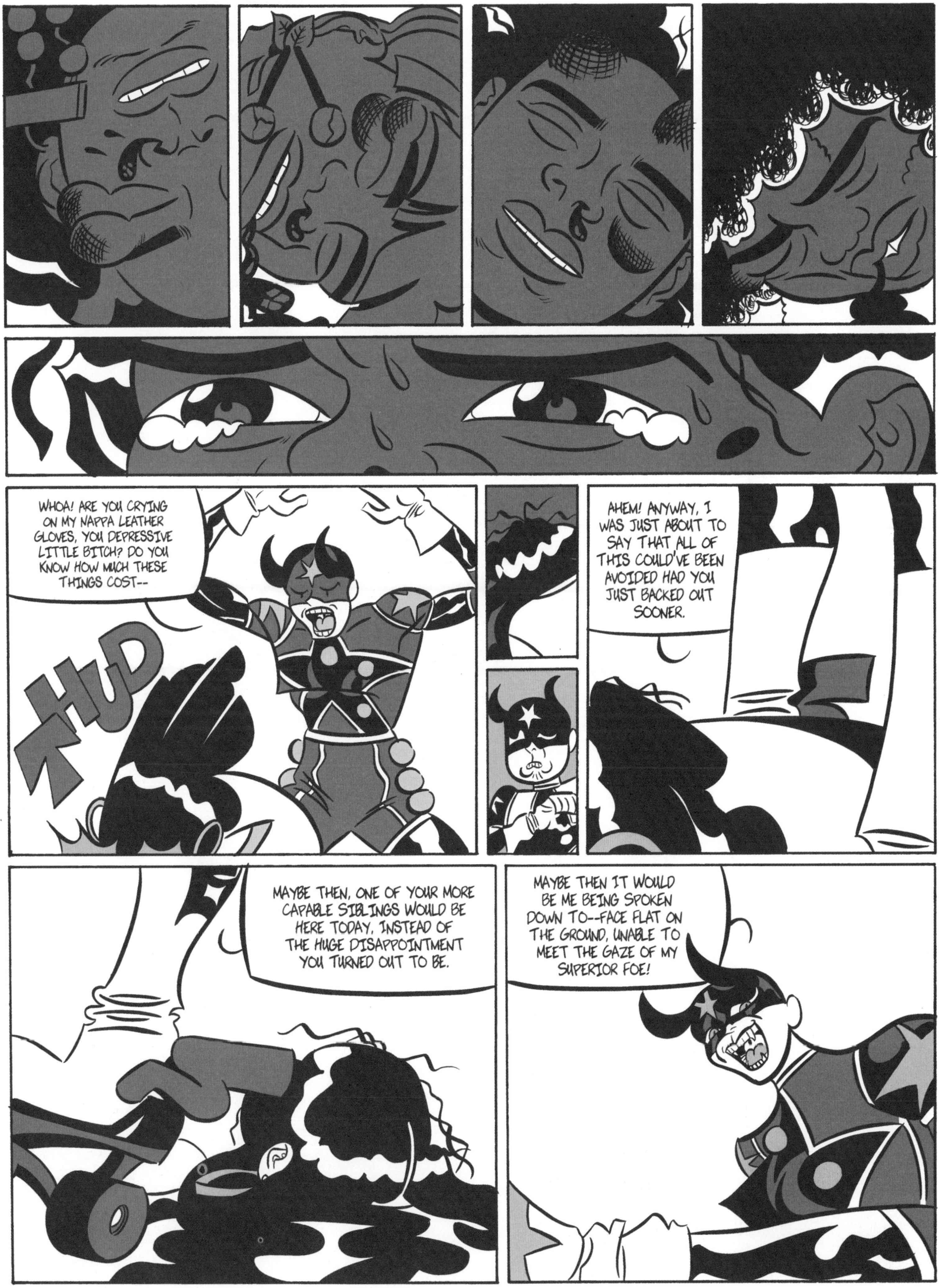
WHOA! ARE YOU CRYING ON MY NAPPA LEATHER GLOVES, YOU DEPRESSIVE LITTLE BITCH? DO YOU KNOW HOW MUCH THESE THINGS COST--
THUD
AHEM! ANYWAY, I WAS JUST ABOUT TO SAY THAT ALL OF THIS COULD'VE BEEN AVOIDED HAD YOU JUST BACKED OUT SOONER.
MAYBE THEN, ONE OF YOUR MORE CAPABLE SIBLINGS WOULD BE HERE TODAY, INSTEAD OF THE HUGE DISAPPOINTMENT YOU TURNED OUT TO BE.
MAYBE THEN IT WOULD BE ME BEING SPOKEN DOWN TO--FACE FLAT ON THE GROUND, UNABLE TO MEET THE GAZE OF MY SUPERIOR FOE!

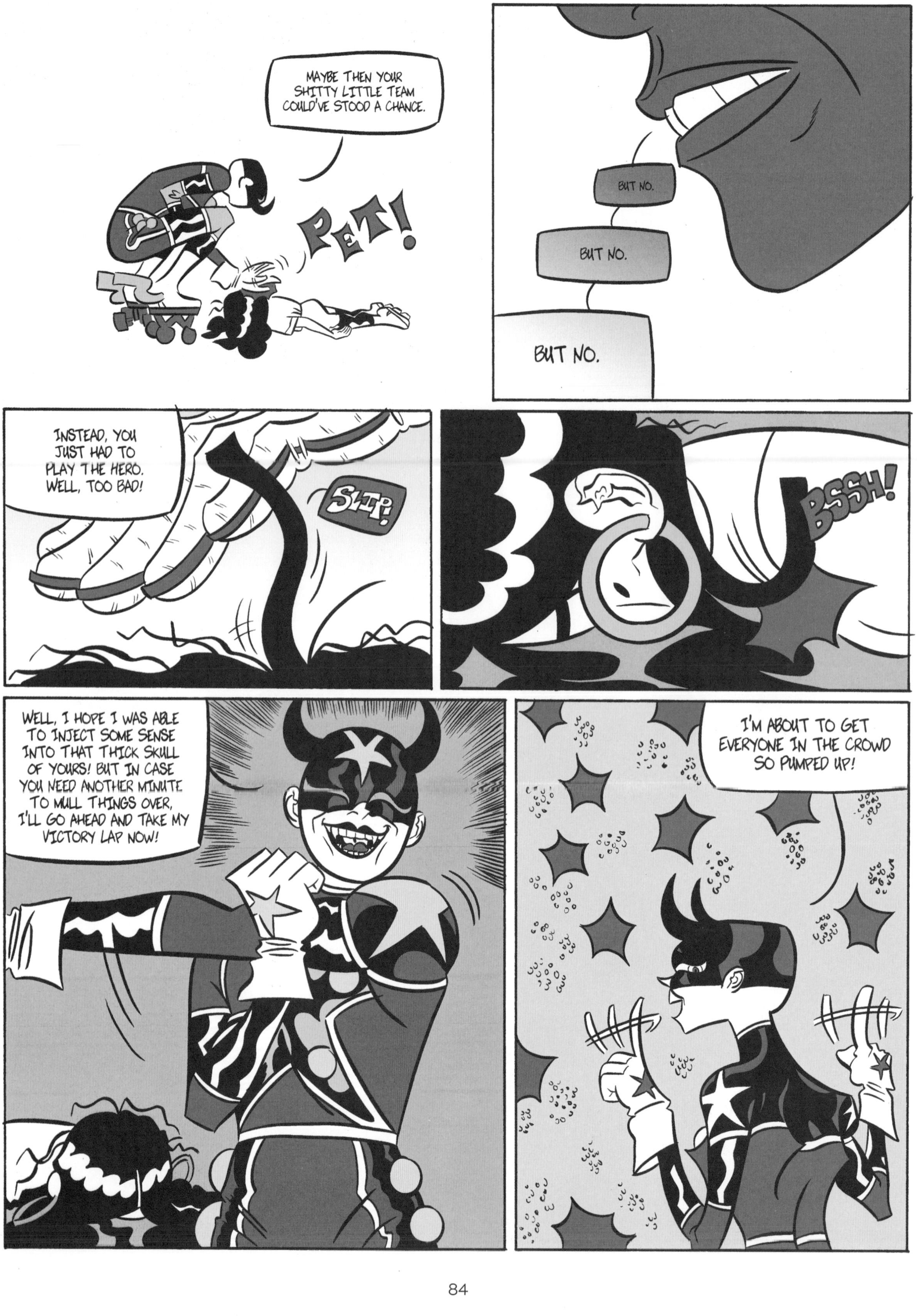
MAYBE THEN YOUR SHITTY LITTLE TEAM COULD'VE STOOD A CHANCE.
PET!
BUT NO.
BUT NO.
BUT NO.
INSTEAD, YOU JUST HAD TO PLAY THE HERO. WELL, TOO BAD!
SLIP!
BSSH!
WELL, I HOPE I WAS ABLE TO INJECT SOME SENSE INTO THAT THICK SKULL OF YOURS! BUT IN CASE YOU NEED ANOTHER MINUTE TO MULL THINGS OVER, I'LL GO AHEAD AND TAKE MY VICTORY LAP NOW!
I'M ABOUT TO GET EVERYONE IN THE CROWD SO PUMPED UP!

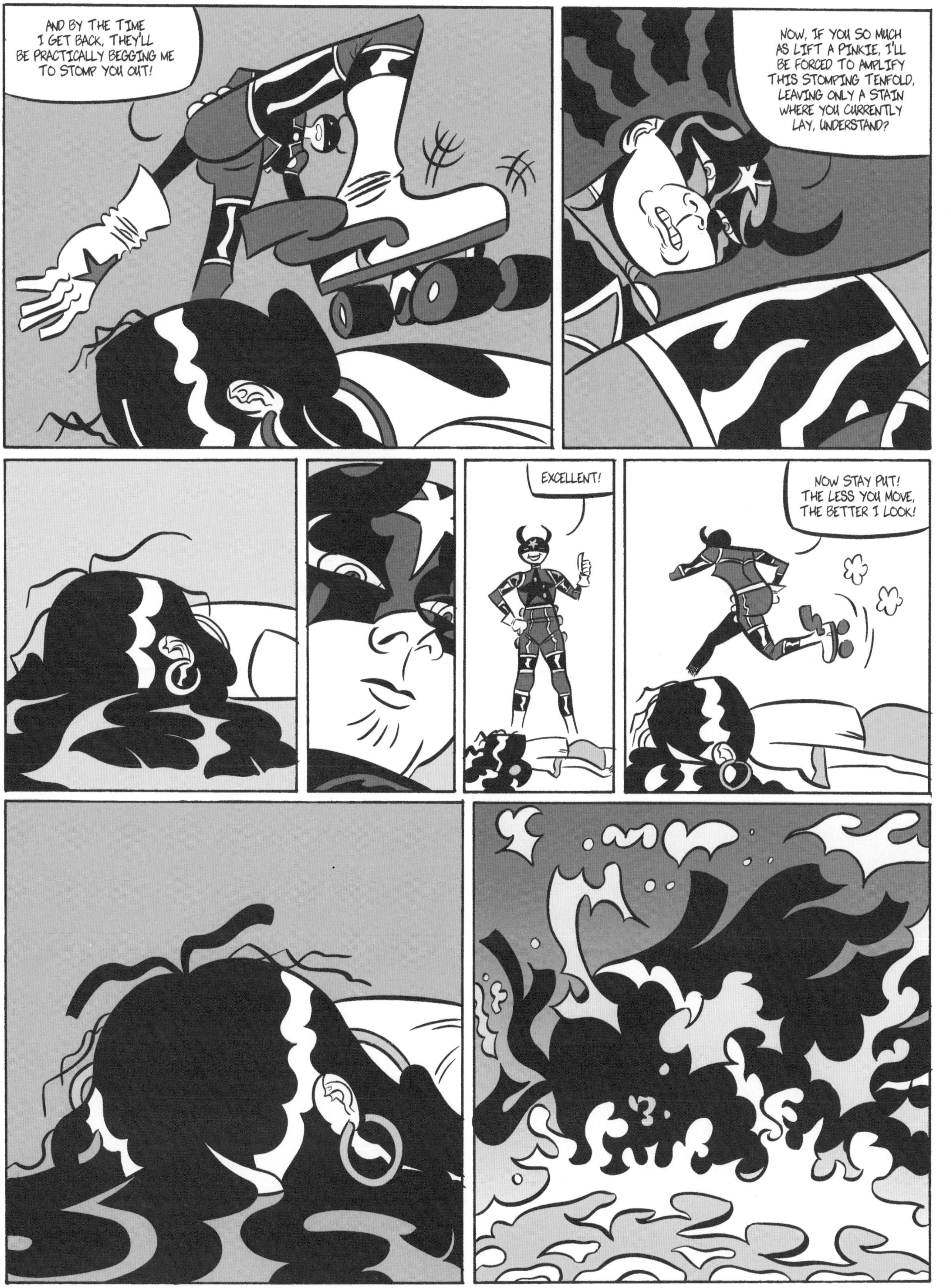
AND BY THE TIME I GET BACK, THEY'LL BE PRACTICALLY BEGGING ME TO STOMP YOU OUT!
NOW, IF YOU SO MUCH AS LIFT A PINKIE, I'LL BE FORCED TO AMPLIFY THIS STOMPING TENFOLD, LEAVING ONLY A STAIN WHERE YOU CURRENTLY LAY, UNDERSTAND?
EXCELLENT!
NOW STAY PUT! THE LESS YOU MOVE, THE BETTER I LOOK!

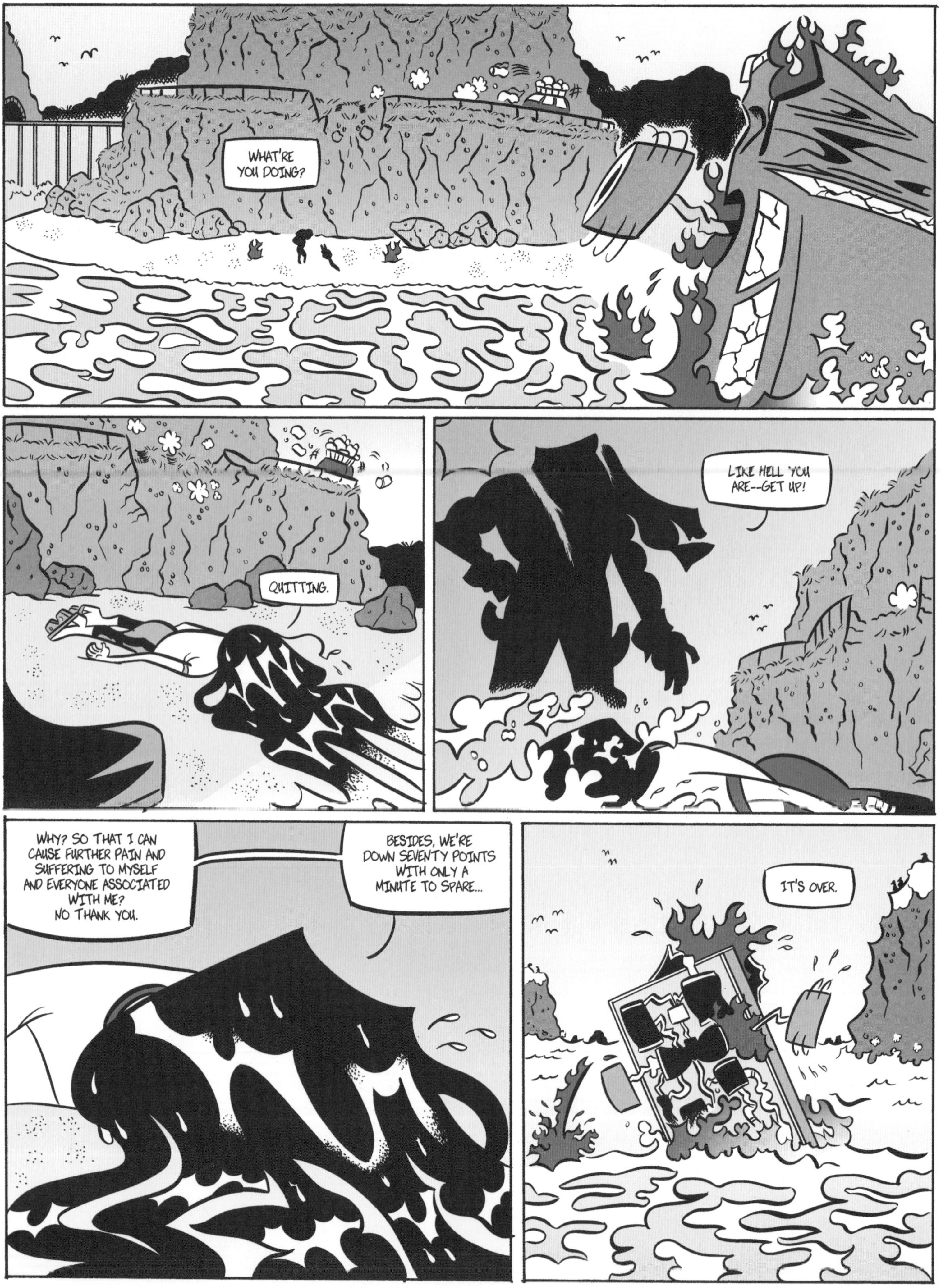
WHAT'RE YOU DOING?
QUITTING.
LIKE HELL YOU ARE--GET UP!
WHY? SO THAT I CAN CAUSE FURTHER PAIN AND SUFFERING TO MYSELF AND EVERYONE ASSOCIATED WITH ME? NO THANK YOU.
BESIDES, WE'RE DOWN SEVENTY POINTS WITH ONLY A MINUTE TO SPARE...
IT'S OVER.

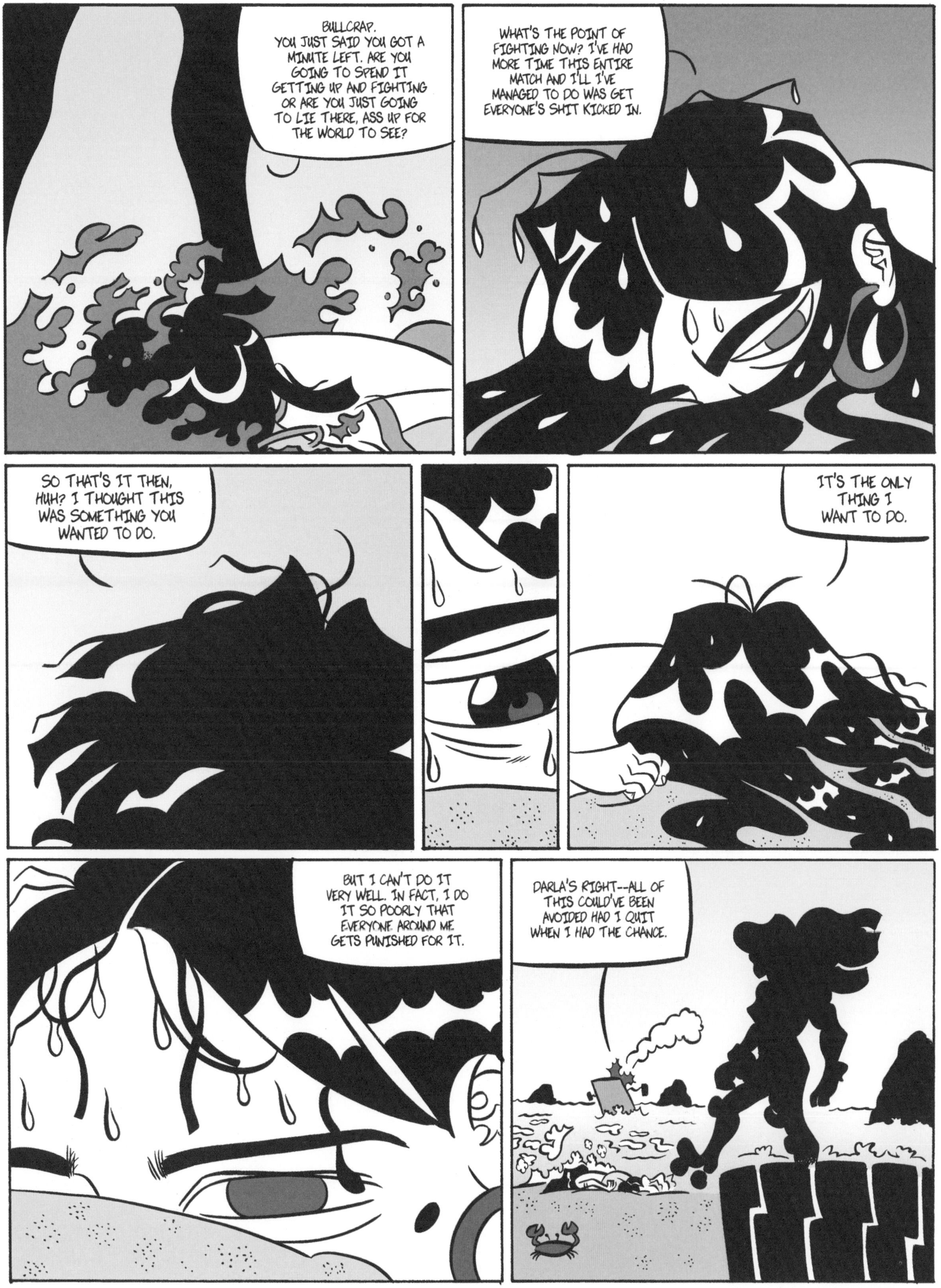
BULLCRAP. YOU JUST SAID YOU GOT A MINUTE LEFT. ARE YOU GOING TO SPEND IT GETTING UP AND FIGHTING OR ARE YOU JUST GOING TO LIE THERE, ASS UP FOR THE WORLD TO SEE?
WHAT'S THE POINT OF FIGHTING NOW? I'VE HAD MORE TIME THIS ENTIRE MATCH AND I'LL I'VE MANAGED TO DO WAS GET EVERYONE'S SHIT KICKED IN.
SO THAT'S IT THEN, HUH? I THOUGHT THIS WAS SOMETHING YOU WANTED TO DO.
IT'S THE ONLY THING I WANT TO DO.
BUT I CAN'T DO IT VERY WELL. IN FACT, I DO IT SO POORLY THAT EVERYONE AROUND ME GETS PUNISHED FOR IT.
DARLA'S RIGHT--ALL OF THIS COULD'VE BEEN AVOIDED HAD I QUIT WHEN I HAD THE CHANCE.

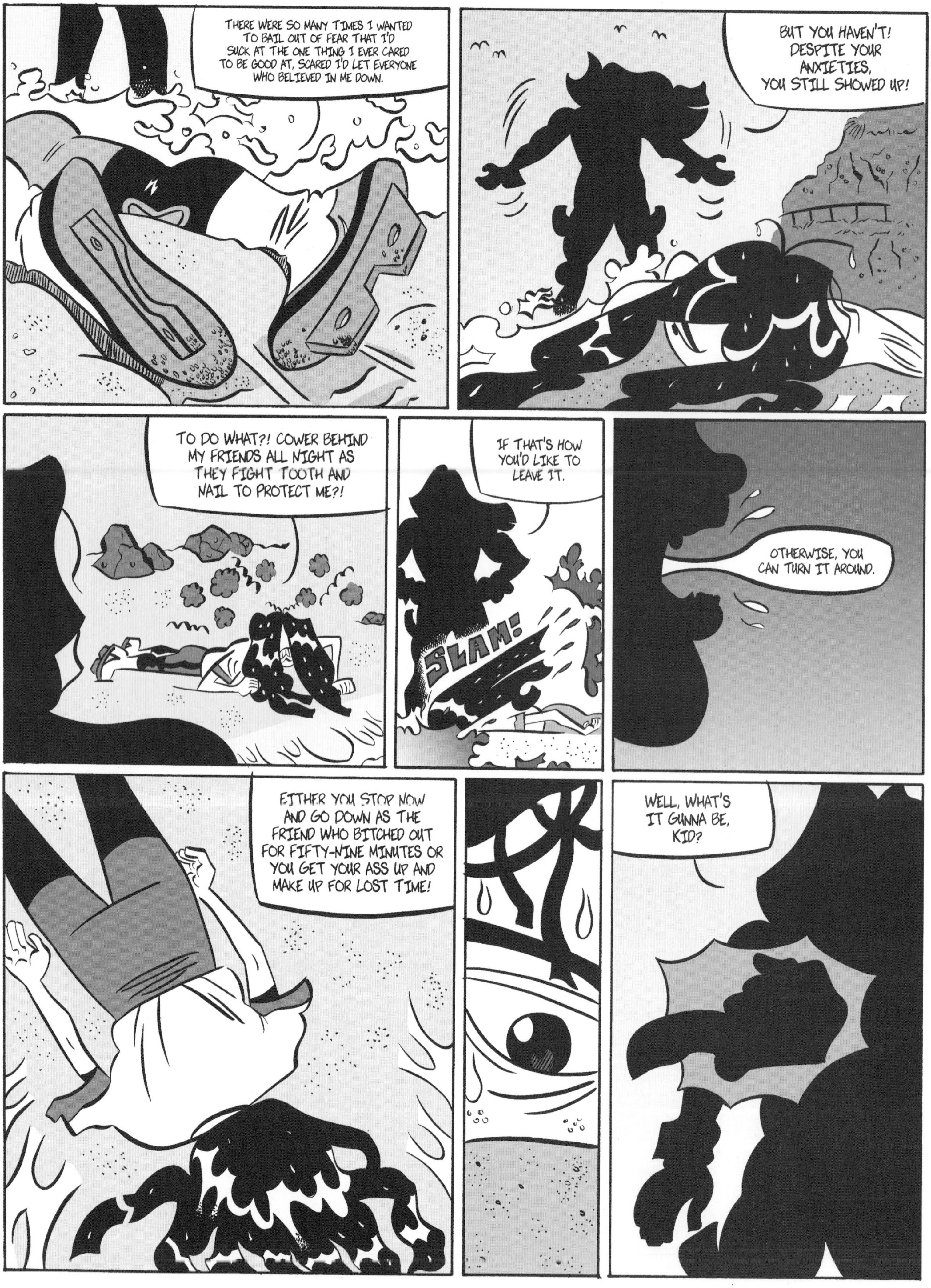
THERE WERE SO MANY TIMES I WANTED TO BAIL OUT OF FEAR THAT I'D SUCK AT THE ONE THING I EVER CARED TO BE GOOD AT, SCARED I'D LET EVERYONE WHO BELIEVED IN ME DOWN.
BUT YOU HAVEN'T! DESPITE YOUR ANXIETIES, YOU STILL SHOWED UP!
TO DO WHAT?! COWER BEHIND MY FRIENDS ALL NIGHT AS THEY FIGHT TOOTH AND NAIL TO PROTECT ME?!
IF THAT'S HOW YOU'D LIKE TO LEAVE IT.
SLAM!
OTHERWISE, YOU CAN TURN IT AROUND.
EITHER YOU STOP NOW AND GO DOWN AS THE FRIEND WHO BITCHED OUT FOR FIFTY-NINE MINUTES OR YOU GET YOUR ASS UP AND MAKE UP FOR LOST TIME!
WELL, WHAT'S IT GUNNA BE, KID?

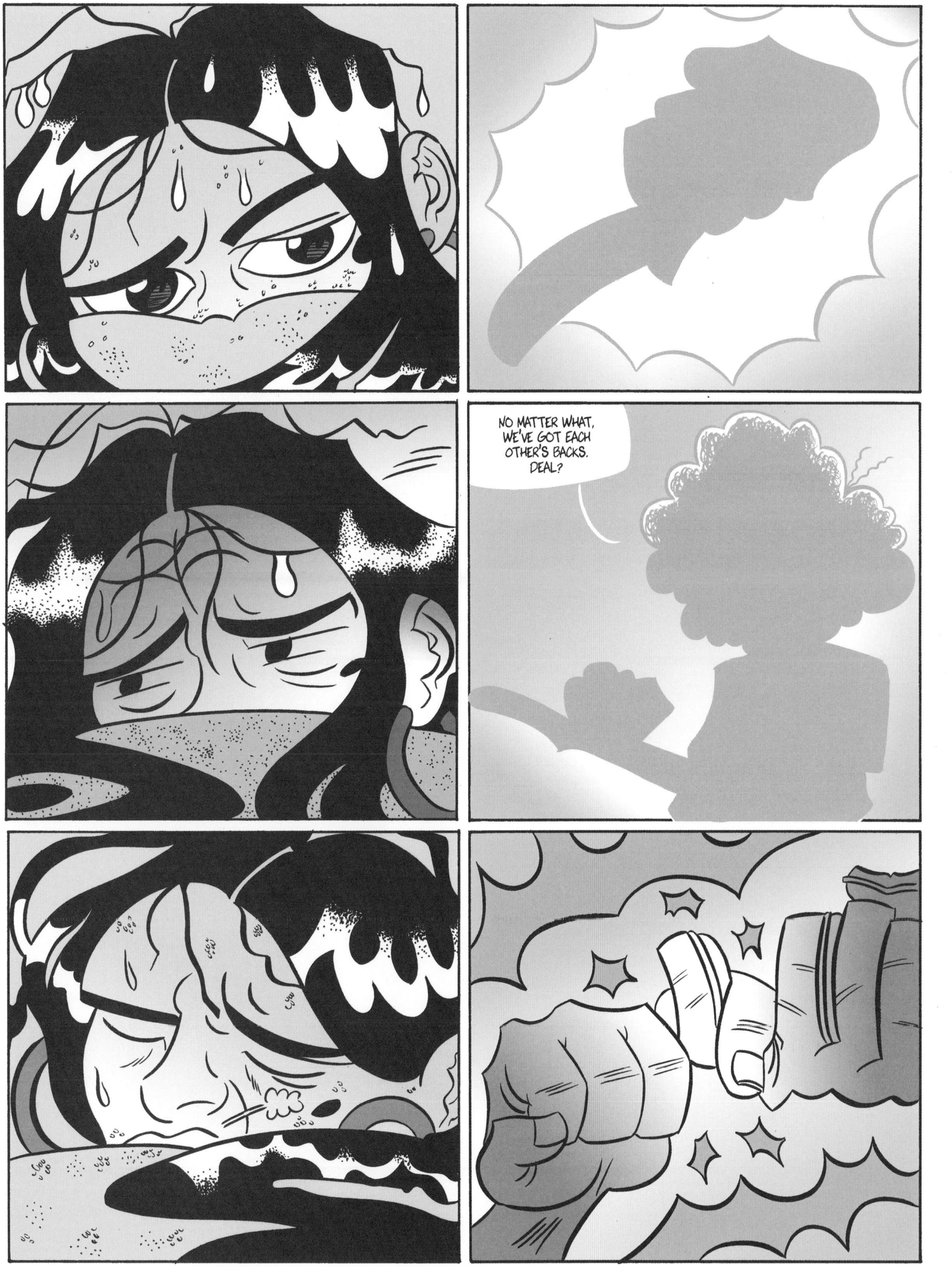
NO MATTER WHAT, WE'VE GOT EACH OTHER'S BACKS. DEAL?

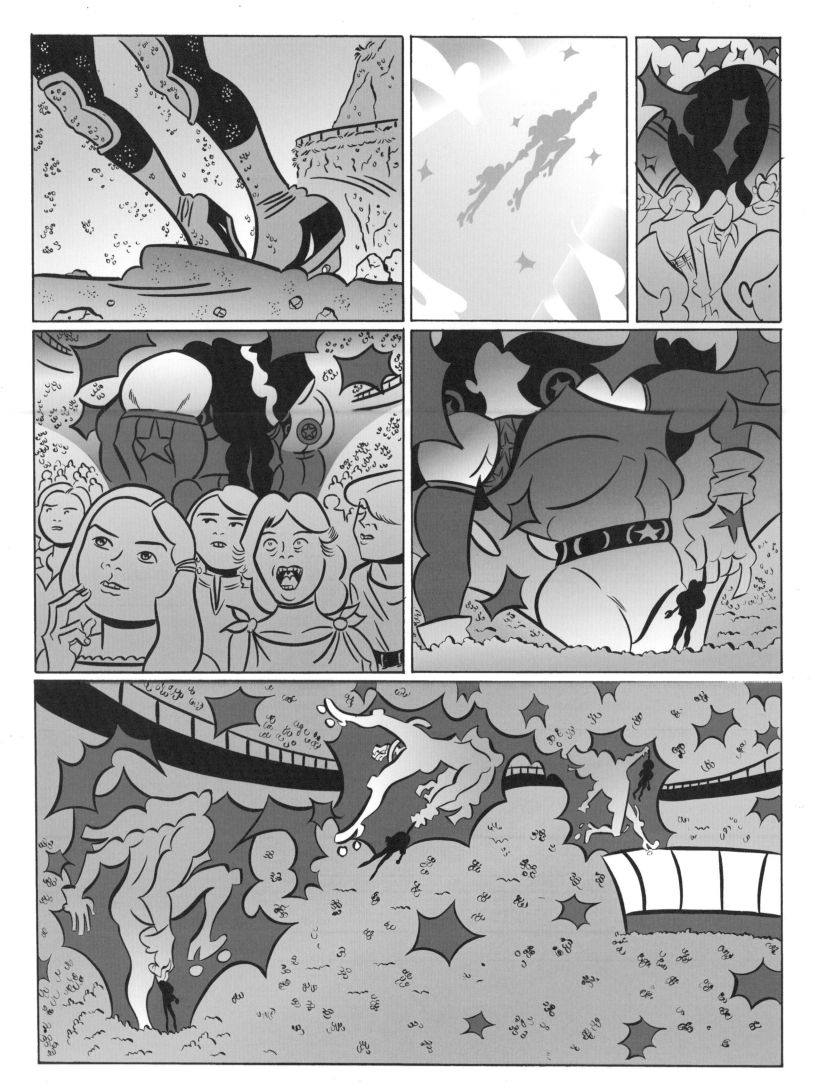

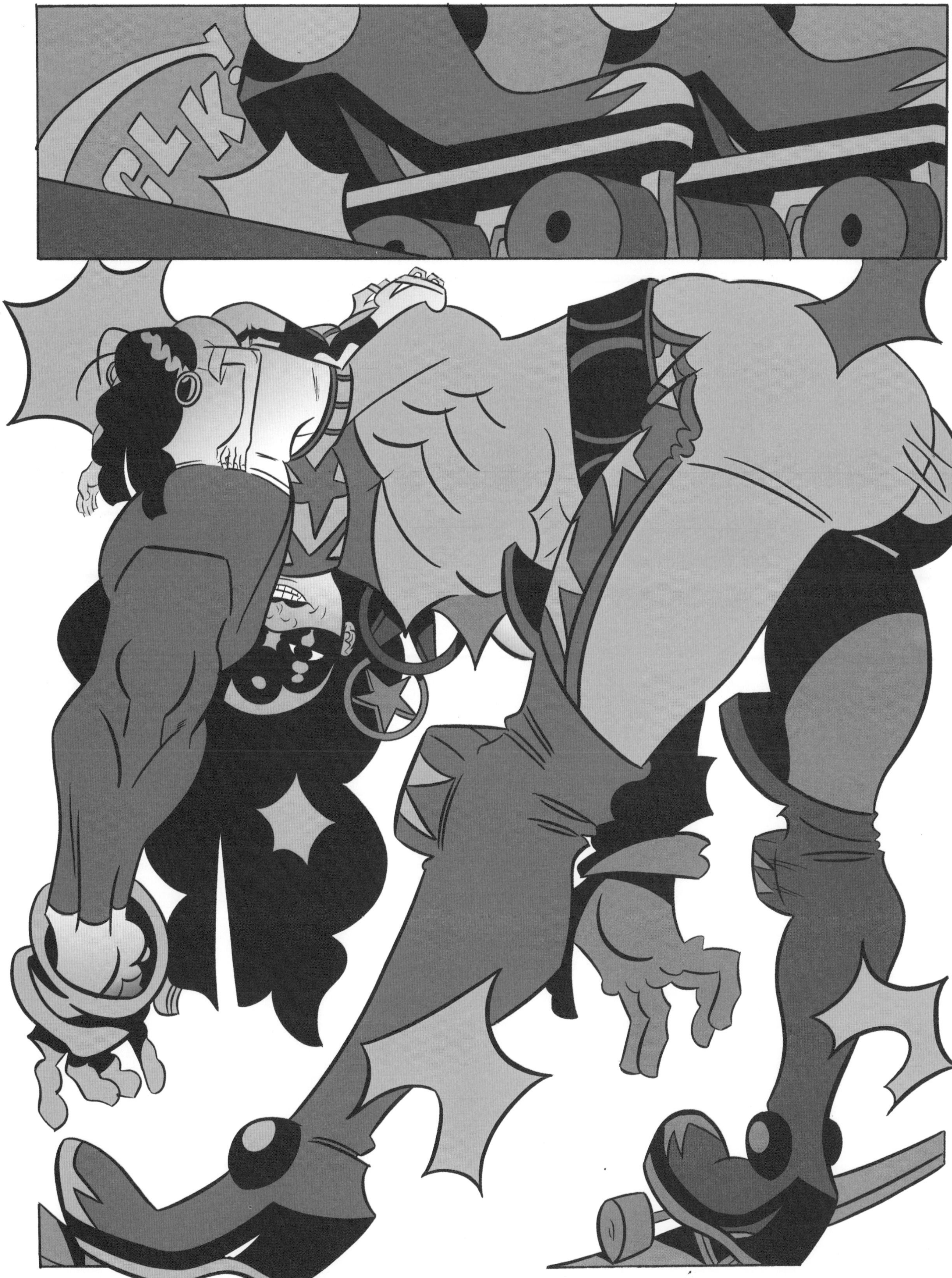
GLK!

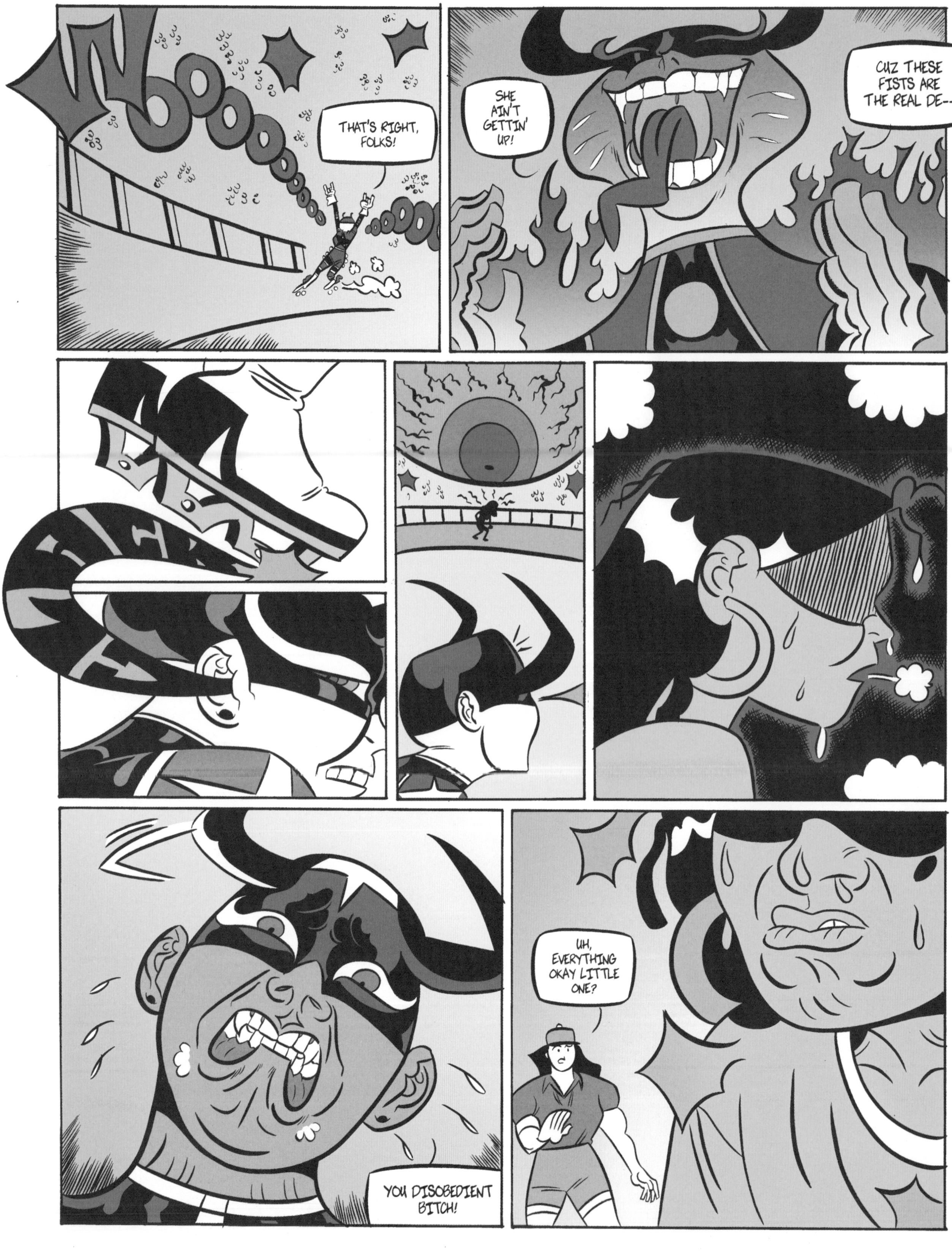
THAT'S RIGHT, FOLKS!
SHE AIN'T GETTIN' UP!
CUZ THESE FISTS ARE THE REAL DE--
YOU DISOBEDIENT BITCH!
UH, EVERYTHING OKAY LITTLE ONE?

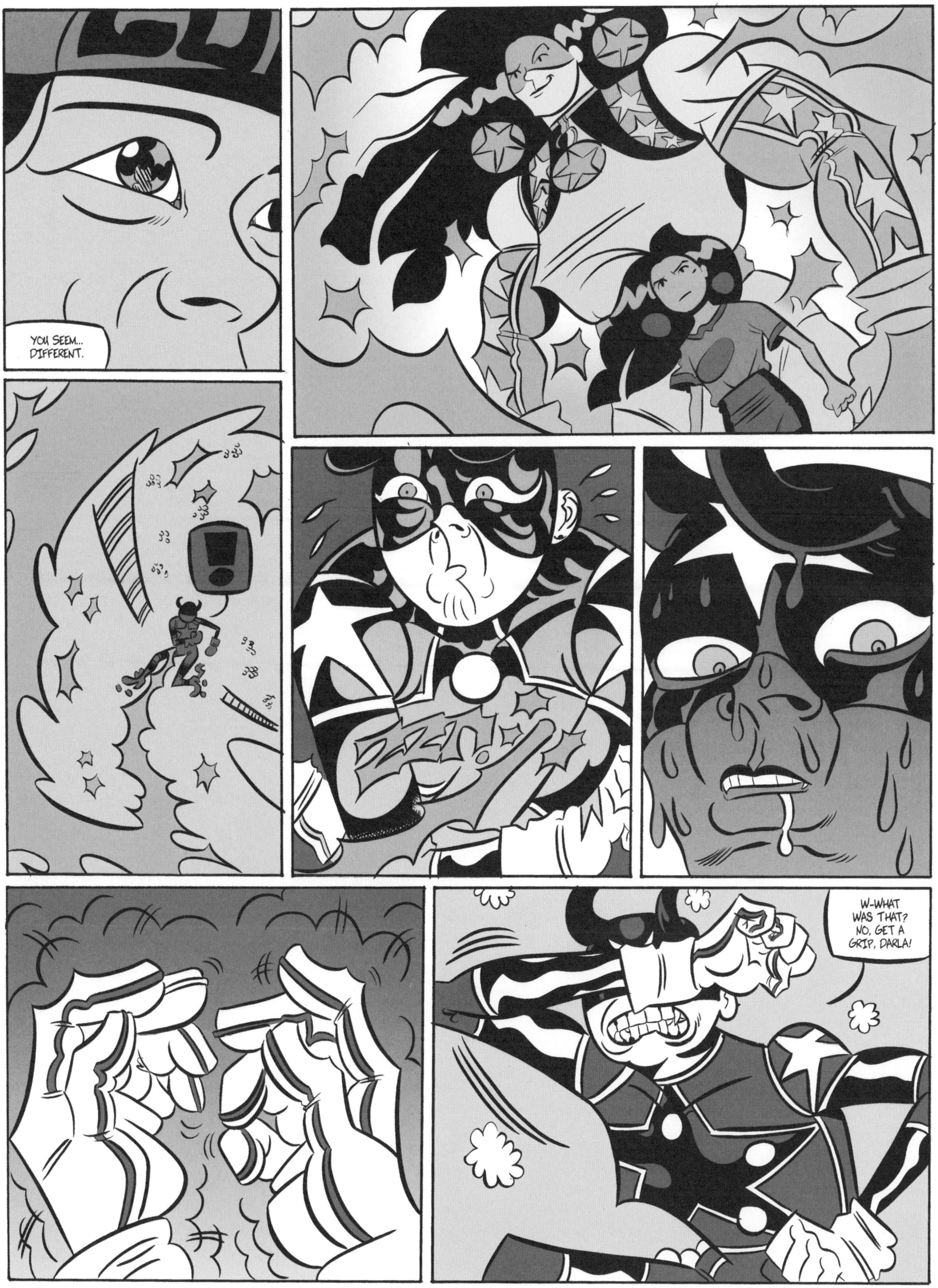
YOU SEEM... DIFFERENT.
W-WHAT WAS THAT? NO, GET A GRIP, DARLA!

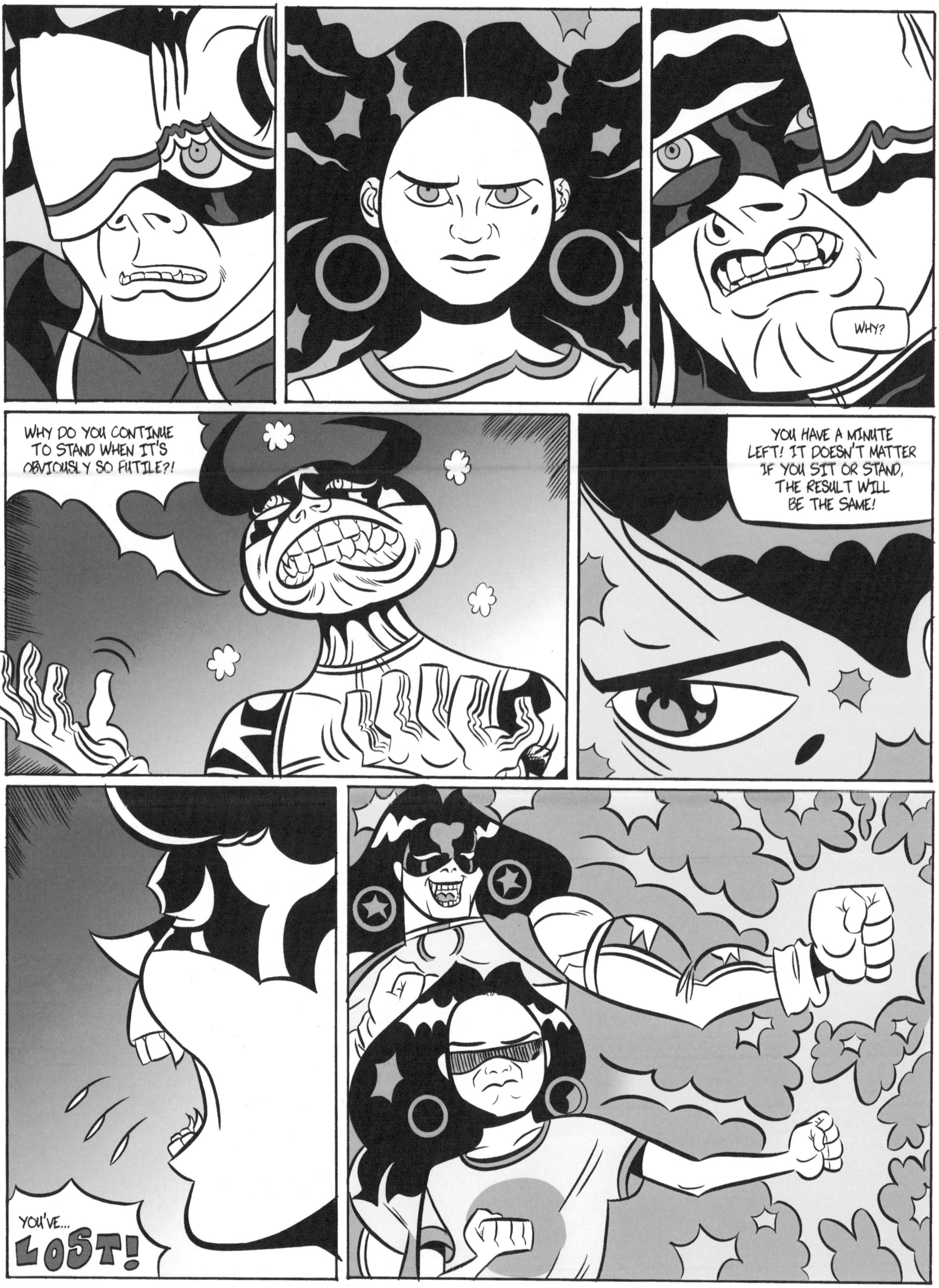

WHY?
WHY DO YOU CONTINUE TO STAND WHEN IT'S OBVIOUSLY SO FUTILE?!
YOU HAVE A MINUTE LEFT! IT DOESN'T MATTER IF YOU SIT OR STAND, THE RESULT WILL BE THE SAME!
YOU'VE... LOST!

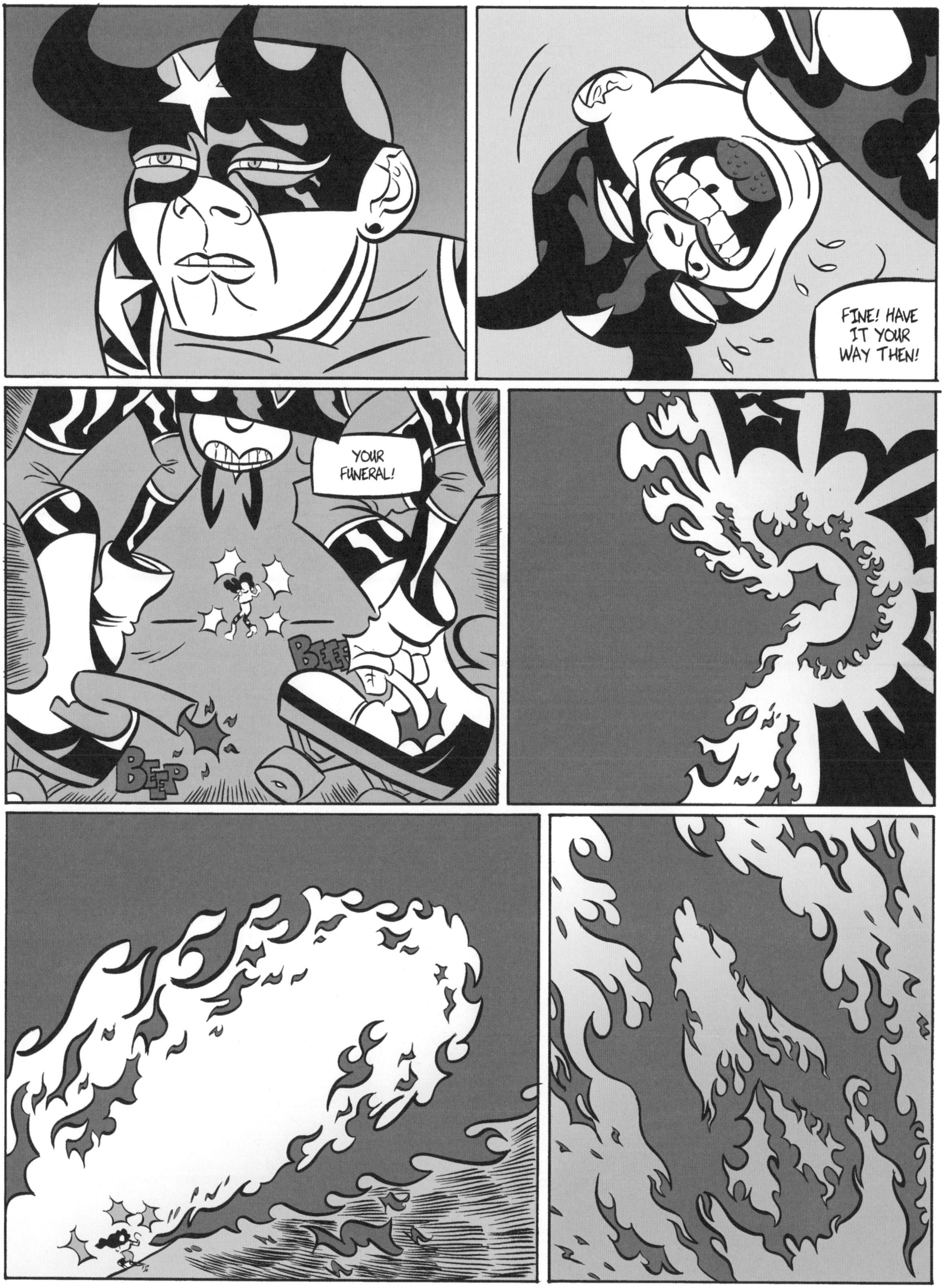
FINE! HAVE IT YOUR WAY THEN!
YOUR FUNERAL!
BEEP
BEEP

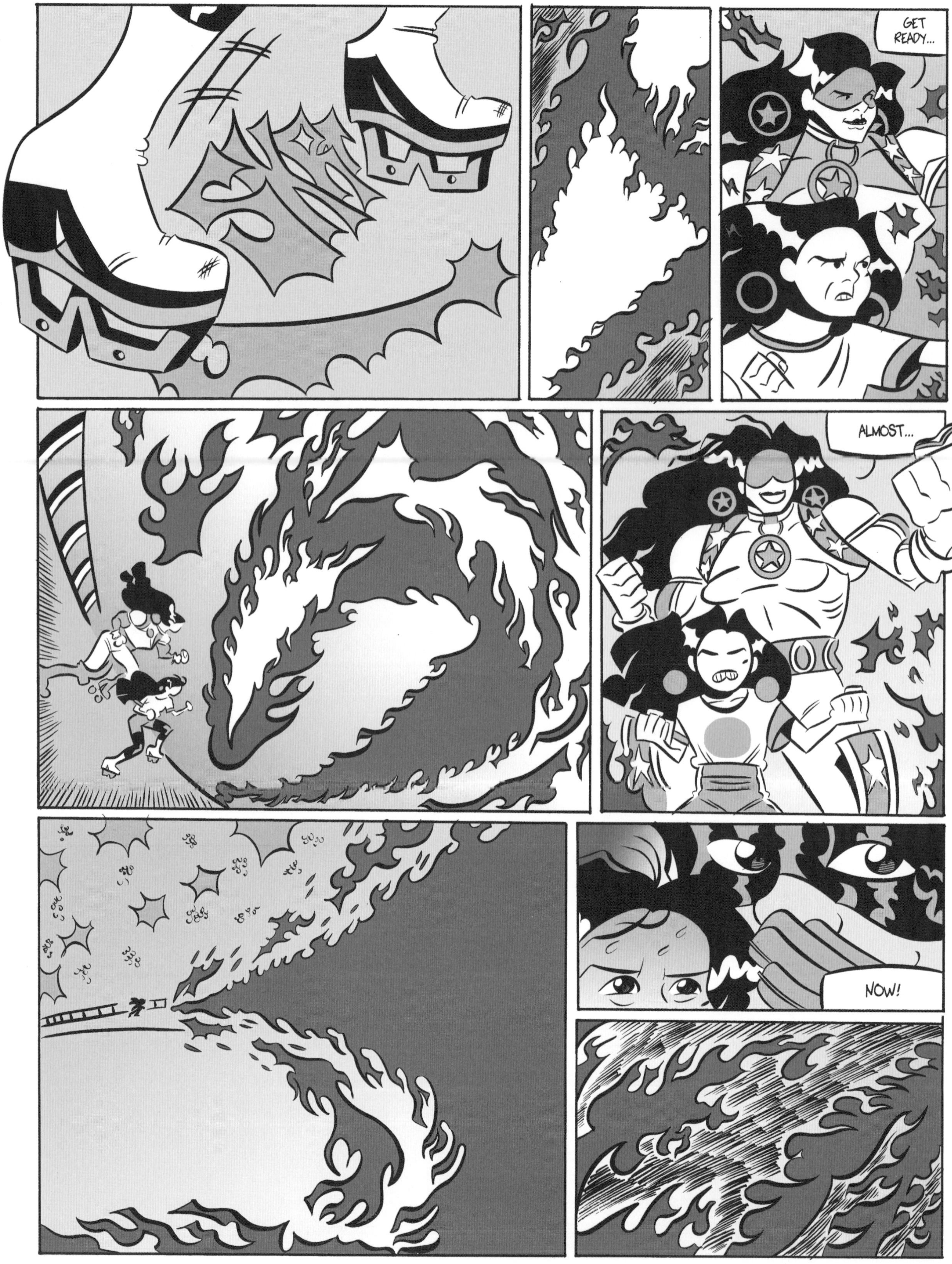
GET READY...
ALMOST...
NOW!

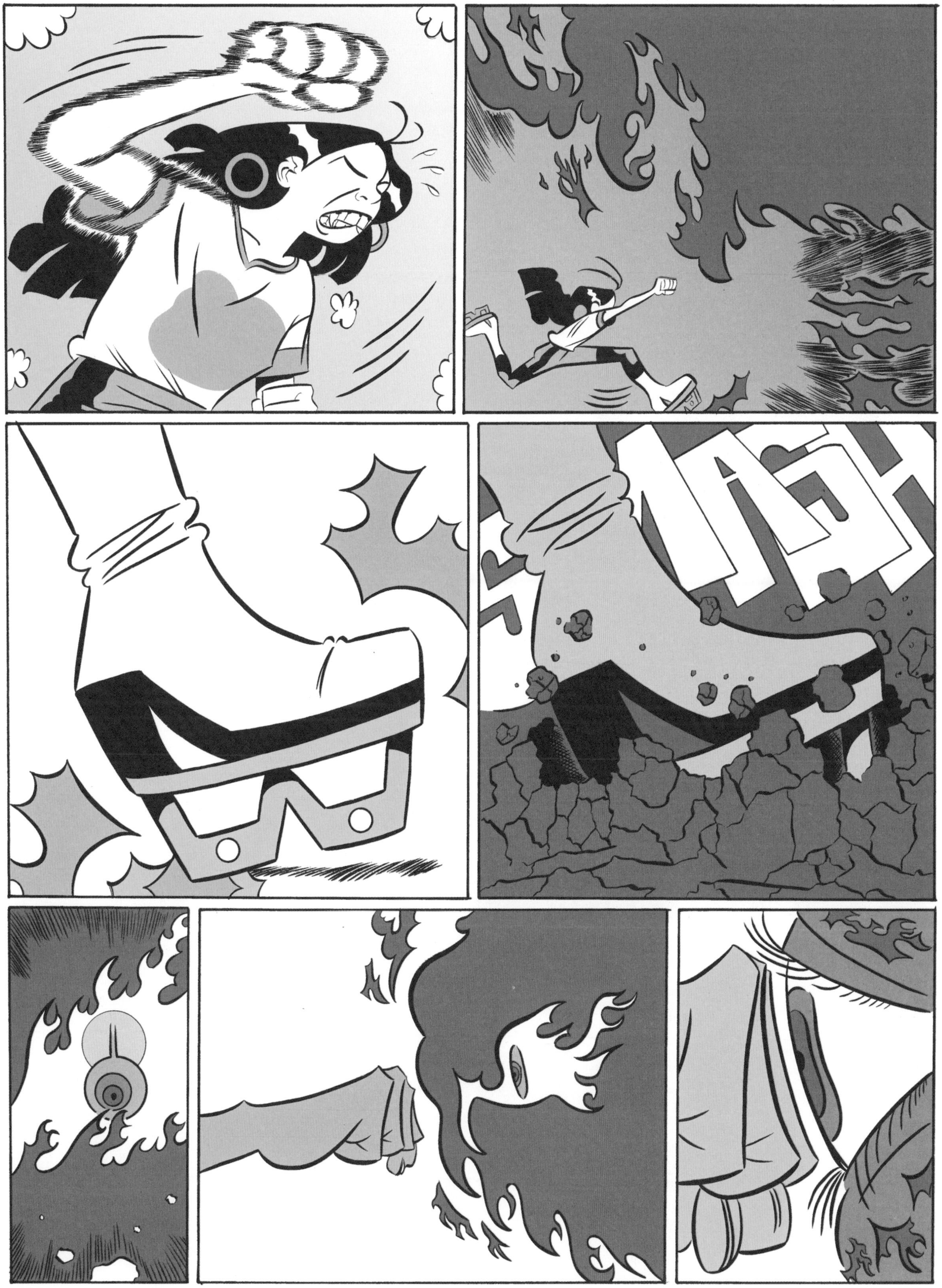

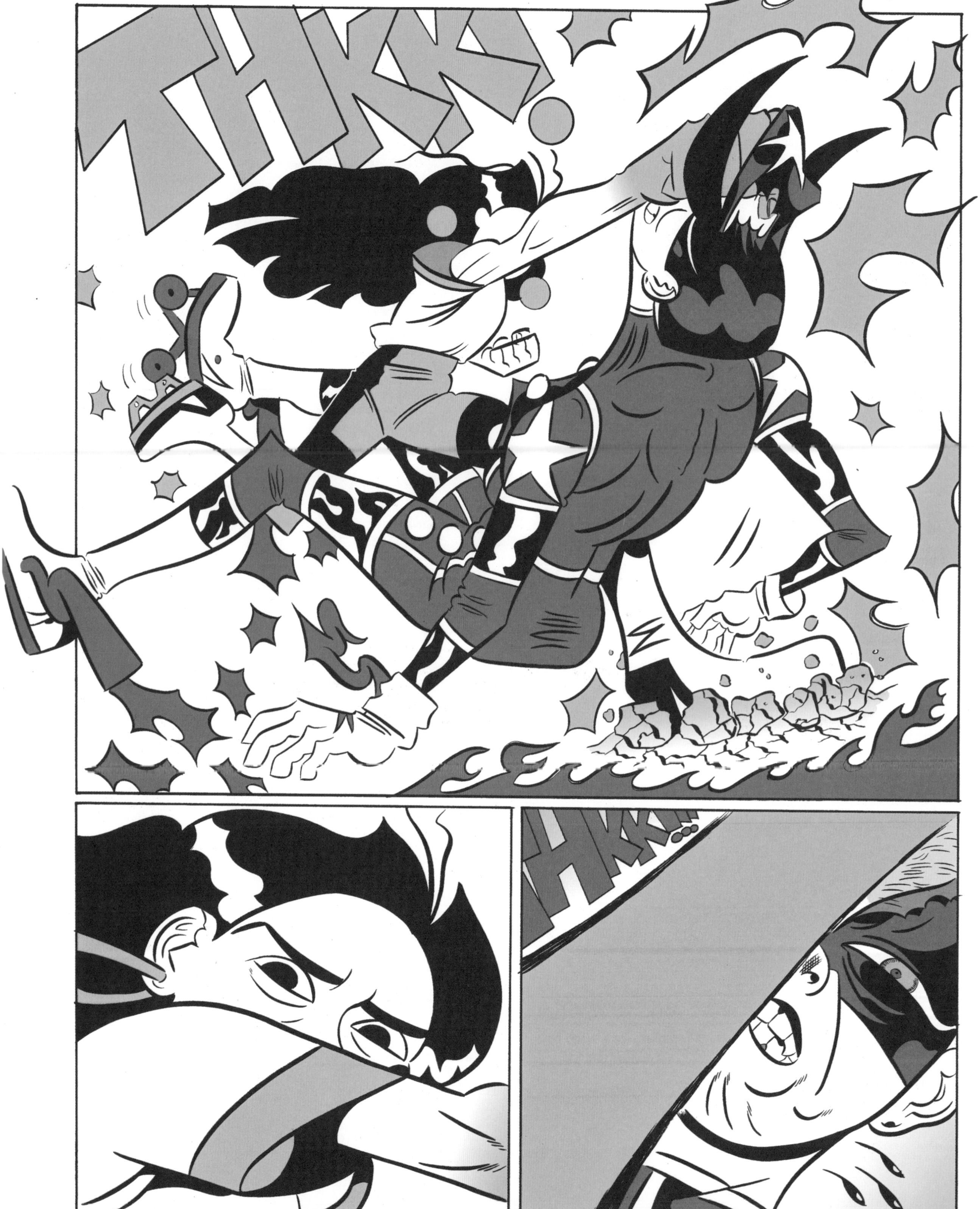
THKK!

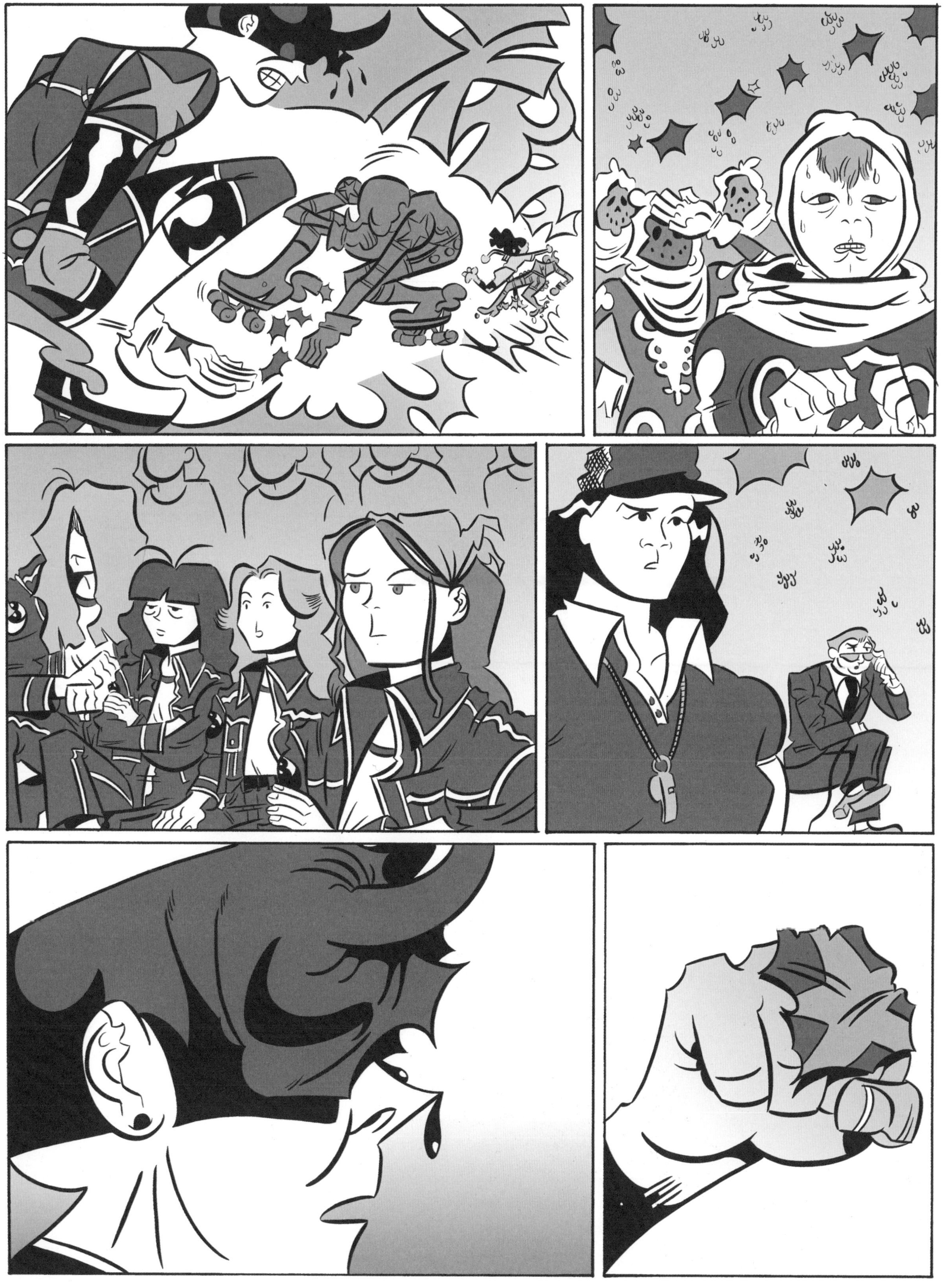

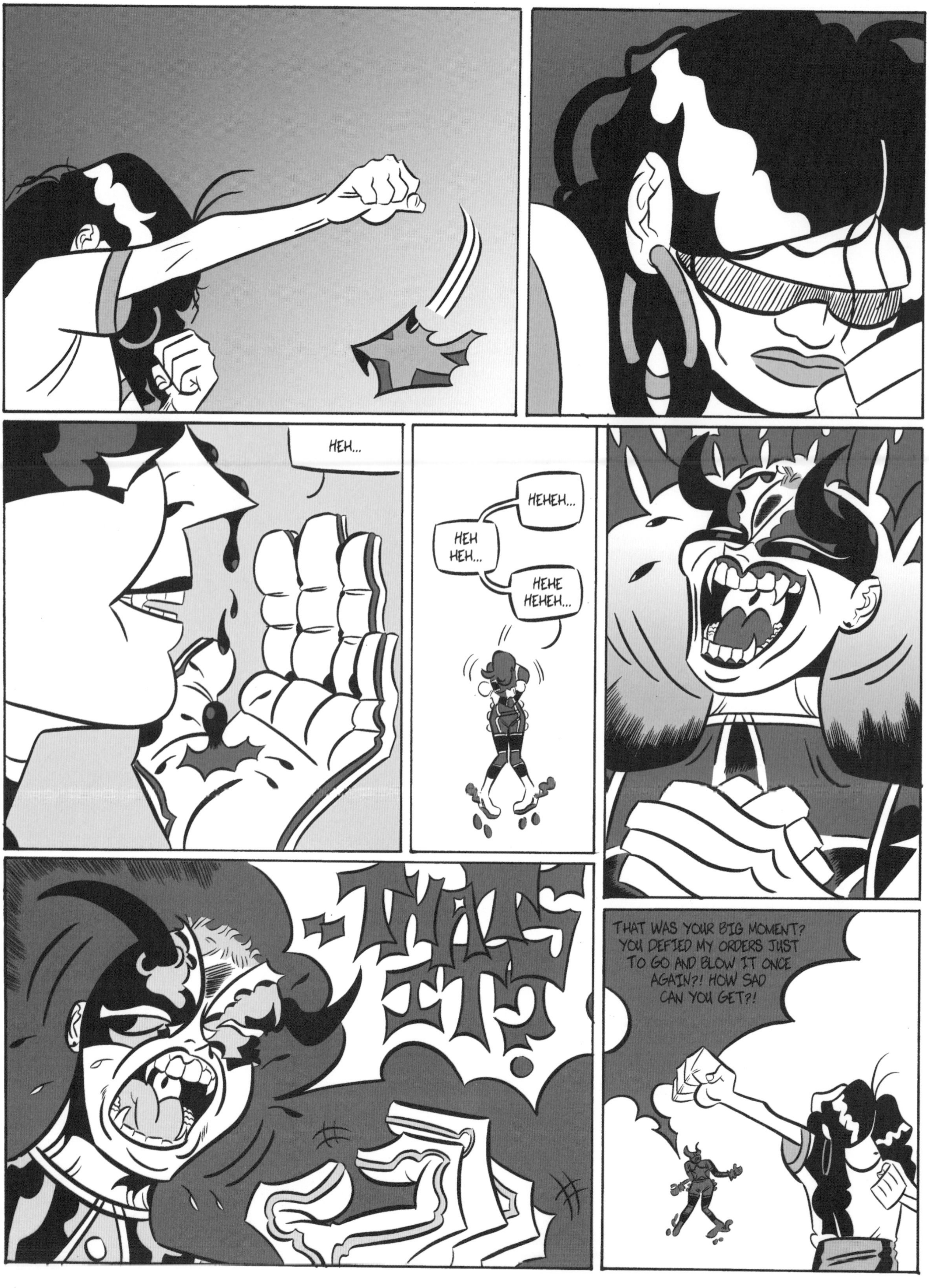
HEH...
HEHEH...
HEH HEH...
HEHE HEHEH...
THAT'S IT!
THAT WAS YOUR BIG MOMENT? YOU DEFIED MY ORDERS JUST TO GO AND BLOW IT ONCE AGAIN?! HOW SAD CAN YOU GET?!

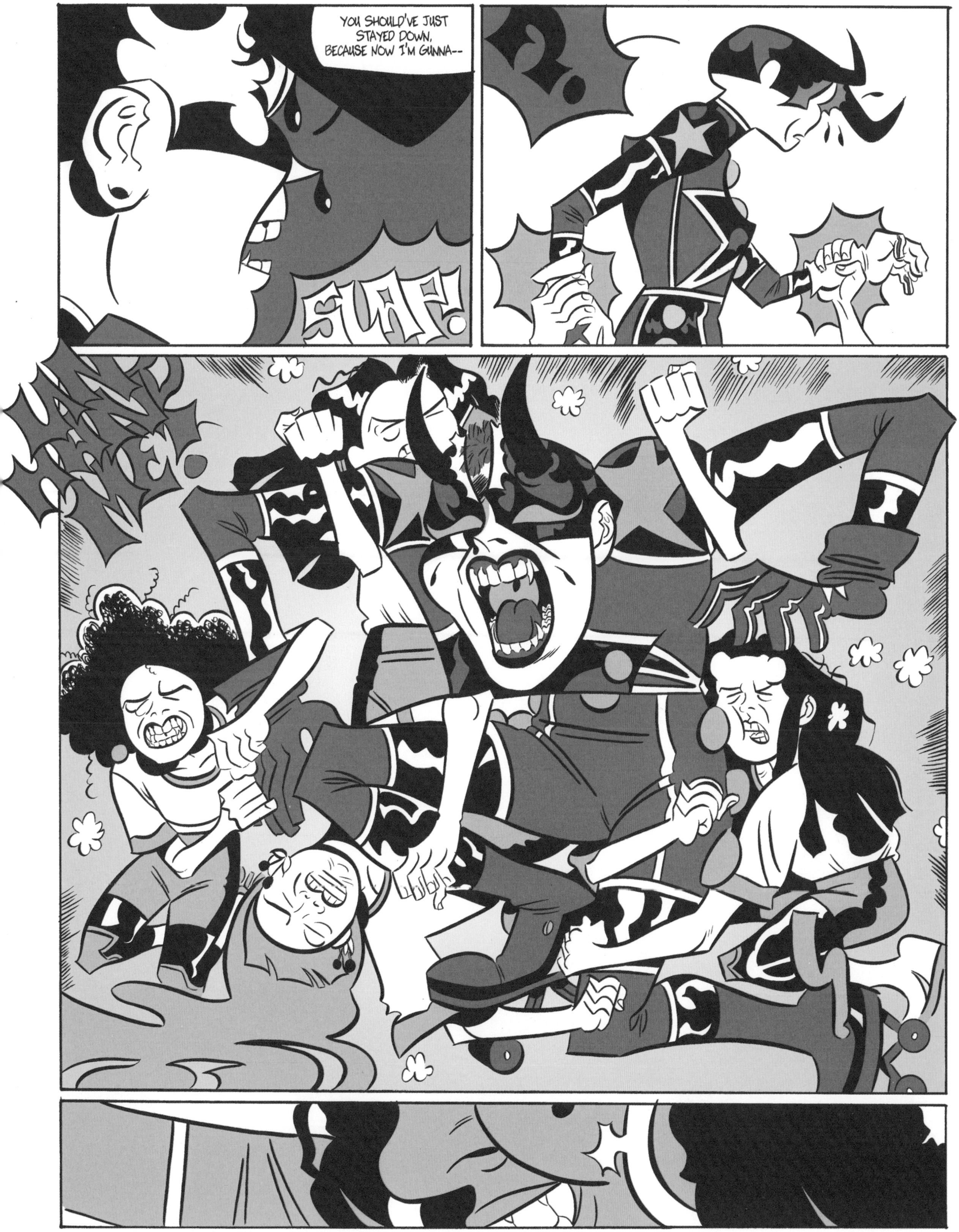
YOU SHOULD'VE JUST STAYED DOWN, BECAUSE NOW I'M GUNNA--
SLAP!

I'M HAPPY YOU SHOWED UP TODAY, BECAUSE IF YOU HADN'T, NONE OF US COULD'VE KNOCKED THIS BITCH OUT!
DON'T YOU DARE, WORM.
LET'S END THIS ONCE AND FOR ALL!

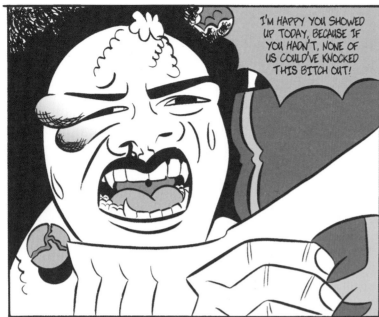

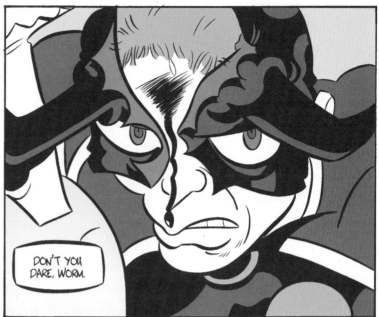

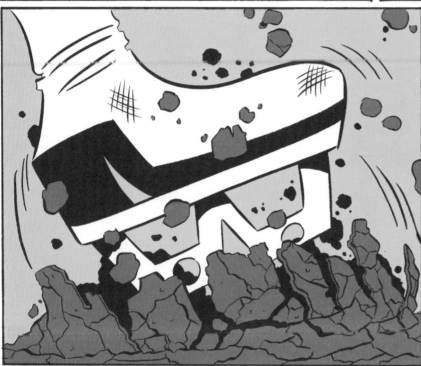

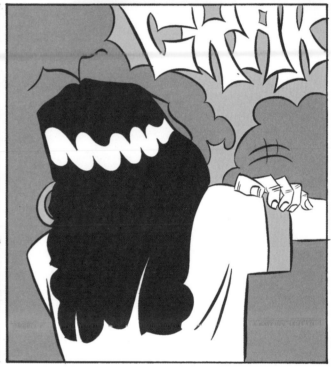

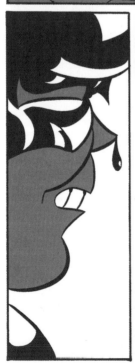

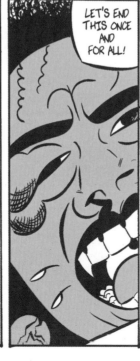

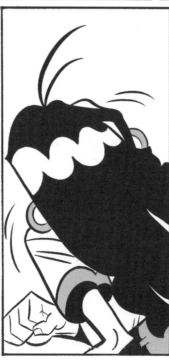

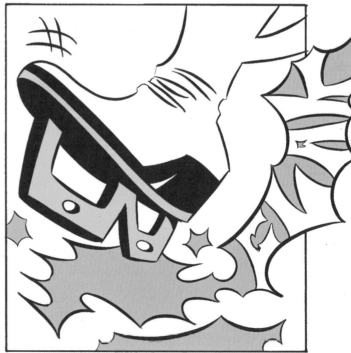

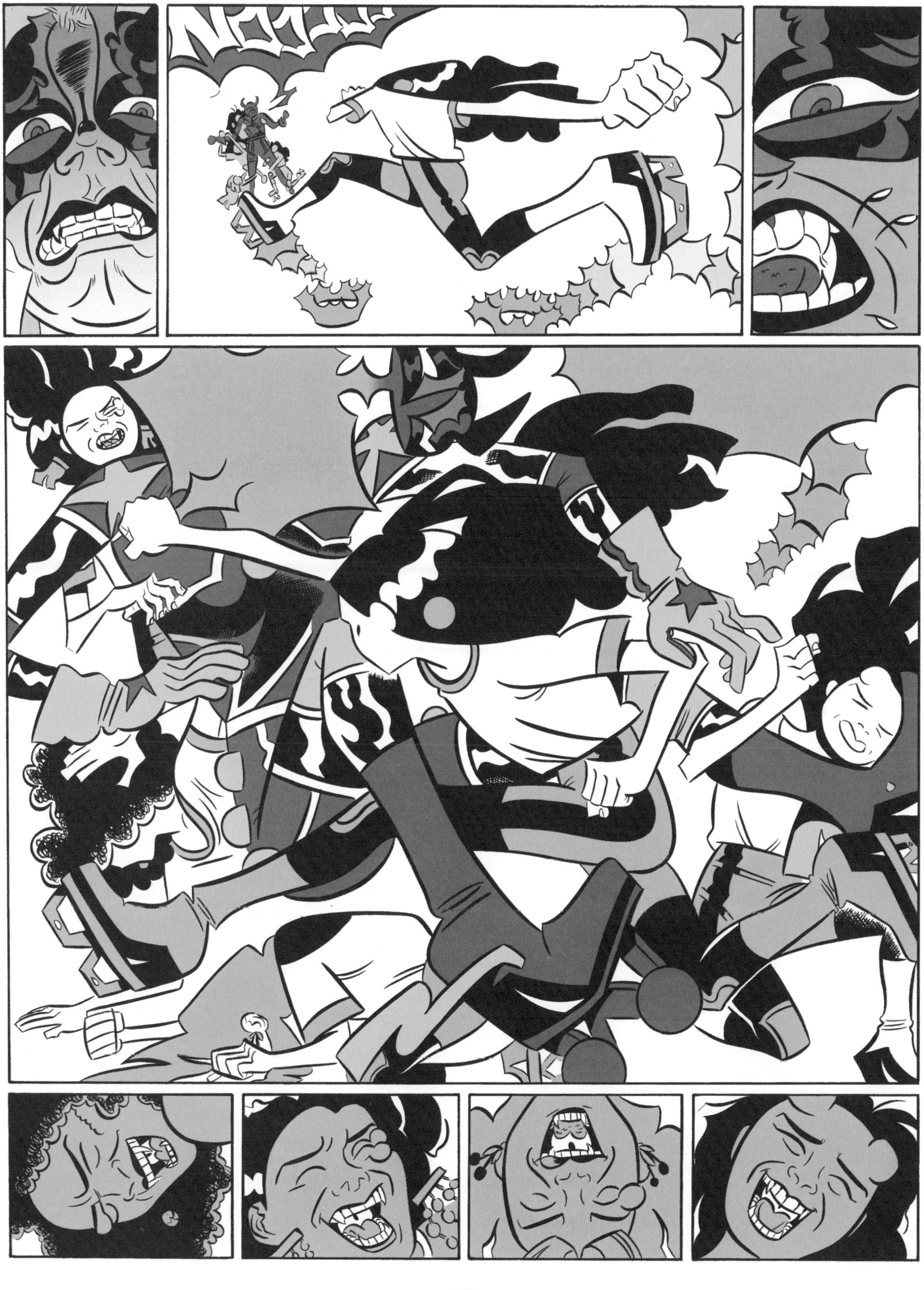

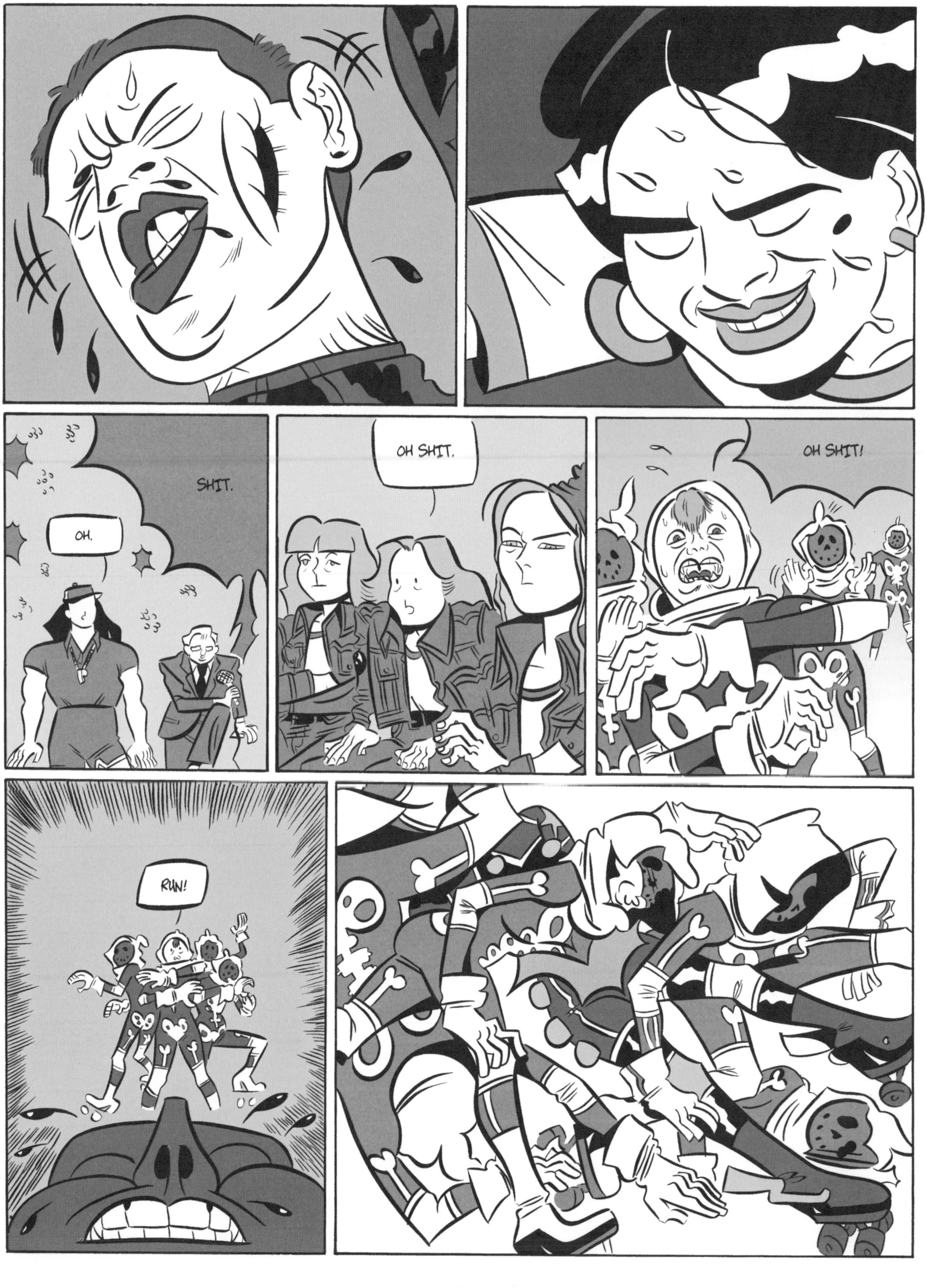
OH.
SHIT.
OH SHIT.
OH SHIT!
RUN!

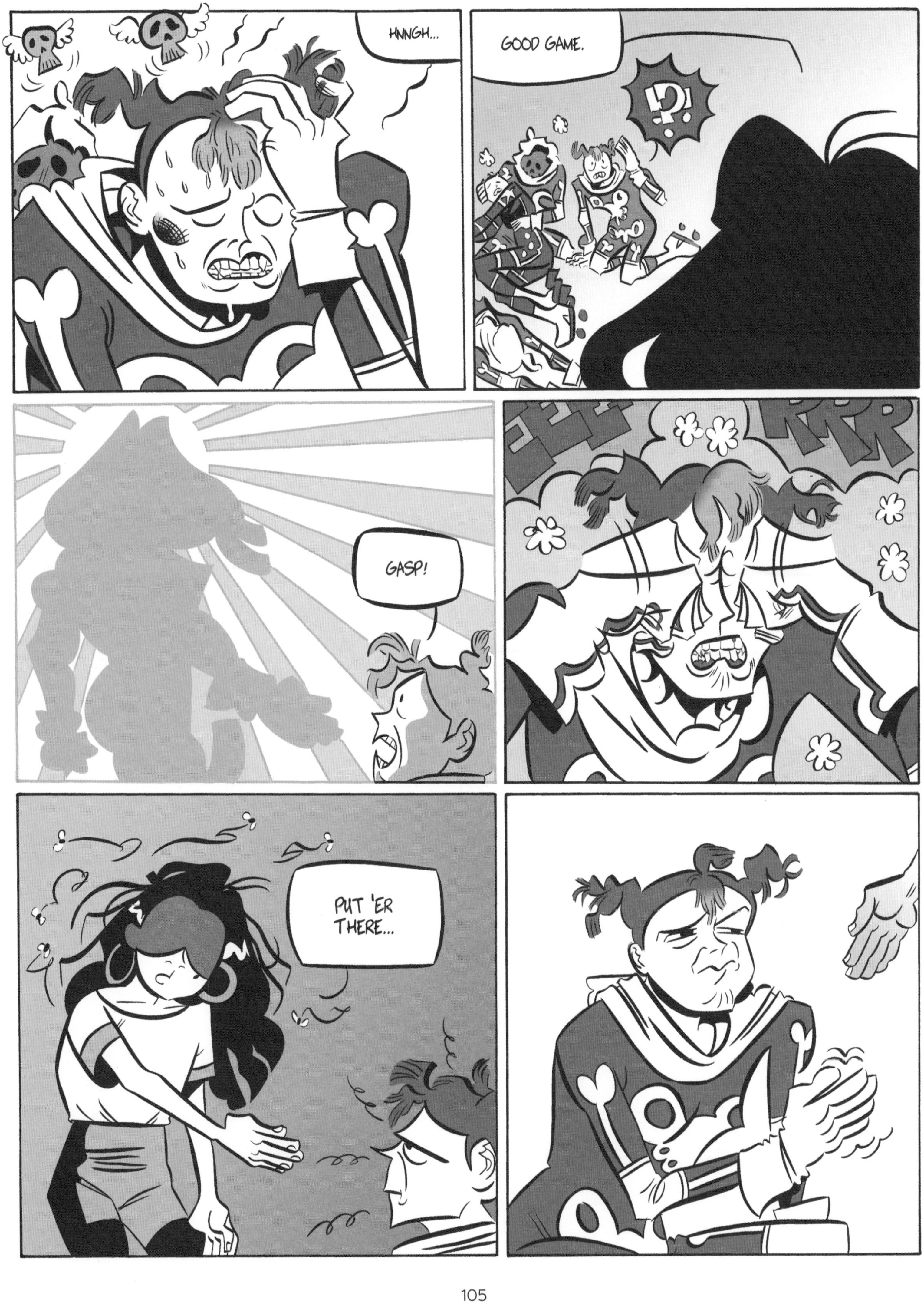
HNNGH...
GOOD GAME.
!?
GASP!
RRR
PUT 'ER THERE...

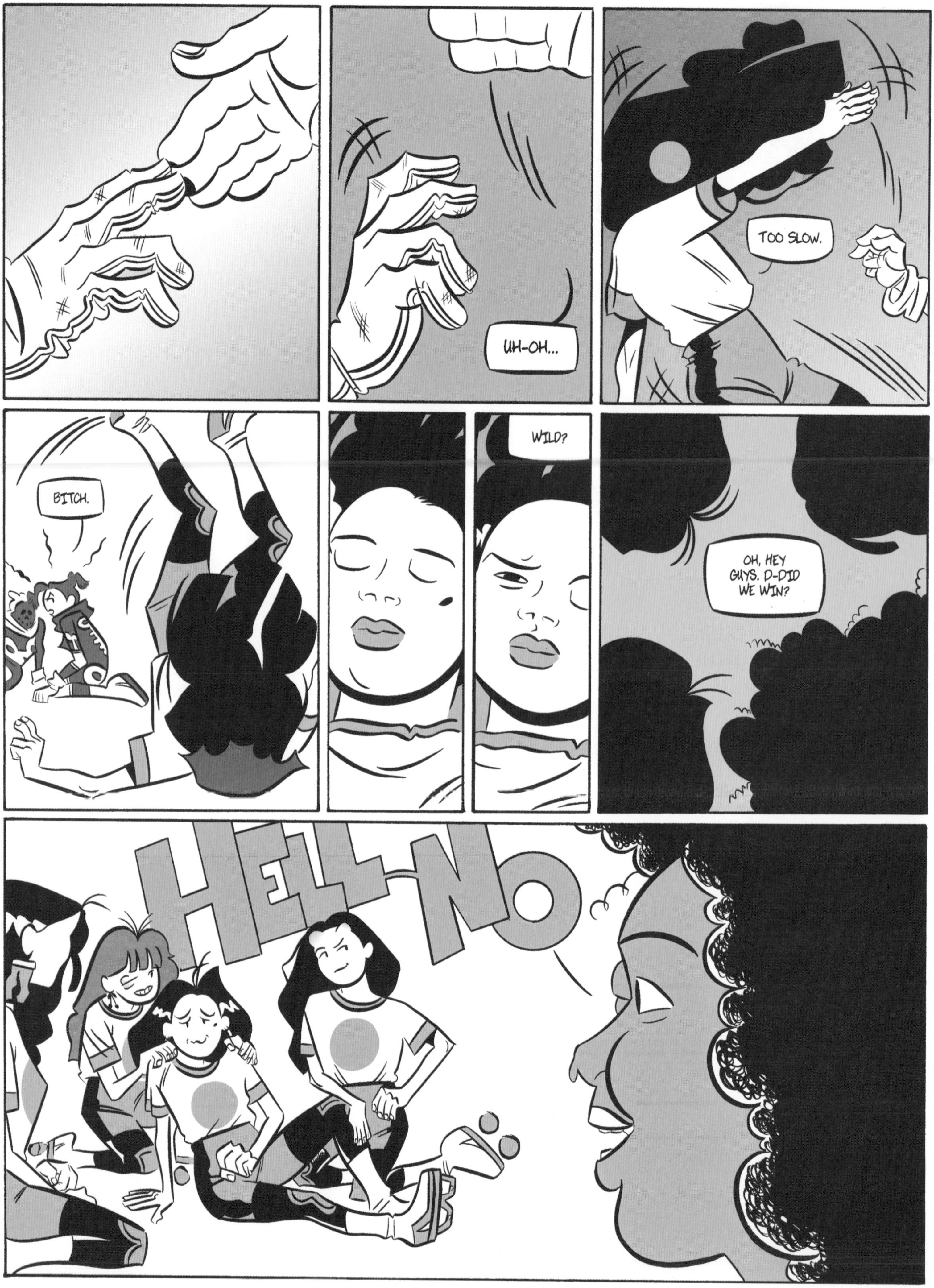
UH-OH...
TOO SLOW.
BITCH.
WILD?
OH, HEY GUYS. D-DID WE WIN?
HELL NO

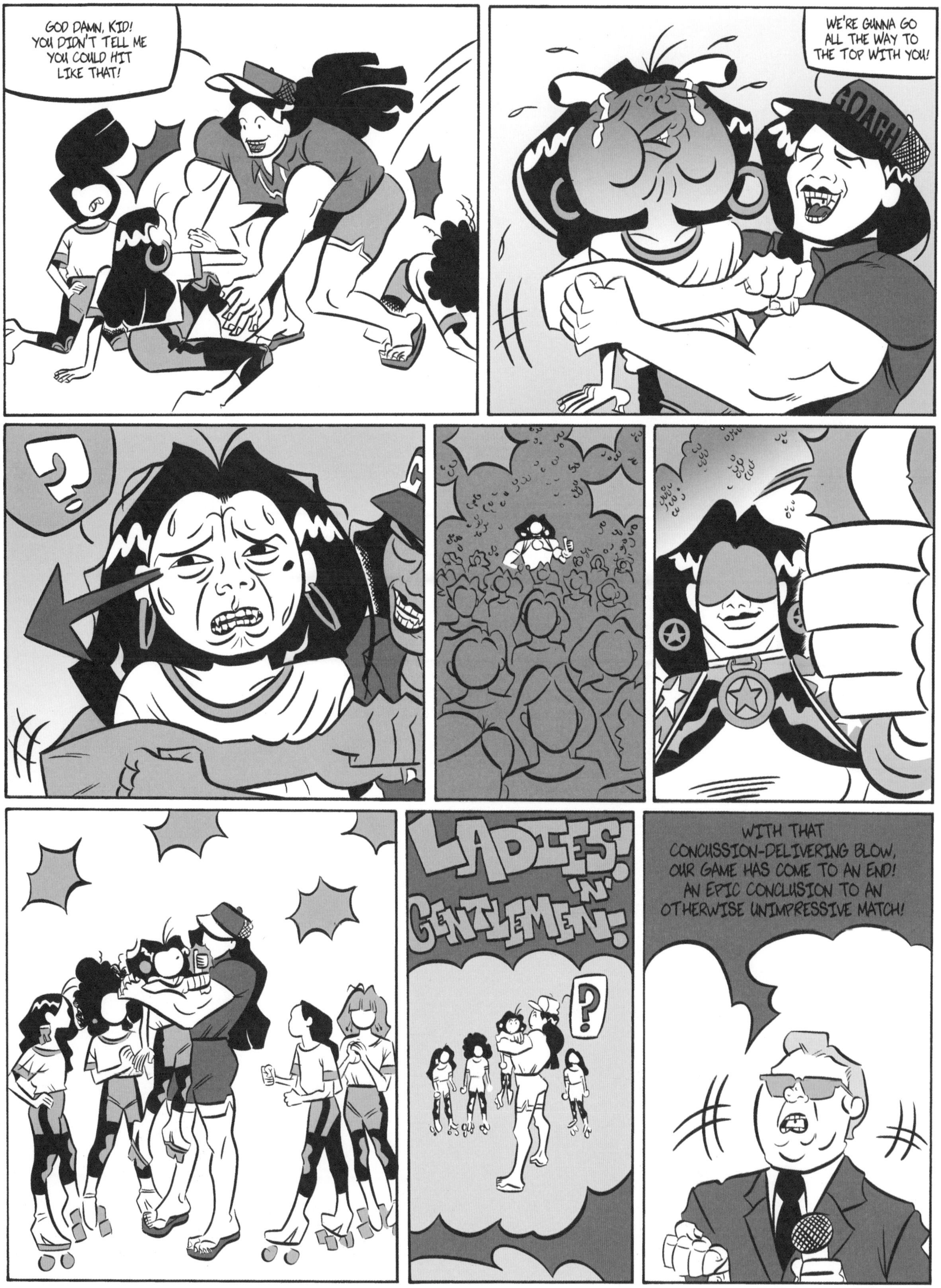
GOD DAMN, KID! YOU DIDN'T TELL ME YOU COULD HIT LIKE THAT!
WE'RE GUNNA GO ALL THE WAY TO THE TOP WITH YOU!
COACH
?
?
LADIES! 'N' GENTLEMEN:
WITH THAT CONCUSSION-DELIVERING BLOW, OUR GAME HAS COME TO AN END! AN EPIC CONCLUSION TO AN OTHERWISE UNIMPRESSIVE MATCH!

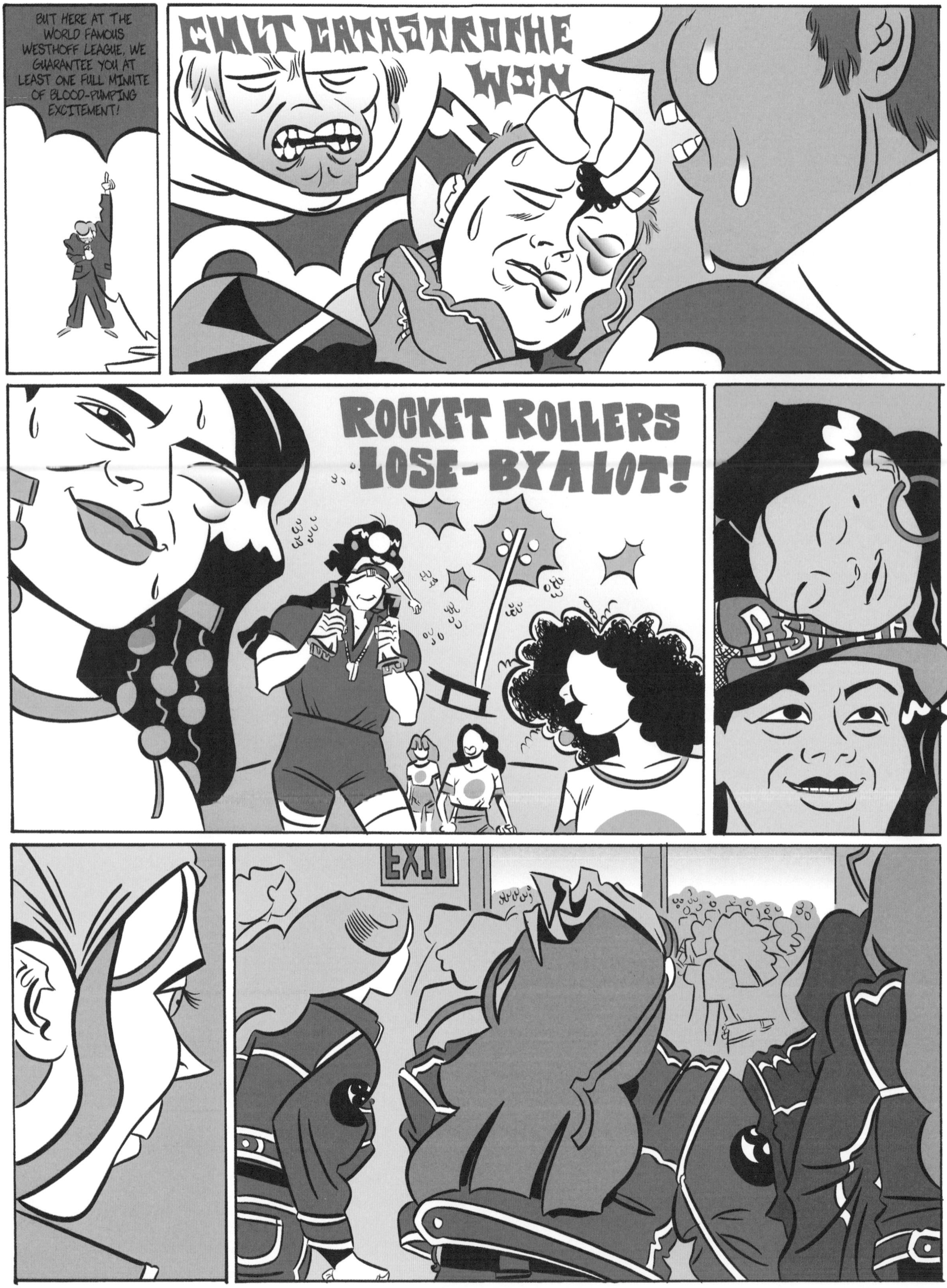
BUT HERE AT THE WORLD FAMOUS WESTHOFF LEAGUE, WE GUARANTEE YOU AT LEAST ONE FULL MINUTE OF BLOOD-PUMPING EXCITEMENT!
CULT CATASTROPHE WIN
ROCKET ROLLERS LOSE- BY A LOT!
EXIT

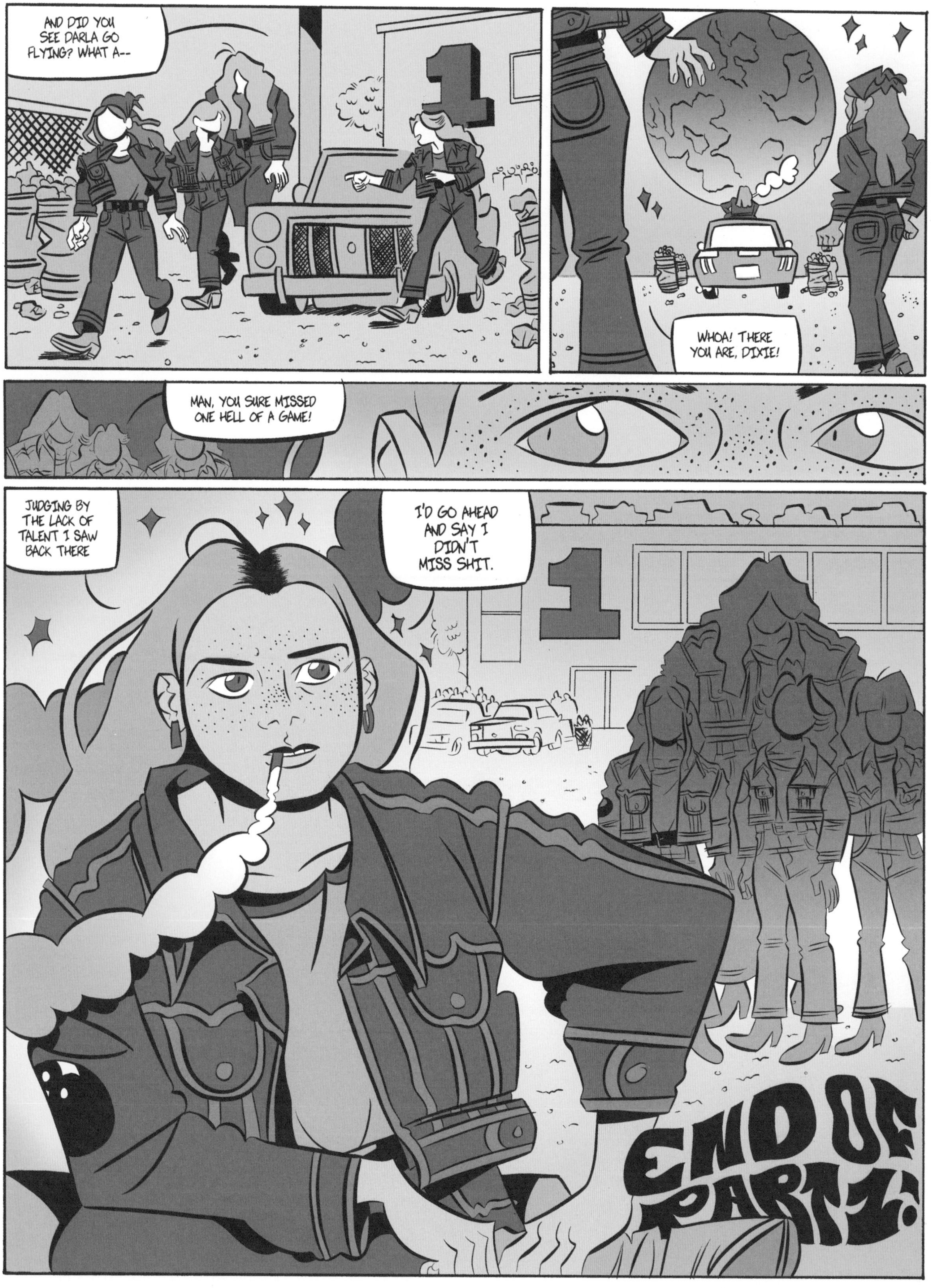
AND DID YOU SEE DARLA GO FLYING? WHAT A--
WHOA! THERE YOU ARE, DIXIE!
MAN, YOU SURE MISSED ONE HELL OF A GAME!
JUDGING BY THE LACK OF TALENT I SAW BACK THERE
I'D GO AHEAD AND SAY I DIDN'T MISS SHIT.
END OF PART 1!

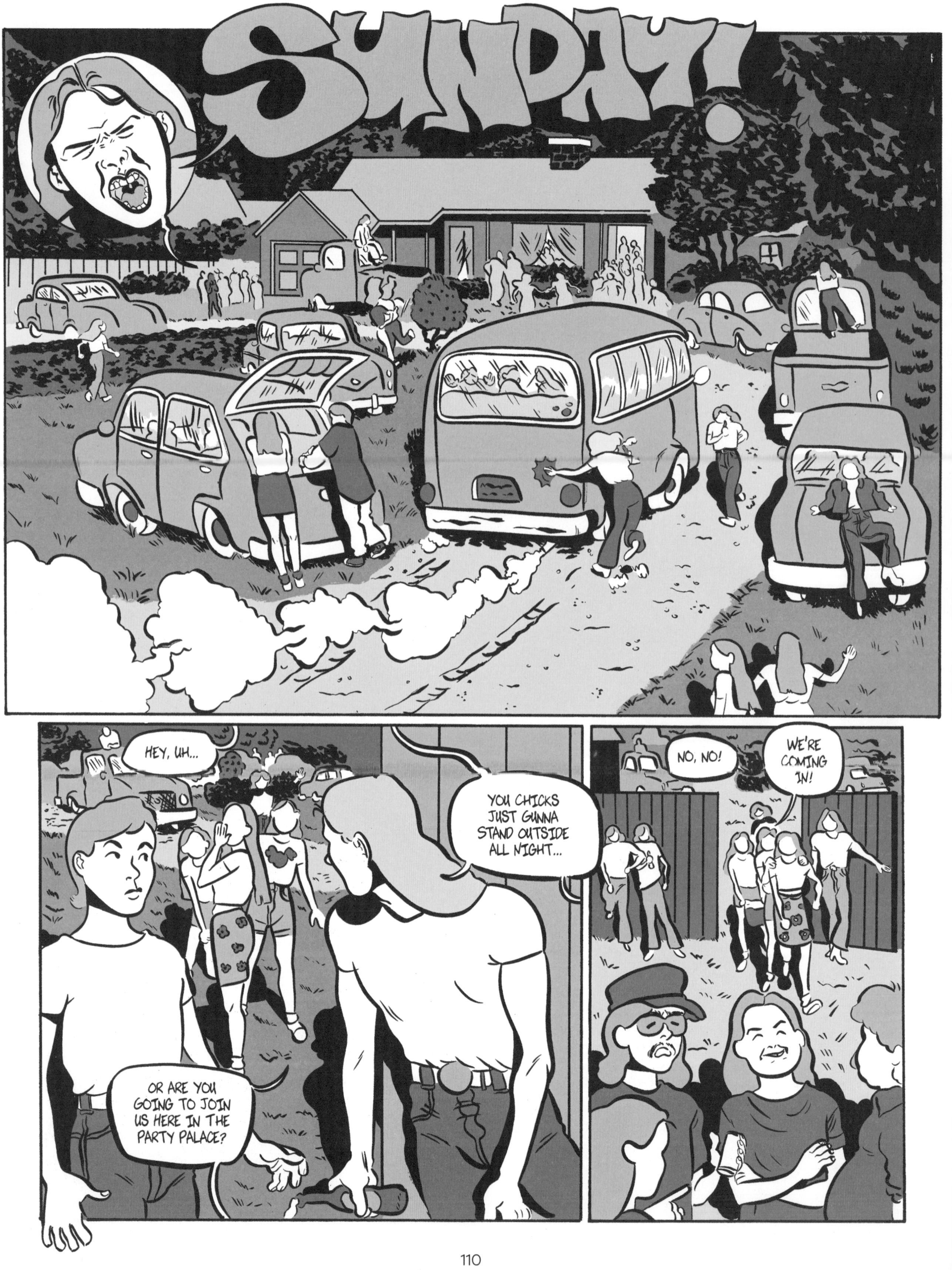
SUNDAY!
HEY, UH...
YOU CHICKS JUST GUNNA STAND OUTSIDE ALL NIGHT...
OR ARE YOU GOING TO JOIN US HERE IN THE PARTY PALACE?
NO, NO!
WE'RE COMING IN!

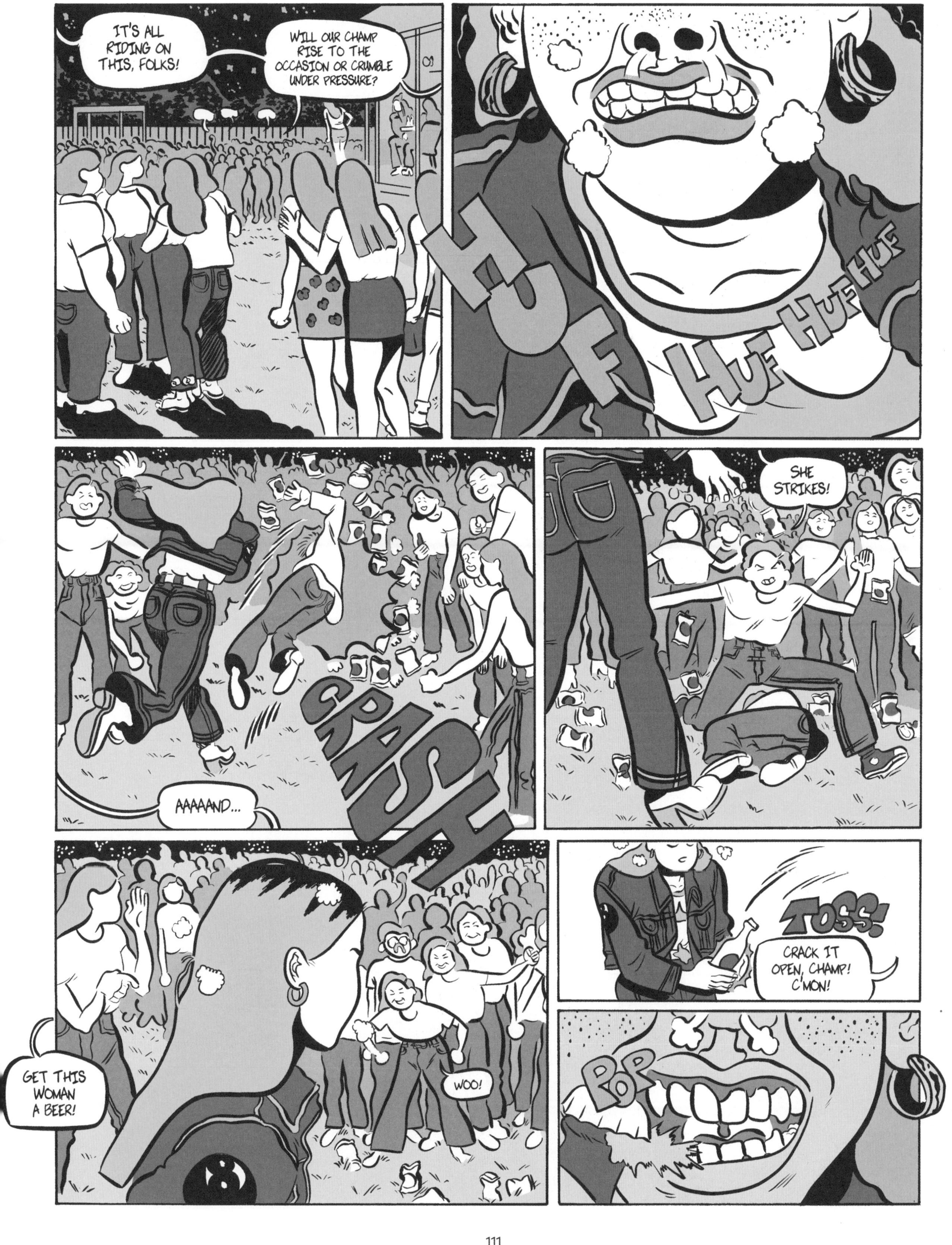
IT'S ALL RIDING ON THIS, FOLKS!
WILL OUR CHAMP RISE TO THE OCCASION OR CRUMBLE UNDER PRESSURE?
HUF
HUF HUF HUF
CRASH
AAAAAND...
SHE STRIKES!
GET THIS WOMAN A BEER!
WOO!
TOSS!
CRACK IT OPEN, CHAMP! C'MON!
POP

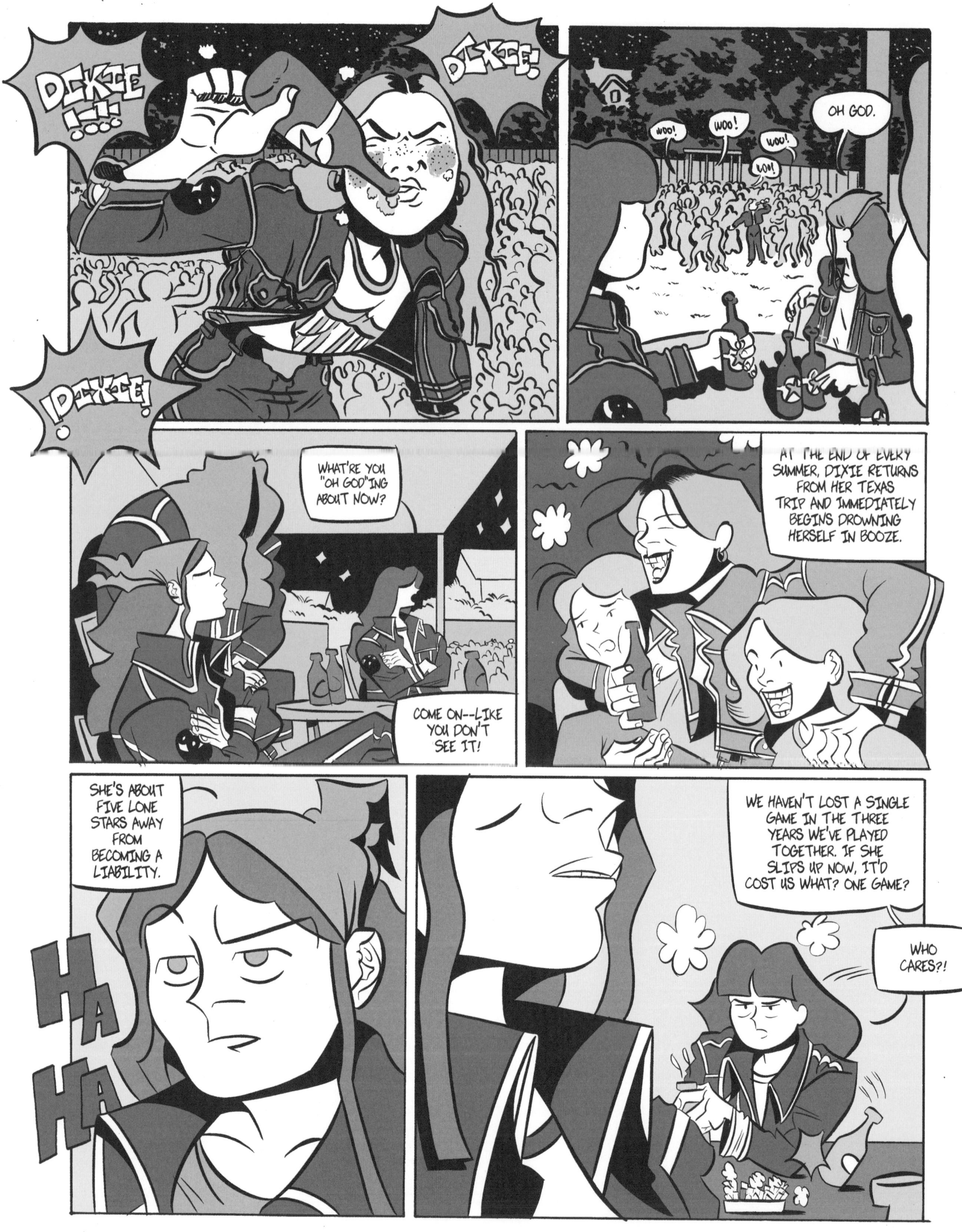
DIXIE
DIXIE!
DIXIE!
WOO!
WOO!
WOO!
WOO!
OH GOD.
WHAT'RE YOU "OH GOD"ING ABOUT NOW?
COME ON--LIKE YOU DON'T SEE IT!
AT THE END OF EVERY SUMMER, DIXIE RETURNS FROM HER TEXAS TRIP AND IMMEDIATELY BEGINS DROWNING HERSELF IN BOOZE.
SHE'S ABOUT FIVE LONE STARS AWAY FROM BECOMING A LIABILITY.
HA HA HA
WE HAVEN'T LOST A SINGLE GAME IN THE THREE YEARS WE'VE PLAYED TOGETHER. IF SHE SLIPS UP NOW, IT'D COST US WHAT? ONE GAME?
WHO CARES?!

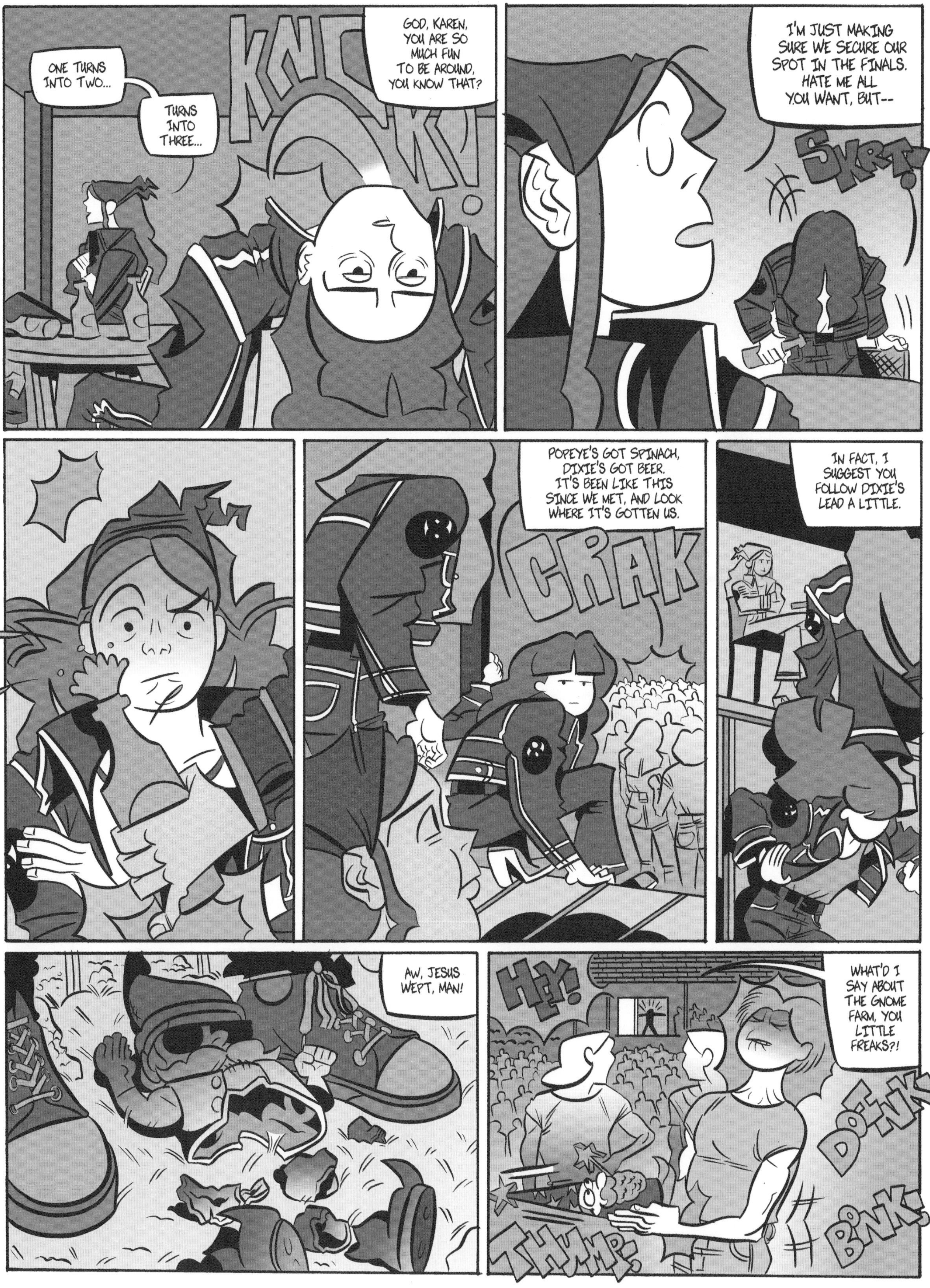
KNOCK
ONE TURNS INTO TWO...
TURNS INTO THREE...
GOD, KAREN, YOU ARE SO MUCH FUN TO BE AROUND, YOU KNOW THAT?
I'M JUST MAKING SURE WE SECURE OUR SPOT IN THE FINALS. HATE ME ALL YOU WANT, BUT--
SKRT!
POPEYE'S GOT SPINACH, DIXIE'S GOT BEER. IT'S BEEN LIKE THIS SINCE WE MET, AND LOOK WHERE IT'S GOTTEN US.
CRAK
IN FACT, I SUGGEST YOU FOLLOW DIXIE'S LEAD A LITTLE.
AW, JESUS WEPT, MAN!
HEY!
WHAT'D I SAY ABOUT THE GNOME FARM, YOU LITTLE FREAKS?!
DOINK!
BONK!
THUMP!

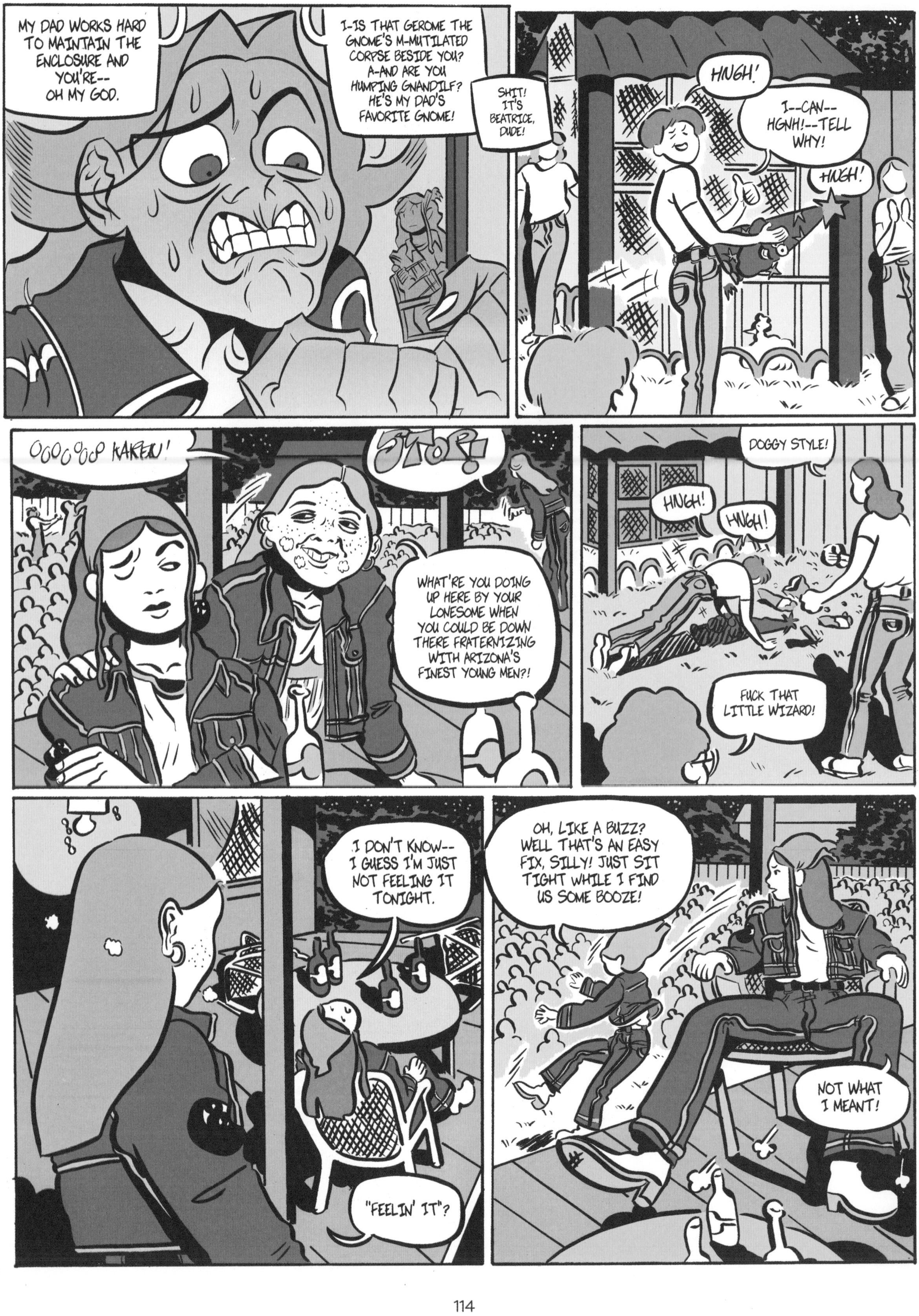

MY DAD WORKS HARD TO MAINTAIN THE ENCLOSURE AND YOU'RE-- OH MY GOD.
I-IS THAT GEROME THE GNOME'S M-MUTILATED CORPSE BESIDE YOU? A-AND ARE YOU HUMPING GNANDILF? HE'S MY DAD'S FAVORITE GNOME!
SHIT! IT'S BEATRICE, DUDE!
HNGH!
I--CAN-- HGNH!--TELL WHY!
HNGH!
OOOOOOP KAREN!
STOP!
WHAT'RE YOU DOING UP HERE BY YOUR LONESOME WHEN YOU COULD BE DOWN THERE FRATERNIZING WITH ARIZONA'S FINEST YOUNG MEN?!
DOGGY STYLE!
HNGH!
HNGH!
FUCK THAT LITTLE WIZARD!
I DON'T KNOW-- I GUESS I'M JUST NOT FEELING IT TONIGHT.
"FEELIN' IT"?
OH, LIKE A BUZZ? WELL THAT'S AN EASY FIX, SILLY! JUST SIT TIGHT WHILE I FIND US SOME BOOZE!
NOT WHAT I MEANT!

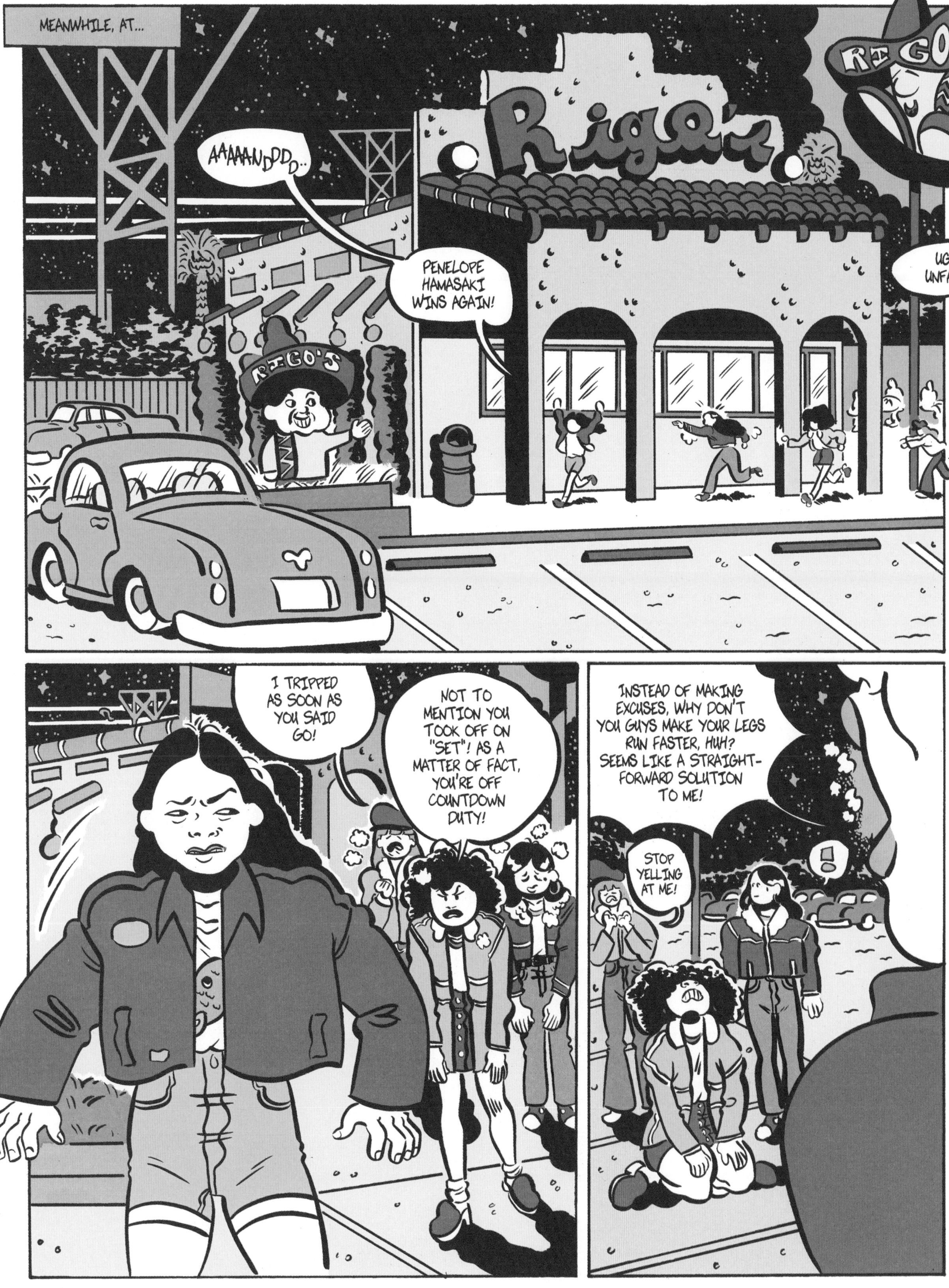
MEANWHILE, AT...
AAAAANDDDD...
PENELOPE HAMASAKI WINS AGAIN!
UGH! UNFAIR!
I TRIPPED AS SOON AS YOU SAID GO!
NOT TO MENTION YOU TOOK OFF ON "SET"! AS A MATTER OF FACT, YOU'RE OFF COUNTDOWN DUTY!
INSTEAD OF MAKING EXCUSES, WHY DON'T YOU GUYS MAKE YOUR LEGS RUN FASTER, HUH? SEEMS LIKE A STRAIGHT-FORWARD SOLUTION TO ME!
STOP YELLING AT ME!
!

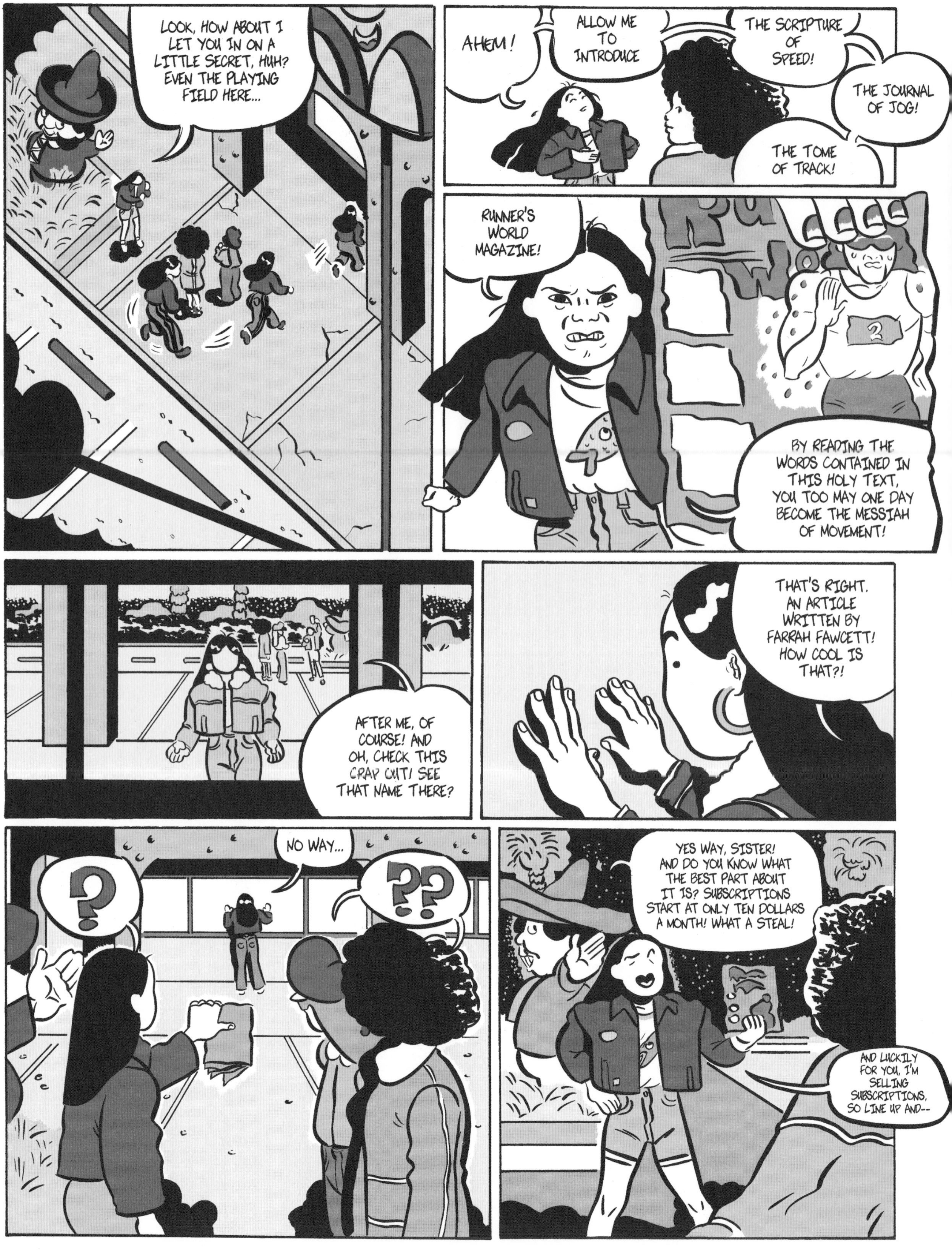
LOOK, HOW ABOUT I LET YOU IN ON A LITTLE SECRET, HUH? EVEN THE PLAYING FIELD HERE...
AHEM!
ALLOW ME TO INTRODUCE
THE SCRIPTURE OF SPEED!
THE JOURNAL OF JOG!
THE TOME OF TRACK!
RUNNER'S WORLD MAGAZINE!
BY READING THE WORDS CONTAINED IN THIS HOLY TEXT, YOU TOO MAY ONE DAY BECOME THE MESSIAH OF MOVEMENT!
AFTER ME, OF COURSE! AND OH, CHECK THIS CRAP OUT! SEE THAT NAME THERE?
THAT'S RIGHT. AN ARTICLE WRITTEN BY FARRAH FAWCETT! HOW COOL IS THAT?!
?
NO WAY...
??
YES WAY, SISTER! AND DO YOU KNOW WHAT THE BEST PART ABOUT IT IS? SUBSCRIPTIONS START AT ONLY TEN DOLLARS A MONTH! WHAT A STEAL!
AND LUCKILY FOR YOU, I'M SELLING SUBSCRIPTIONS, SO LINE UP AND--

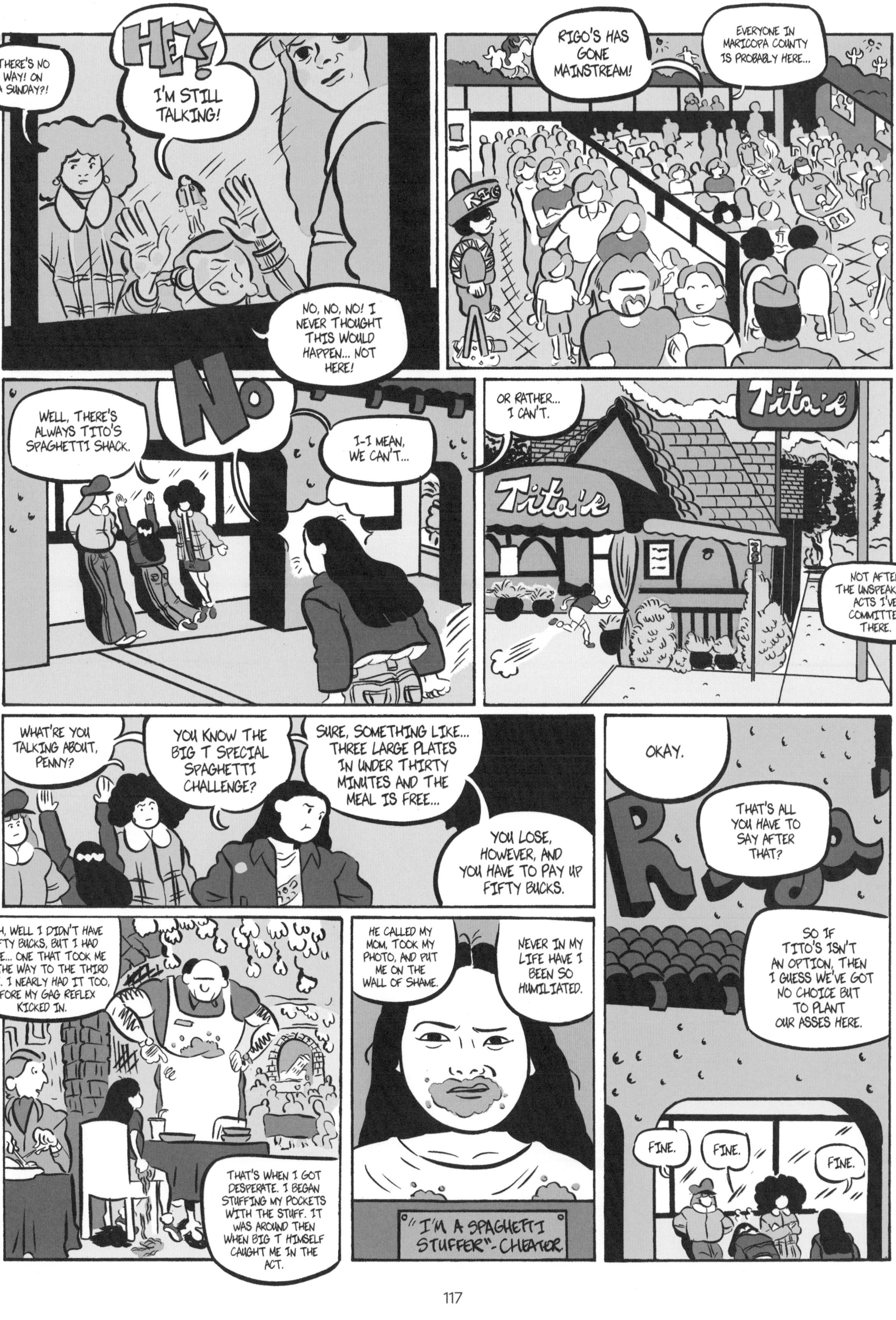

THERE'S NO WAY! ON A SUNDAY?!
HEY!
I'M STILL TALKING!
NO, NO, NO! I NEVER THOUGHT THIS WOULD HAPPEN... NOT HERE!
RIGO'S HAS GONE MAINSTREAM!
EVERYONE IN MARICOPA COUNTY IS PROBABLY HERE...
WELL, THERE'S ALWAYS TITO'S SPAGHETTI SHACK.
NO
I-I MEAN, WE CAN'T...
OR RATHER... I CAN'T.
Tito's
NOT AFTER THE UNSPEAKABLE ACTS I'VE COMMITTED THERE.
WHAT'RE YOU TALKING ABOUT, PENNY?
YOU KNOW THE BIG T SPECIAL SPAGHETTI CHALLENGE?
SURE, SOMETHING LIKE... THREE LARGE PLATES IN UNDER THIRTY MINUTES AND THE MEAL IS FREE...
YOU LOSE, HOWEVER, AND YOU HAVE TO PAY UP FIFTY BUCKS.
YEAH, WELL I DIDN'T HAVE FIFTY BUCKS, BUT I HAD DRIVE... ONE THAT TOOK ME ALL THE WAY TO THE THIRD PLATE. I NEARLY HAD IT TOO, BEFORE MY GAG REFLEX KICKED IN.
THAT'S WHEN I GOT DESPERATE. I BEGAN STUFFING MY POCKETS WITH THE STUFF. IT WAS AROUND THEN WHEN BIG T HIMSELF CAUGHT ME IN THE ACT.
HE CALLED MY MOM, TOOK MY PHOTO, AND PUT ME ON THE WALL OF SHAME.
NEVER IN MY LIFE HAVE I BEEN SO HUMILIATED.
"I'M A SPAGHETTI STUFFER"-CHEATER
OKAY.
THAT'S ALL YOU HAVE TO SAY AFTER THAT?
SO IF TITO'S ISN'T AN OPTION, THEN I GUESS WE'VE GOT NO CHOICE BUT TO PLANT OUR ASSES HERE.
FINE.
FINE.
FINE.

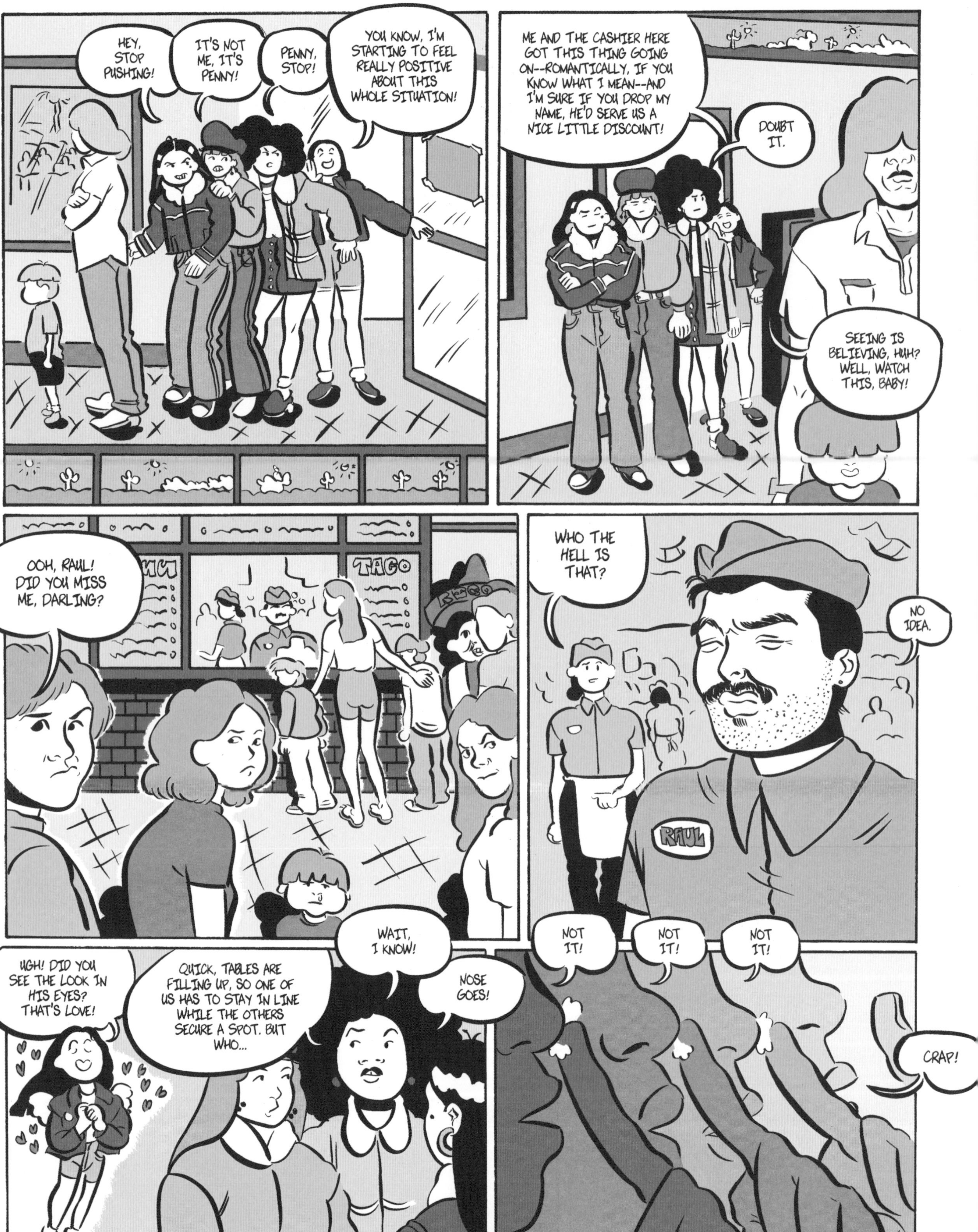
HEY, STOP PUSHING!
IT'S NOT ME, IT'S PENNY!
PENNY, STOP!
YOU KNOW, I'M STARTING TO FEEL REALLY POSITIVE ABOUT THIS WHOLE SITUATION!
ME AND THE CASHIER HERE GOT THIS THING GOING ON--ROMANTICALLY, IF YOU KNOW WHAT I MEAN--AND I'M SURE IF YOU DROP MY NAME, HE'D SERVE US A NICE LITTLE DISCOUNT!
DOUBT IT.
SEEING IS BELIEVING, HUH? WELL, WATCH THIS, BABY!
TACO
OOH, RAUL! DID YOU MISS ME, DARLING?
WHO THE HELL IS THAT?
NO IDEA.
RAUL
UGH! DID YOU SEE THE LOOK IN HIS EYES? THAT'S LOVE!
QUICK, TABLES ARE FILLING UP, SO ONE OF US HAS TO STAY IN LINE WHILE THE OTHERS SECURE A SPOT. BUT WHO...
WAIT, I KNOW!
NOSE GOES!
NOT IT!
NOT IT!
NOT IT!
CRAP!

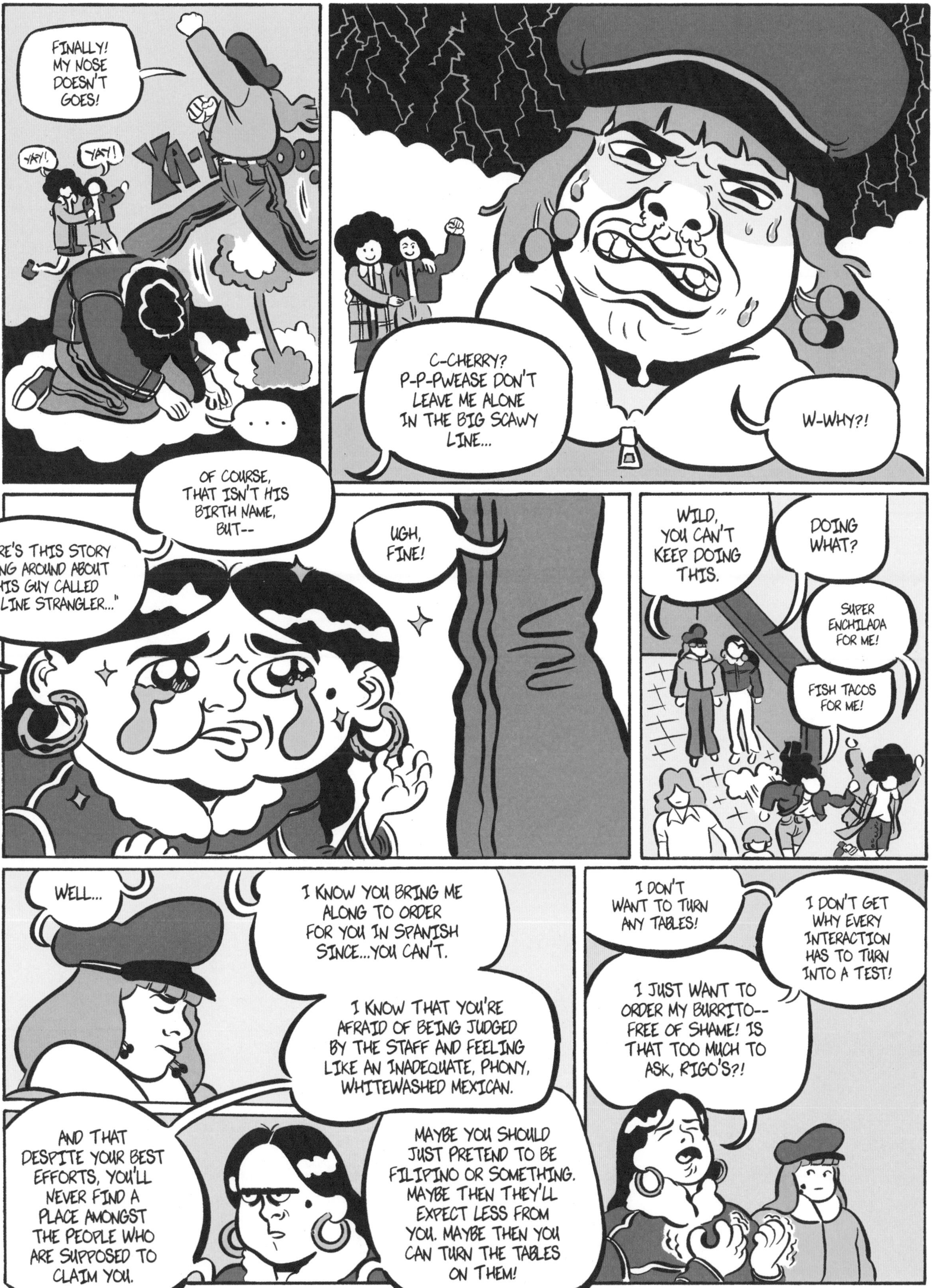
FINALLY! MY NOSE DOESN'T GOES!
YAY!
YAY!
YA-HOO!
...
C-CHERRY? P-P-PWEASE DON'T LEAVE ME ALONE IN THE BIG SCAWY LINE...
W-WHY?!
THERE'S THIS STORY GOING AROUND ABOUT THIS GUY CALLED "THE LINE STRANGLER..."
OF COURSE, THAT ISN'T HIS BIRTH NAME, BUT--
UGH, FINE!
WILD, YOU CAN'T KEEP DOING THIS.
DOING WHAT?
SUPER ENCHILADA FOR ME!
FISH TACOS FOR ME!
WELL...
I KNOW YOU BRING ME ALONG TO ORDER FOR YOU IN SPANISH SINCE...YOU CAN'T.
I KNOW THAT YOU'RE AFRAID OF BEING JUDGED BY THE STAFF AND FEELING LIKE AN INADEQUATE, PHONY, WHITEWASHED MEXICAN.
AND THAT DESPITE YOUR BEST EFFORTS, YOU'LL NEVER FIND A PLACE AMONGST THE PEOPLE WHO ARE SUPPOSED TO CLAIM YOU.
MAYBE YOU SHOULD JUST PRETEND TO BE FILIPINO OR SOMETHING. MAYBE THEN THEY'LL EXPECT LESS FROM YOU. MAYBE THEN YOU CAN TURN THE TABLES ON THEM!
I DON'T WANT TO TURN ANY TABLES!
I DON'T GET WHY EVERY INTERACTION HAS TO TURN INTO A TEST!
I JUST WANT TO ORDER MY BURRITO-- FREE OF SHAME! IS THAT TOO MUCH TO ASK, RIGO'S?!

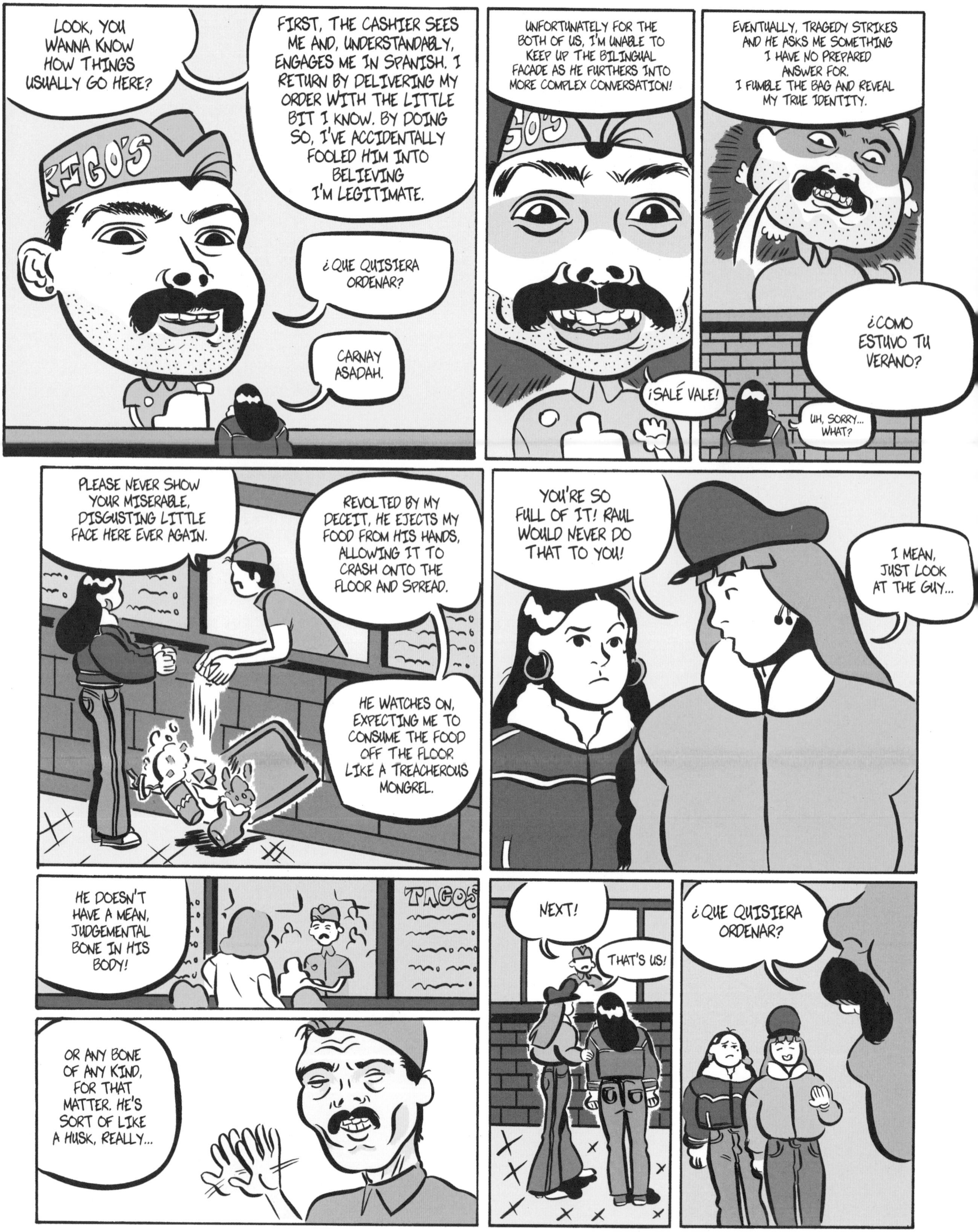
LOOK, YOU WANNA KNOW HOW THINGS USUALLY GO HERE?
FIRST, THE CASHIER SEES ME AND, UNDERSTANDABLY, ENGAGES ME IN SPANISH. I RETURN BY DELIVERING MY ORDER WITH THE LITTLE BIT I KNOW. BY DOING SO, I'VE ACCIDENTALLY FOOLED HIM INTO BELIEVING I'M LEGITIMATE.
RIGO'S
¿QUE QUISIERA ORDENAR?
CARNAY ASADAH.
UNFORTUNATELY FOR THE BOTH OF US, I'M UNABLE TO KEEP UP THE BILINGUAL FACADE AS HE FURTHERS INTO MORE COMPLEX CONVERSATION!
¡SALÉ VALE!
EVENTUALLY, TRAGEDY STRIKES AND HE ASKS ME SOMETHING I HAVE NO PREPARED ANSWER FOR. I FUMBLE THE BAG AND REVEAL MY TRUE IDENTITY.
¿COMO ESTUVO TU VERANO?
UH, SORRY... WHAT?
PLEASE NEVER SHOW YOUR MISERABLE, DISGUSTING LITTLE FACE HERE EVER AGAIN.
REVOLTED BY MY DECEIT, HE EJECTS MY FOOD FROM HIS HANDS, ALLOWING IT TO CRASH ONTO THE FLOOR AND SPREAD.
HE WATCHES ON, EXPECTING ME TO CONSUME THE FOOD OFF THE FLOOR LIKE A TREACHEROUS MONGREL.
YOU'RE SO FULL OF IT! RAUL WOULD NEVER DO THAT TO YOU!
I MEAN, JUST LOOK AT THE GUY...
HE DOESN'T HAVE A MEAN, JUDGEMENTAL BONE IN HIS BODY!
TACOS
OR ANY BONE OF ANY KIND, FOR THAT MATTER. HE'S SORT OF LIKE A HUSK, REALLY...
NEXT!
THAT'S US!
¿QUE QUISIERA ORDENAR?

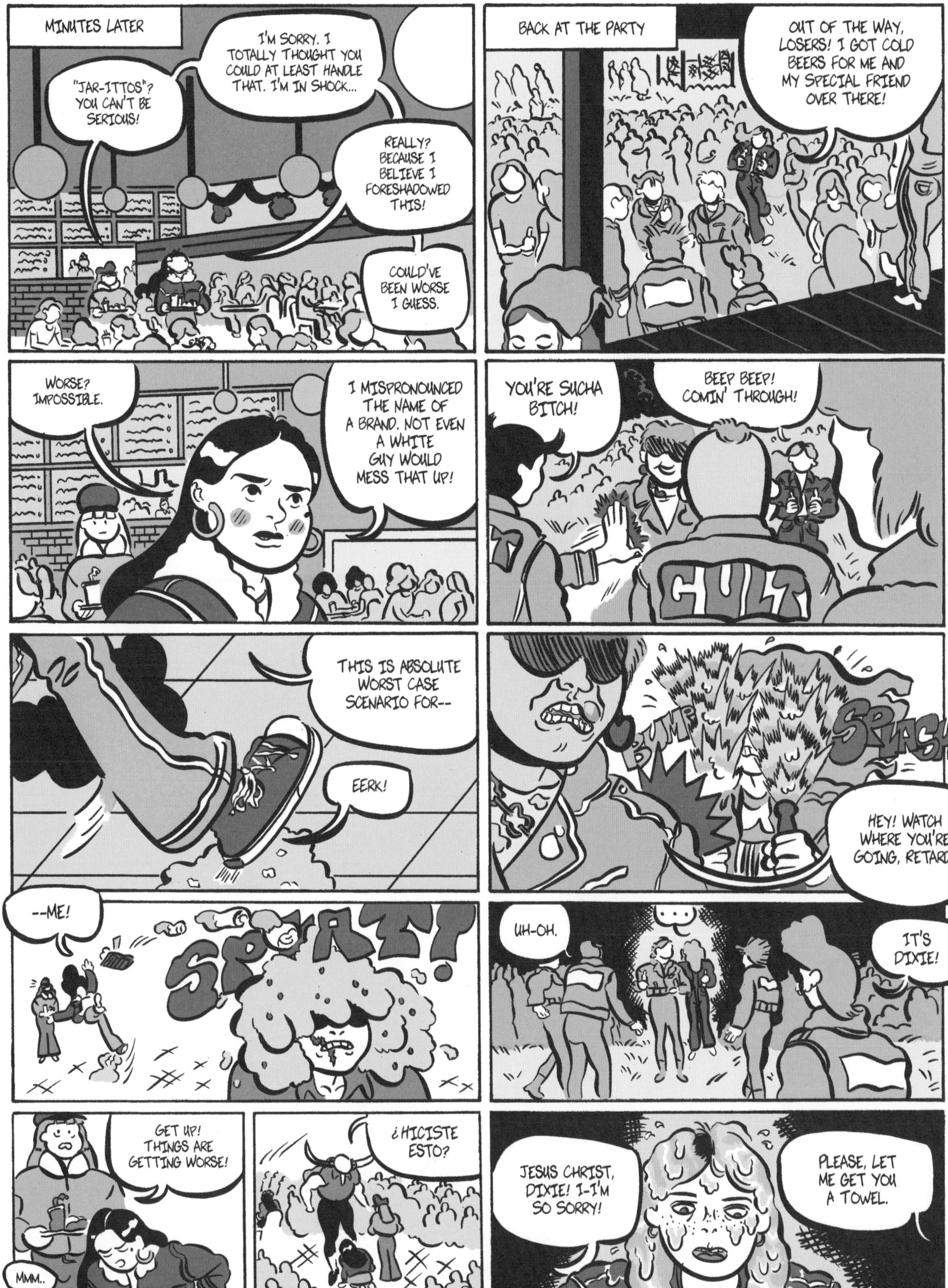
MINUTES LATER
"JAR-ITTOS"? YOU CAN'T BE SERIOUS!
I'M SORRY. I TOTALLY THOUGHT YOU COULD AT LEAST HANDLE THAT. I'M IN SHOCK...
REALLY? BECAUSE I BELIEVE I FORESHADOWED THIS!
COULD'VE BEEN WORSE I GUESS.
BACK AT THE PARTY
OUT OF THE WAY, LOSERS! I GOT COLD BEERS FOR ME AND MY SPECIAL FRIEND OVER THERE!
WORSE? IMPOSSIBLE.
I MISPRONOUNCED THE NAME OF A BRAND. NOT EVEN A WHITE GUY WOULD MESS THAT UP!
YOU'RE SUCHA BITCH!
BEEP BEEP! COMIN' THROUGH!
CULT
THIS IS ABSOLUTE WORST CASE SCENARIO FOR--
EERK!
BUMP
SPLASH!
HEY! WATCH WHERE YOU'RE GOING, RETARD!
--ME!
SPLAT!
UH-OH.
IT'S DIXIE!
GET UP! THINGS ARE GETTING WORSE!
MMM..
¿HICISTE ESTO?
JESUS CHRIST, DIXIE! I-I'M SO SORRY!
PLEASE, LET ME GET YOU A TOWEL.

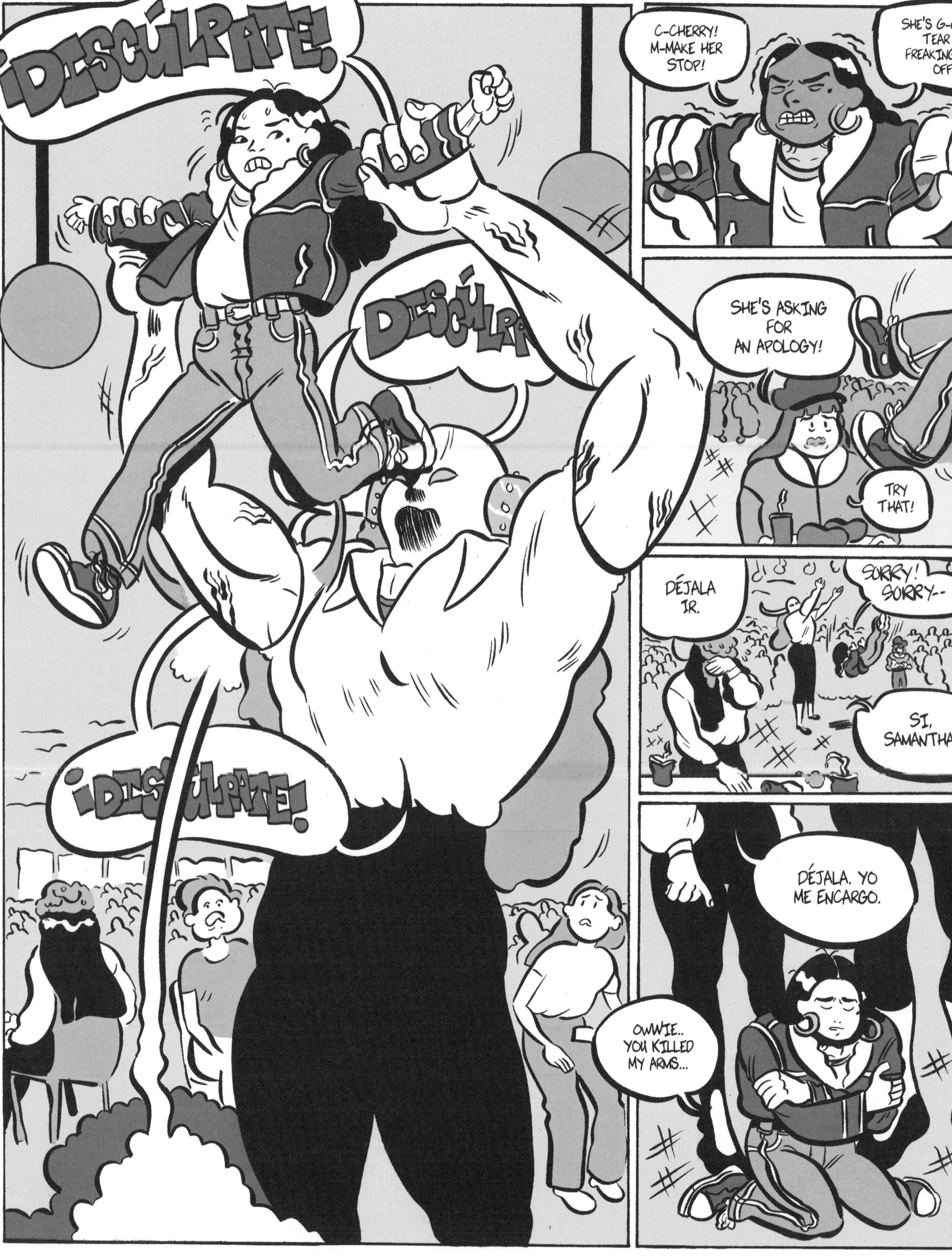
¡DISCÚLPATE!
DISCÚLP
¡DISCÚLPATE!
C-CHERRY! M-MAKE HER STOP!
SHE'S G-GUNNA.. TEAR MY FREAKING ARMS OFF!
SHE'S ASKING FOR AN APOLOGY!
TRY THAT!
DÉJALA IR.
SORRY! SORRY--
SI, SAMANTHA.
DÉJALA. YO ME ENCARGO.
OWWIE.. YOU KILLED MY ARMS...

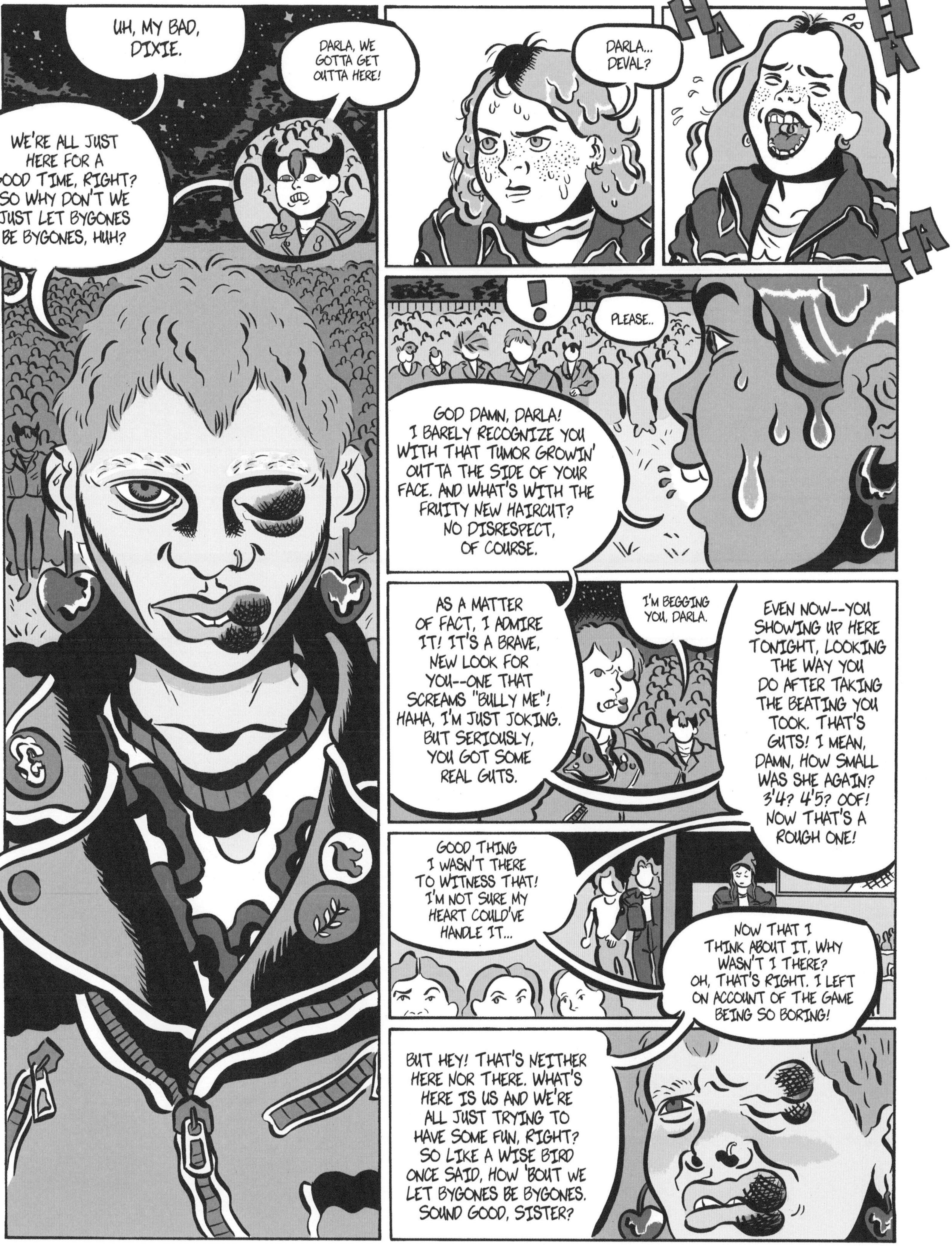
UH, MY BAD, DIXIE.
DARLA, WE GOTTA GET OUTTA HERE!
WE'RE ALL JUST HERE FOR A GOOD TIME, RIGHT? SO WHY DON'T WE JUST LET BYGONES BE BYGONES, HUH?
DARLA... DEVAL?
HA HA HA
!
PLEASE..
GOD DAMN, DARLA! I BARELY RECOGNIZE YOU WITH THAT TUMOR GROWIN' OUTTA THE SIDE OF YOUR FACE. AND WHAT'S WITH THE FRUITY NEW HAIRCUT? NO DISRESPECT, OF COURSE.
AS A MATTER OF FACT, I ADMIRE IT! IT'S A BRAVE, NEW LOOK FOR YOU--ONE THAT SCREAMS "BULLY ME"! HAHA, I'M JUST JOKING. BUT SERIOUSLY, YOU GOT SOME REAL GUTS.
I'M BEGGING YOU, DARLA.
EVEN NOW--YOU SHOWING UP HERE TONIGHT, LOOKING THE WAY YOU DO AFTER TAKING THE BEATING YOU TOOK. THAT'S GUTS! I MEAN, DAMN, HOW SMALL WAS SHE AGAIN? 3'4? 4'5? OOF! NOW THAT'S A ROUGH ONE!
GOOD THING I WASN'T THERE TO WITNESS THAT! I'M NOT SURE MY HEART COULD'VE HANDLE IT...
NOW THAT I THINK ABOUT IT, WHY WASN'T I THERE? OH, THAT'S RIGHT. I LEFT ON ACCOUNT OF THE GAME BEING SO BORING!
BUT HEY! THAT'S NEITHER HERE NOR THERE. WHAT'S HERE IS US AND WE'RE ALL JUST TRYING TO HAVE SOME FUN, RIGHT? SO LIKE A WISE BIRD ONCE SAID, HOW 'BOUT WE LET BYGONES BE BYGONES. SOUND GOOD, SISTER?

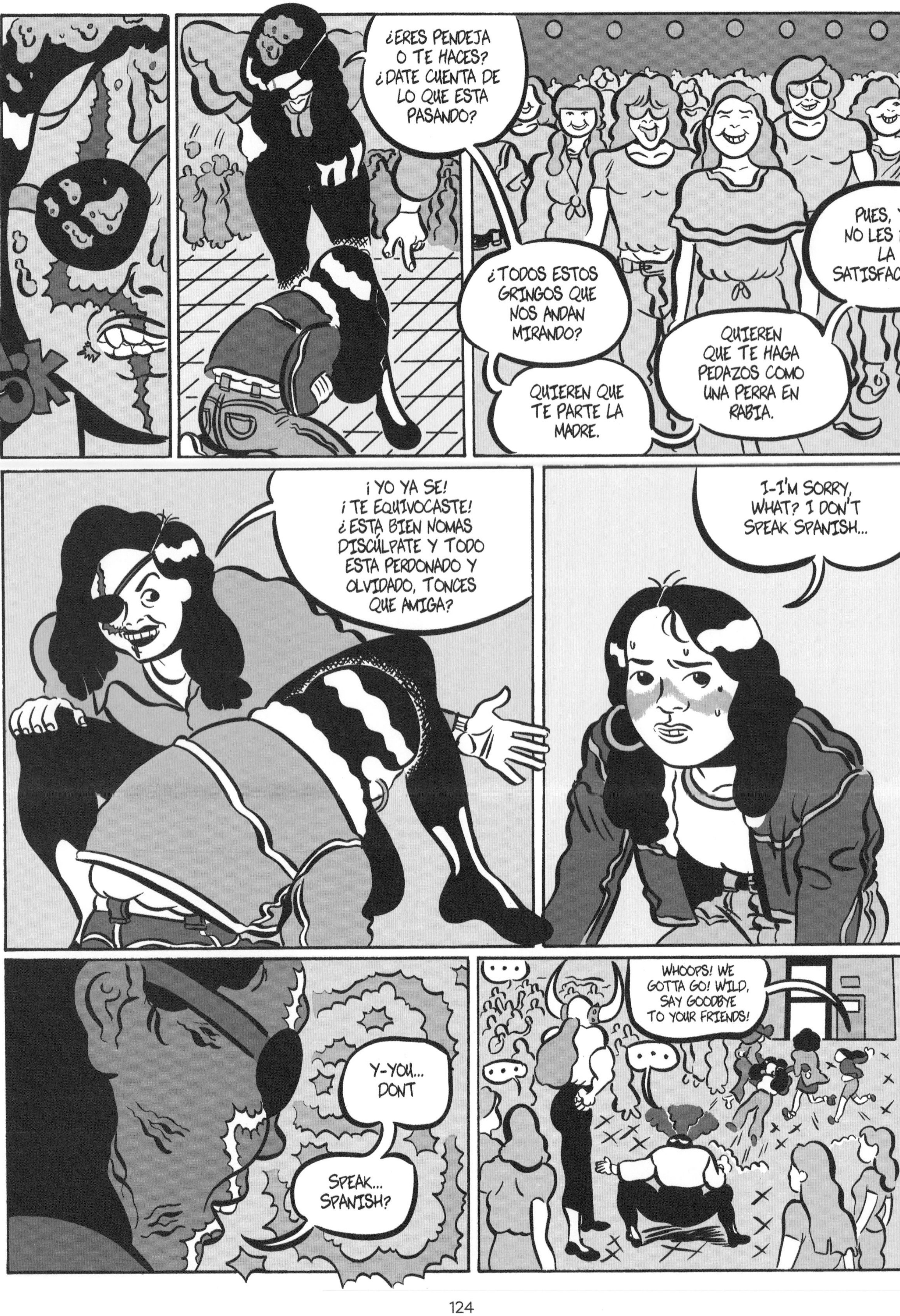
TSK
¿ERES PENDEJA O TE HACES? ¿DATE CUENTA DE LO QUE ESTA PASANDO?
¿TODOS ESTOS GRINGOS QUE NOS ANDAN MIRANDO?
QUIEREN QUE TE PARTE LA MADRE.
QUIEREN QUE TE HAGA PEDAZOS COMO UNA PERRA EN RABIA.
PUES, YO NO LES DOY LA SATISFACCIÓN.
¡YO YA SE! ¡TE EQUIVOCASTE! ¿ESTA BIEN NOMAS DISCÚLPATE Y TODO ESTA PERDONADO Y OLVIDADO, TONCES QUE AMIGA?
I-I'M SORRY, WHAT? I DON'T SPEAK SPANISH...
Y-YOU... DONT
SPEAK... SPANISH?
WHOOPS! WE GOTTA GO! WILD, SAY GOODBYE TO YOUR FRIENDS!

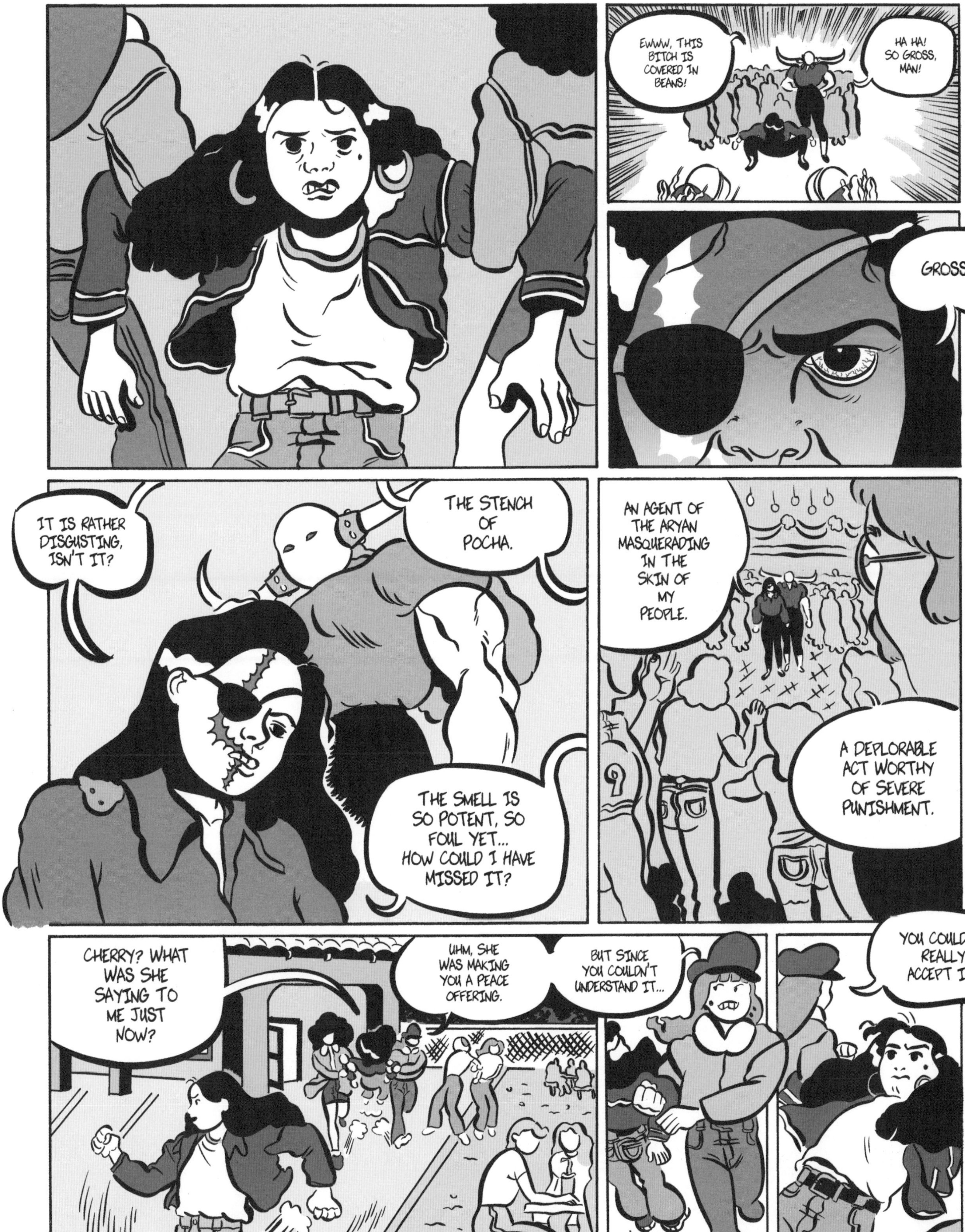
EWWW, THIS BITCH IS COVERED IN BEANS!
HA HA! SO GROSS, MAN!
GROSS?
IT IS RATHER DISGUSTING, ISN'T IT?
THE STENCH OF POCHA.
THE SMELL IS SO POTENT, SO FOUL YET... HOW COULD I HAVE MISSED IT?
AN AGENT OF THE ARYAN MASQUERADING IN THE SKIN OF MY PEOPLE.
A DEPLORABLE ACT WORTHY OF SEVERE PUNISHMENT.
CHERRY? WHAT WAS SHE SAYING TO ME JUST NOW?
UHM, SHE WAS MAKING YOU A PEACE OFFERING.
BUT SINCE YOU COULDN'T UNDERSTAND IT...
YOU COULDN'T REALLY ACCEPT IT!

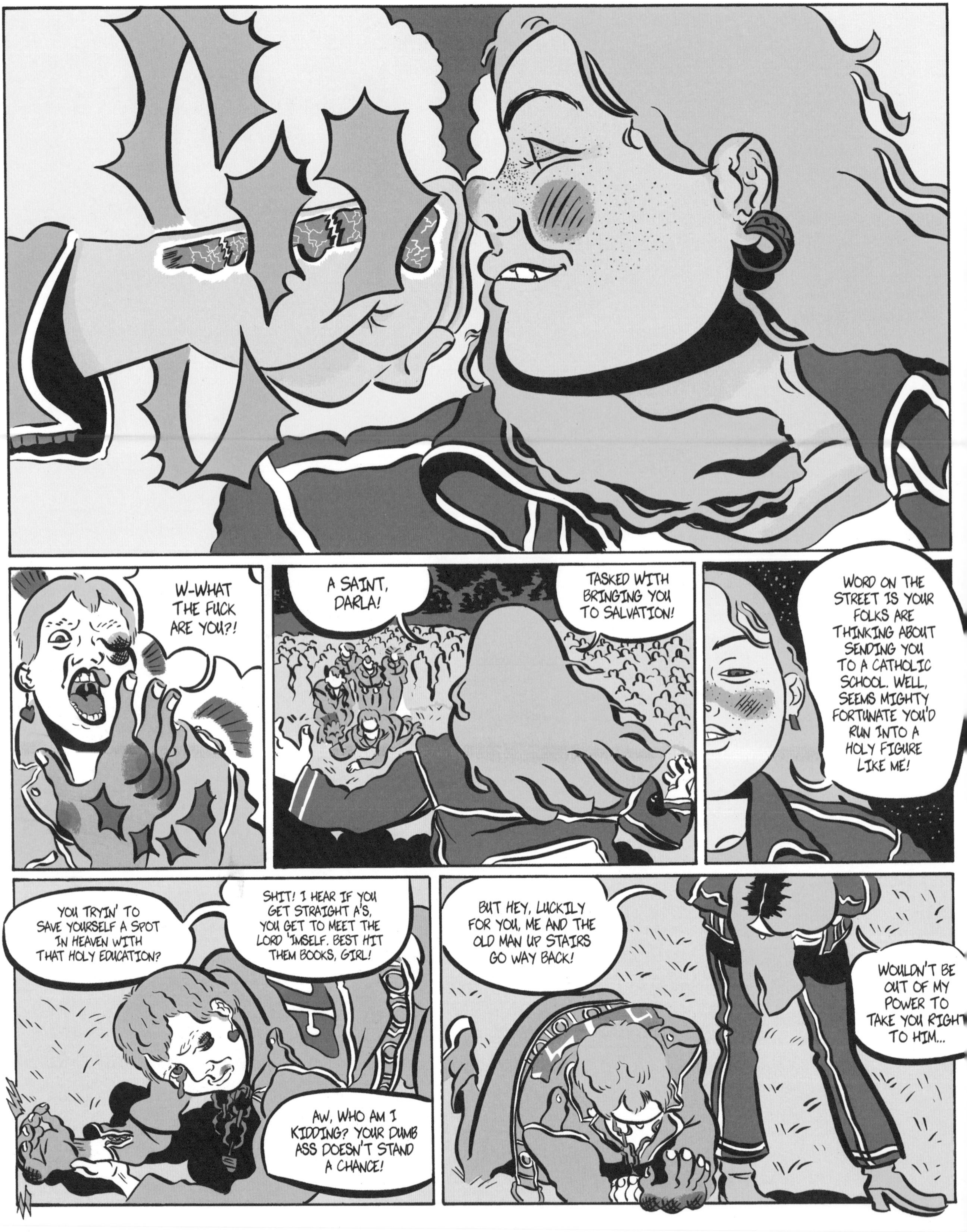
W-WHAT THE FUCK ARE YOU?!
A SAINT, DARLA!
TASKED WITH BRINGING YOU TO SALVATION!
WORD ON THE STREET IS YOUR FOLKS ARE THINKING ABOUT SENDING YOU TO A CATHOLIC SCHOOL. WELL, SEEMS MIGHTY FORTUNATE YOU'D RUN INTO A HOLY FIGURE LIKE ME!
YOU TRYIN' TO SAVE YOURSELF A SPOT IN HEAVEN WITH THAT HOLY EDUCATION?
SHIT! I HEAR IF YOU GET STRAIGHT A'S, YOU GET TO MEET THE LORD 'IMSELF. BEST HIT THEM BOOKS, GIRL!
AW, WHO AM I KIDDING? YOUR DUMB ASS DOESN'T STAND A CHANCE!
BUT HEY, LUCKILY FOR YOU, ME AND THE OLD MAN UP STAIRS GO WAY BACK!
WOULDN'T BE OUT OF MY POWER TO TAKE YOU RIGHT TO HIM...

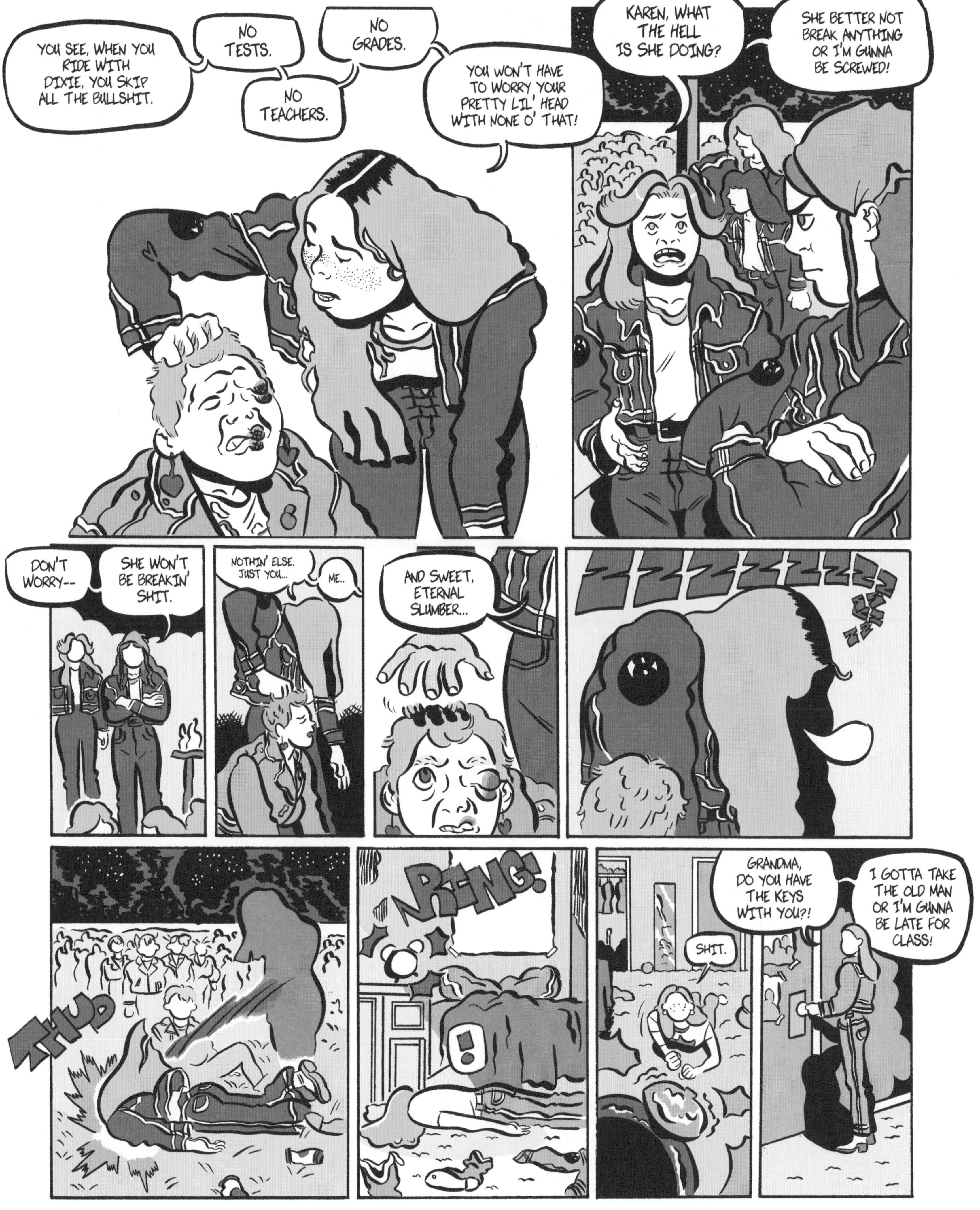
YOU SEE, WHEN YOU RIDE WITH DIXIE, YOU SKIP ALL THE BULLSHIT.
NO TESTS.
NO TEACHERS.
NO GRADES.
YOU WON'T HAVE TO WORRY YOUR PRETTY LIL' HEAD WITH NONE O' THAT!
KAREN, WHAT THE HELL IS SHE DOING?
SHE BETTER NOT BREAK ANYTHING OR I'M GUNNA BE SCREWED!
DON'T WORRY--
SHE WON'T BE BREAKIN' SHIT.
NOTHIN' ELSE. JUST YOU...
ME..
AND SWEET, ETERNAL SLUMBER...
ZZZZZZZZZZZ
THUD
RING!
SHIT.
GRANDMA, DO YOU HAVE THE KEYS WITH YOU?!
I GOTTA TAKE THE OLD MAN OR I'M GUNNA BE LATE FOR CLASS!

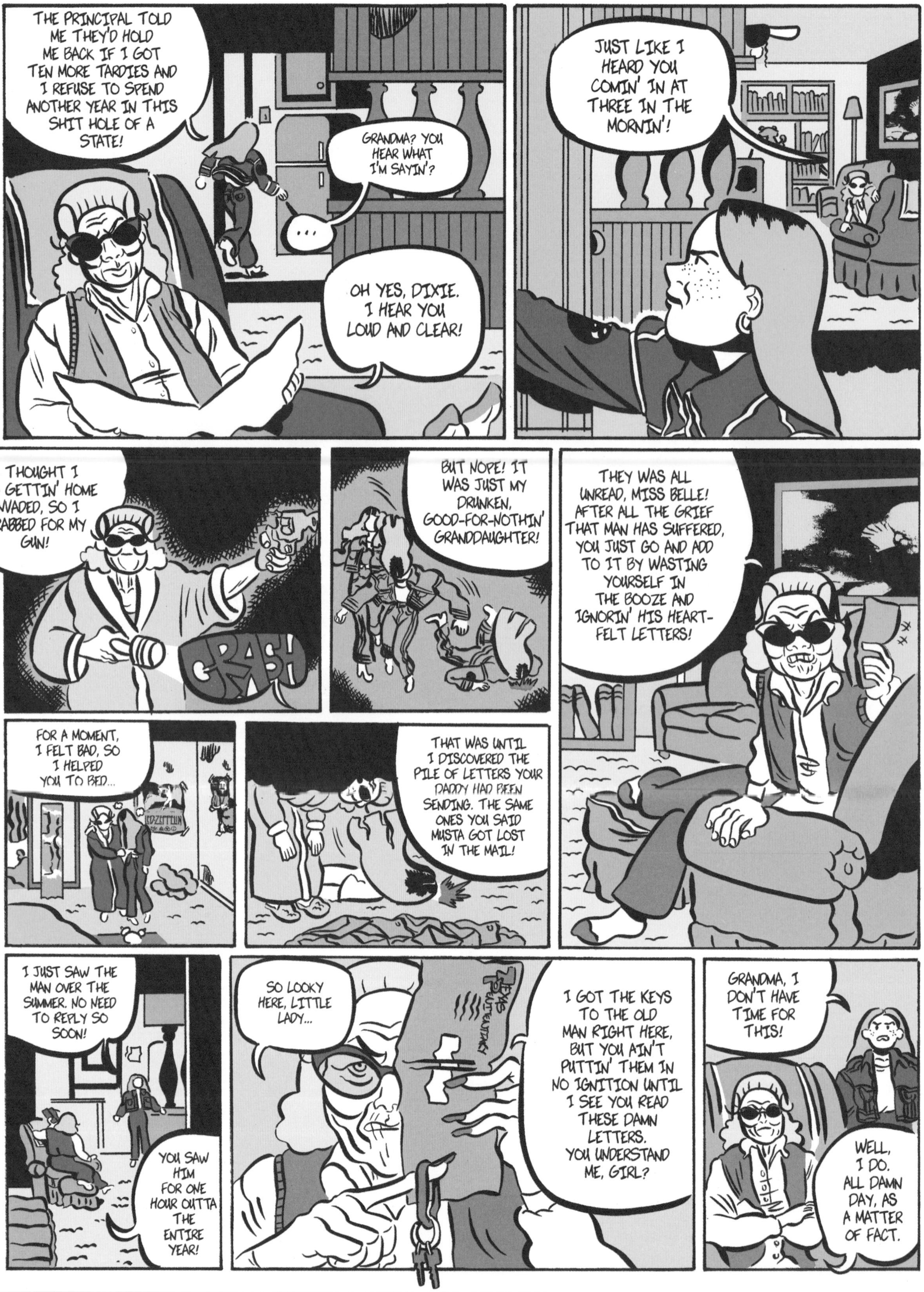
THE PRINCIPAL TOLD ME THEY'D HOLD ME BACK IF I GOT TEN MORE TARDIES AND I REFUSE TO SPEND ANOTHER YEAR IN THIS SHIT HOLE OF A STATE!
GRANDMA? YOU HEAR WHAT I'M SAYIN'?
...
OH YES, DIXIE. I HEAR YOU LOUD AND CLEAR!
JUST LIKE I HEARD YOU COMIN' IN AT THREE IN THE MORNIN'!
I THOUGHT I WAS GETTIN' HOME INVADED, SO I GRABBED FOR MY GUN!
CRASH
BUT NOPE! IT WAS JUST MY DRUNKEN, GOOD-FOR-NOTHIN' GRANDDAUGHTER!
THEY WAS ALL UNREAD, MISS BELLE! AFTER ALL THE GRIEF THAT MAN HAS SUFFERED, YOU JUST GO AND ADD TO IT BY WASTING YOURSELF IN THE BOOZE AND IGNORIN' HIS HEART-FELT LETTERS!
FOR A MOMENT, I FELT BAD, SO I HELPED YOU TO BED...
LED ZEPPELIN
THAT WAS UNTIL I DISCOVERED THE PILE OF LETTERS YOUR DADDY HAD BEEN SENDING. THE SAME ONES YOU SAID MUSTA GOT LOST IN THE MAIL!
I JUST SAW THE MAN OVER THE SUMMER. NO NEED TO REPLY SO SOON!
YOU SAW HIM FOR ONE HOUR OUTTA THE ENTIRE YEAR!
SO LOOKY HERE, LITTLE LADY...
I GOT THE KEYS TO THE OLD MAN RIGHT HERE, BUT YOU AIN'T PUTTIN' THEM IN NO IGNITION UNTIL I SEE YOU READ THESE DAMN LETTERS. YOU UNDERSTAND ME, GIRL?
GRANDMA, I DON'T HAVE TIME FOR THIS!
WELL, I DO. ALL DAMN DAY, AS A MATTER OF FACT.

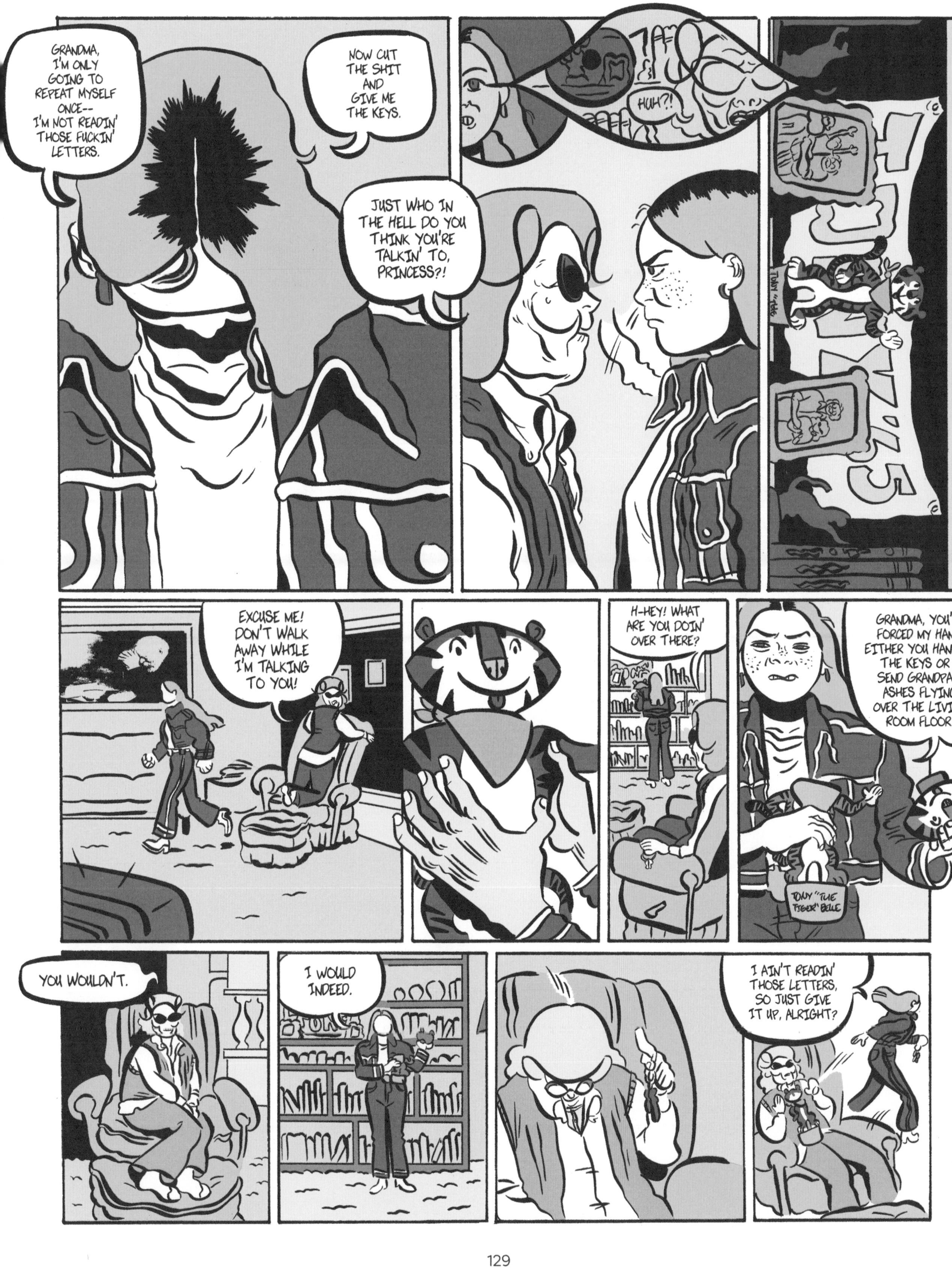
GRANDMA, I'M ONLY GOING TO REPEAT MYSELF ONCE-- I'M NOT READIN' THOSE FUCKIN' LETTERS.
NOW CUT THE SHIT AND GIVE ME THE KEYS.
HUH?!
JUST WHO IN THE HELL DO YOU THINK YOU'RE TALKIN' TO, PRINCESS?!
EXCUSE ME! DON'T WALK AWAY WHILE I'M TALKING TO YOU!
H-HEY! WHAT ARE YOU DOIN' OVER THERE?
GRANDMA, YOU'VE FORCED MY HAND. EITHER YOU HAND ME THE KEYS OR I SEND GRANDPA'S ASHES FLYING OVER THE LIVING ROOM FLOOR.
TONY "THE TIGER" BELLE
YOU WOULDN'T.
I WOULD INDEED.
I AIN'T READIN' THOSE LETTERS, SO JUST GIVE IT UP, ALRIGHT?

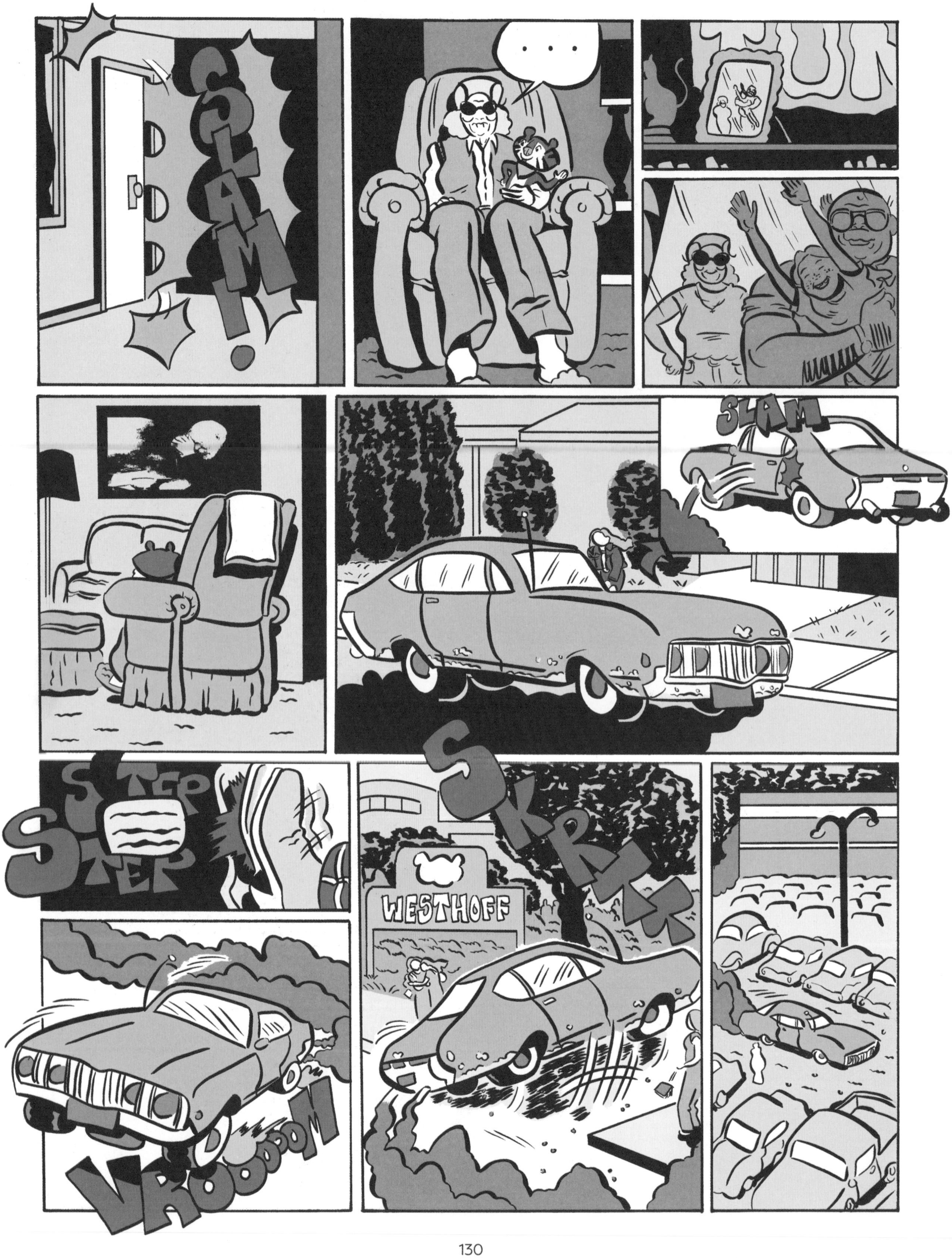
SLAM!
. . .
SLAM
STEP STEP
SKRKK
WESTHOFF
VROOOOOOM

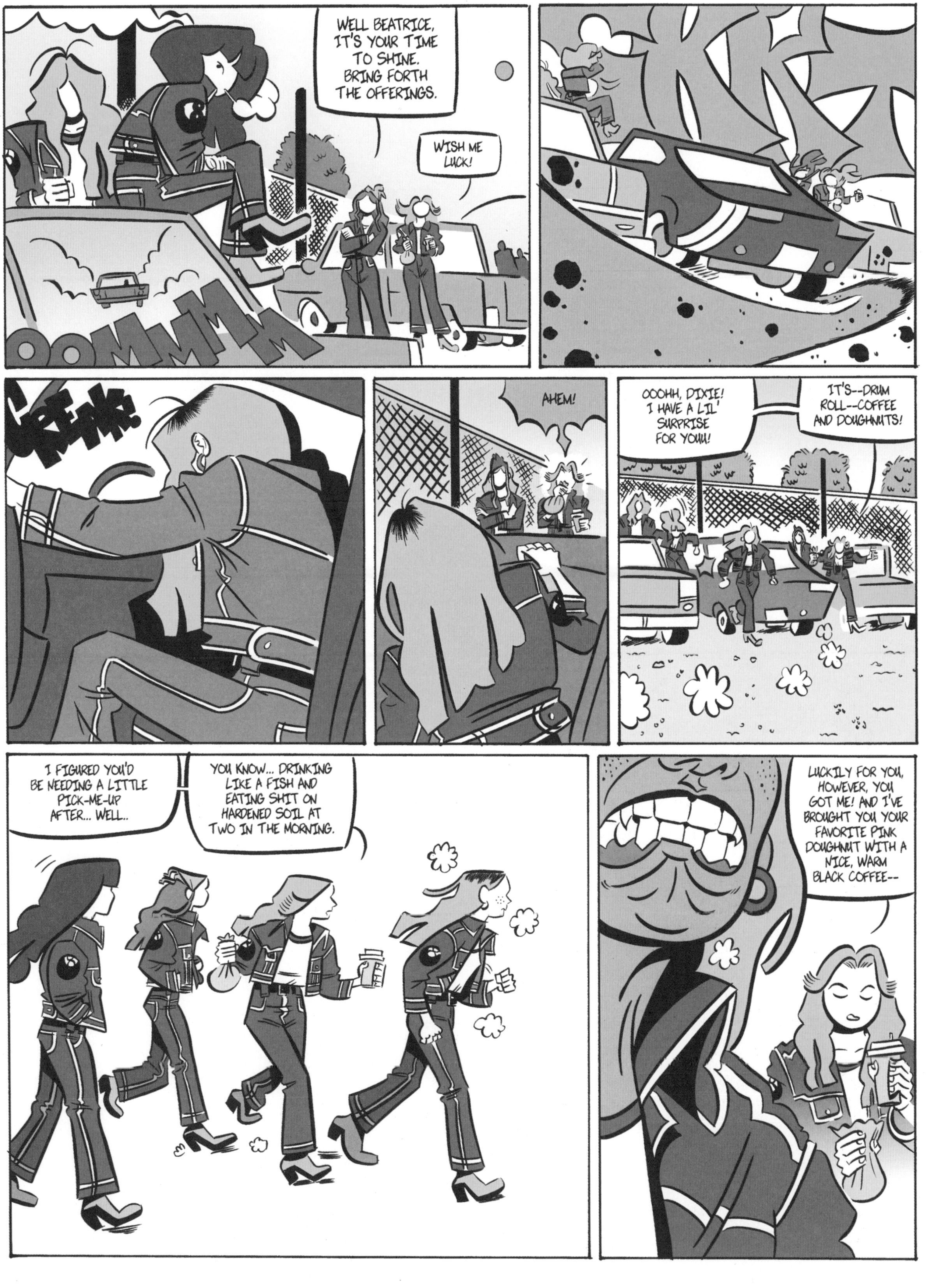
WELL BEATRICE, IT'S YOUR TIME TO SHINE. BRING FORTH THE OFFERINGS.
WISH ME LUCK!
OOMMMM
AHEM!
OOOHH, DIXIE! I HAVE A LIL' SURPRISE FOR YOUU!
IT'S--DRUM ROLL--COFFEE AND DOUGHNUTS!
I FIGURED YOU'D BE NEEDING A LITTLE PICK-ME-UP AFTER... WELL..
YOU KNOW... DRINKING LIKE A FISH AND EATING SHIT ON HARDENED SOIL AT TWO IN THE MORNING.
LUCKILY FOR YOU, HOWEVER, YOU GOT ME! AND I'VE BROUGHT YOU YOUR FAVORITE PINK DOUGHNUT WITH A NICE, WARM BLACK COFFEE--

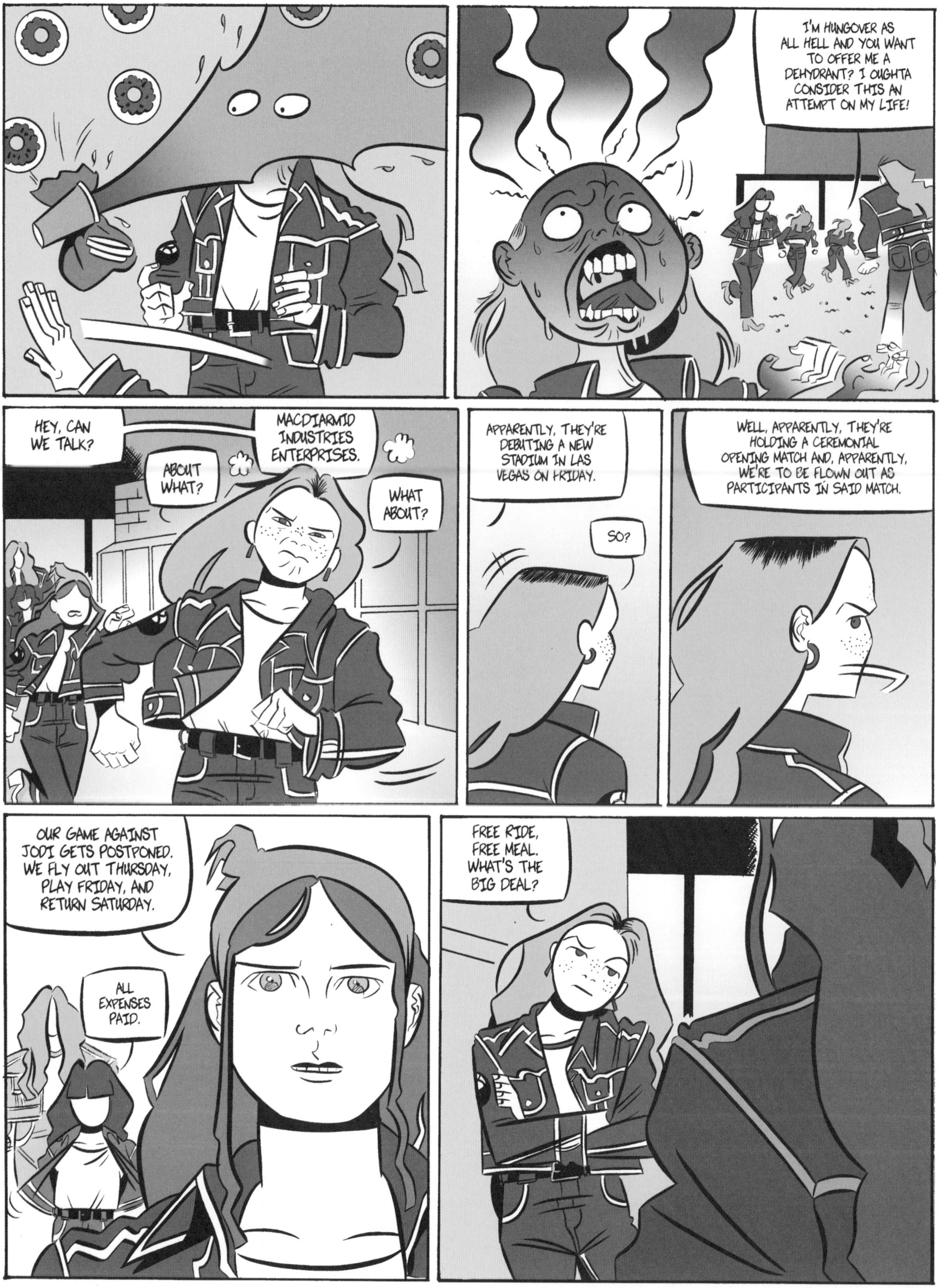

I'M HUNGOVER AS ALL HELL AND YOU WANT TO OFFER ME A DEHYDRANT? I OUGHTA CONSIDER THIS AN ATTEMPT ON MY LIFE!
HEY, CAN WE TALK?
ABOUT WHAT?
MACDIARMID INDUSTRIES ENTERPRISES.
WHAT ABOUT?
APPARENTLY, THEY'RE DEBUTING A NEW STADIUM IN LAS VEGAS ON FRIDAY.
SO?
WELL, APPARENTLY, THEY'RE HOLDING A CEREMONIAL OPENING MATCH AND, APPARENTLY, WE'RE TO BE FLOWN OUT AS PARTICIPANTS IN SAID MATCH.
OUR GAME AGAINST JODI GETS POSTPONED. WE FLY OUT THURSDAY, PLAY FRIDAY, AND RETURN SATURDAY.
ALL EXPENSES PAID.
FREE RIDE, FREE MEAL. WHAT'S THE BIG DEAL?

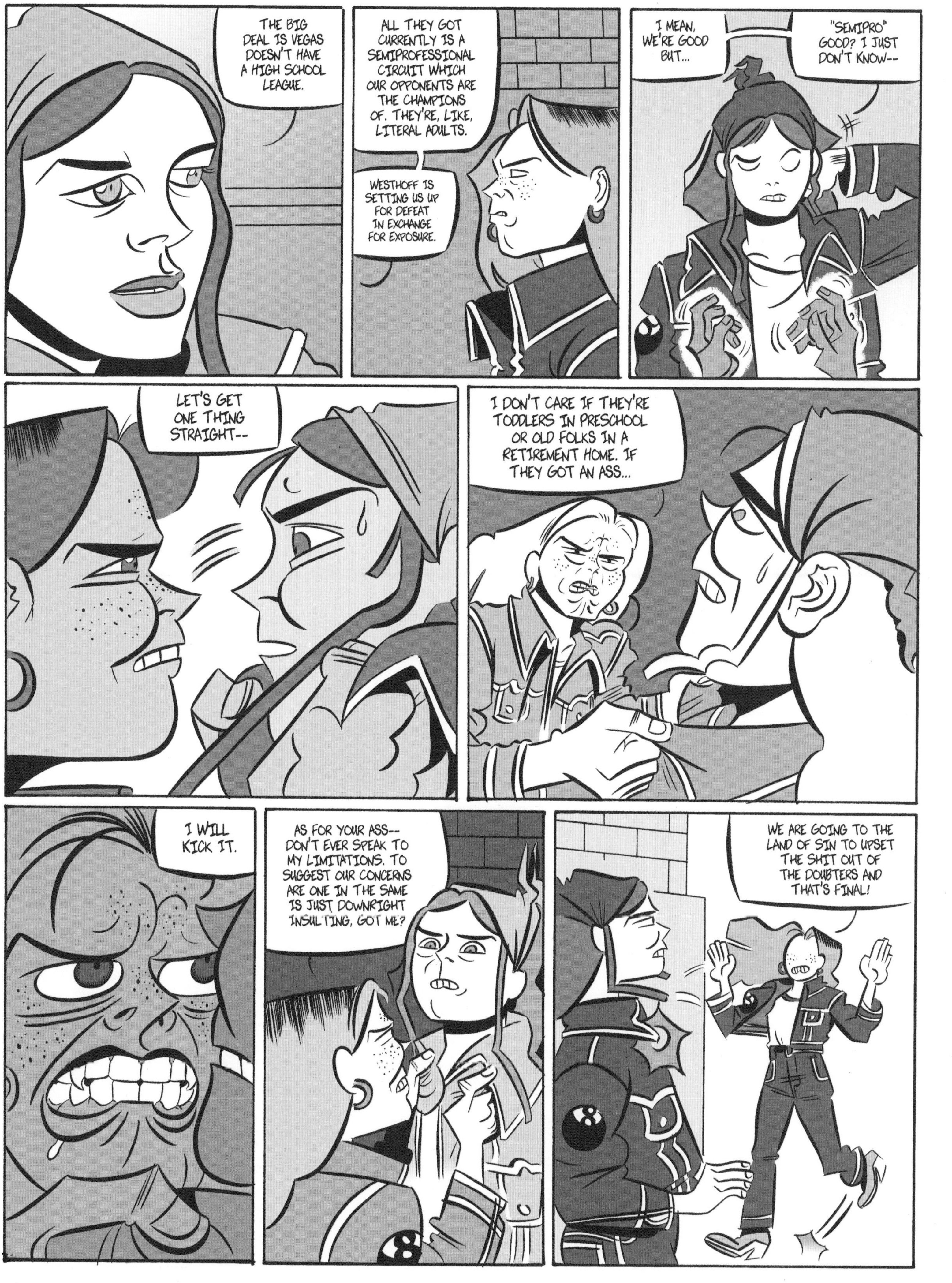
THE BIG DEAL IS VEGAS DOESN'T HAVE A HIGH SCHOOL LEAGUE.
ALL THEY GOT CURRENTLY IS A SEMIPROFESSIONAL CIRCUIT WHICH OUR OPPONENTS ARE THE CHAMPIONS OF. THEY'RE, LIKE, LITERAL ADULTS.
WESTHOFF IS SETTING US UP FOR DEFEAT IN EXCHANGE FOR EXPOSURE.
I MEAN, WE'RE GOOD BUT...
"SEMIPRO" GOOD? I JUST DON'T KNOW--
LET'S GET ONE THING STRAIGHT--
I DON'T CARE IF THEY'RE TODDLERS IN PRESCHOOL OR OLD FOLKS IN A RETIREMENT HOME. IF THEY GOT AN ASS...
I WILL KICK IT.
AS FOR YOUR ASS-- DON'T EVER SPEAK TO MY LIMITATIONS. TO SUGGEST OUR CONCERNS ARE ONE IN THE SAME IS JUST DOWNRIGHT INSULTING, GOT ME?
WE ARE GOING TO THE LAND OF SIN TO UPSET THE SHIT OUT OF THE DOUBTERS AND THAT'S FINAL!

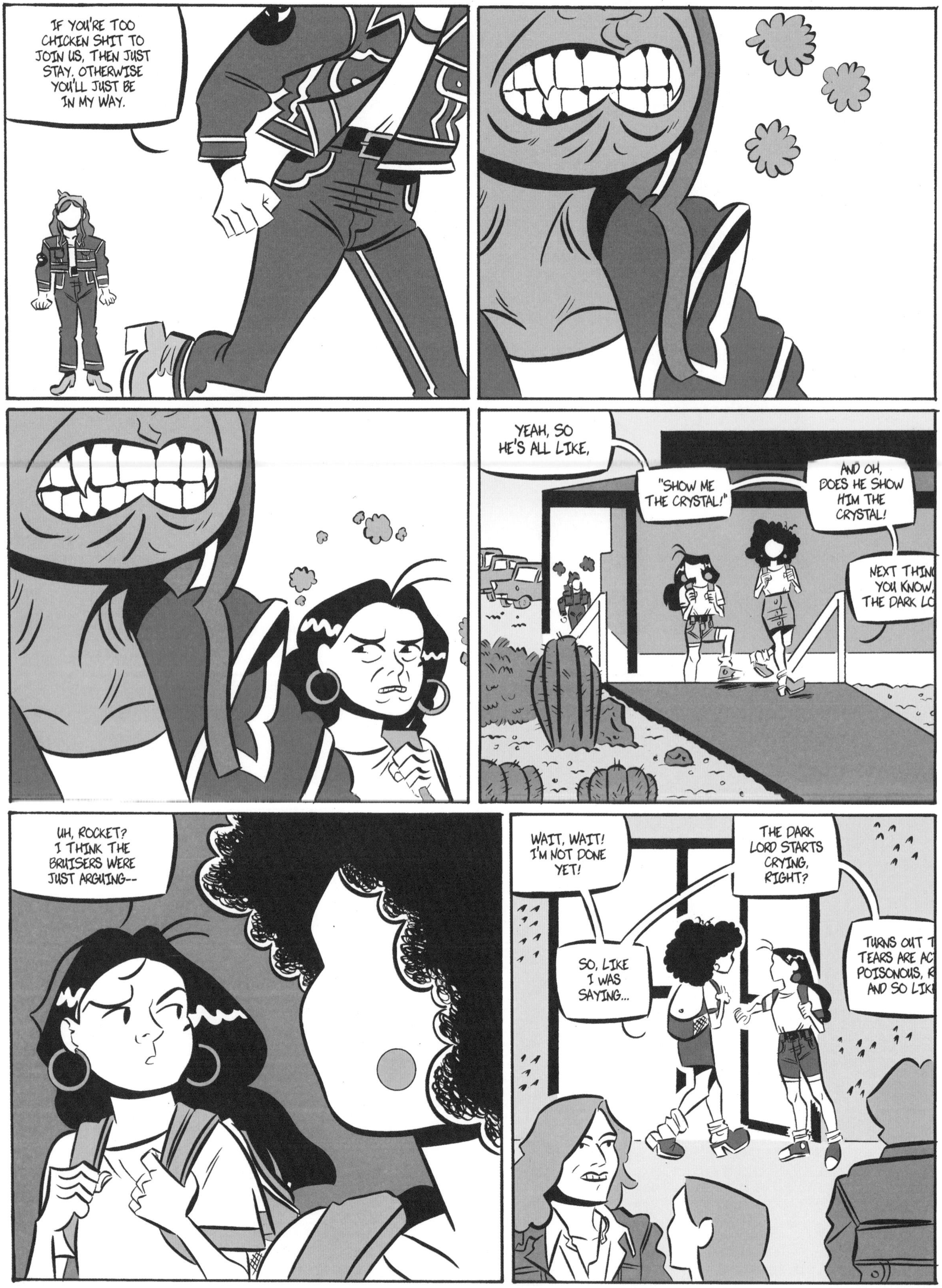
IF YOU'RE TOO CHICKEN SHIT TO JOIN US, THEN JUST STAY. OTHERWISE YOU'LL JUST BE IN MY WAY.
YEAH, SO HE'S ALL LIKE,
"SHOW ME THE CRYSTAL!"
AND OH, DOES HE SHOW HIM THE CRYSTAL!
NEXT THING YOU KNOW, THE DARK LO
UH, ROCKET? I THINK THE BRUISERS WERE JUST ARGUING--
WAIT, WAIT! I'M NOT DONE YET!
THE DARK LORD STARTS CRYING, RIGHT?
SO, LIKE I WAS SAYING...
TURNS OUT T TEARS ARE ACT POISONOUS, R AND SO LIKE

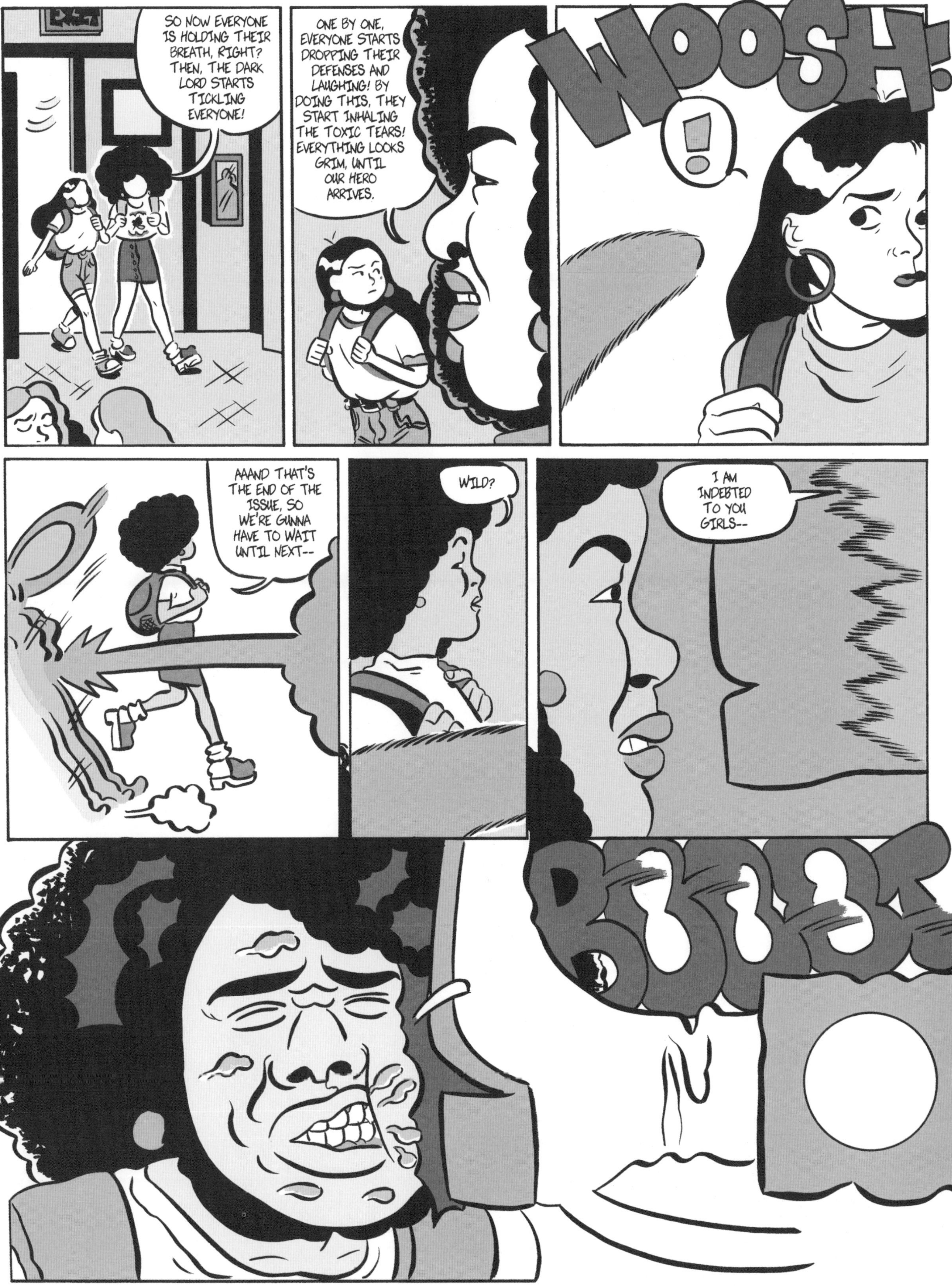
SO NOW EVERYONE IS HOLDING THEIR BREATH, RIGHT? THEN, THE DARK LORD STARTS TICKLING EVERYONE!
ONE BY ONE, EVERYONE STARTS DROPPING THEIR DEFENSES AND LAUGHING! BY DOING THIS, THEY START INHALING THE TOXIC TEARS! EVERYTHING LOOKS GRIM, UNTIL OUR HERO ARRIVES.
WOOSH!
!
AAAND THAT'S THE END OF THE ISSUE, SO WE'RE GUNNA HAVE TO WAIT UNTIL NEXT--
WILD?
I AM INDEBTED TO YOU GIRLS--

YOU HAVE OPENED MY EYES--GIVEN ME PURPOSE!
YOU SEE, LAST NIGHT I WAS SAMANTHA RIVERA...
BUT TODAY, I AM NOTHING BUT THE FINAL DESTINATION OF YOUR LIFE'S JOURNEY!
I KNOW NOW I AM THE UNAVOIDABLE FATE FROM WHICH YOU FLEE!

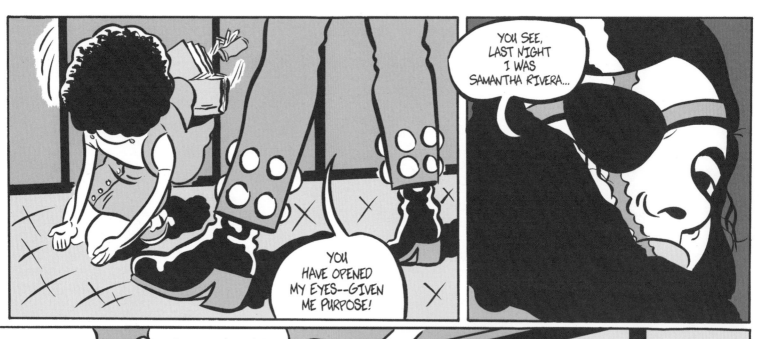

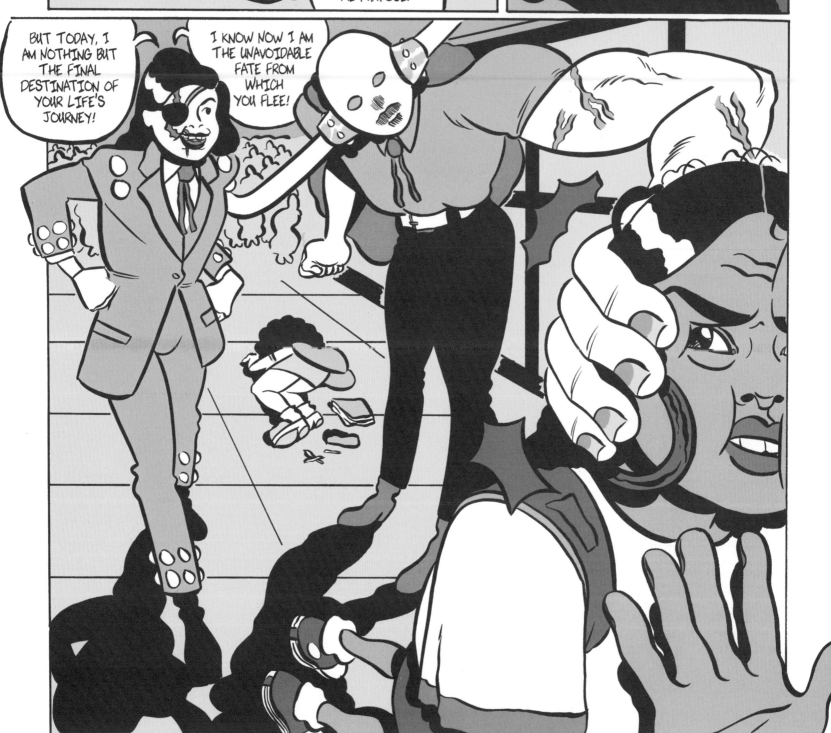

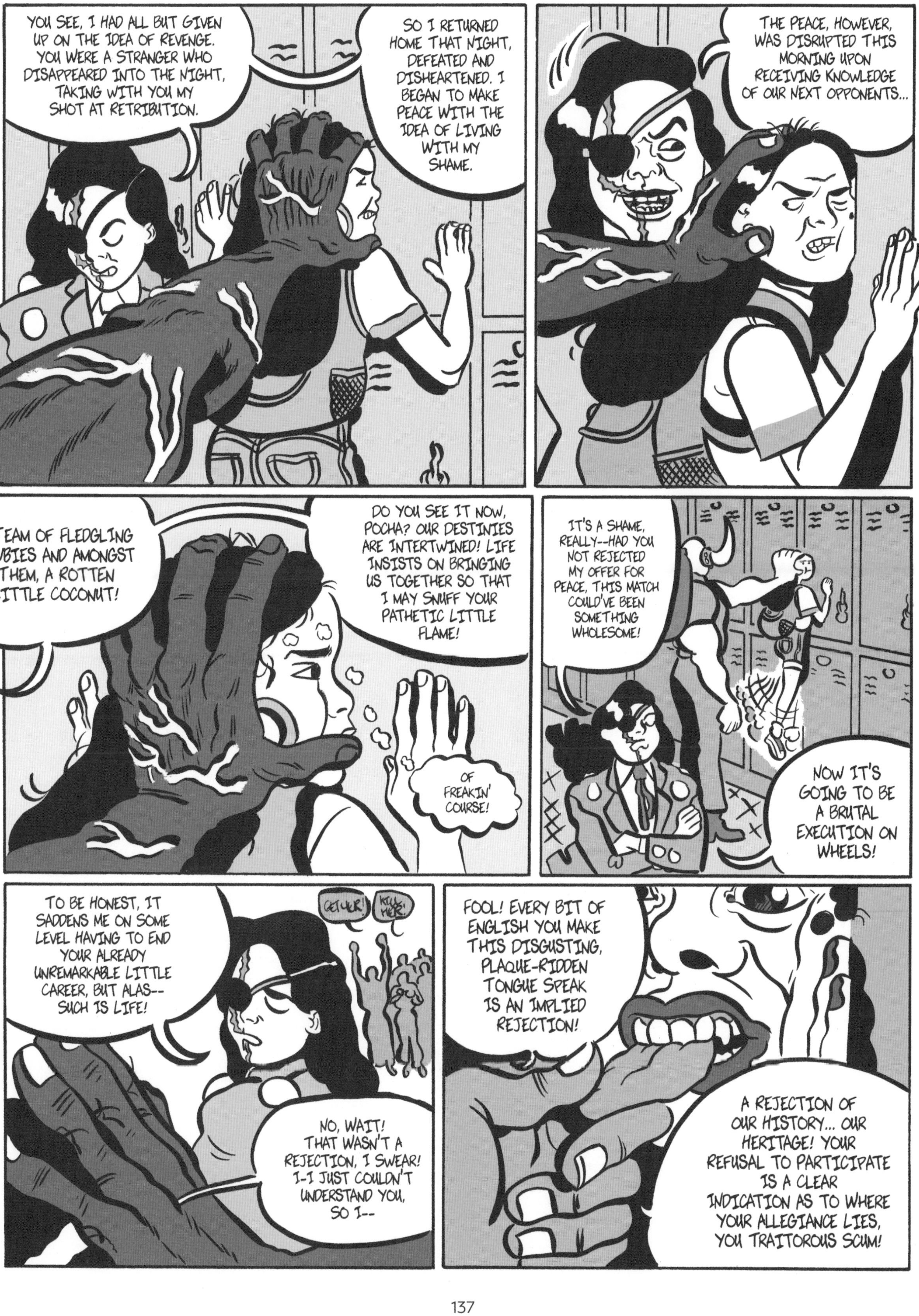
YOU SEE, I HAD ALL BUT GIVEN UP ON THE IDEA OF REVENGE. YOU WERE A STRANGER WHO DISAPPEARED INTO THE NIGHT, TAKING WITH YOU MY SHOT AT RETRIBUTION.
SO I RETURNED HOME THAT NIGHT, DEFEATED AND DISHEARTENED. I BEGAN TO MAKE PEACE WITH THE IDEA OF LIVING WITH MY SHAME.
THE PEACE, HOWEVER, WAS DISRUPTED THIS MORNING UPON RECEIVING KNOWLEDGE OF OUR NEXT OPPONENTS...
A TEAM OF FLEDGLING NEWBIES AND AMONGST THEM, A ROTTEN LITTLE COCONUT!
DO YOU SEE IT NOW, POCHA? OUR DESTINIES ARE INTERTWINED! LIFE INSISTS ON BRINGING US TOGETHER SO THAT I MAY SNUFF YOUR PATHETIC LITTLE FLAME!
OF FREAKIN' COURSE!
IT'S A SHAME, REALLY--HAD YOU NOT REJECTED MY OFFER FOR PEACE, THIS MATCH COULD'VE BEEN SOMETHING WHOLESOME!
NOW IT'S GOING TO BE A BRUTAL EXECUTION ON WHEELS!
TO BE HONEST, IT SADDENS ME ON SOME LEVEL HAVING TO END YOUR ALREADY UNREMARKABLE LITTLE CAREER, BUT ALAS-- SUCH IS LIFE!
GET HER!
KILL HER!
NO, WAIT! THAT WASN'T A REJECTION, I SWEAR! I-I JUST COULDN'T UNDERSTAND YOU, SO I--
FOOL! EVERY BIT OF ENGLISH YOU MAKE THIS DISGUSTING, PLAQUE-RIDDEN TONGUE SPEAK IS AN IMPLIED REJECTION!
A REJECTION OF OUR HISTORY... OUR HERITAGE! YOUR REFUSAL TO PARTICIPATE IS A CLEAR INDICATION AS TO WHERE YOUR ALLEGIANCE LIES, YOU TRAITOROUS SCUM!

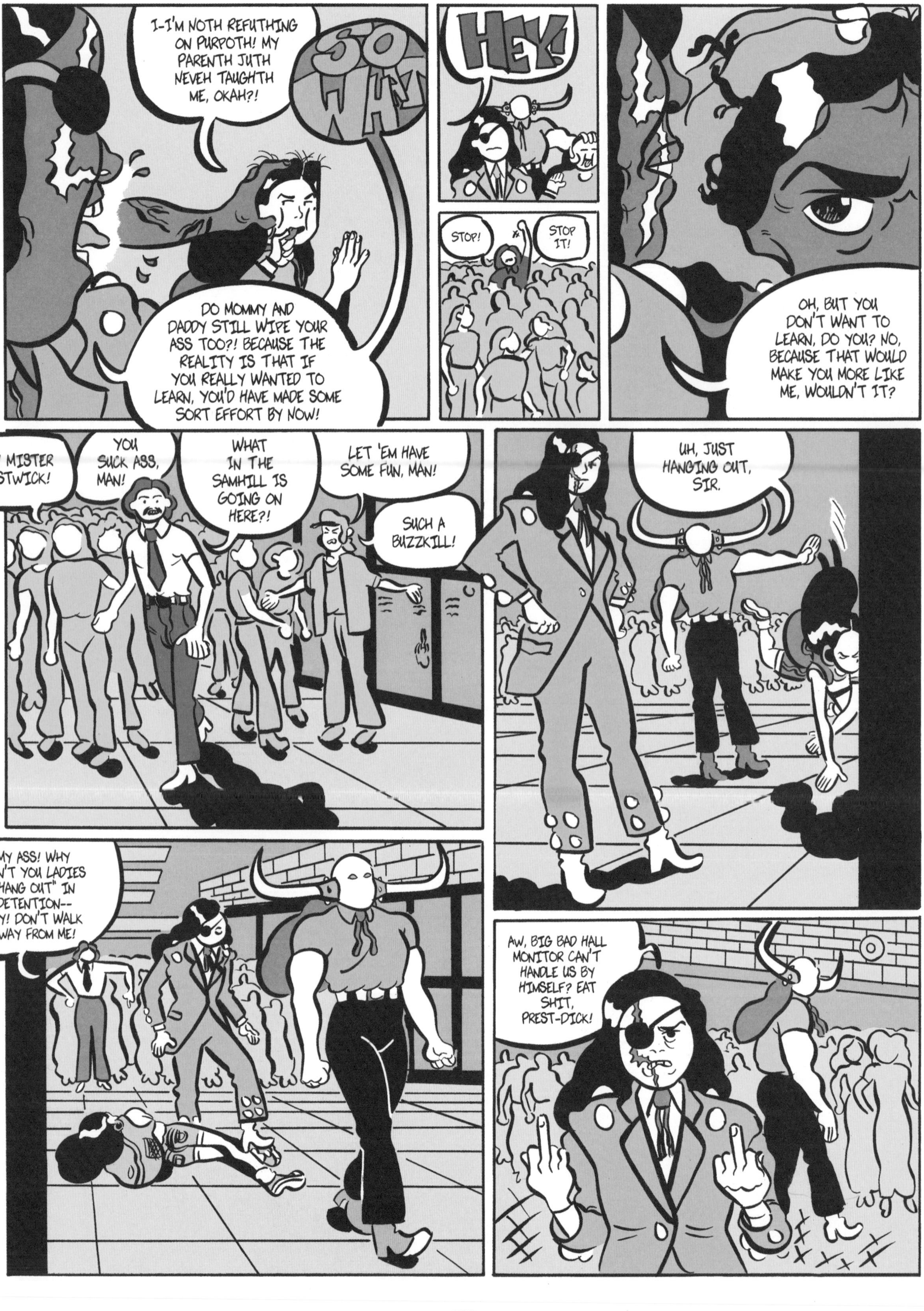

I-I'M NOTH REFUTHING ON PURPOTH! MY PARENTH JUTH NEVEH TAUGHTH ME, OKAH?!
SO WHAT
DO MOMMY AND DADDY STILL WIPE YOUR ASS TOO?! BECAUSE THE REALITY IS THAT IF YOU REALLY WANTED TO LEARN, YOU'D HAVE MADE SOME SORT EFFORT BY NOW!
HEY!
STOP!
STOP IT!
OH, BUT YOU DON'T WANT TO LEARN, DO YOU? NO, BECAUSE THAT WOULD MAKE YOU MORE LIKE ME, WOULDN'T IT?
UGH! MISTER PRESTWICK!
YOU SUCK ASS, MAN!
WHAT IN THE SAMHILL IS GOING ON HERE?!
LET 'EM HAVE SOME FUN, MAN!
SUCH A BUZZKILL!
UH, JUST HANGING OUT, SIR.
MY ASS! WHY DON'T YOU LADIES "HANG OUT" IN DETENTION-- HEY! DON'T WALK AWAY FROM ME!
AW, BIG BAD HALL MONITOR CAN'T HANDLE US BY HIMSELF? EAT SHIT, PREST-DICK!

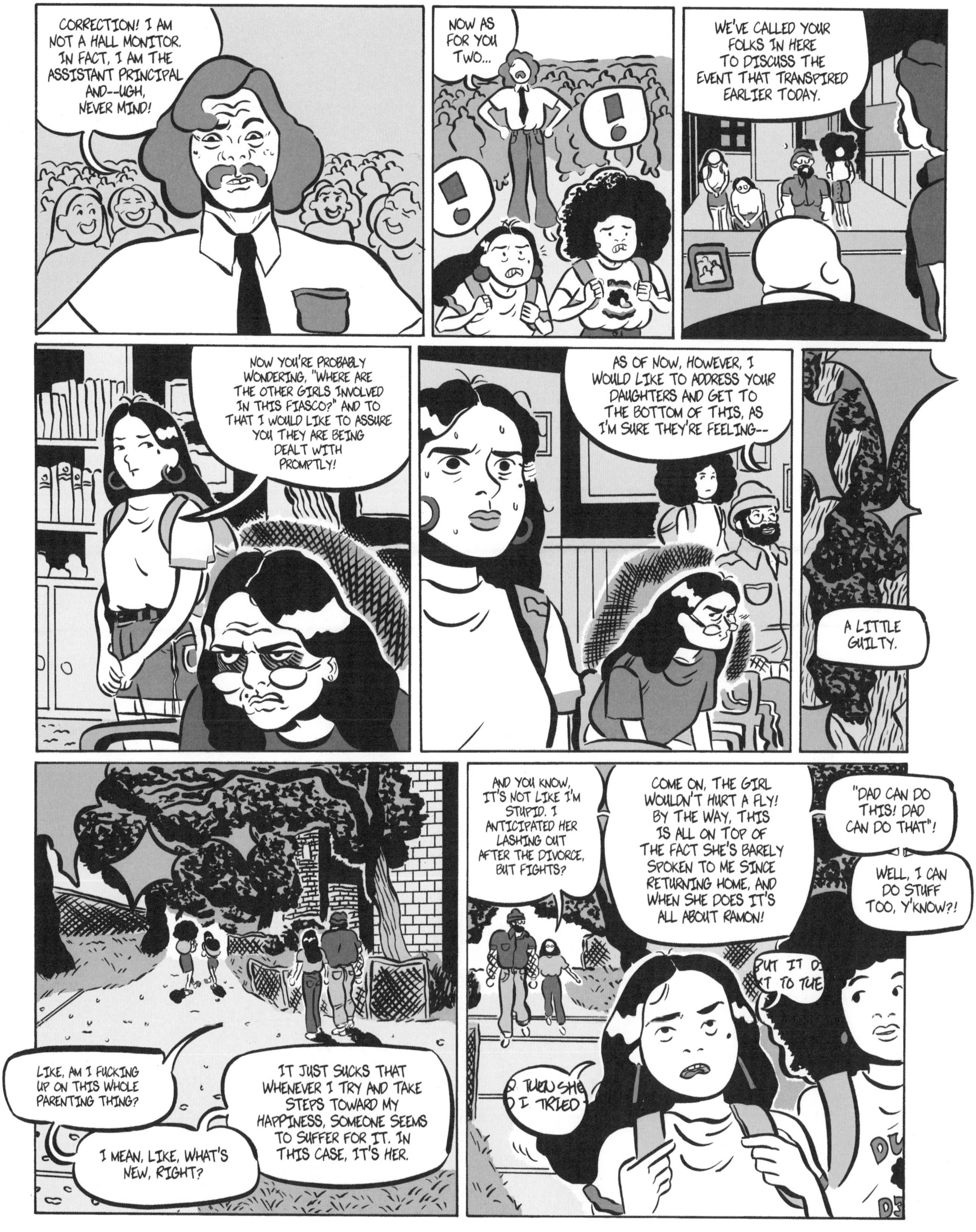
CORRECTION! I AM NOT A HALL MONITOR. IN FACT, I AM THE ASSISTANT PRINCIPAL AND--UGH, NEVER MIND!
NOW AS FOR YOU TWO...
WE'VE CALLED YOUR FOLKS IN HERE TO DISCUSS THE EVENT THAT TRANSPIRED EARLIER TODAY.
NOW YOU'RE PROBABLY WONDERING, "WHERE ARE THE OTHER GIRLS INVOLVED IN THIS FIASCO?" AND TO THAT I WOULD LIKE TO ASSURE YOU THEY ARE BEING DEALT WITH PROMPTLY!
AS OF NOW, HOWEVER, I WOULD LIKE TO ADDRESS YOUR DAUGHTERS AND GET TO THE BOTTOM OF THIS, AS I'M SURE THEY'RE FEELING--
A LITTLE GUILTY.
LIKE, AM I FUCKING UP ON THIS WHOLE PARENTING THING?
I MEAN, LIKE, WHAT'S NEW, RIGHT?
IT JUST SUCKS THAT WHENEVER I TRY AND TAKE STEPS TOWARD MY HAPPINESS, SOMEONE SEEMS TO SUFFER FOR IT. IN THIS CASE, IT'S HER.
AND YOU KNOW, IT'S NOT LIKE I'M STUPID. I ANTICIPATED HER LASHING OUT AFTER THE DIVORCE, BUT FIGHTS?
COME ON, THE GIRL WOULDN'T HURT A FLY! BY THE WAY, THIS IS ALL ON TOP OF THE FACT SHE'S BARELY SPOKEN TO ME SINCE RETURNING HOME, AND WHEN SHE DOES IT'S ALL ABOUT RAMON!
"DAD CAN DO THIS! DAD CAN DO THAT"!
WELL, I CAN DO STUFF TOO, Y'KNOW?!

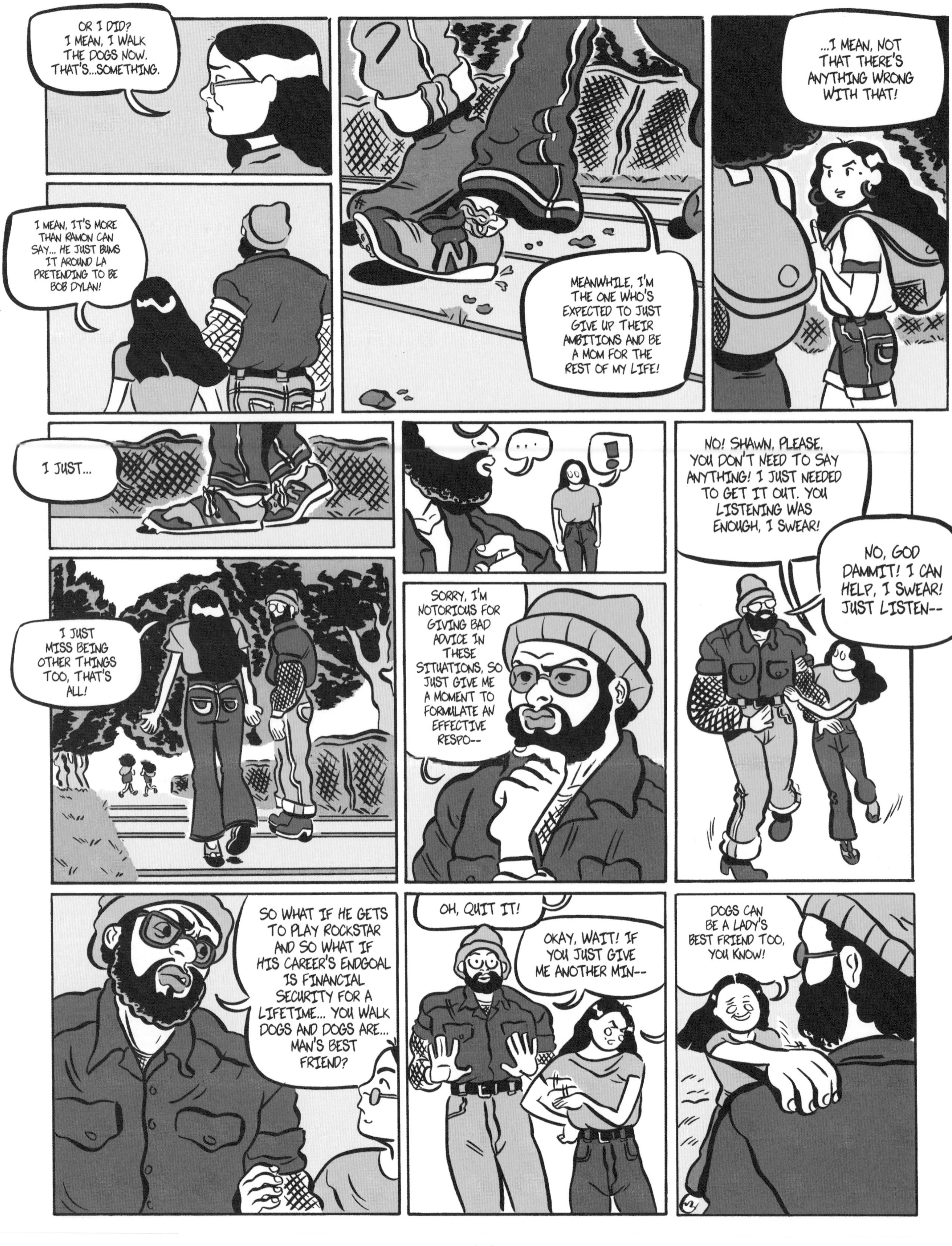
OR I DID? I MEAN, I WALK THE DOGS NOW. THAT'S...SOMETHING.
I MEAN, IT'S MORE THAN RAMON CAN SAY... HE JUST BUMS IT AROUND LA PRETENDING TO BE BOB DYLAN!
MEANWHILE, I'M THE ONE WHO'S EXPECTED TO JUST GIVE UP THEIR AMBITIONS AND BE A MOM FOR THE REST OF MY LIFE!
...I MEAN, NOT THAT THERE'S ANYTHING WRONG WITH THAT!
I JUST...
...
!
NO! SHAWN, PLEASE, YOU DON'T NEED TO SAY ANYTHING! I JUST NEEDED TO GET IT OUT. YOU LISTENING WAS ENOUGH, I SWEAR!
I JUST MISS BEING OTHER THINGS TOO, THAT'S ALL!
SORRY, I'M NOTORIOUS FOR GIVING BAD ADVICE IN THESE SITUATIONS, SO JUST GIVE ME A MOMENT TO FORMULATE AN EFFECTIVE RESPO--
NO, GOD DAMMIT! I CAN HELP, I SWEAR! JUST LISTEN--
SO WHAT IF HE GETS TO PLAY ROCKSTAR AND SO WHAT IF HIS CAREER'S ENDGOAL IS FINANCIAL SECURITY FOR A LIFETIME... YOU WALK DOGS AND DOGS ARE... MAN'S BEST FRIEND?
OH, QUIT IT!
OKAY, WAIT! IF YOU JUST GIVE ME ANOTHER MIN--
DOGS CAN BE A LADY'S BEST FRIEND TOO, YOU KNOW!

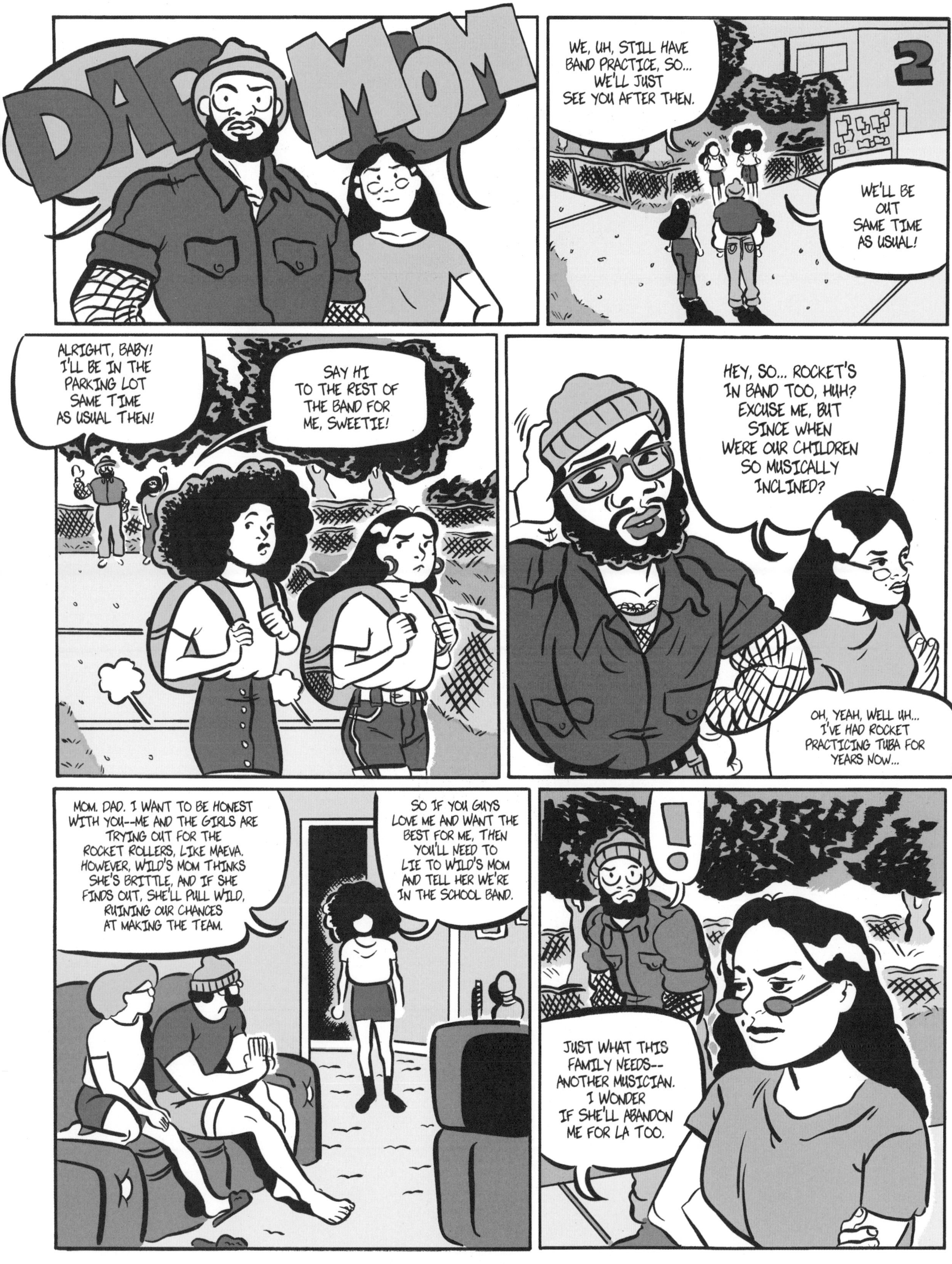
DAD
MOM
WE, UH, STILL HAVE BAND PRACTICE, SO... WE'LL JUST SEE YOU AFTER THEN.
WE'LL BE OUT SAME TIME AS USUAL!
2
ALRIGHT, BABY! I'LL BE IN THE PARKING LOT SAME TIME AS USUAL THEN!
SAY HI TO THE REST OF THE BAND FOR ME, SWEETIE!
HEY, SO... ROCKET'S IN BAND TOO, HUH? EXCUSE ME, BUT SINCE WHEN WERE OUR CHILDREN SO MUSICALLY INCLINED?
OH, YEAH, WELL UH... I'VE HAD ROCKET PRACTICING TUBA FOR YEARS NOW...
MOM. DAD. I WANT TO BE HONEST WITH YOU--ME AND THE GIRLS ARE TRYING OUT FOR THE ROCKET ROLLERS, LIKE MAEVA. HOWEVER, WILD'S MOM THINKS SHE'S BRITTLE, AND IF SHE FINDS OUT, SHE'LL PULL WILD, RUINING OUR CHANCES AT MAKING THE TEAM.
SO IF YOU GUYS LOVE ME AND WANT THE BEST FOR ME, THEN YOU'LL NEED TO LIE TO WILD'S MOM AND TELL HER WE'RE IN THE SCHOOL BAND.
!
JUST WHAT THIS FAMILY NEEDS--ANOTHER MUSICIAN. I WONDER IF SHE'LL ABANDON ME FOR LA TOO.

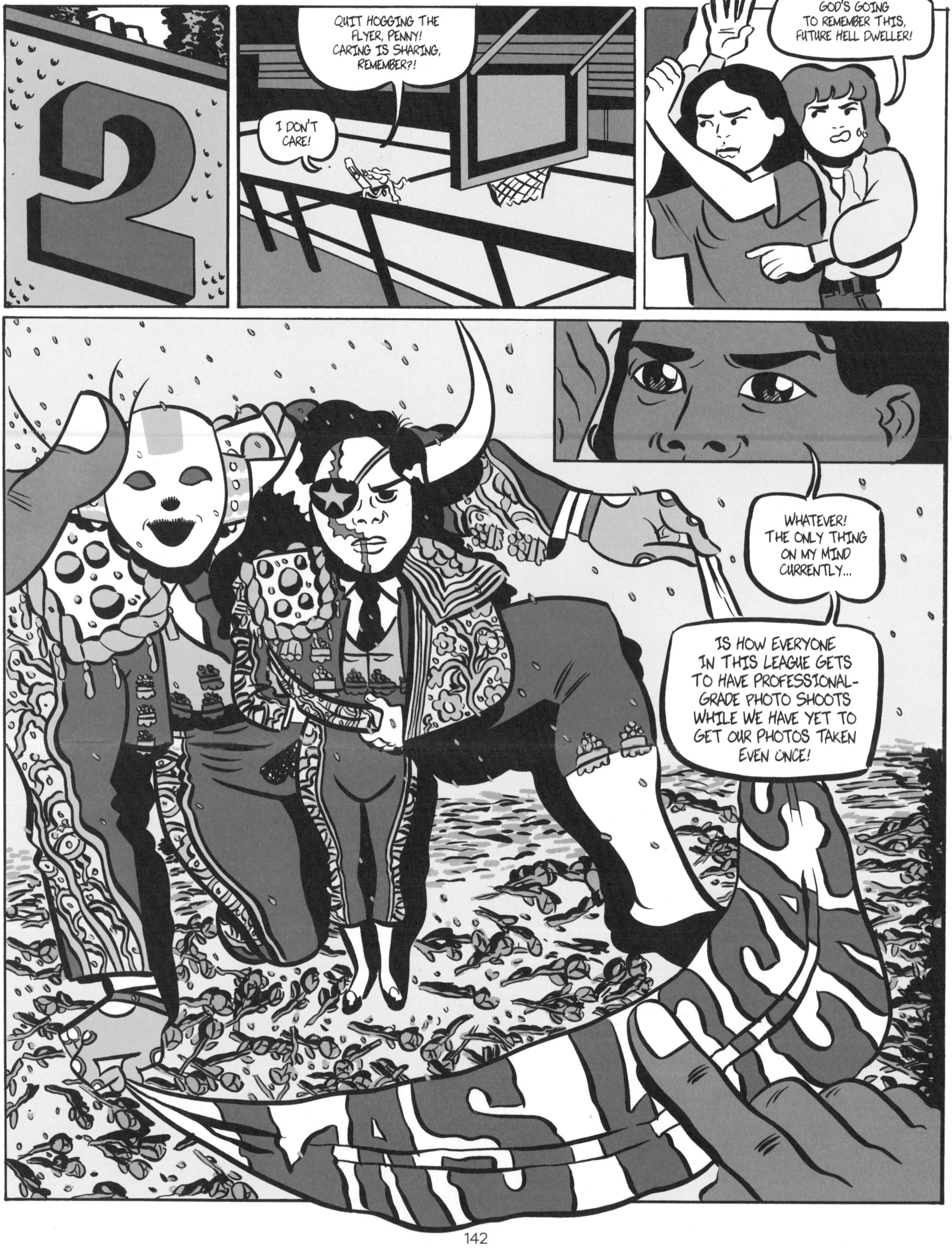
QUIT HOGGING THE FLYER, PENNY! CARING IS SHARING, REMEMBER?!
I DON'T CARE!
GOD'S GOING TO REMEMBER THIS, FUTURE HELL DWELLER!
WHATEVER! THE ONLY THING ON MY MIND CURRENTLY...
IS HOW EVERYONE IN THIS LEAGUE GETS TO HAVE PROFESSIONAL-GRADE PHOTO SHOOTS WHILE WE HAVE YET TO GET OUR PHOTOS TAKEN EVEN ONCE!

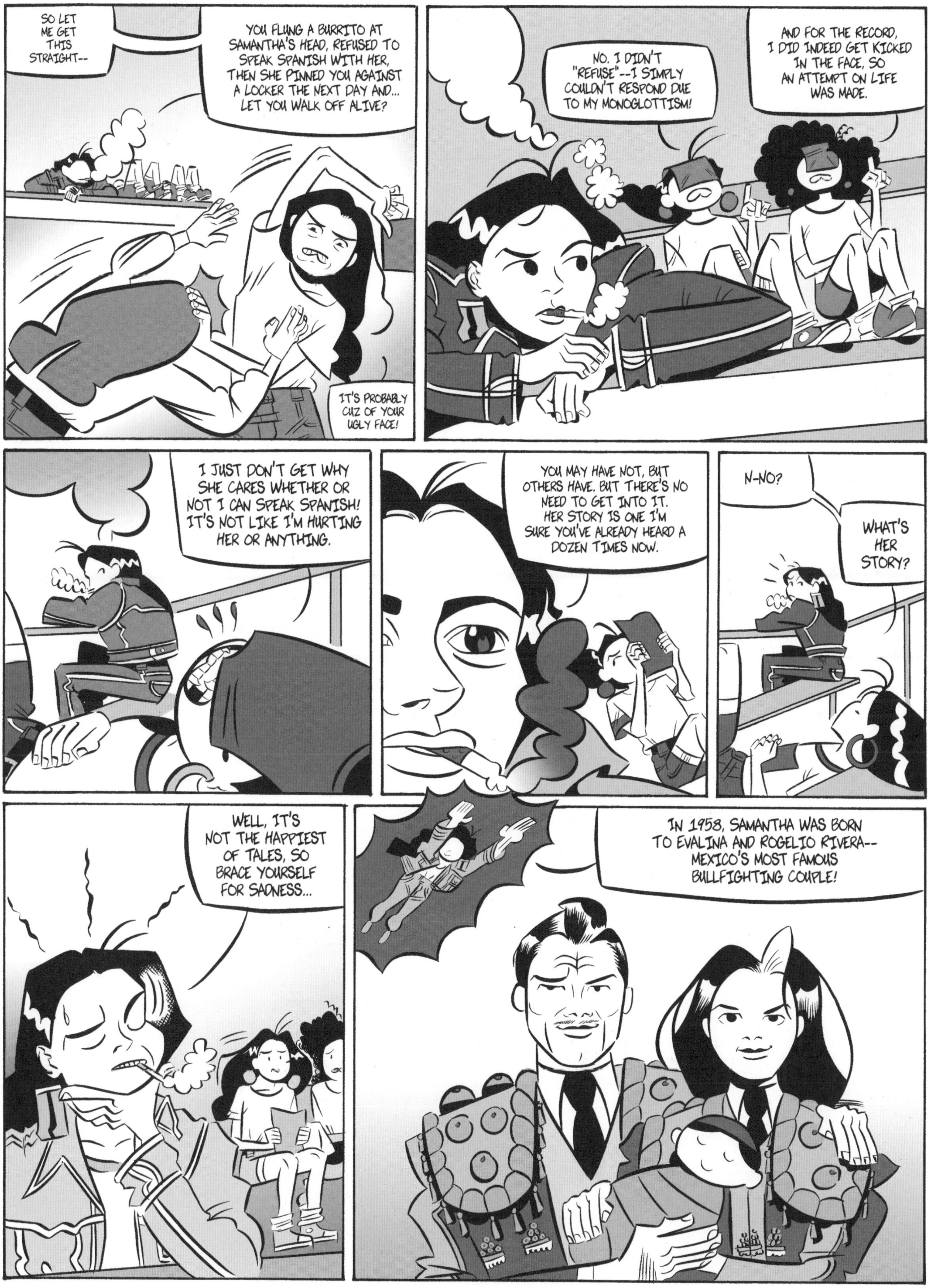
SO LET ME GET THIS STRAIGHT--
YOU FLUNG A BURRITO AT SAMANTHA'S HEAD, REFUSED TO SPEAK SPANISH WITH HER, THEN SHE PINNED YOU AGAINST A LOCKER THE NEXT DAY AND... LET YOU WALK OFF ALIVE?
IT'S PROBABLY CUZ OF YOUR UGLY FACE!
NO. I DIDN'T "REFUSE"--I SIMPLY COULDN'T RESPOND DUE TO MY MONOGLOTTISM!
AND FOR THE RECORD, I DID INDEED GET KICKED IN THE FACE, SO AN ATTEMPT ON LIFE WAS MADE.
I JUST DON'T GET WHY SHE CARES WHETHER OR NOT I CAN SPEAK SPANISH! IT'S NOT LIKE I'M HURTING HER OR ANYTHING.
YOU MAY HAVE NOT, BUT OTHERS HAVE. BUT THERE'S NO NEED TO GET INTO IT. HER STORY IS ONE I'M SURE YOU'VE ALREADY HEARD A DOZEN TIMES NOW.
N-NO?
WHAT'S HER STORY?
WELL, IT'S NOT THE HAPPIEST OF TALES, SO BRACE YOURSELF FOR SADNESS...
IN 1958, SAMANTHA WAS BORN TO EVALINA AND ROGELIO RIVERA--MEXICO'S MOST FAMOUS BULLFIGHTING COUPLE!

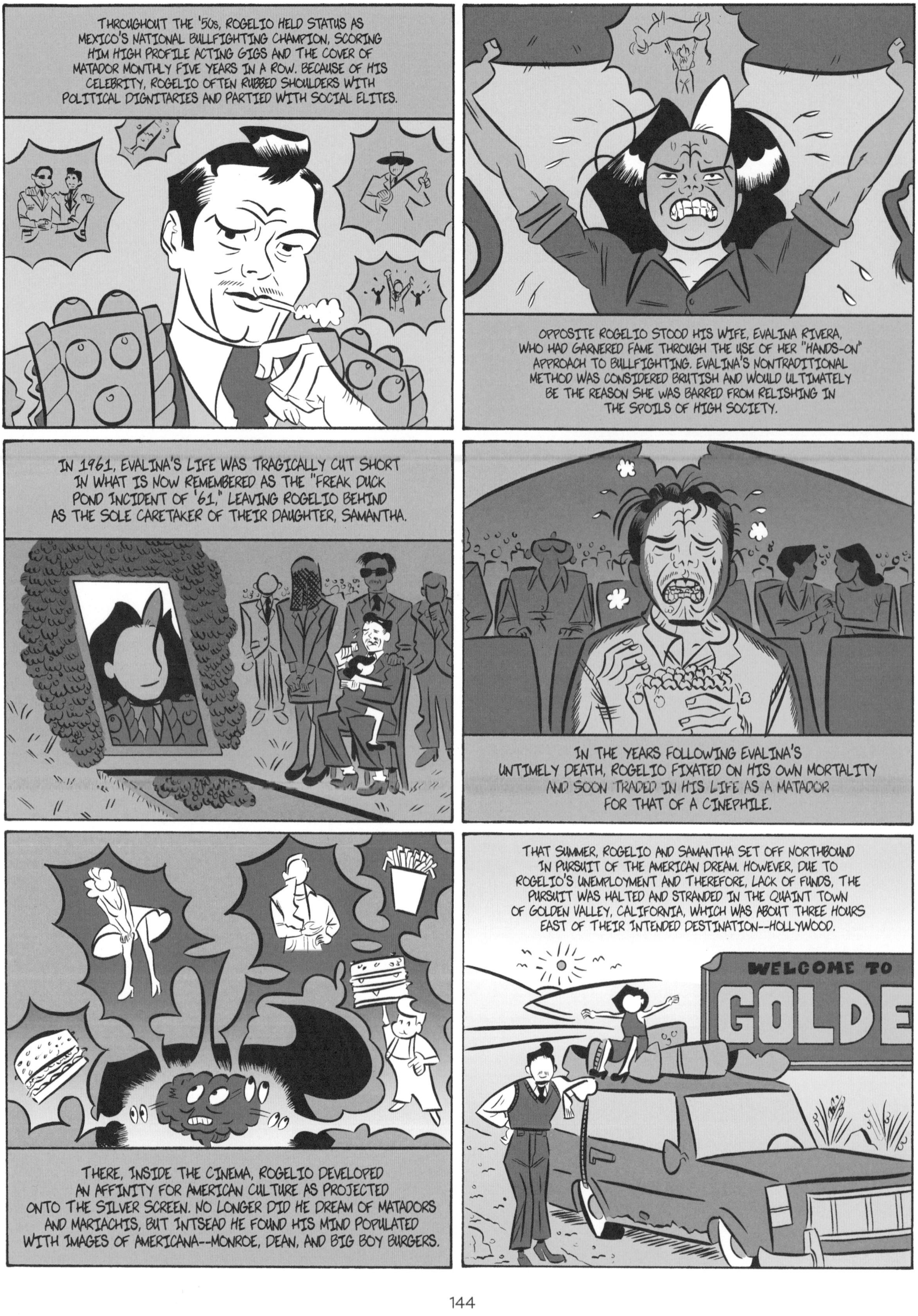
THROUGHOUT THE '50s, ROGELIO HELD STATUS AS MEXICO'S NATIONAL BULLFIGHTING CHAMPION, SCORING HIM HIGH PROFILE ACTING GIGS AND THE COVER OF MATADOR MONTHLY FIVE YEARS IN A ROW. BECAUSE OF HIS CELEBRITY, ROGELIO OFTEN RUBBED SHOULDERS WITH POLITICAL DIGNITARIES AND PARTIED WITH SOCIAL ELITES.
OPPOSITE ROGELIO STOOD HIS WIFE, EVALINA RIVERA, WHO HAD GARNERED FAME THROUGH THE USE OF HER "HANDS-ON" APPROACH TO BULLFIGHTING. EVALINA'S NONTRADITIONAL METHOD WAS CONSIDERED BRUTISH AND WOULD ULTIMATELY BE THE REASON SHE WAS BARRED FROM RELISHING IN THE SPOILS OF HIGH SOCIETY.
IN 1961, EVALINA'S LIFE WAS TRAGICALLY CUT SHORT IN WHAT IS NOW REMEMBERED AS THE "FREAK DUCK POND INCIDENT OF '61," LEAVING ROGELIO BEHIND AS THE SOLE CARETAKER OF THEIR DAUGHTER, SAMANTHA.
IN THE YEARS FOLLOWING EVALINA'S UNTIMELY DEATH, ROGELIO FIXATED ON HIS OWN MORTALITY AND SOON TRADED IN HIS LIFE AS A MATADOR FOR THAT OF A CINEPHILE.
THERE, INSIDE THE CINEMA, ROGELIO DEVELOPED AN AFFINITY FOR AMERICAN CULTURE AS PROJECTED ONTO THE SILVER SCREEN. NO LONGER DID HE DREAM OF MATADORS AND MARIACHIS, BUT INTSEAD HE FOUND HIS MIND POPULATED WITH IMAGES OF AMERICANA--MONROE, DEAN, AND BIG BOY BURGERS.
THAT SUMMER, ROGELIO AND SAMANTHA SET OFF NORTHBOUND IN PURSUIT OF THE AMERICAN DREAM. HOWEVER, DUE TO ROGELIO'S UNEMPLOYMENT AND THEREFORE, LACK OF FUNDS, THE PURSUIT WAS HALTED AND STRANDED IN THE QUAINT TOWN OF GOLDEN VALLEY, CALIFORNIA, WHICH WAS ABOUT THREE HOURS EAST OF THEIR INTENDED DESTINATION--HOLLYWOOD.
WELCOME TO
GOLDE

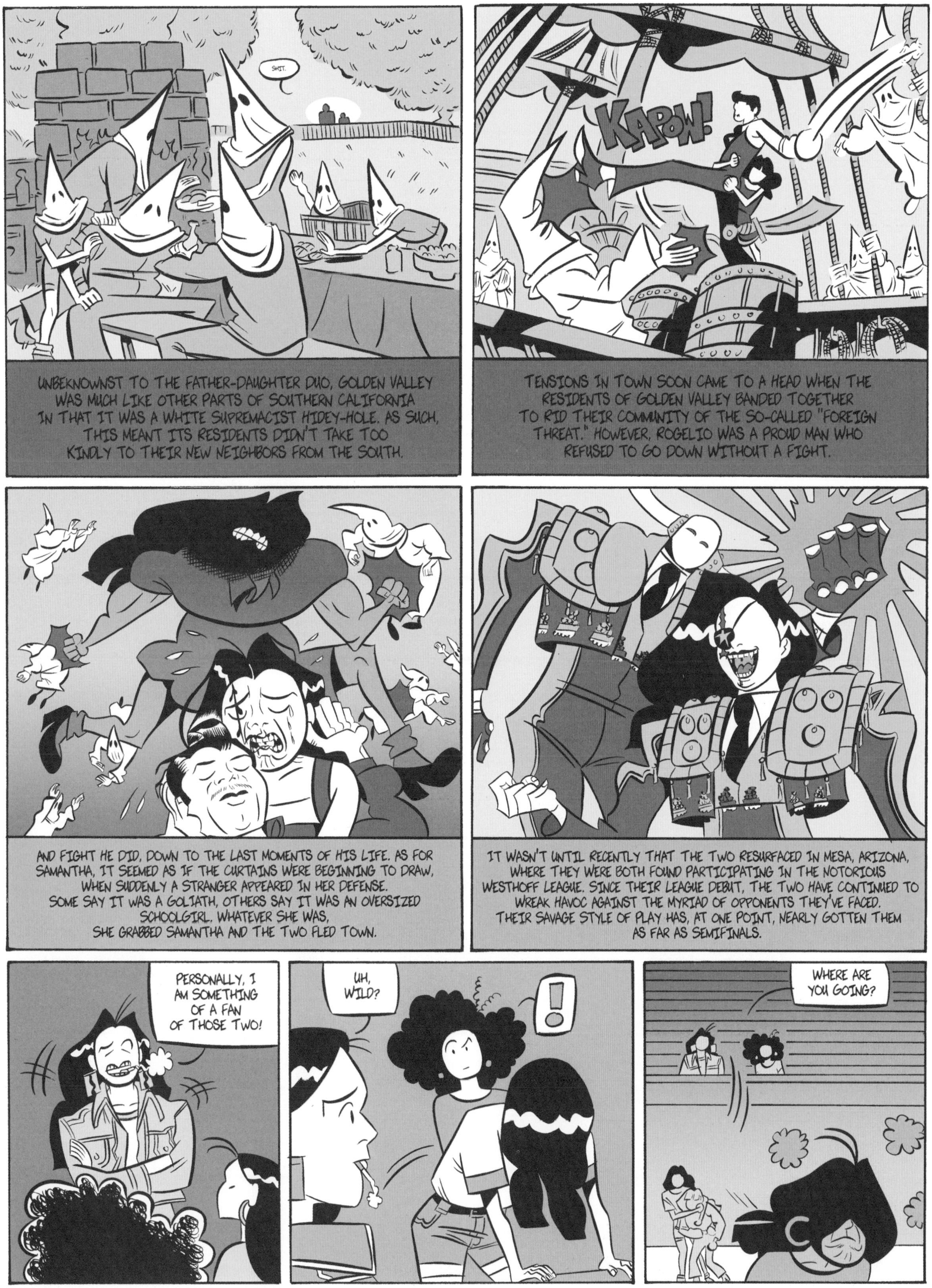
SHIT.
UNBEKNOWNST TO THE FATHER-DAUGHTER DUO, GOLDEN VALLEY WAS MUCH LIKE OTHER PARTS OF SOUTHERN CALIFORNIA IN THAT IT WAS A WHITE SUPREMACIST HIDEY-HOLE. AS SUCH, THIS MEANT ITS RESIDENTS DIDN'T TAKE TOO KINDLY TO THEIR NEW NEIGHBORS FROM THE SOUTH.
KAPOW!
TENSIONS IN TOWN SOON CAME TO A HEAD WHEN THE RESIDENTS OF GOLDEN VALLEY BANDED TOGETHER TO RID THEIR COMMUNITY OF THE SO-CALLED "FOREIGN THREAT." HOWEVER, ROGELIO WAS A PROUD MAN WHO REFUSED TO GO DOWN WITHOUT A FIGHT.
AND FIGHT HE DID, DOWN TO THE LAST MOMENTS OF HIS LIFE. AS FOR SAMANTHA, IT SEEMED AS IF THE CURTAINS WERE BEGINNING TO DRAW, WHEN SUDDENLY A STRANGER APPEARED IN HER DEFENSE. SOME SAY IT WAS A GOLIATH, OTHERS SAY IT WAS AN OVERSIZED SCHOOLGIRL. WHATEVER SHE WAS, SHE GRABBED SAMANTHA AND THE TWO FLED TOWN.
IT WASN'T UNTIL RECENTLY THAT THE TWO RESURFACED IN MESA, ARIZONA, WHERE THEY WERE BOTH FOUND PARTICIPATING IN THE NOTORIOUS WESTHOFF LEAGUE. SINCE THEIR LEAGUE DEBUT, THE TWO HAVE CONTINUED TO WREAK HAVOC AGAINST THE MYRIAD OF OPPONENTS THEY'VE FACED. THEIR SAVAGE STYLE OF PLAY HAS, AT ONE POINT, NEARLY GOTTEN THEM AS FAR AS SEMIFINALS.
PERSONALLY, I AM SOMETHING OF A FAN OF THOSE TWO!
UH, WILD?
!
WHERE ARE YOU GOING?

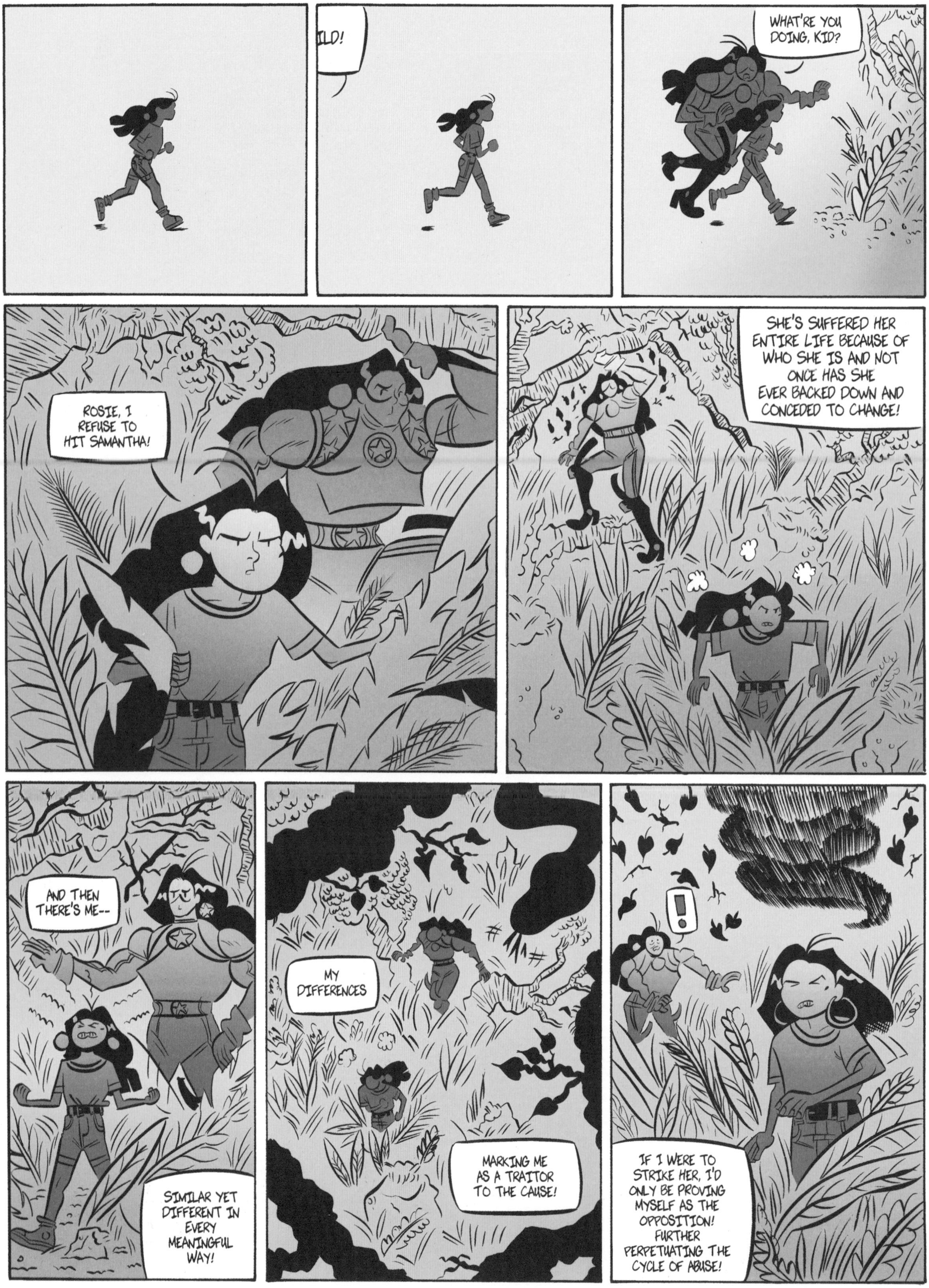
ILD!
WHAT'RE YOU DOING, KID?
ROSIE, I REFUSE TO HIT SAMANTHA!
SHE'S SUFFERED HER ENTIRE LIFE BECAUSE OF WHO SHE IS AND NOT ONCE HAS SHE EVER BACKED DOWN AND CONCEDED TO CHANGE!
AND THEN THERE'S ME--
SIMILAR YET DIFFERENT IN EVERY MEANINGFUL WAY!
MY DIFFERENCES
MARKING ME AS A TRAITOR TO THE CAUSE!
!
IF I WERE TO STRIKE HER, I'D ONLY BE PROVING MYSELF AS THE OPPOSITION! FURTHER PERPETUATING THE CYCLE OF ABUSE!

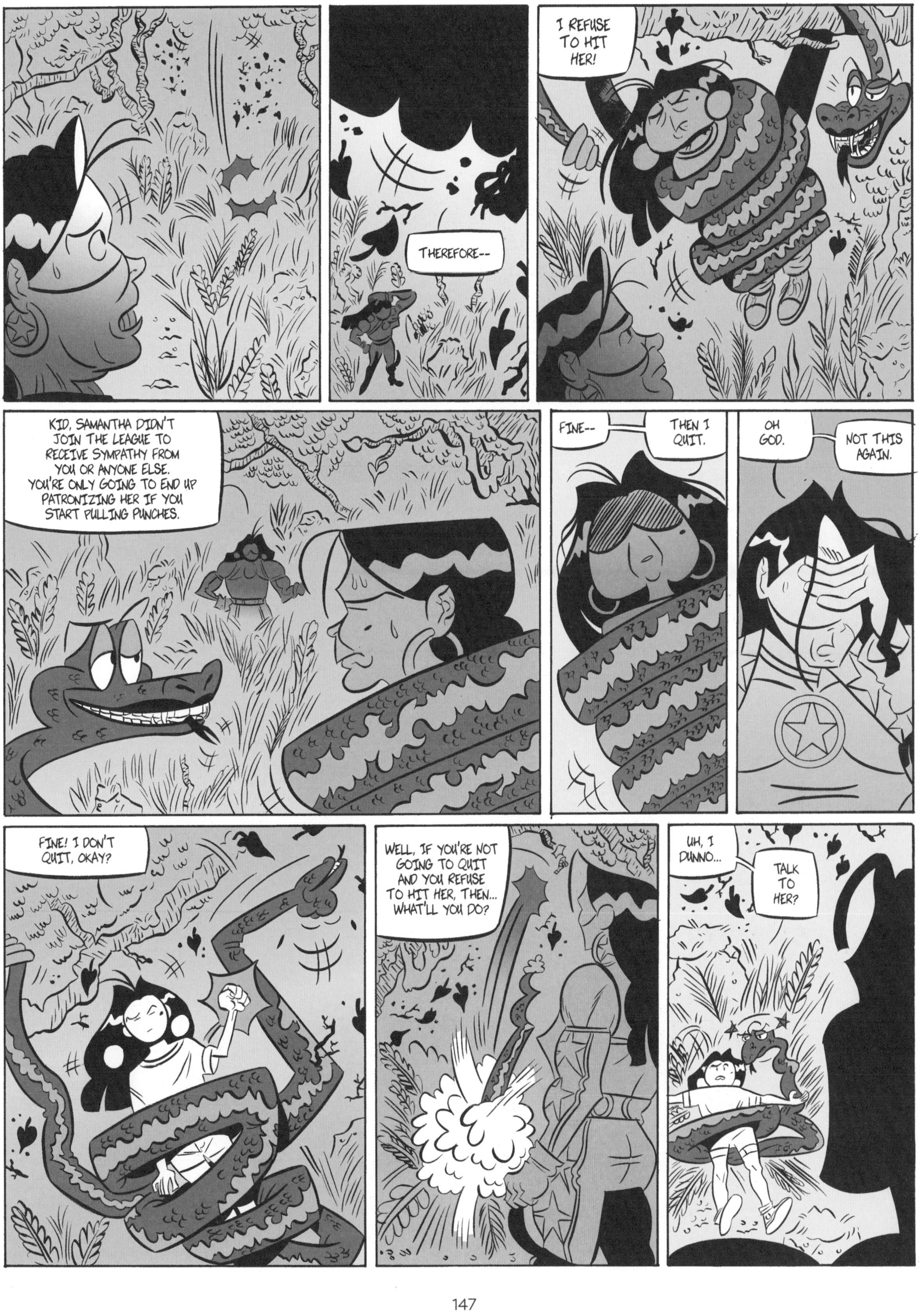
THEREFORE--
I REFUSE TO HIT HER!
KID, SAMANTHA DIDN'T JOIN THE LEAGUE TO RECEIVE SYMPATHY FROM YOU OR ANYONE ELSE. YOU'RE ONLY GOING TO END UP PATRONIZING HER IF YOU START PULLING PUNCHES.
FINE--
THEN I QUIT.
OH GOD.
NOT THIS AGAIN.
FINE! I DON'T QUIT, OKAY?
WELL, IF YOU'RE NOT GOING TO QUIT AND YOU REFUSE TO HIT HER, THEN... WHAT'LL YOU DO?
UH, I DUNNO...
TALK TO HER?

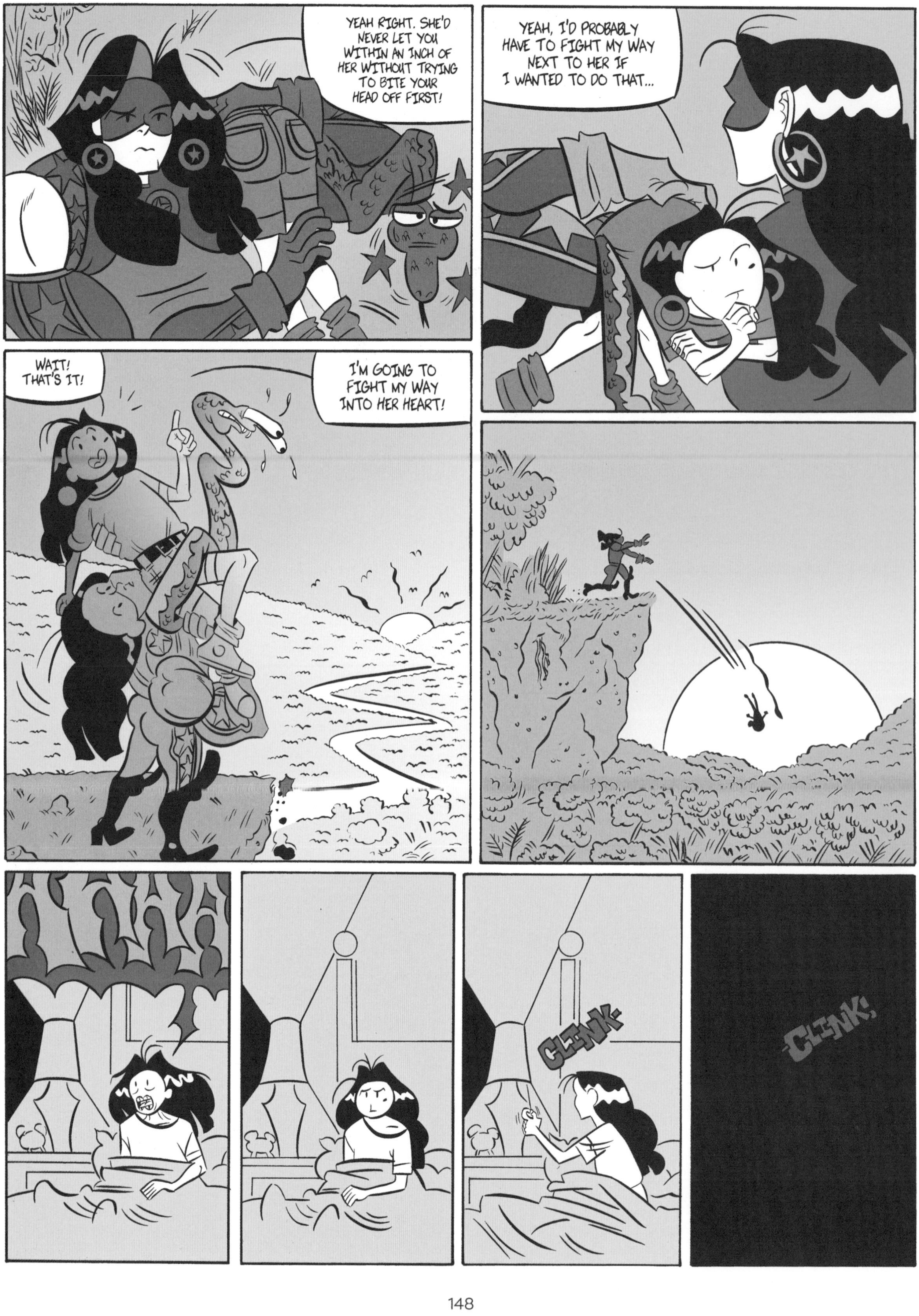
YEAH RIGHT. SHE'D NEVER LET YOU WITHIN AN INCH OF HER WITHOUT TRYING TO BITE YOUR HEAD OFF FIRST!
YEAH, I'D PROBABLY HAVE TO FIGHT MY WAY NEXT TO HER IF I WANTED TO DO THAT...
WAIT! THAT'S IT!
I'M GOING TO FIGHT MY WAY INTO HER HEART!
CLINK!
CLINK!

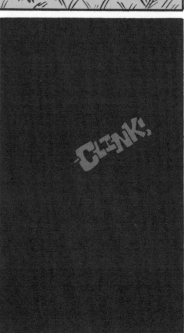

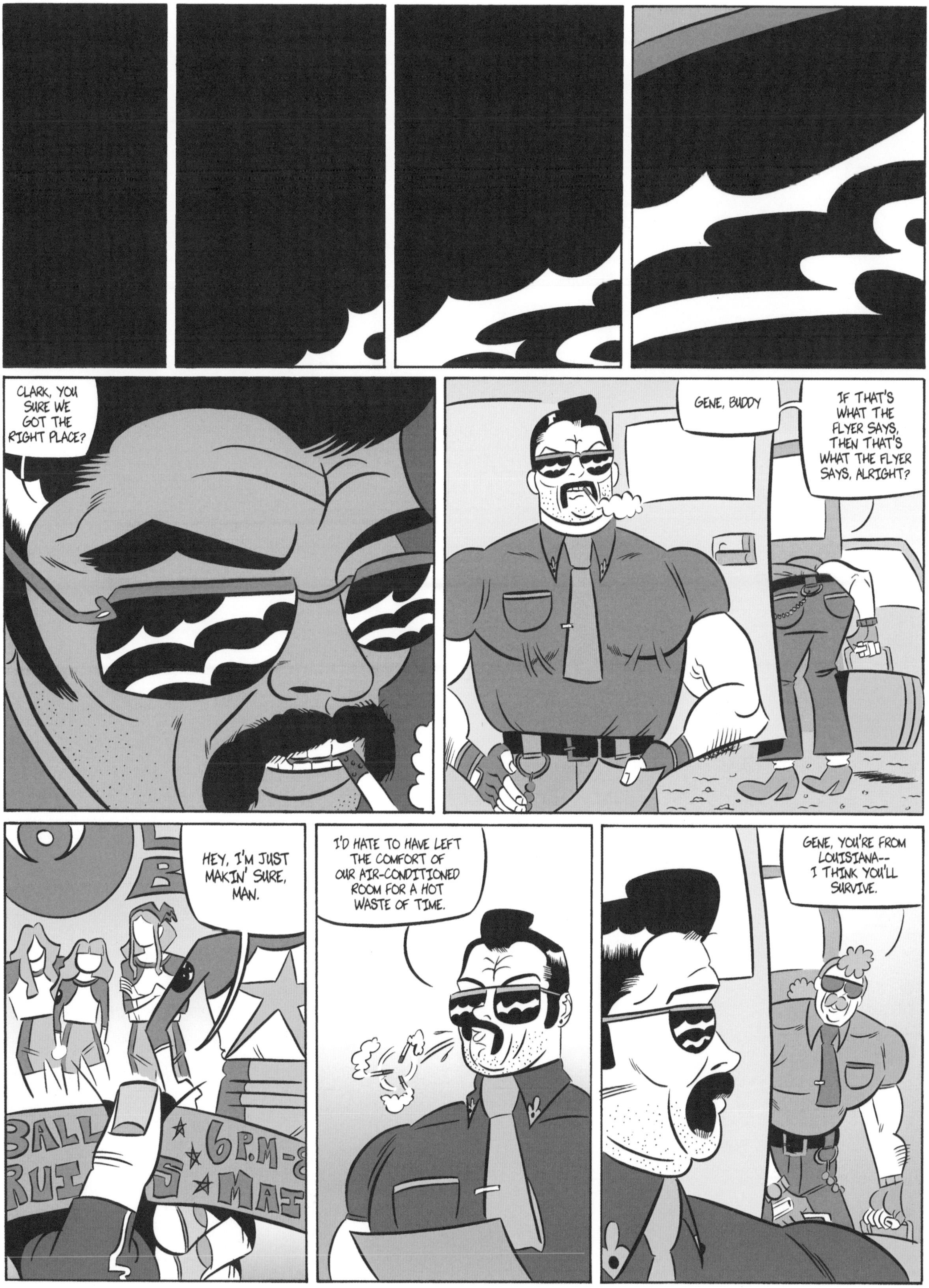
CLARK, YOU SURE WE GOT THE RIGHT PLACE?
GENE, BUDDY
IF THAT'S WHAT THE FLYER SAYS, THEN THAT'S WHAT THE FLYER SAYS, ALRIGHT?
HEY, I'M JUST MAKIN' SURE, MAN.
I'D HATE TO HAVE LEFT THE COMFORT OF OUR AIR-CONDITIONED ROOM FOR A HOT WASTE OF TIME.
GENE, YOU'RE FROM LOUISIANA-- I THINK YOU'LL SURVIVE.

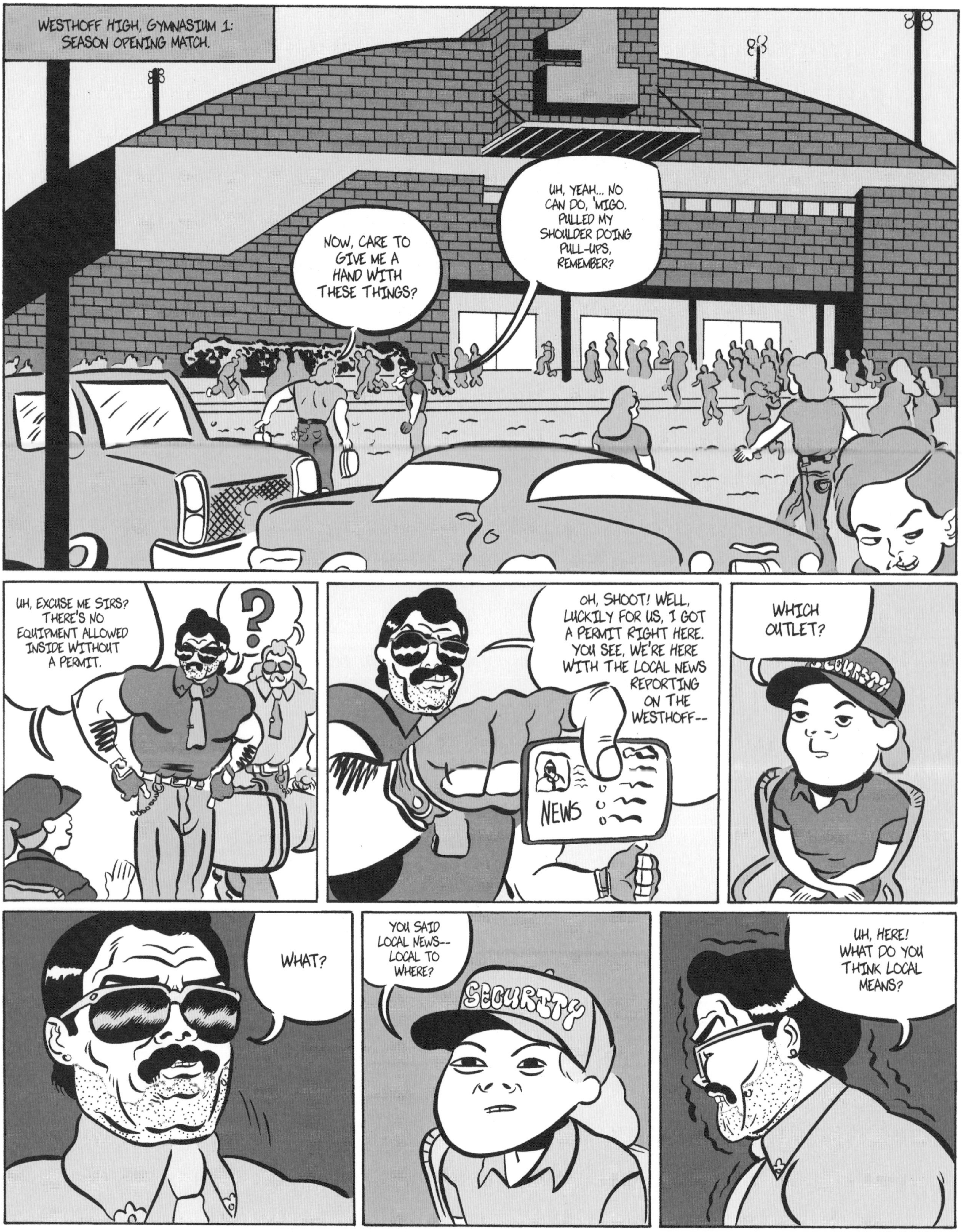
WESTHOFF HIGH, GYMNASIUM 1: SEASON OPENING MATCH.
NOW, CARE TO GIVE ME A HAND WITH THESE THINGS?
UH, YEAH... NO CAN DO, 'MIGO. PULLED MY SHOULDER DOING PULL-UPS, REMEMBER?
UH, EXCUSE ME SIRS? THERE'S NO EQUIPMENT ALLOWED INSIDE WITHOUT A PERMIT.
?
OH, SHOOT! WELL, LUCKILY FOR US, I GOT A PERMIT RIGHT HERE. YOU SEE, WE'RE HERE WITH THE LOCAL NEWS REPORTING ON THE WESTHOFF--
NEWS
WHICH OUTLET?
WHAT?
YOU SAID LOCAL NEWS-- LOCAL TO WHERE?
SECURITY
UH, HERE! WHAT DO YOU THINK LOCAL MEANS?

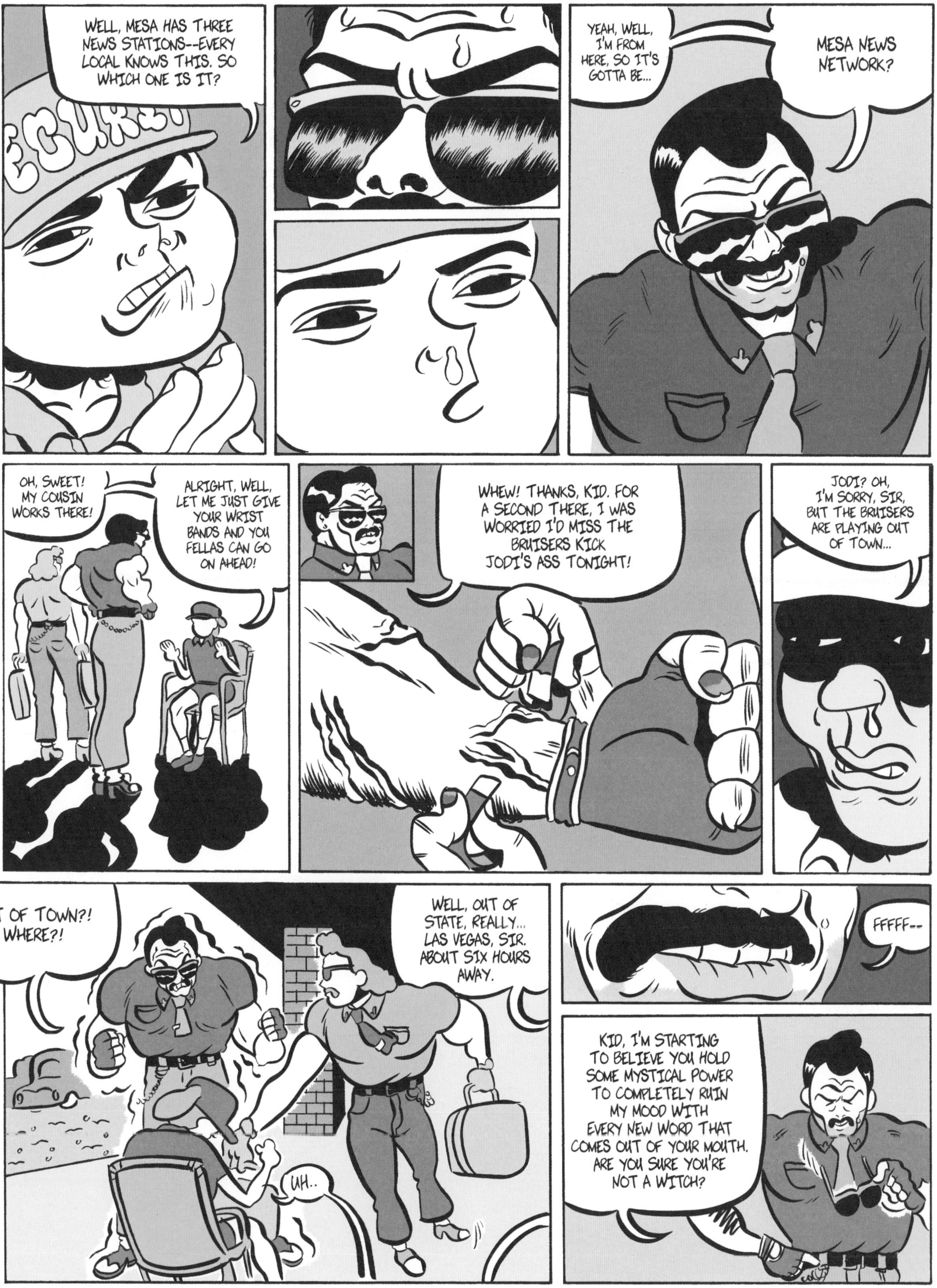

WELL, MESA HAS THREE NEWS STATIONS--EVERY LOCAL KNOWS THIS. SO WHICH ONE IS IT?
YEAH, WELL, I'M FROM HERE, SO IT'S GOTTA BE...
MESA NEWS NETWORK?
OH, SWEET! MY COUSIN WORKS THERE!
ALRIGHT, WELL, LET ME JUST GIVE YOUR WRIST BANDS AND YOU FELLAS CAN GO ON AHEAD!
WHEW! THANKS, KID. FOR A SECOND THERE, I WAS WORRIED I'D MISS THE BRUISERS KICK JODI'S ASS TONIGHT!
JODI? OH, I'M SORRY, SIR, BUT THE BRUISERS ARE PLAYING OUT OF TOWN...
OUT OF TOWN?! WHERE?!
WELL, OUT OF STATE, REALLY... LAS VEGAS, SIR. ABOUT SIX HOURS AWAY.
UH..
FFFFF--
KID, I'M STARTING TO BELIEVE YOU HOLD SOME MYSTICAL POWER TO COMPLETELY RUIN MY MOOD WITH EVERY NEW WORD THAT COMES OUT OF YOUR MOUTH. ARE YOU SURE YOU'RE NOT A WITCH?

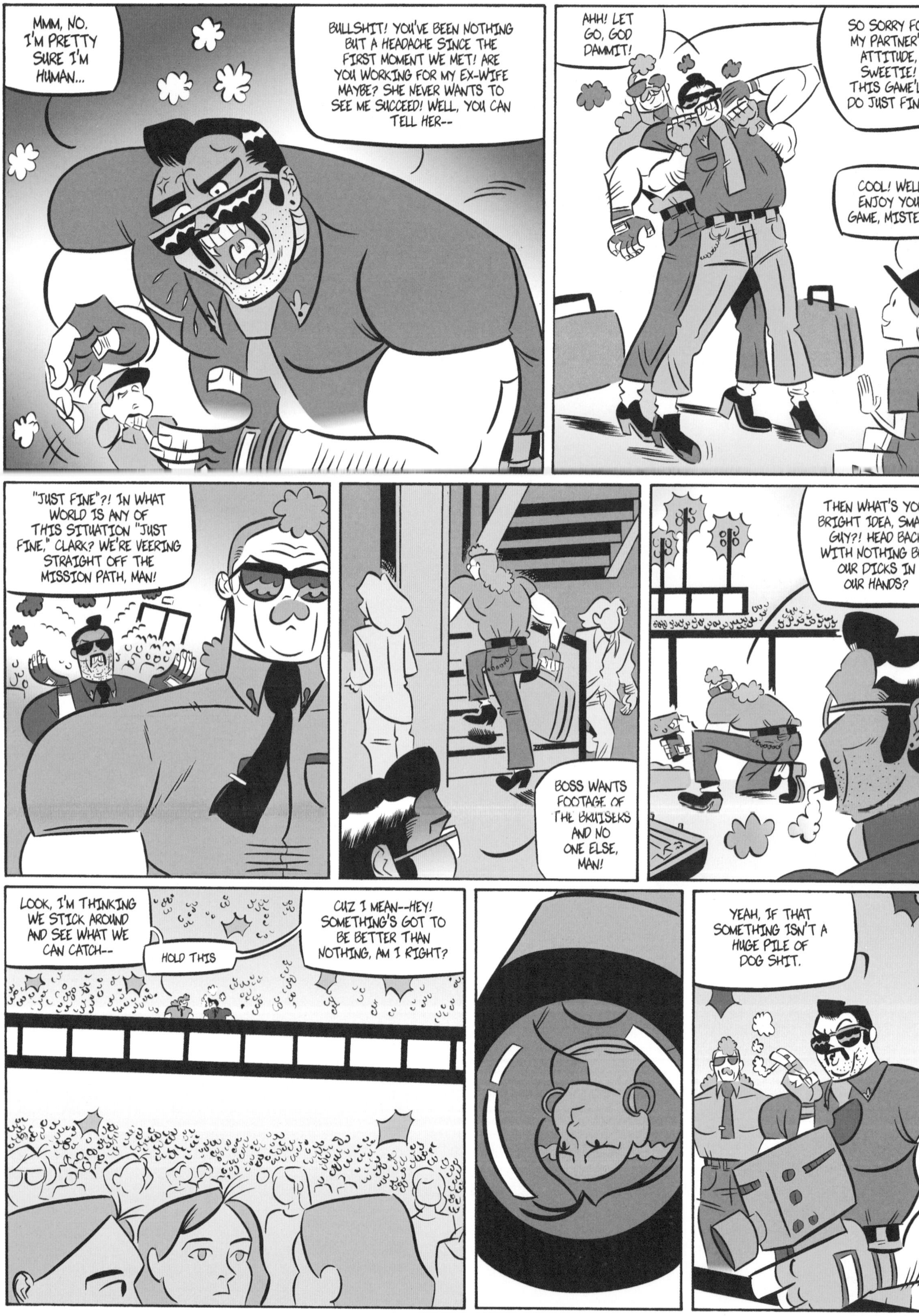

MMM, NO. I'M PRETTY SURE I'M HUMAN...
BULLSHIT! YOU'VE BEEN NOTHING BUT A HEADACHE SINCE THE FIRST MOMENT WE MET! ARE YOU WORKING FOR MY EX-WIFE MAYBE? SHE NEVER WANTS TO SEE ME SUCCEED! WELL, YOU CAN TELL HER--
AHH! LET GO, GOD DAMMIT!
SO SORRY FOR MY PARTNER'S ATTITUDE, SWEETIE! THIS GAME'LL DO JUST FINE!
COOL! WELL, ENJOY YOUR GAME, MISTERS!
"JUST FINE"?! IN WHAT WORLD IS ANY OF THIS SITUATION "JUST FINE," CLARK? WE'RE VEERING STRAIGHT OFF THE MISSION PATH, MAN!
BOSS WANTS FOOTAGE OF THE BRUISERS AND NO ONE ELSE, MAN!
THEN WHAT'S YOUR BRIGHT IDEA, SMART GUY?! HEAD BACK WITH NOTHING BUT OUR DICKS IN OUR HANDS?
LOOK, I'M THINKING WE STICK AROUND AND SEE WHAT WE CAN CATCH--
HOLD THIS
CUZ I MEAN--HEY! SOMETHING'S GOT TO BE BETTER THAN NOTHING, AM I RIGHT?
YEAH, IF THAT SOMETHING ISN'T A HUGE PILE OF DOG SHIT.

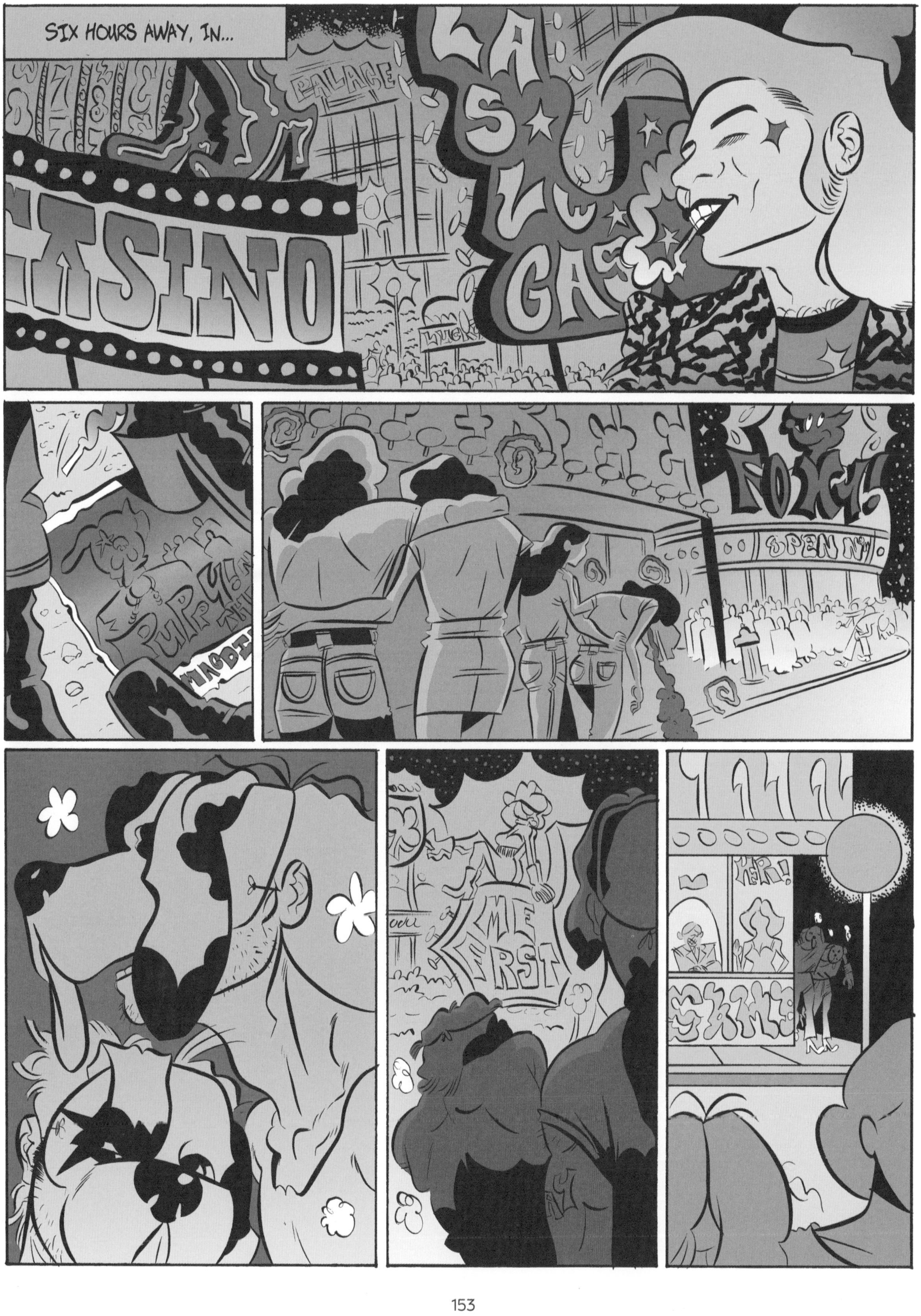
SIX HOURS AWAY, IN...
LAS VEGAS
CASINO
PALACE
LUCK
OPEN
FOXY!
ME FIRST

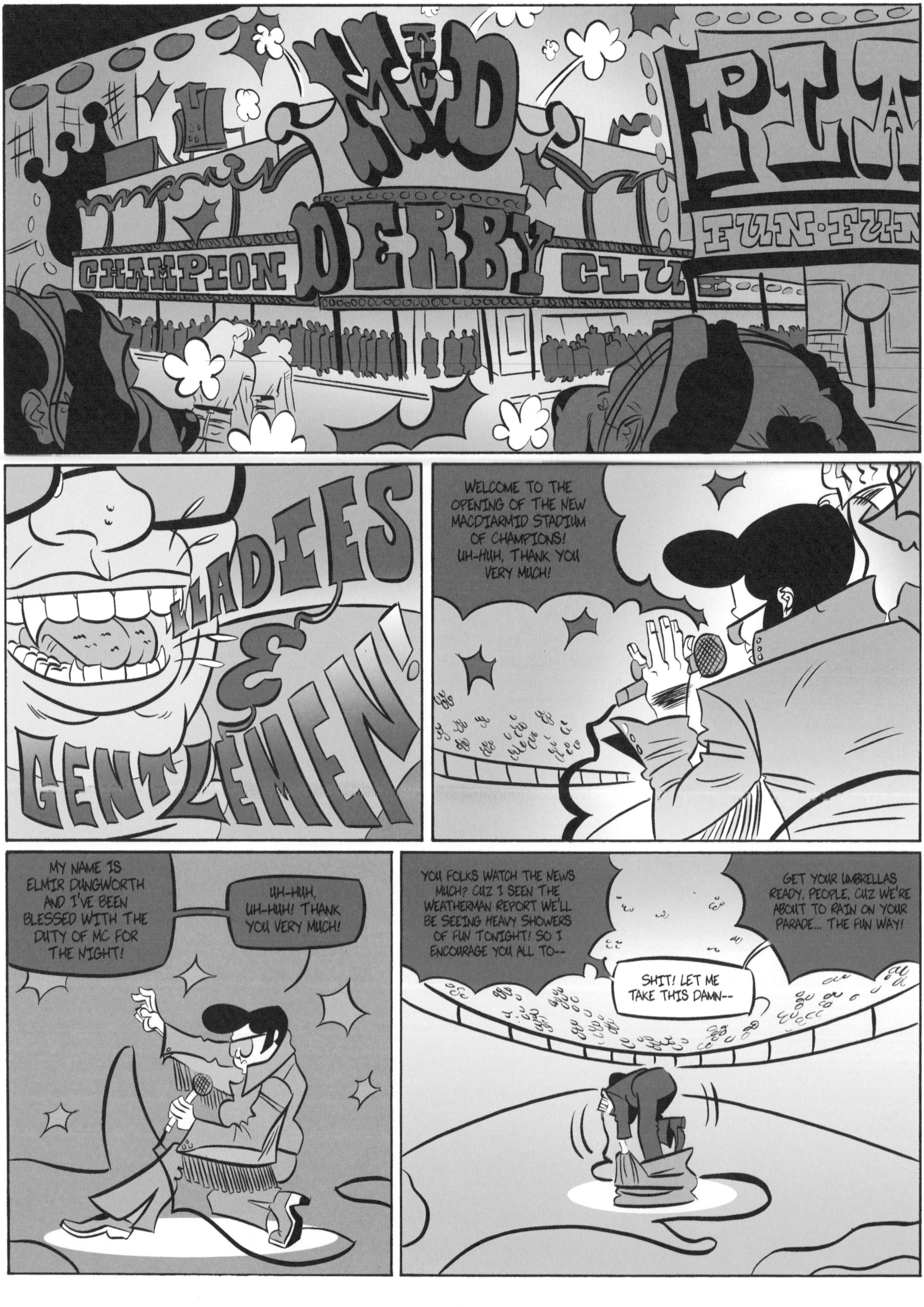

MAC
MAD
PLA
FUN·FUN
CHAMPION
DERBY
CLU
LADIES
&
GENTLEMEN!
WELCOME TO THE OPENING OF THE NEW MACDIARMID STADIUM OF CHAMPIONS! UH-HUH, THANK YOU VERY MUCH!
MY NAME IS ELMIR DUNGWORTH AND I'VE BEEN BLESSED WITH THE DUTY OF MC FOR THE NIGHT!
UH-HUH, UH-HUH! THANK YOU VERY MUCH!
YOU FOLKS WATCH THE NEWS MUCH? CUZ I SEEN THE WEATHERMAN REPORT WE'LL BE SEEING HEAVY SHOWERS OF FUN TONIGHT! SO I ENCOURAGE YOU ALL TO--
GET YOUR UMBRELLAS READY, PEOPLE, CUZ WE'RE ABOUT TO RAIN ON YOUR PARADE... THE FUN WAY!
SHIT! LET ME TAKE THIS DAMN--

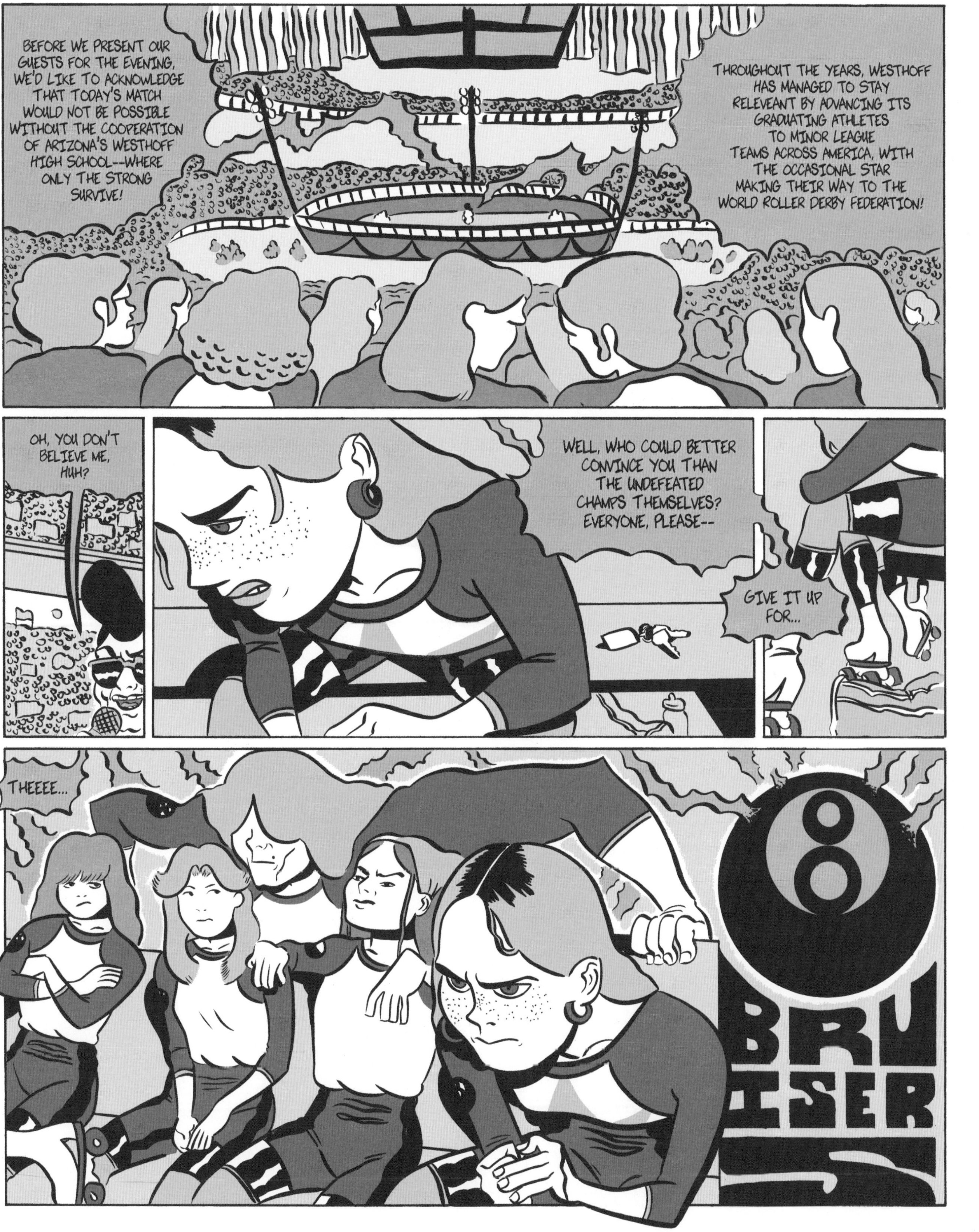
BEFORE WE PRESENT OUR GUESTS FOR THE EVENING, WE'D LIKE TO ACKNOWLEDGE THAT TODAY'S MATCH WOULD NOT BE POSSIBLE WITHOUT THE COOPERATION OF ARIZONA'S WESTHOFF HIGH SCHOOL--WHERE ONLY THE STRONG SURVIVE!
THROUGHOUT THE YEARS, WESTHOFF HAS MANAGED TO STAY RELEVEANT BY ADVANCING ITS GRADUATING ATHLETES TO MINOR LEAGUE TEAMS ACROSS AMERICA, WITH THE OCCASIONAL STAR MAKING THEIR WAY TO THE WORLD ROLLER DERBY FEDERATION!
OH, YOU DON'T BELIEVE ME, HUH?
WELL, WHO COULD BETTER CONVINCE YOU THAN THE UNDEFEATED CHAMPS THEMSELVES? EVERYONE, PLEASE--
GIVE IT UP FOR...
THEEEE...
8
BRUISER

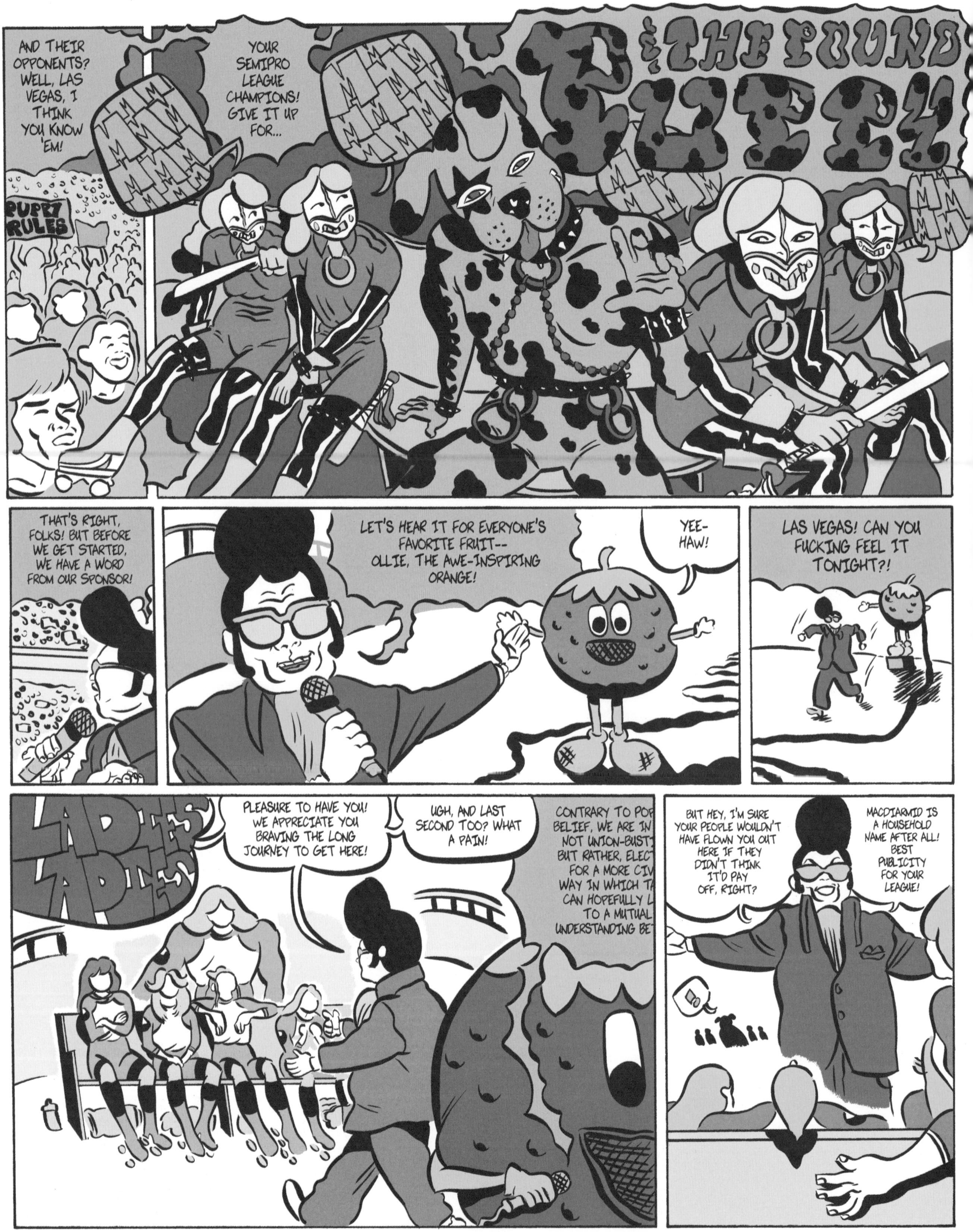
AND THEIR OPPONENTS? WELL, LAS VEGAS, I THINK YOU KNOW 'EM!
YOUR SEMIPRO LEAGUE CHAMPIONS! GIVE IT UP FOR...
& THE POUND
PUPPY RULES
THAT'S RIGHT, FOLKS! BUT BEFORE WE GET STARTED, WE HAVE A WORD FROM OUR SPONSOR!
LET'S HEAR IT FOR EVERYONE'S FAVORITE FRUIT-- OLLIE, THE AWE-INSPIRING ORANGE!
YEE-HAW!
LAS VEGAS! CAN YOU FUCKING FEEL IT TONIGHT?!
LADIES LADIES
PLEASURE TO HAVE YOU! WE APPRECIATE YOU BRAVING THE LONG JOURNEY TO GET HERE!
UGH, AND LAST SECOND TOO? WHAT A PAIN!
CONTRARY TO POP
BELIEF, WE ARE IN
NOT UNION-BUSTI
BUT RATHER, ELECT
FOR A MORE CIV
WAY IN WHICH TA
CAN HOPEFULLY L
TO A MUTUAL
UNDERSTANDING BE
BUT HEY, I'M SURE YOUR PEOPLE WOULDN'T HAVE FLOWN YOU OUT HERE IF THEY DIDN'T THINK IT'D PAY OFF, RIGHT?
MACDIARMID IS A HOUSEHOLD NAME AFTER ALL! BEST PUBLICITY FOR YOUR LEAGUE!

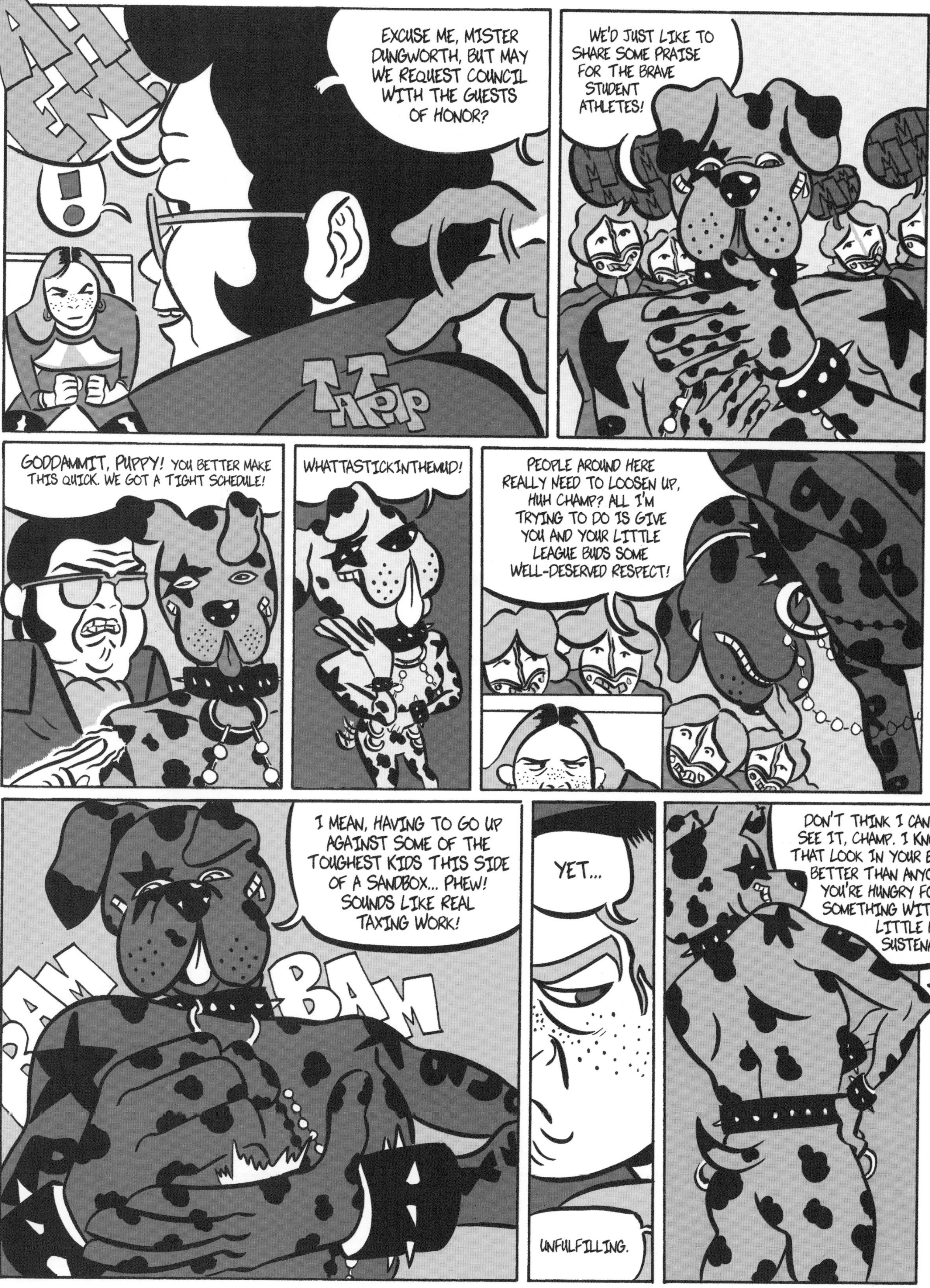
EXCUSE ME, MISTER DUNGWORTH, BUT MAY WE REQUEST COUNCIL WITH THE GUESTS OF HONOR?
WE'D JUST LIKE TO SHARE SOME PRAISE FOR THE BRAVE STUDENT ATHLETES!
GODDAMMIT, PUPPY! YOU BETTER MAKE THIS QUICK. WE GOT A TIGHT SCHEDULE!
WHATTASTICKINTHEMUD!
PEOPLE AROUND HERE REALLY NEED TO LOOSEN UP, HUH CHAMP? ALL I'M TRYING TO DO IS GIVE YOU AND YOUR LITTLE LEAGUE BUDS SOME WELL-DESERVED RESPECT!
I MEAN, HAVING TO GO UP AGAINST SOME OF THE TOUGHEST KIDS THIS SIDE OF A SANDBOX... PHEW! SOUNDS LIKE REAL TAXING WORK!
BAM
BAM
YET...
UNFULFILLING.
DON'T THINK I CAN'T SEE IT, CHAMP. I KNOW THAT LOOK IN YOUR EYES BETTER THAN ANYONE. YOU'RE HUNGRY FOR SOMETHING WITH A LITTLE MORE SUSTENANCE.

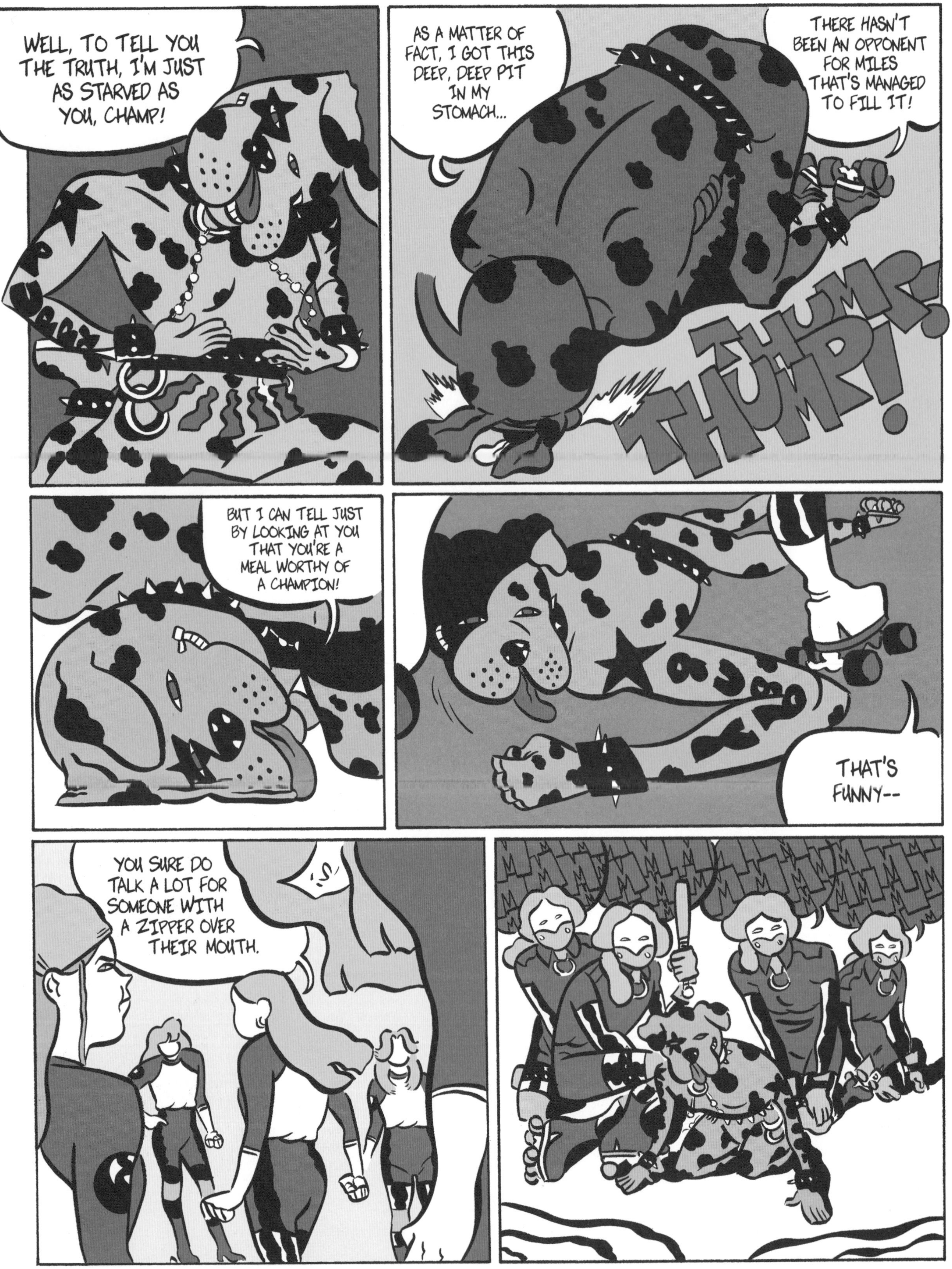
WELL, TO TELL YOU THE TRUTH, I'M JUST AS STARVED AS YOU, CHAMP!
AS A MATTER OF FACT, I GOT THIS DEEP, DEEP PIT IN MY STOMACH...
THERE HASN'T BEEN AN OPPONENT FOR MILES THAT'S MANAGED TO FILL IT!
THUMP! THUMP!
BUT I CAN TELL JUST BY LOOKING AT YOU THAT YOU'RE A MEAL WORTHY OF A CHAMPION!
THAT'S FUNNY--
YOU SURE DO TALK A LOT FOR SOMEONE WITH A ZIPPER OVER THEIR MOUTH.

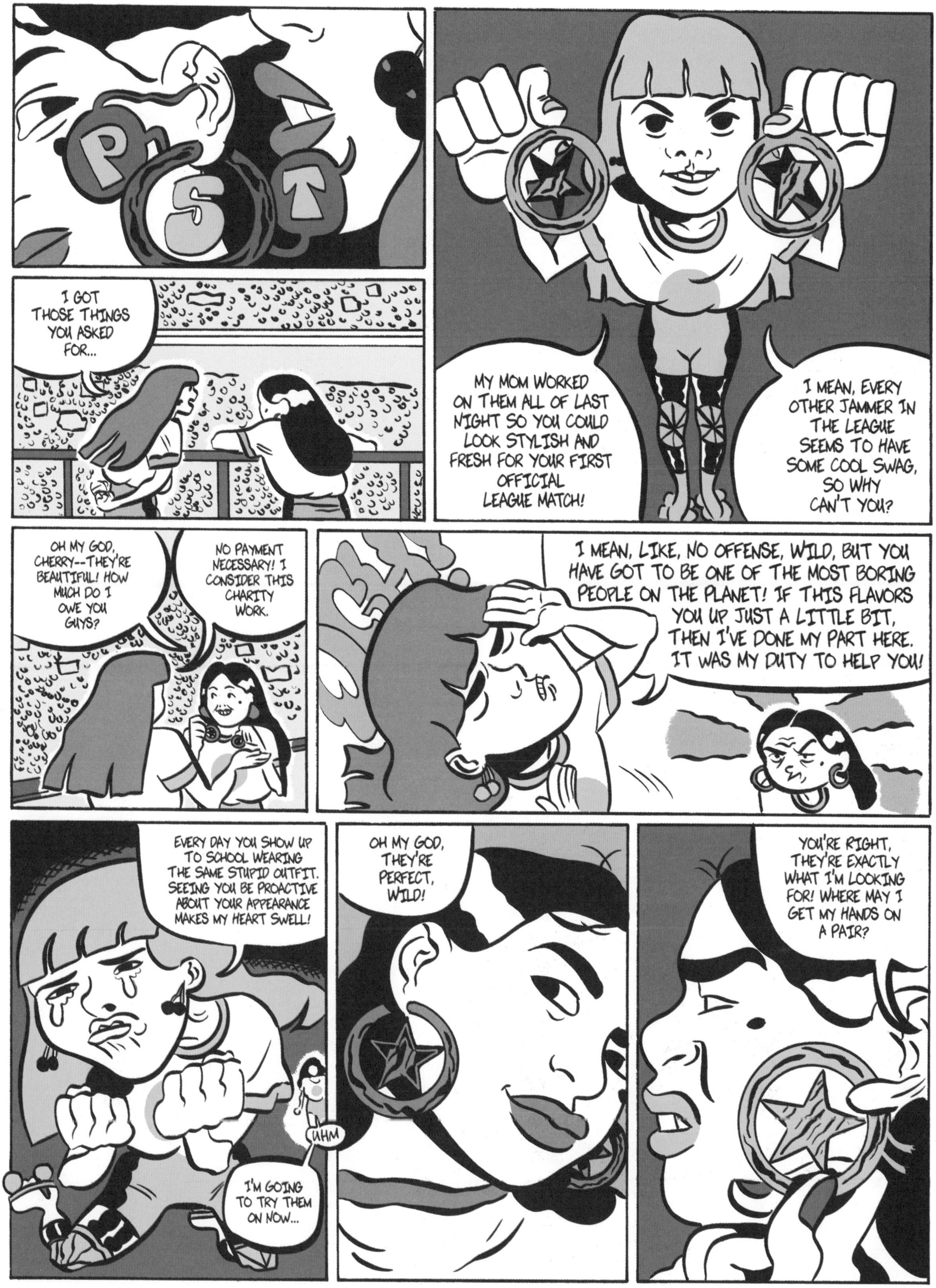
PSST
I GOT THOSE THINGS YOU ASKED FOR...
MY MOM WORKED ON THEM ALL OF LAST NIGHT SO YOU COULD LOOK STYLISH AND FRESH FOR YOUR FIRST OFFICIAL LEAGUE MATCH!
I MEAN, EVERY OTHER JAMMER IN THE LEAGUE SEEMS TO HAVE SOME COOL SWAG, SO WHY CAN'T YOU?
OH MY GOD, CHERRY--THEY'RE BEAUTIFUL! HOW MUCH DO I OWE YOU GUYS?
NO PAYMENT NECESSARY! I CONSIDER THIS CHARITY WORK.
I MEAN, LIKE, NO OFFENSE, WILD, BUT YOU HAVE GOT TO BE ONE OF THE MOST BORING PEOPLE ON THE PLANET! IF THIS FLAVORS YOU UP JUST A LITTLE BIT, THEN I'VE DONE MY PART HERE. IT WAS MY DUTY TO HELP YOU!
EVERY DAY YOU SHOW UP TO SCHOOL WEARING THE SAME STUPID OUTFIT. SEEING YOU BE PROACTIVE ABOUT YOUR APPEARANCE MAKES MY HEART SWELL!
UHM
I'M GOING TO TRY THEM ON NOW...
OH MY GOD, THEY'RE PERFECT, WILD!
YOU'RE RIGHT, THEY'RE EXACTLY WHAT I'M LOOKING FOR! WHERE MAY I GET MY HANDS ON A PAIR?

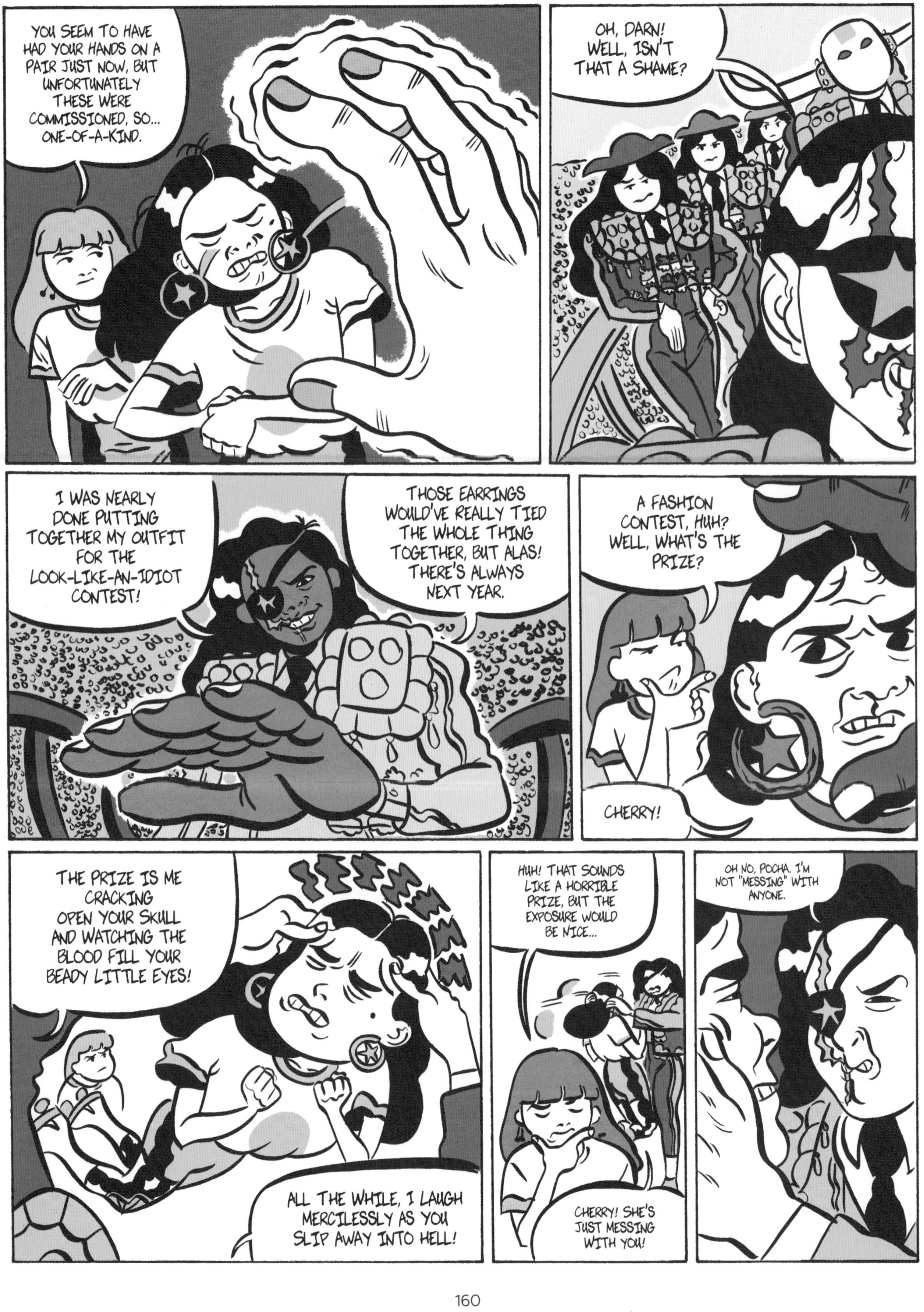
YOU SEEM TO HAVE HAD YOUR HANDS ON A PAIR JUST NOW, BUT UNFORTUNATELY THESE WERE COMMISSIONED, SO... ONE-OF-A-KIND.
OH, DARN! WELL, ISN'T THAT A SHAME?
I WAS NEARLY DONE PUTTING TOGETHER MY OUTFIT FOR THE LOOK-LIKE-AN-IDIOT CONTEST!
THOSE EARRINGS WOULD'VE REALLY TIED THE WHOLE THING TOGETHER, BUT ALAS! THERE'S ALWAYS NEXT YEAR.
A FASHION CONTEST, HUH? WELL, WHAT'S THE PRIZE?
CHERRY!
THE PRIZE IS ME CRACKING OPEN YOUR SKULL AND WATCHING THE BLOOD FILL YOUR BEADY LITTLE EYES!
ALL THE WHILE, I LAUGH MERCILESSLY AS YOU SLIP AWAY INTO HELL!
HUH! THAT SOUNDS LIKE A HORRIBLE PRIZE, BUT THE EXPOSURE WOULD BE NICE...
CHERRY! SHE'S JUST MESSING WITH YOU!
OH NO, POCHA. I'M NOT "MESSING" WITH ANYONE.

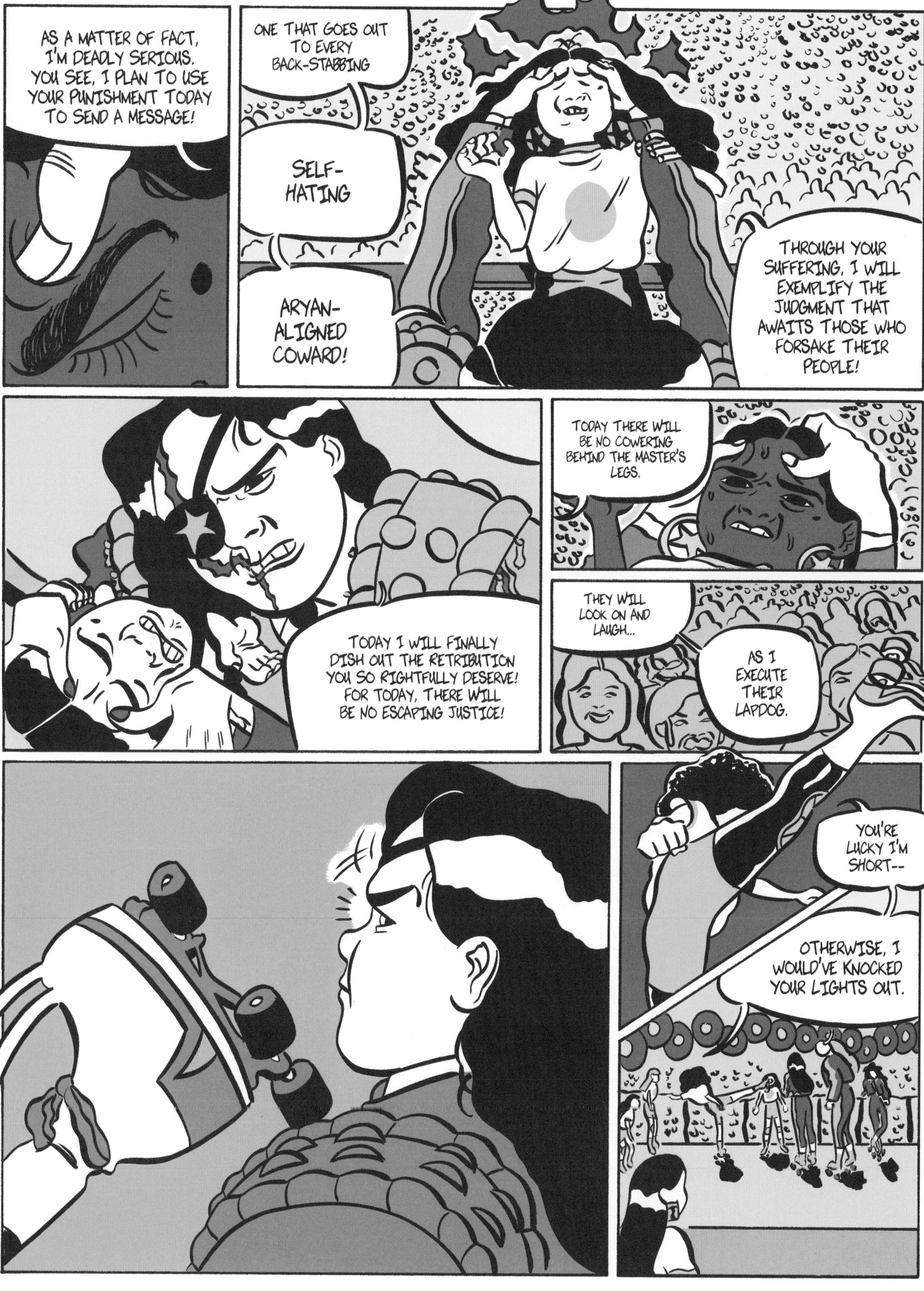
AS A MATTER OF FACT, I'M DEADLY SERIOUS. YOU SEE, I PLAN TO USE YOUR PUNISHMENT TODAY TO SEND A MESSAGE!
ONE THAT GOES OUT TO EVERY BACK-STABBING
SELF-HATING
ARYAN-ALIGNED COWARD!
THROUGH YOUR SUFFERING, I WILL EXEMPLIFY THE JUDGMENT THAT AWAITS THOSE WHO FORSAKE THEIR PEOPLE!
TODAY I WILL FINALLY DISH OUT THE RETRIBUTION YOU SO RIGHTFULLY DESERVE! FOR TODAY, THERE WILL BE NO ESCAPING JUSTICE!
TODAY THERE WILL BE NO COWERING BEHIND THE MASTER'S LEGS.
THEY WILL LOOK ON AND LAUGH...
AS I EXECUTE THEIR LAPDOG.
YOU'RE LUCKY I'M SHORT--
OTHERWISE, I WOULD'VE KNOCKED YOUR LIGHTS OUT.

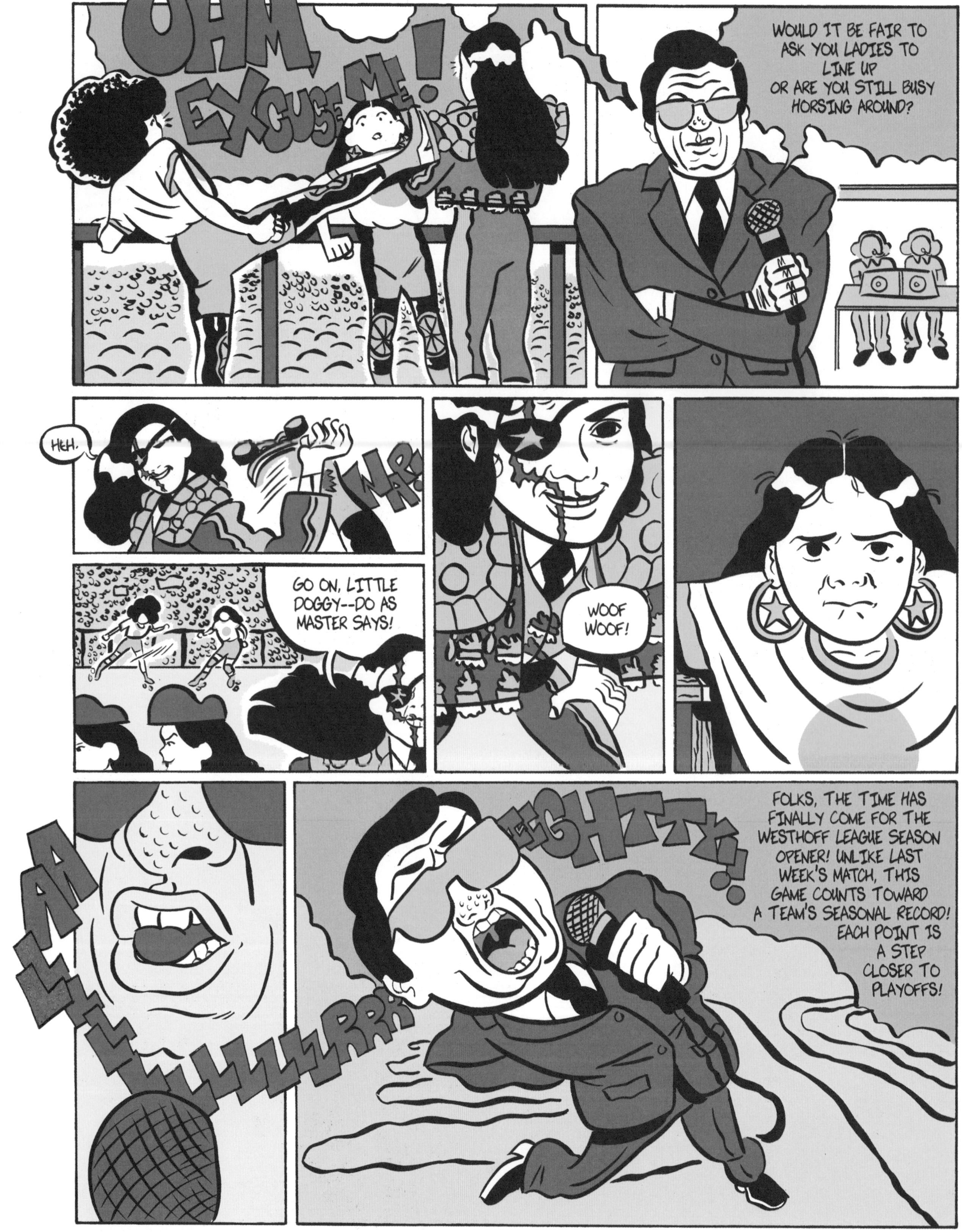
UHM, EXCUSE ME!
WOULD IT BE FAIR TO ASK YOU LADIES TO LINE UP OR ARE YOU STILL BUSY HORSING AROUND?
HEH.
GO ON, LITTLE DOGGY--DO AS MASTER SAYS!
WOOF WOOF!
AALLLLLLLLLRRR
EIGHTTTY!!
FOLKS, THE TIME HAS FINALLY COME FOR THE WESTHOFF LEAGUE SEASON OPENER! UNLIKE LAST WEEK'S MATCH, THIS GAME COUNTS TOWARD A TEAM'S SEASONAL RECORD! EACH POINT IS A STEP CLOSER TO PLAYOFFS!

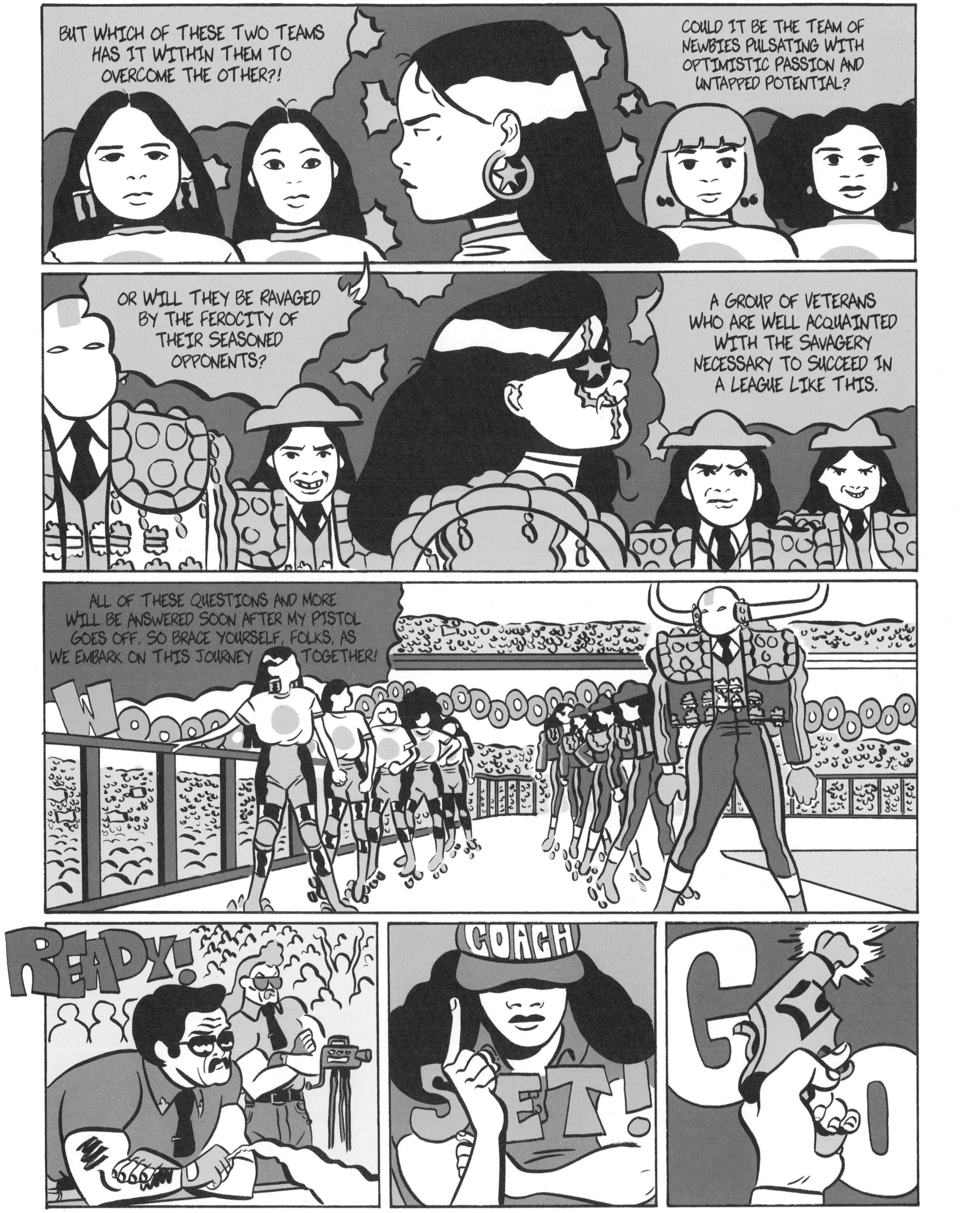
BUT WHICH OF THESE TWO TEAMS HAS IT WITHIN THEM TO OVERCOME THE OTHER?!
COULD IT BE THE TEAM OF NEWBIES PULSATING WITH OPTIMISTIC PASSION AND UNTAPPED POTENTIAL?
OR WILL THEY BE RAVAGED BY THE FEROCITY OF THEIR SEASONED OPPONENTS?
A GROUP OF VETERANS WHO ARE WELL ACQUAINTED WITH THE SAVAGERY NECESSARY TO SUCCEED IN A LEAGUE LIKE THIS.
ALL OF THESE QUESTIONS AND MORE WILL BE ANSWERED SOON AFTER MY PISTOL GOES OFF. SO BRACE YOURSELF, FOLKS, AS WE EMBARK ON THIS JOURNEY TOGETHER!
READY!
COACH
SET!
GO

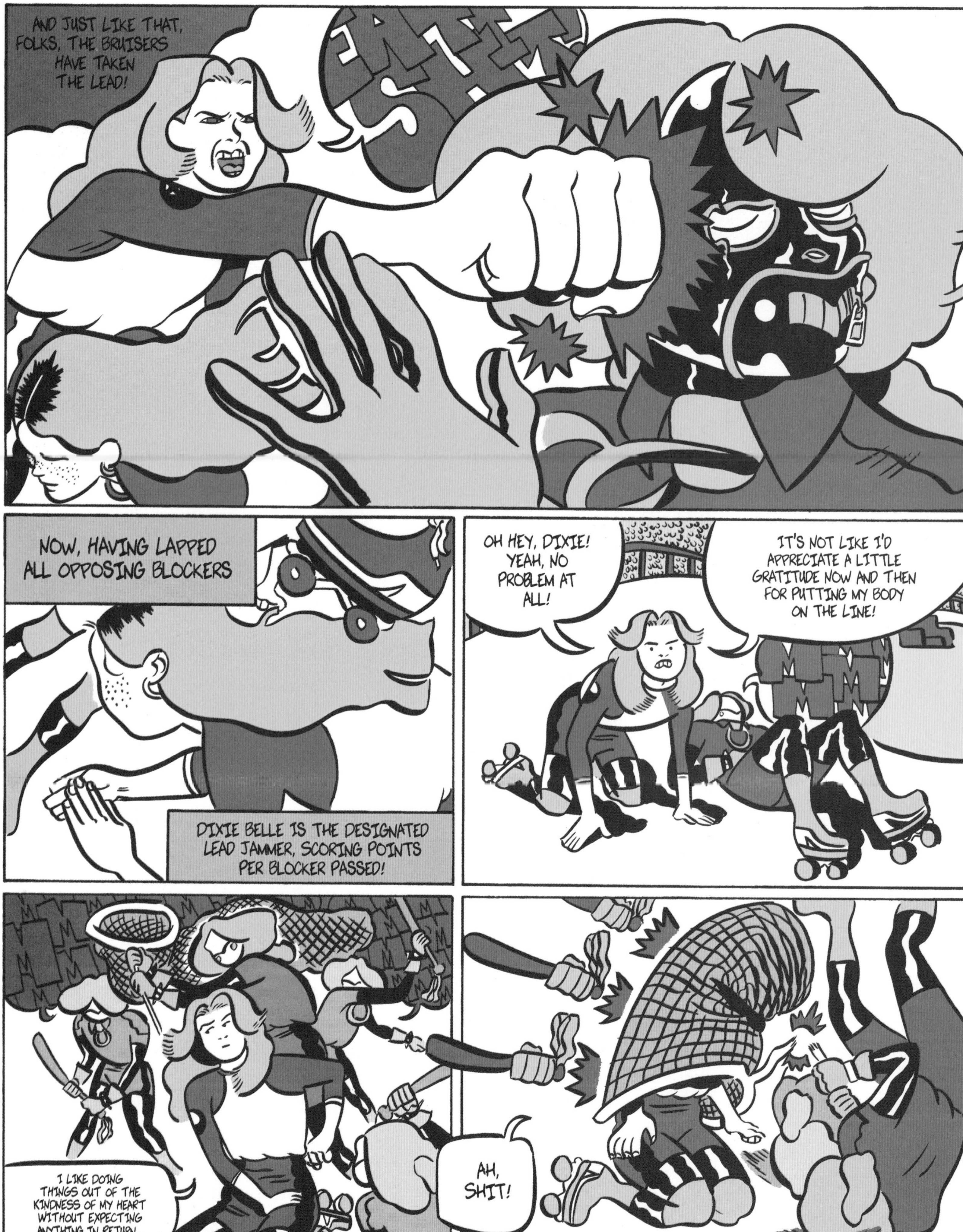
AND JUST LIKE THAT, FOLKS, THE BRUISERS HAVE TAKEN THE LEAD!
NOW, HAVING LAPPED ALL OPPOSING BLOCKERS
DIXIE BELLE IS THE DESIGNATED LEAD JAMMER, SCORING POINTS PER BLOCKER PASSED!
OH HEY, DIXIE! YEAH, NO PROBLEM AT ALL!
IT'S NOT LIKE I'D APPRECIATE A LITTLE GRATITUDE NOW AND THEN FOR PUTTING MY BODY ON THE LINE!
I LIKE DOING THINGS OUT OF THE KINDNESS OF MY HEART WITHOUT EXPECTING ANYTHING IN RETURN...
AH, SHIT!

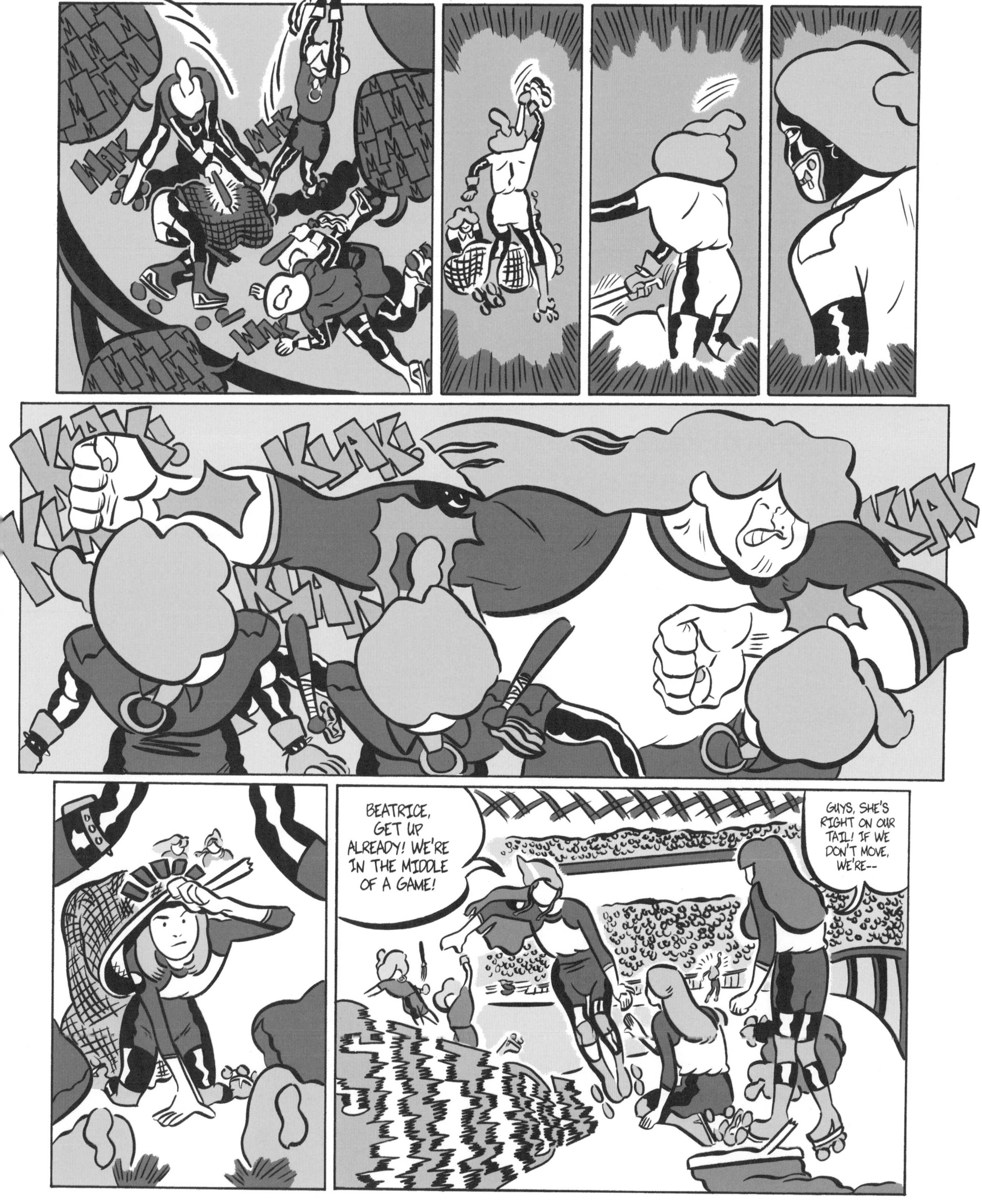
WAK
WAK
WAK
KLAK!
KLAK!
KLAK
BEATRICE, GET UP ALREADY! WE'RE IN THE MIDDLE OF A GAME!
GUYS, SHE'S RIGHT ON OUR TAIL! IF WE DON'T MOVE, WE'RE--

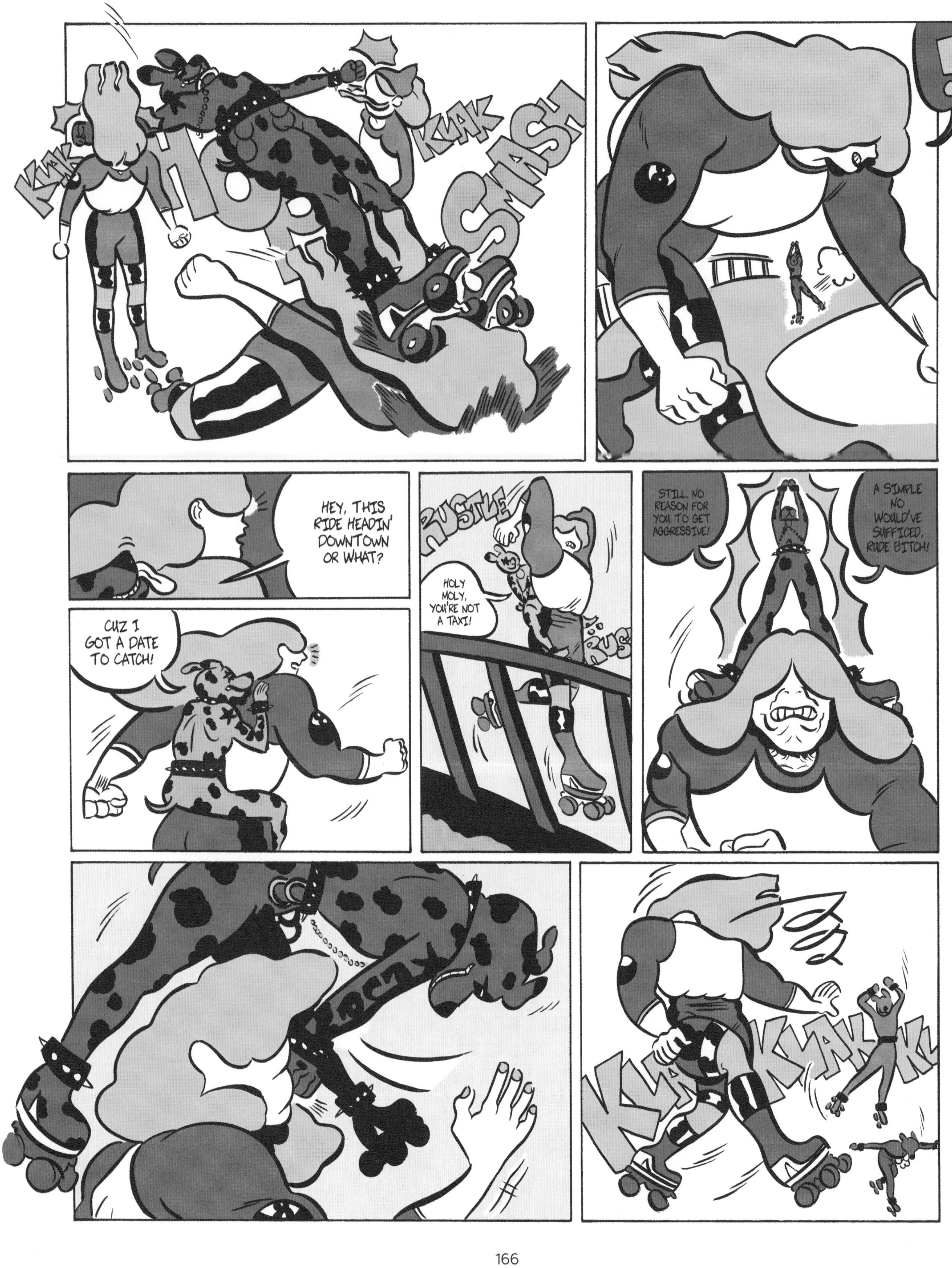
KLAK
HO
KLAK
SMASH
!
HEY, THIS RIDE HEADIN' DOWNTOWN OR WHAT?
BUSTLE
HOLY MOLY, YOU'RE NOT A TAXI!
STILL, NO REASON FOR YOU TO GET AGGRESSIVE!
A SIMPLE NO WOULD'VE SUFFICED, RUDE BITCH!
CUZ I GOT A DATE TO CATCH!
KLAK KLAK KL

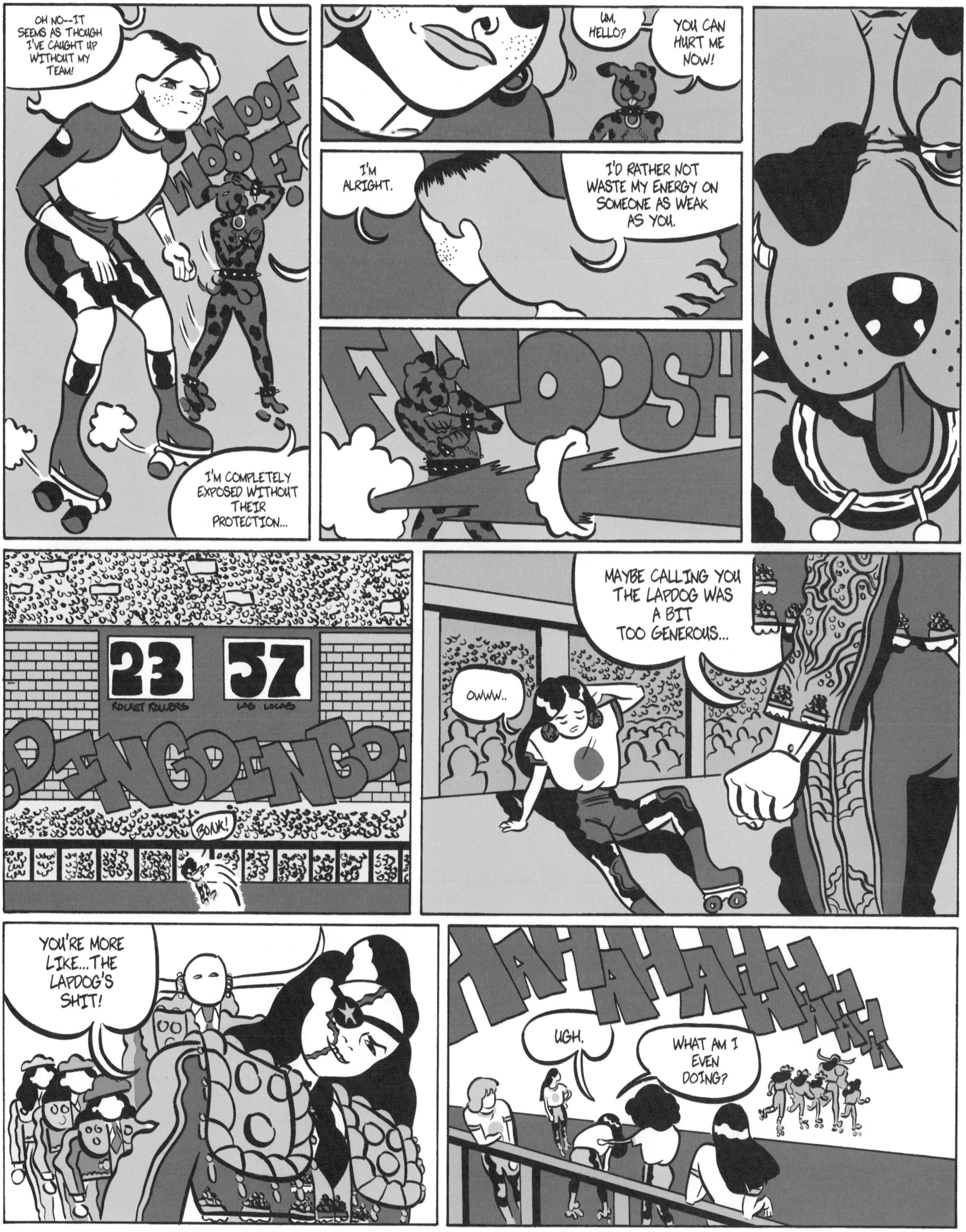
OH NO--IT SEEMS AS THOUGH I'VE CAUGHT UP WITHOUT MY TEAM!
WOOF WOOF!
I'M COMPLETELY EXPOSED WITHOUT THEIR PROTECTION...
UM, HELLO?
YOU CAN HURT ME NOW!
I'M ALRIGHT.
I'D RATHER NOT WASTE MY ENERGY ON SOMEONE AS WEAK AS YOU.
FWOOSH
23
57
ROCKET ROLLERS
LAS LOLAS
DINGDINGDING
BONK!
MAYBE CALLING YOU THE LAPDOG WAS A BIT TOO GENEROUS...
OWWW..
YOU'RE MORE LIKE...THE LAPDOG'S SHIT!
HAHAHAHAHAHAHAHA
UGH.
WHAT AM I EVEN DOING?

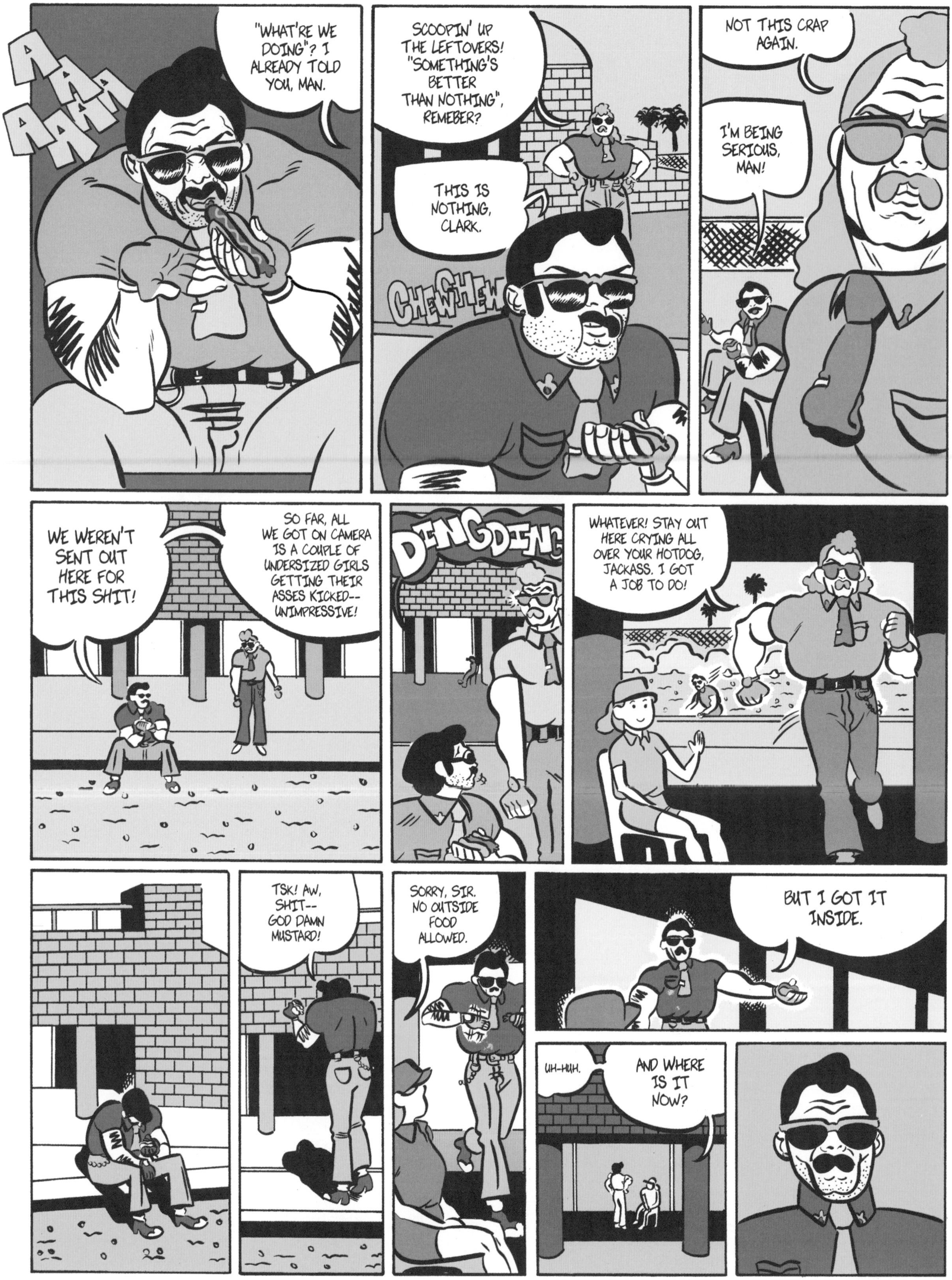
AAAAHH
"WHAT'RE WE DOING"? I ALREADY TOLD YOU, MAN.
SCOOPIN' UP THE LEFTOVERS! "SOMETHING'S BETTER THAN NOTHING", REMEBER?
THIS IS NOTHING, CLARK.
CHEW CHEW
NOT THIS CRAP AGAIN.
I'M BEING SERIOUS, MAN!
WE WEREN'T SENT OUT HERE FOR THIS SHIT!
SO FAR, ALL WE GOT ON CAMERA IS A COUPLE OF UNDERSIZED GIRLS GETTING THEIR ASSES KICKED-- UNIMPRESSIVE!
DING DING
WHATEVER! STAY OUT HERE CRYING ALL OVER YOUR HOTDOG, JACKASS. I GOT A JOB TO DO!
TSK! AW, SHIT-- GOD DAMN MUSTARD!
SORRY, SIR. NO OUTSIDE FOOD ALLOWED.
BUT I GOT IT INSIDE.
UH-HUH.
AND WHERE IS IT NOW?

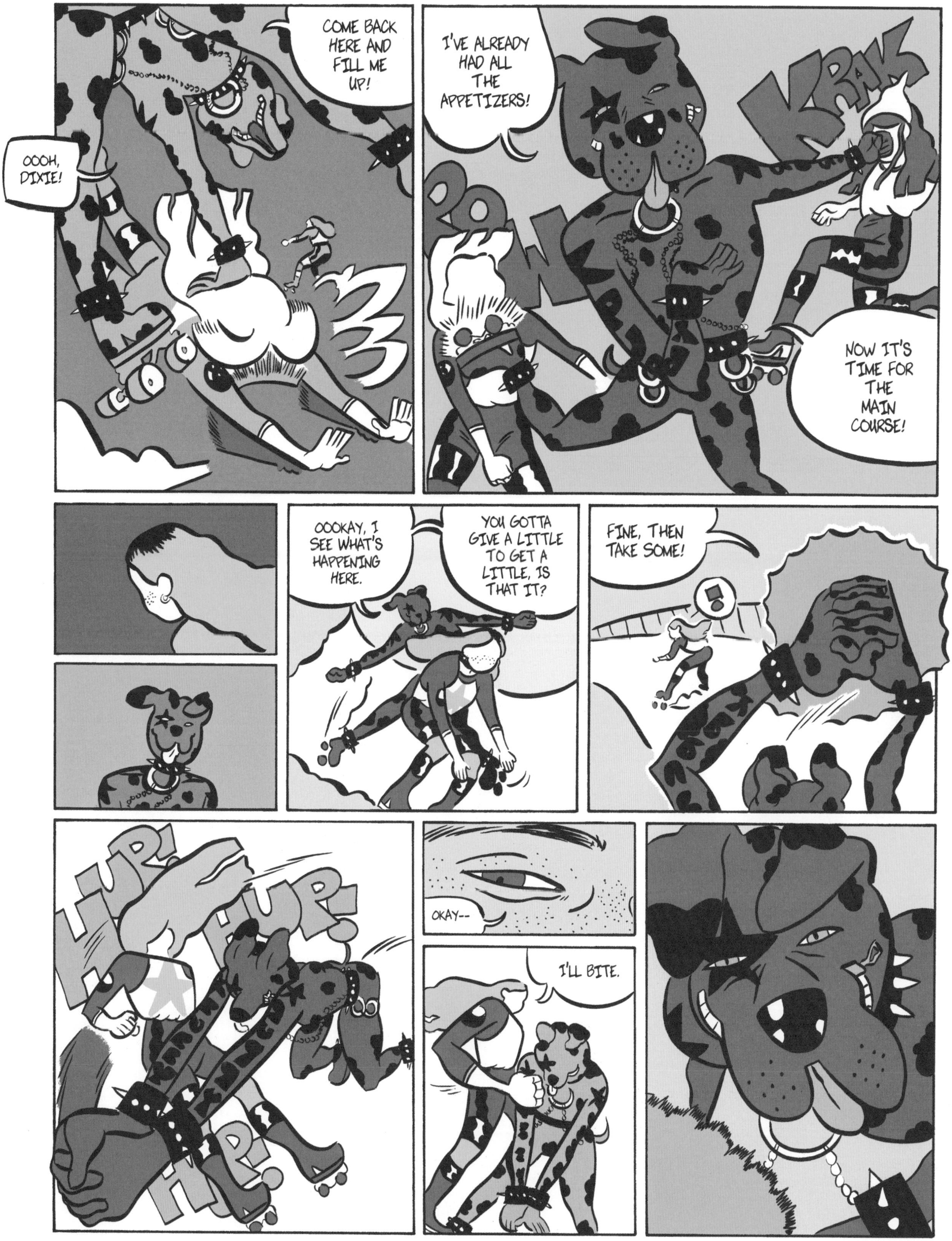
COME BACK HERE AND FILL ME UP!
OOOH, DIXIE!
I'VE ALREADY HAD ALL THE APPETIZERS!
KRAK
POW
NOW IT'S TIME FOR THE MAIN COURSE!
OOOKAY, I SEE WHAT'S HAPPENING HERE.
YOU GOTTA GIVE A LITTLE TO GET A LITTLE, IS THAT IT?
FINE, THEN TAKE SOME!
HUP!
HUP!
HUP!
OKAY--
I'LL BITE.

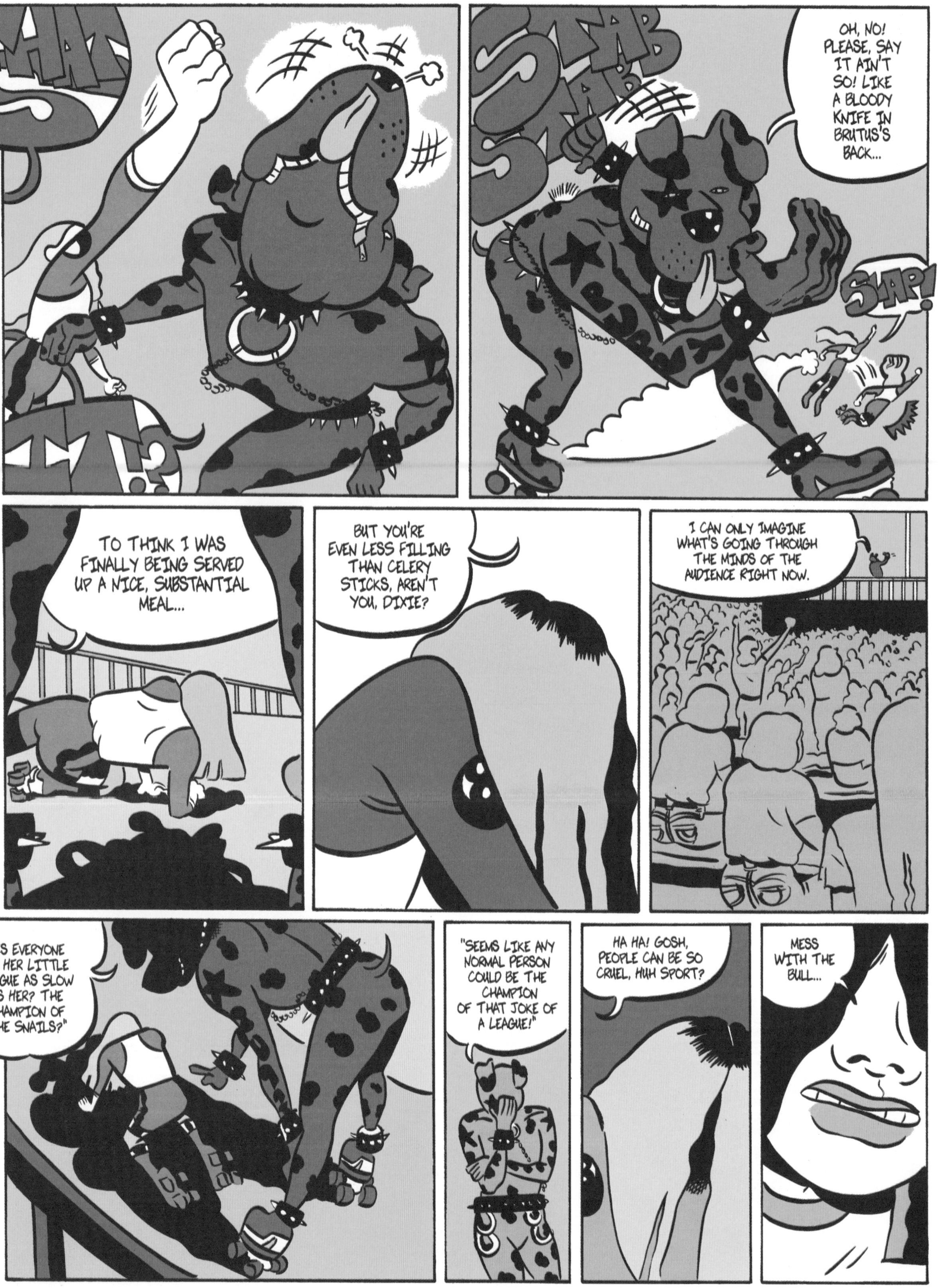
THAT
STAB STAB
OH, NO! PLEASE, SAY IT AIN'T SO! LIKE A BLOODY KNIFE IN BRUTUS'S BACK...
SLAP!
TO THINK I WAS FINALLY BEING SERVED UP A NICE, SUBSTANTIAL MEAL...
BUT YOU'RE EVEN LESS FILLING THAN CELERY STICKS, AREN'T YOU, DIXIE?
I CAN ONLY IMAGINE WHAT'S GOING THROUGH THE MINDS OF THE AUDIENCE RIGHT NOW.
"IS EVERYONE IN HER LITTLE LEAGUE AS SLOW AS HER? THE CHAMPION OF THE SNAILS?"
"SEEMS LIKE ANY NORMAL PERSON COULD BE THE CHAMPION OF THAT JOKE OF A LEAGUE!"
HA HA! GOSH, PEOPLE CAN BE SO CRUEL, HUH SPORT?
MESS WITH THE BULL...

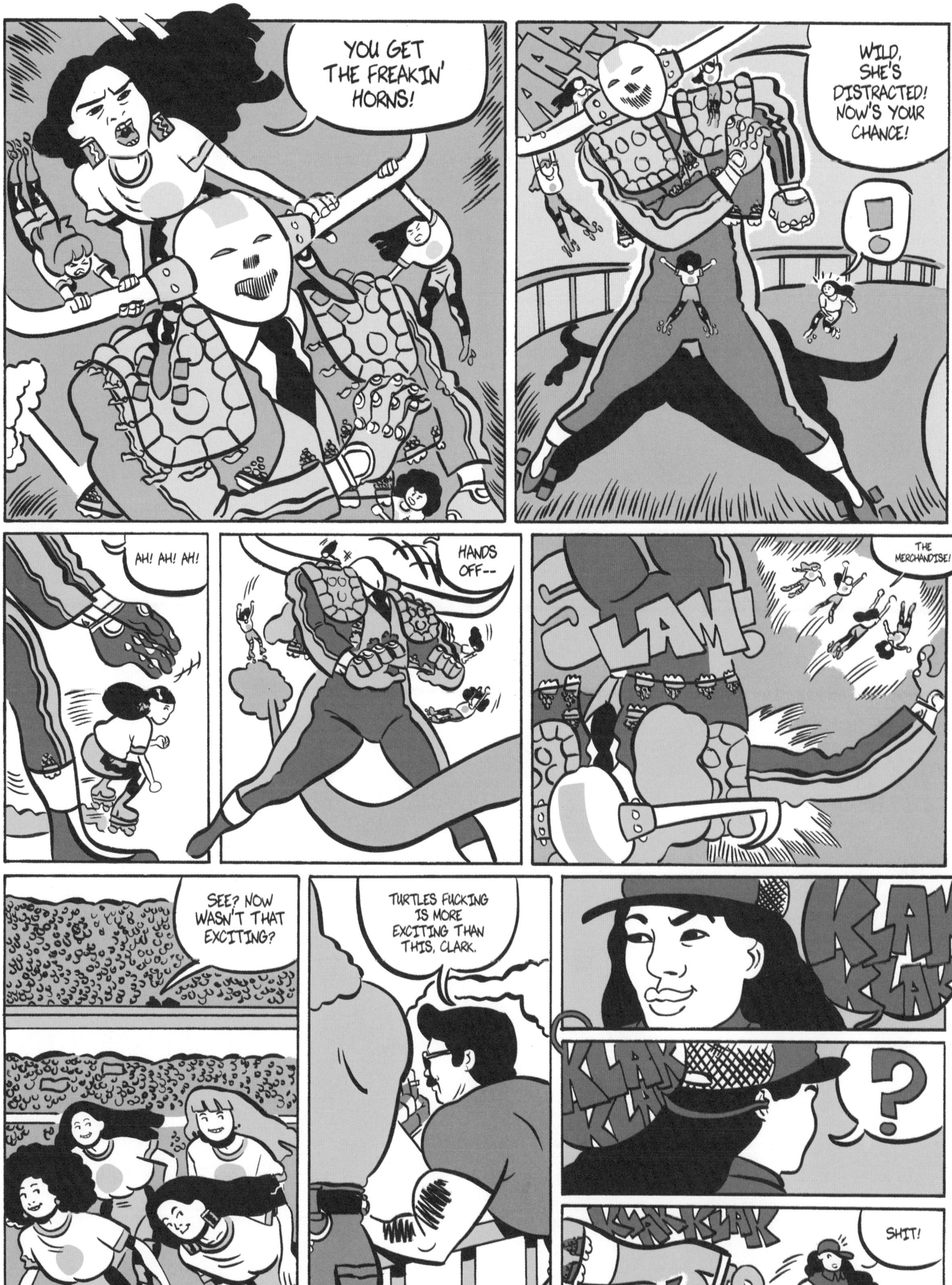
YOU GET THE FREAKIN' HORNS!
WILD, SHE'S DISTRACTED! NOW'S YOUR CHANCE!
!
AH! AH! AH!
HANDS OFF--
SLAM!
THE MERCHANDISE!
SEE? NOW WASN'T THAT EXCITING?
TURTLES FUCKING IS MORE EXCITING THAN THIS, CLARK.
KLAK KLAK
KLAK KLAK
?
KLAK KLAK
KLAK
SHIT!

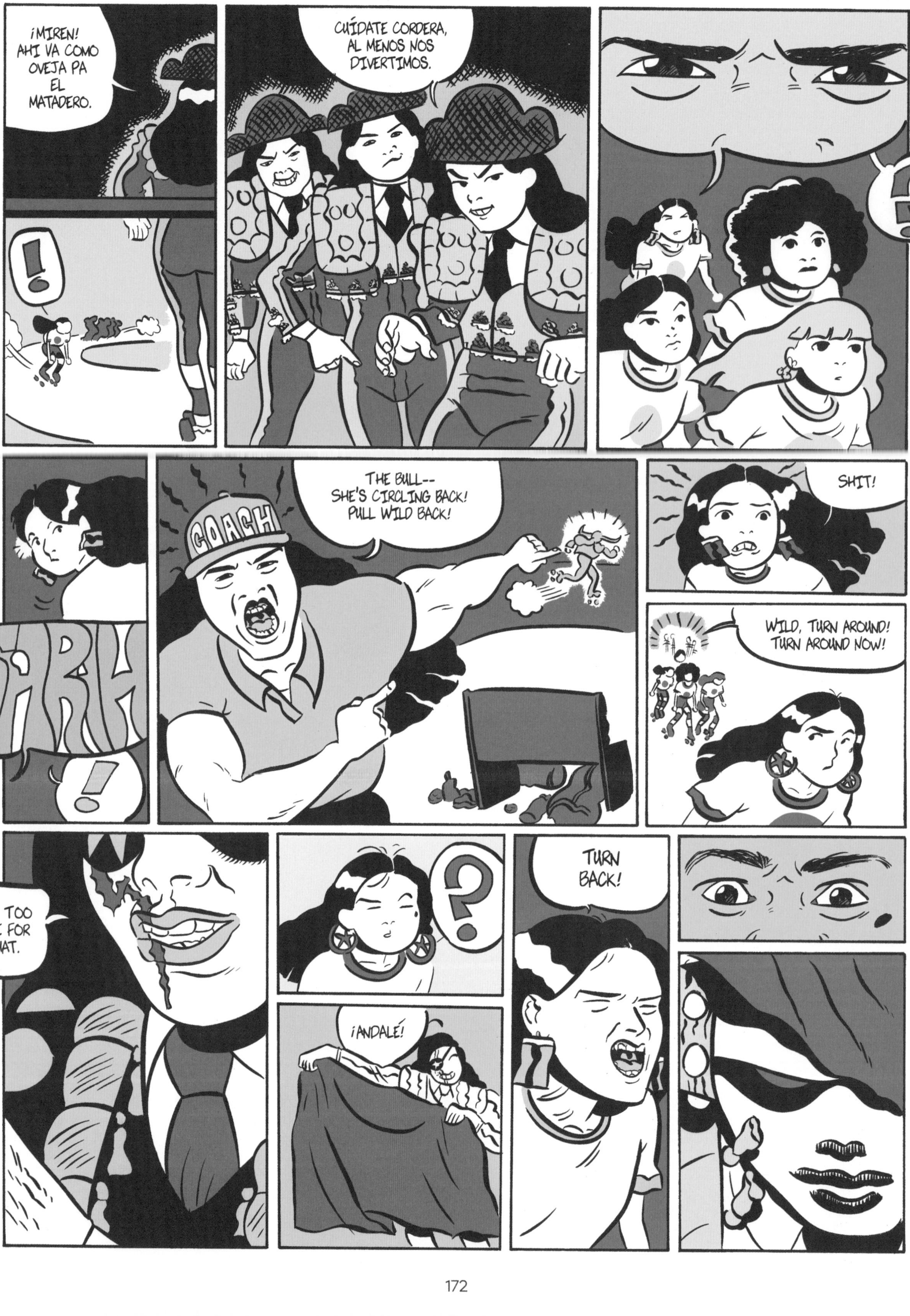

¡MIREN! AHI VA COMO OVEJA PA EL MATADERO.
!
CUÍDATE CORDERA, AL MENOS NOS DIVERTIMOS.
?
SKRH
!
THE BULL-- SHE'S CIRCLING BACK! PULL WILD BACK!
COACH
SHIT!
WILD, TURN AROUND! TURN AROUND NOW!
IT'S TOO LATE FOR THAT.
?
¡ANDALÉ!
TURN BACK!

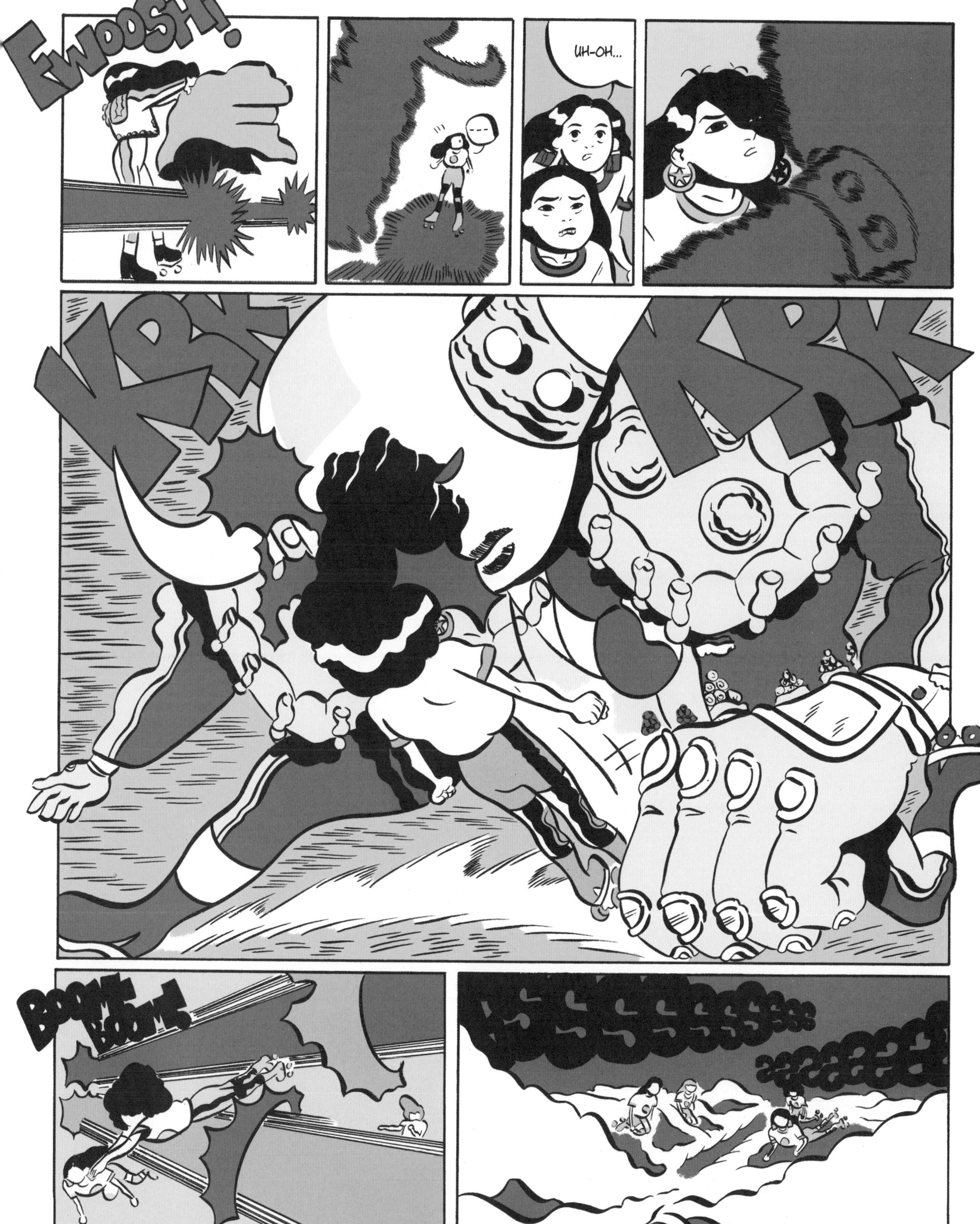
FWOOSH!
UH-OH...
KRK
KRK
BOOM! BOOM!

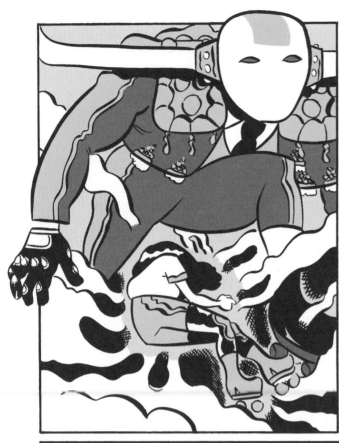

OH MY GOD, SHE FUCKING KILLED HER!

EWWWW! WHAT THE HELL IS THAT THING?!

BADOING!

UH, I HATE TO BE THAT GUY, BUT IF THE GIRL IS UNABLE TO CONTINUE...

THEN YOUR TEAM WILL BE FORCED TO FORFEIT.

OH, SCREW YOU, BOB! I KNOW THE RULES, ALRIGHT?!

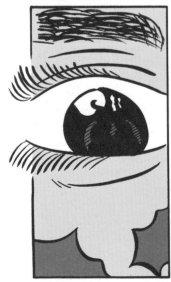

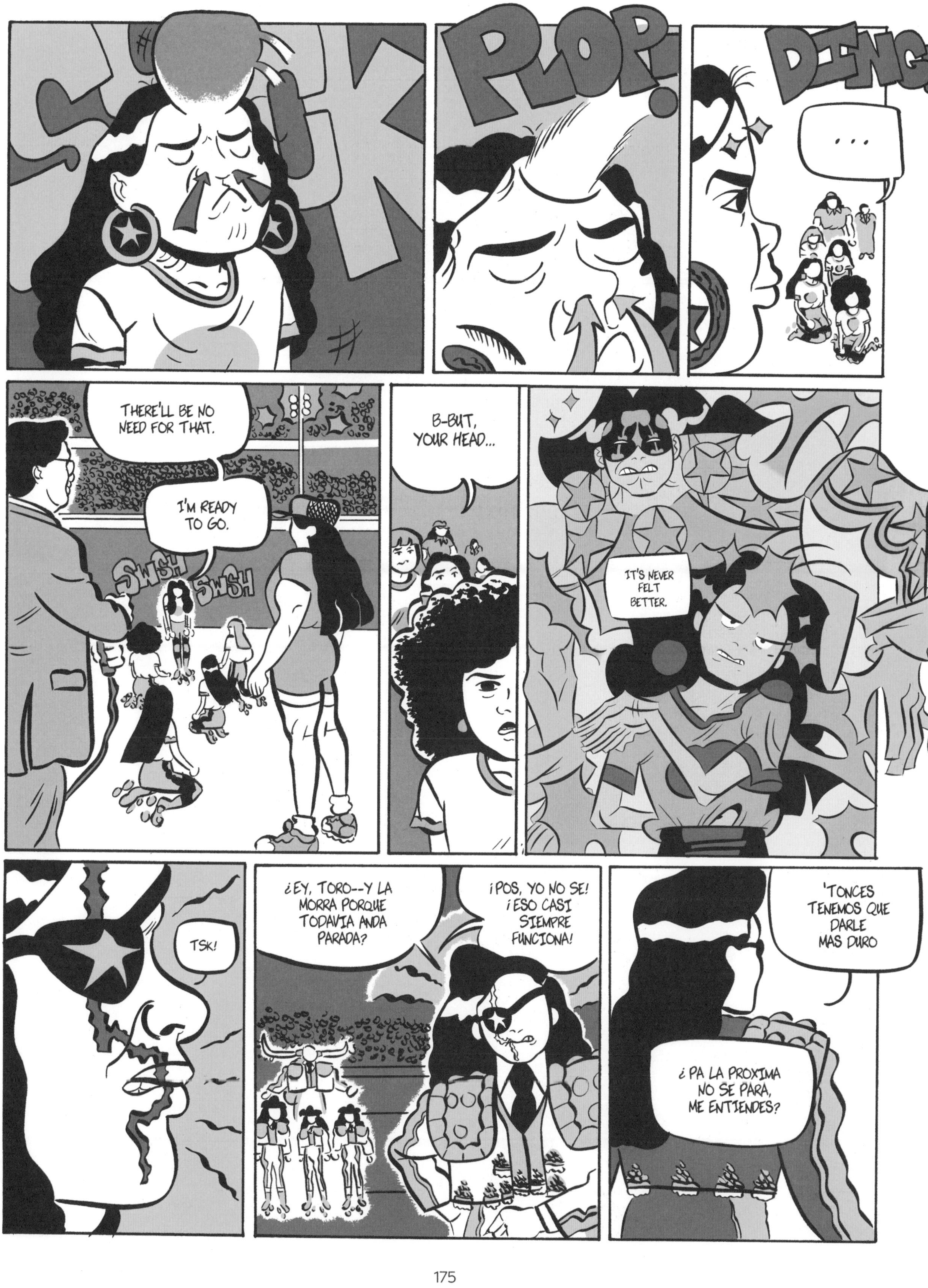
PLOP!
DING!
...
THERE'LL BE NO NEED FOR THAT.
I'M READY TO GO.
SWSH
SWSH
B-BUT, YOUR HEAD...
IT'S NEVER FELT BETTER.
TSK!
¿EY, TORO--Y LA MORRA PORQUE TODAVIA ANDA PARADA?
¡POS, YO NO SE! ¡ESO CASI SIEMPRE FUNCIONA!
'TONCES TENEMOS QUE DARLE MAS DURO
¿PA LA PROXIMA NO SE PARA, ME ENTIENDES?

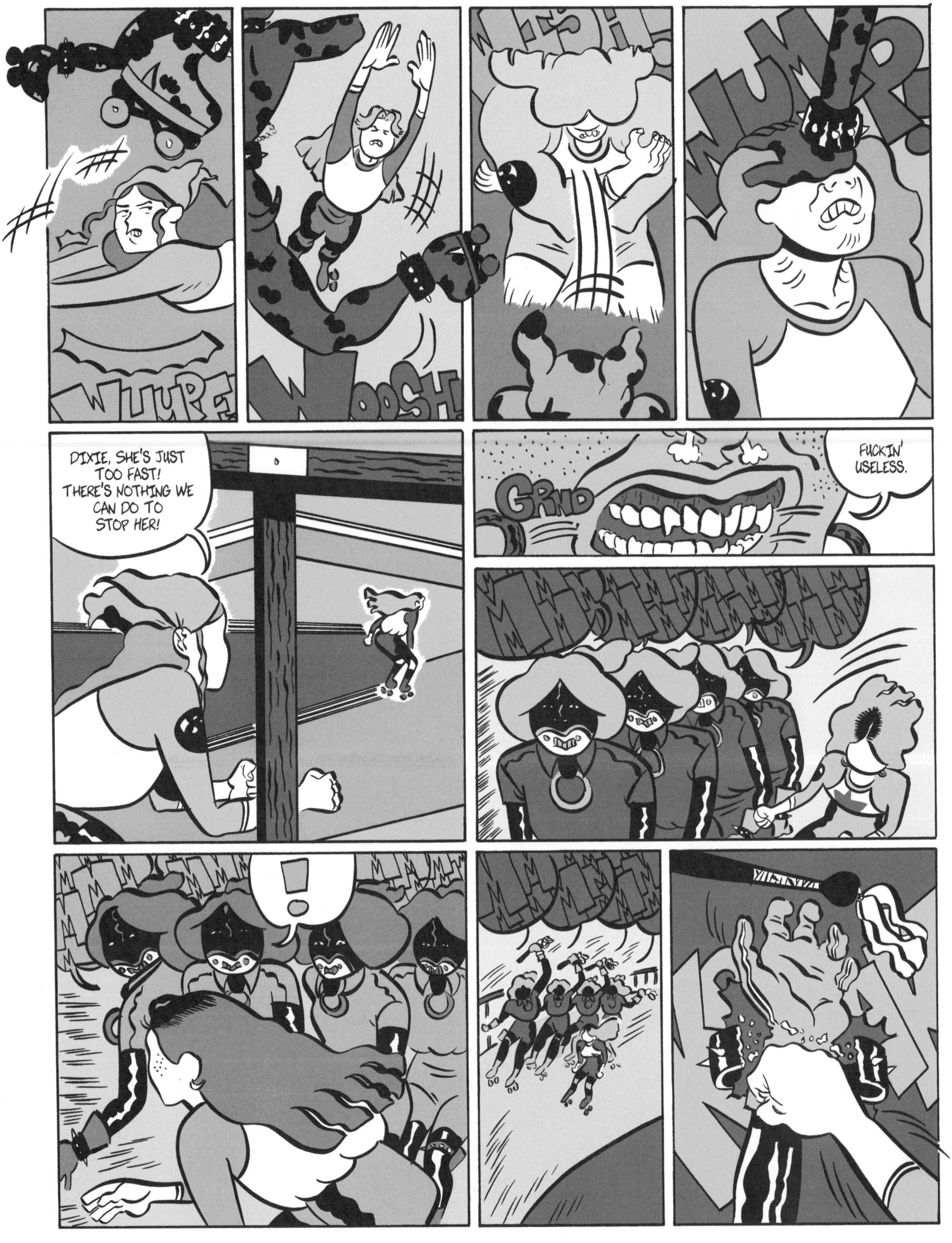
WOOSH!
DIXIE, SHE'S JUST TOO FAST! THERE'S NOTHING WE CAN DO TO STOP HER!
GRND
FUCKIN' USELESS.
!

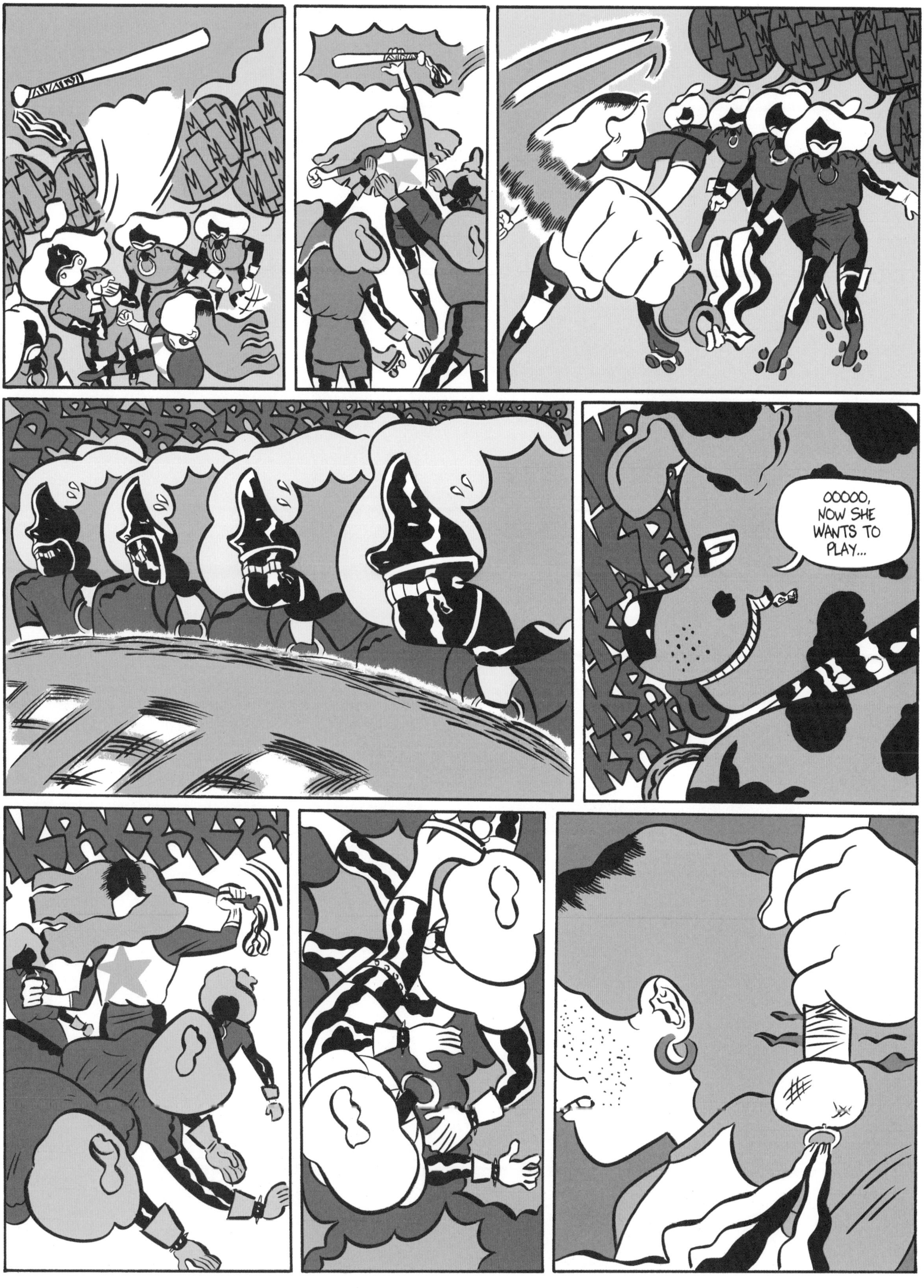
OOOOO, NOW SHE WANTS TO PLAY...

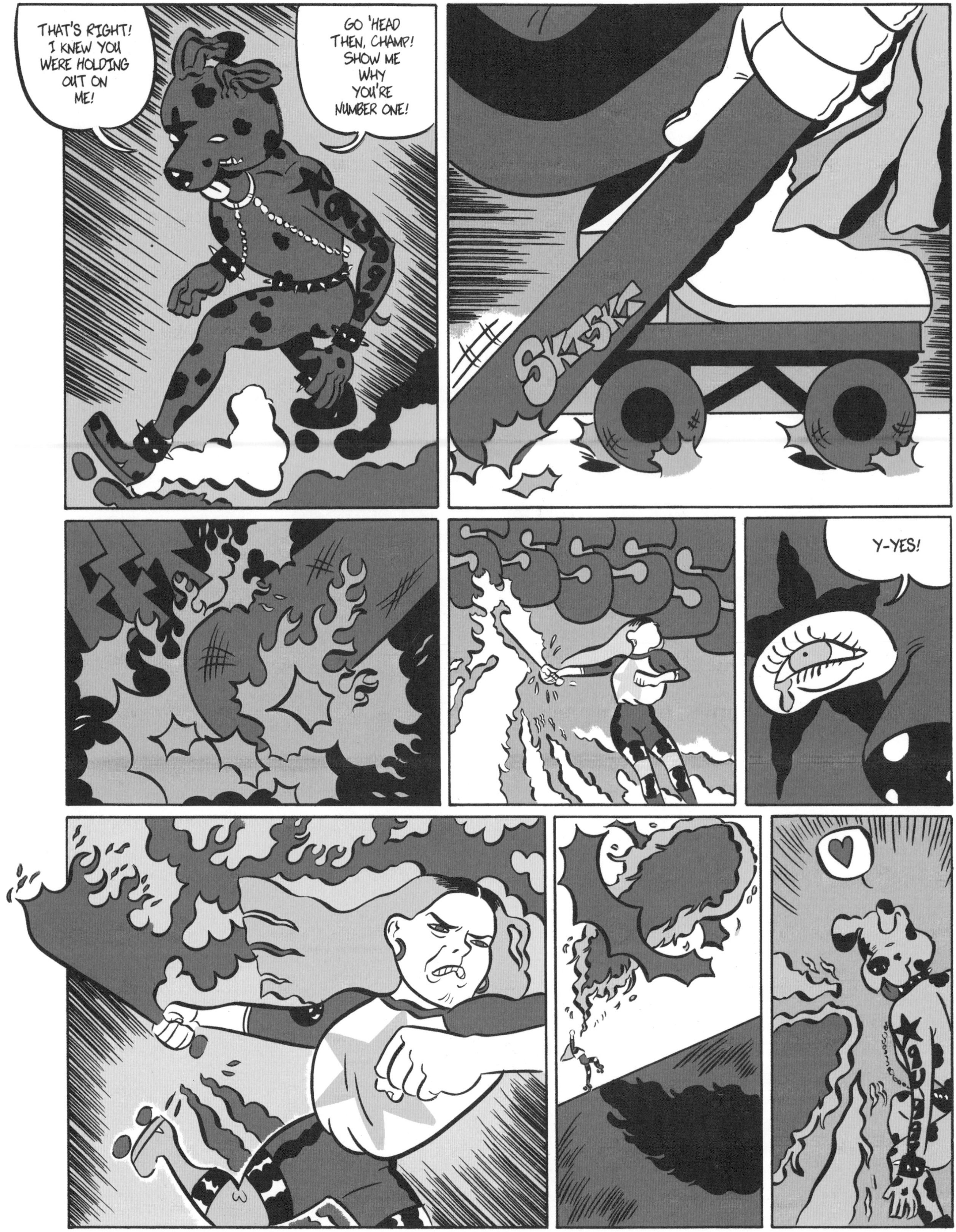
THAT'S RIGHT! I KNEW YOU WERE HOLDING OUT ON ME!
GO 'HEAD THEN, CHAMP! SHOW ME WHY YOU'RE NUMBER ONE!
SKTSK
Y-YES!

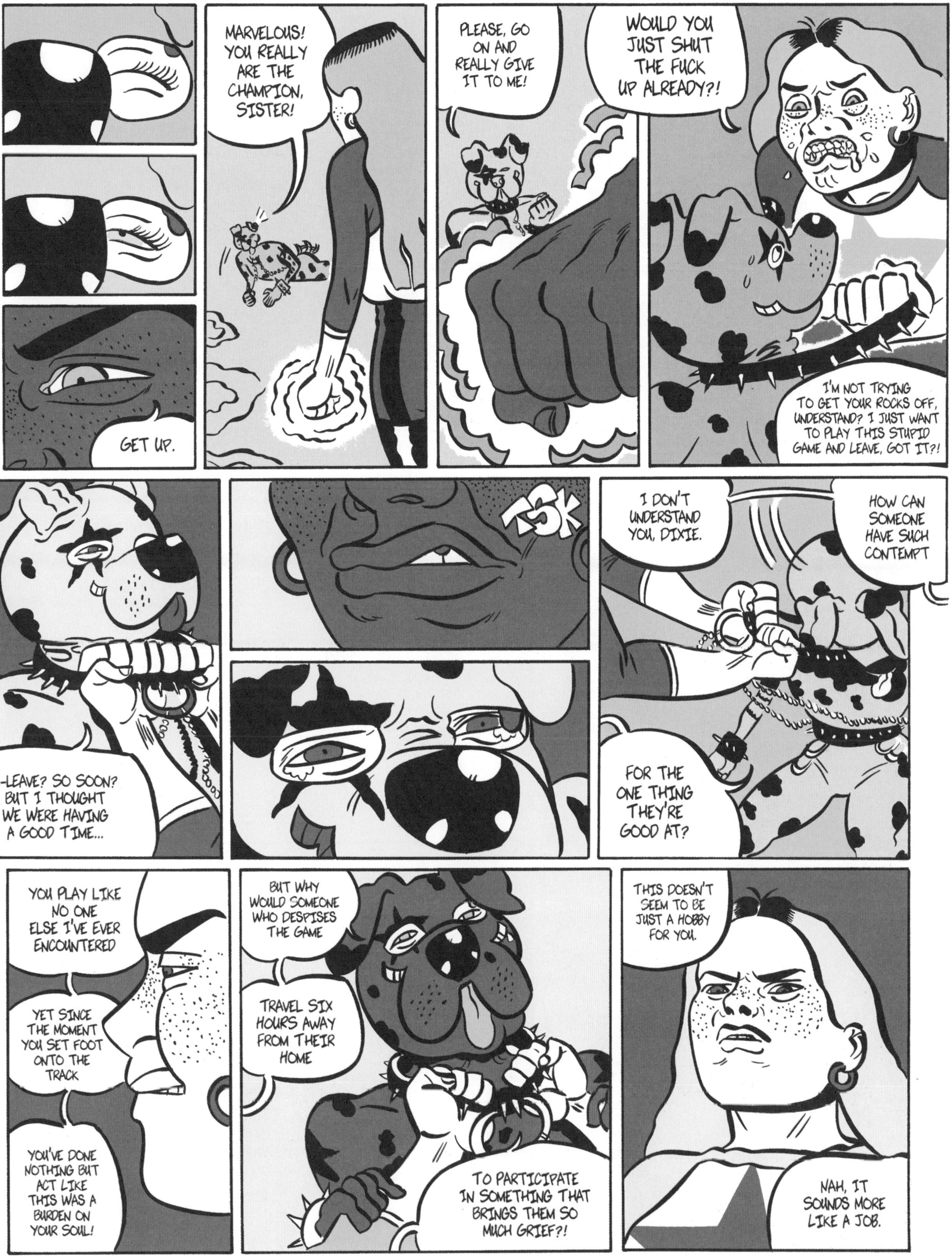
GET UP.
MARVELOUS! YOU REALLY ARE THE CHAMPION, SISTER!
PLEASE, GO ON AND REALLY GIVE IT TO ME!
WOULD YOU JUST SHUT THE FUCK UP ALREADY?!
I'M NOT TRYING TO GET YOUR ROCKS OFF, UNDERSTAND? I JUST WANT TO PLAY THIS STUPID GAME AND LEAVE, GOT IT?!
L-LEAVE? SO SOON? BUT I THOUGHT WE WERE HAVING A GOOD TIME...
TSK
I DON'T UNDERSTAND YOU, DIXIE.
HOW CAN SOMEONE HAVE SUCH CONTEMPT
FOR THE ONE THING THEY'RE GOOD AT?
YOU PLAY LIKE NO ONE ELSE I'VE EVER ENCOUNTERED
YET SINCE THE MOMENT YOU SET FOOT ONTO THE TRACK
YOU'VE DONE NOTHING BUT ACT LIKE THIS WAS A BURDEN ON YOUR SOUL!
BUT WHY WOULD SOMEONE WHO DESPISES THE GAME
TRAVEL SIX HOURS AWAY FROM THEIR HOME
TO PARTICIPATE IN SOMETHING THAT BRINGS THEM SO MUCH GRIEF?!
THIS DOESN'T SEEM TO BE JUST A HOBBY FOR YOU.
NAH, IT SOUNDS MORE LIKE A JOB.

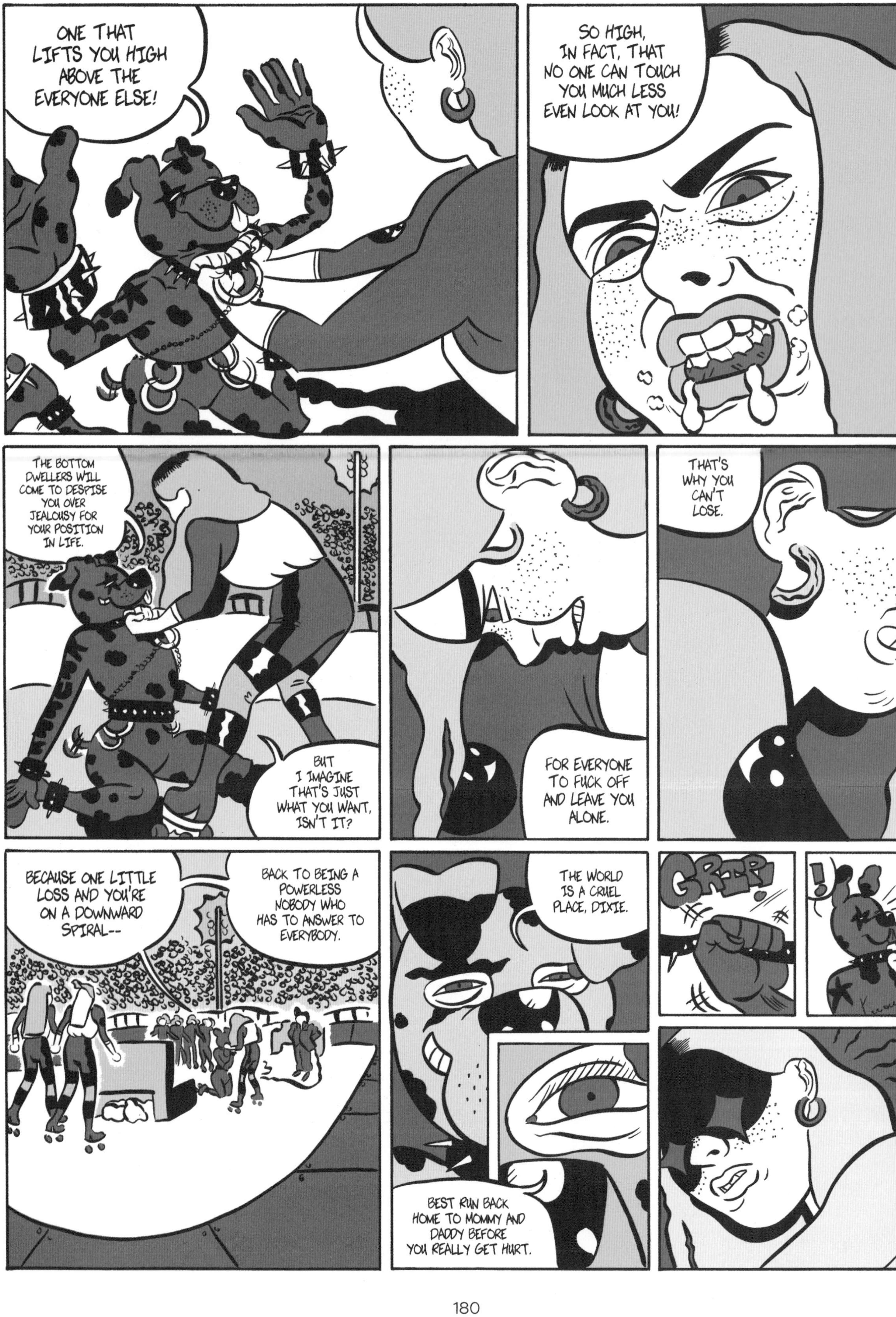

ONE THAT LIFTS YOU HIGH ABOVE THE EVERYONE ELSE!
SO HIGH, IN FACT, THAT NO ONE CAN TOUCH YOU MUCH LESS EVEN LOOK AT YOU!
THE BOTTOM DWELLERS WILL COME TO DESPISE YOU OVER JEALOUSY FOR YOUR POSITION IN LIFE.
BUT I IMAGINE THAT'S JUST WHAT YOU WANT, ISN'T IT?
FOR EVERYONE TO FUCK OFF AND LEAVE YOU ALONE.
THAT'S WHY YOU CAN'T LOSE.
BECAUSE ONE LITTLE LOSS AND YOU'RE ON A DOWNWARD SPIRAL--
BACK TO BEING A POWERLESS NOBODY WHO HAS TO ANSWER TO EVERYBODY.
THE WORLD IS A CRUEL PLACE, DIXIE.
BEST RUN BACK HOME TO MOMMY AND DADDY BEFORE YOU REALLY GET HURT.
GRIP
!

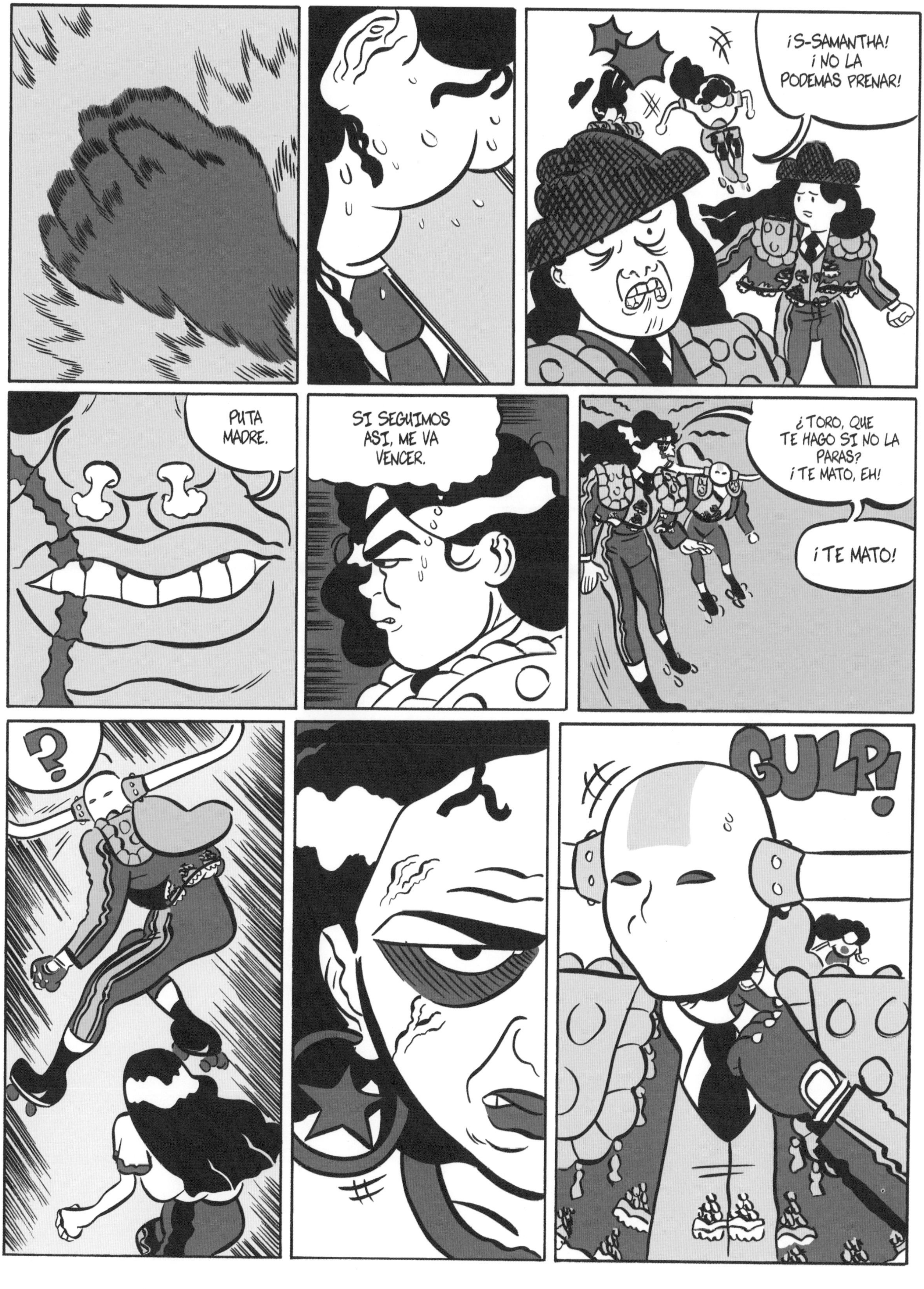
¡S-SAMANTHA! ¡NO LA PODEMAS PRENAR!
PUTA MADRE.
SI SEGUIMOS ASI, ME VA VENCER.
¿TORO, QUE TE HAGO SI NO LA PARAS? ¡TE MATO, EH!
¡TE MATO!
?
GULP!

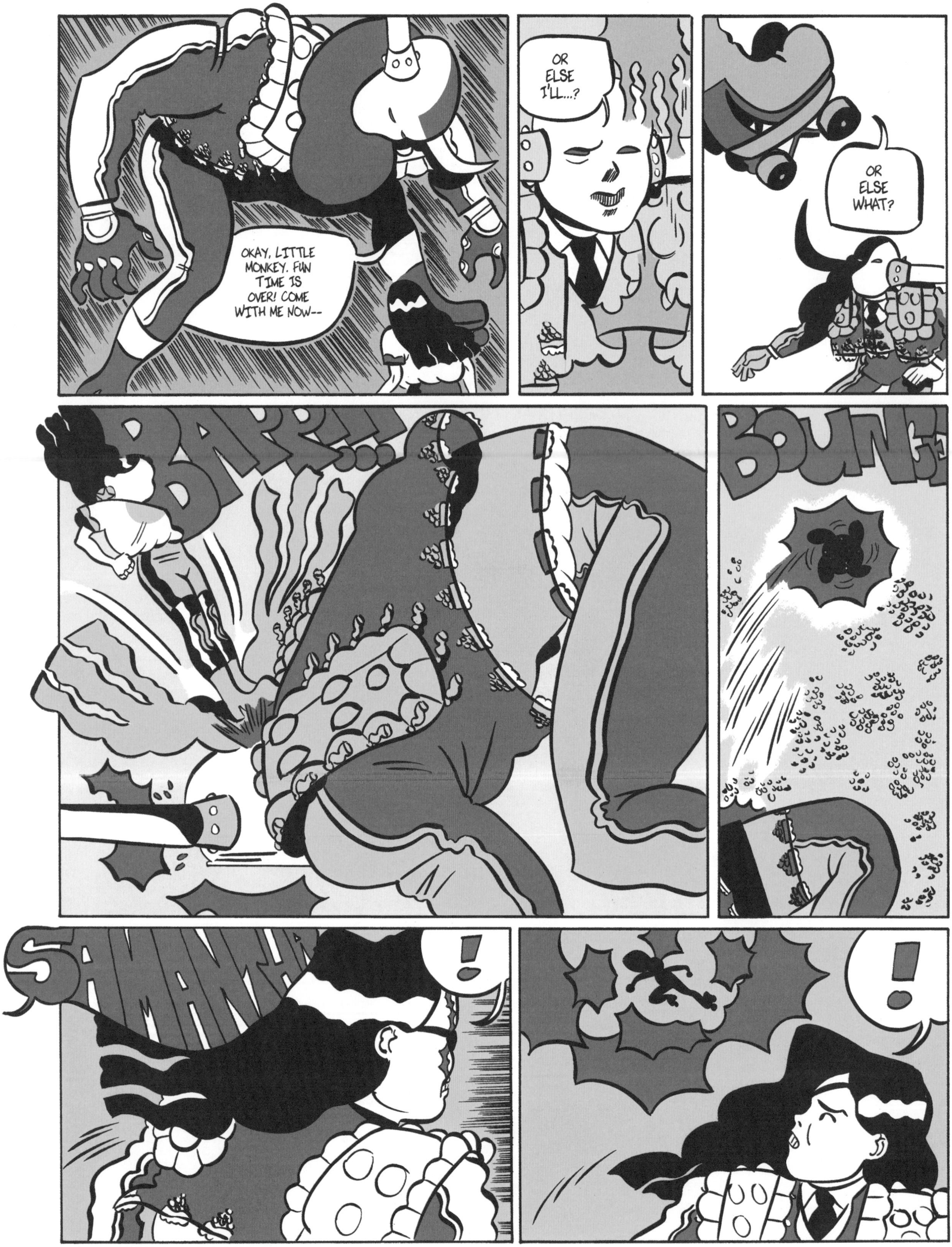
OKAY, LITTLE MONKEY. FUN TIME IS OVER! COME WITH ME NOW--
OR ELSE I'LL...?
OR ELSE WHAT?
BAPP!!...
BOUNCE
SAMANTHA
!
!

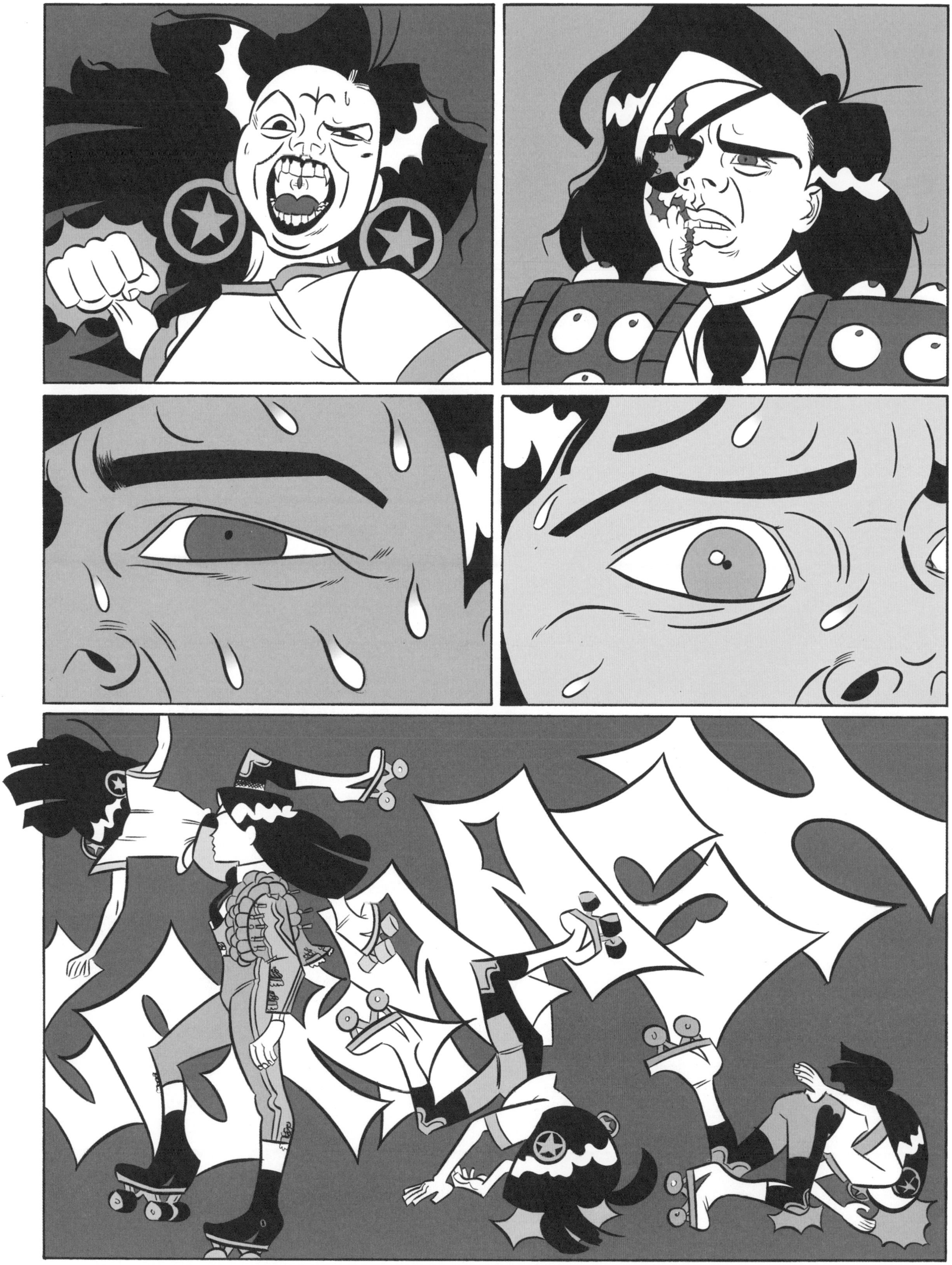

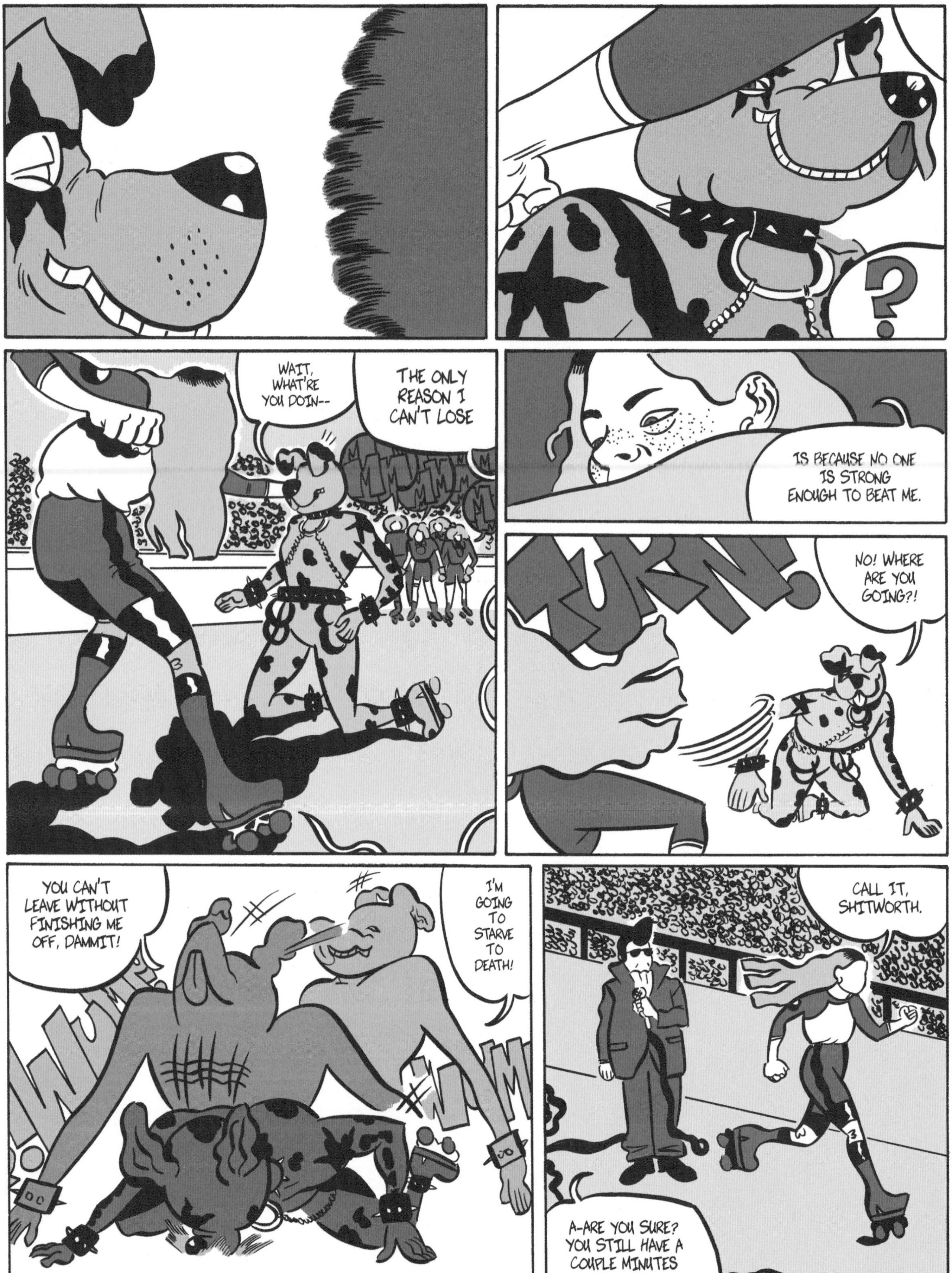
?
WAIT, WHAT'RE YOU DOIN--
THE ONLY REASON I CAN'T LOSE
IS BECAUSE NO ONE IS STRONG ENOUGH TO BEAT ME.
NO! WHERE ARE YOU GOING?!
YOU CAN'T LEAVE WITHOUT FINISHING ME OFF, DAMMIT!
I'M GOING TO STARVE TO DEATH!
CALL IT, SHITWORTH.
A-ARE YOU SURE? YOU STILL HAVE A COUPLE MINUTES LEFT IN THE GAME...

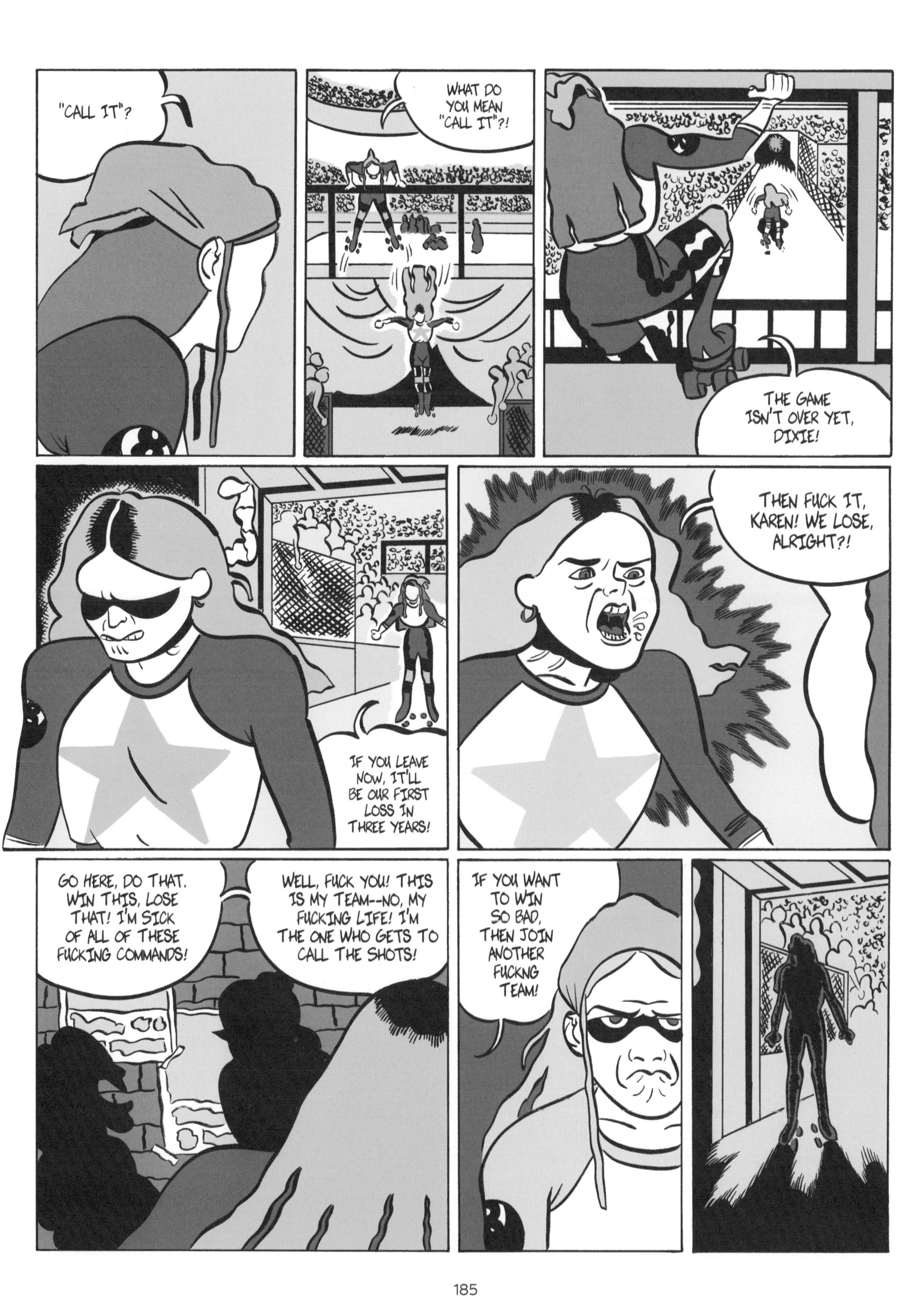
"CALL IT"?
WHAT DO YOU MEAN "CALL IT"?!
THE GAME ISN'T OVER YET, DIXIE!
IF YOU LEAVE NOW, IT'LL BE OUR FIRST LOSS IN THREE YEARS!
THEN FUCK IT, KAREN! WE LOSE, ALRIGHT?!
GO HERE, DO THAT. WIN THIS, LOSE THAT! I'M SICK OF ALL OF THESE FUCKING COMMANDS!
WELL, FUCK YOU! THIS IS MY TEAM--NO, MY FUCKING LIFE! I'M THE ONE WHO GETS TO CALL THE SHOTS!
IF YOU WANT TO WIN SO BAD, THEN JOIN ANOTHER FUCKNG TEAM!

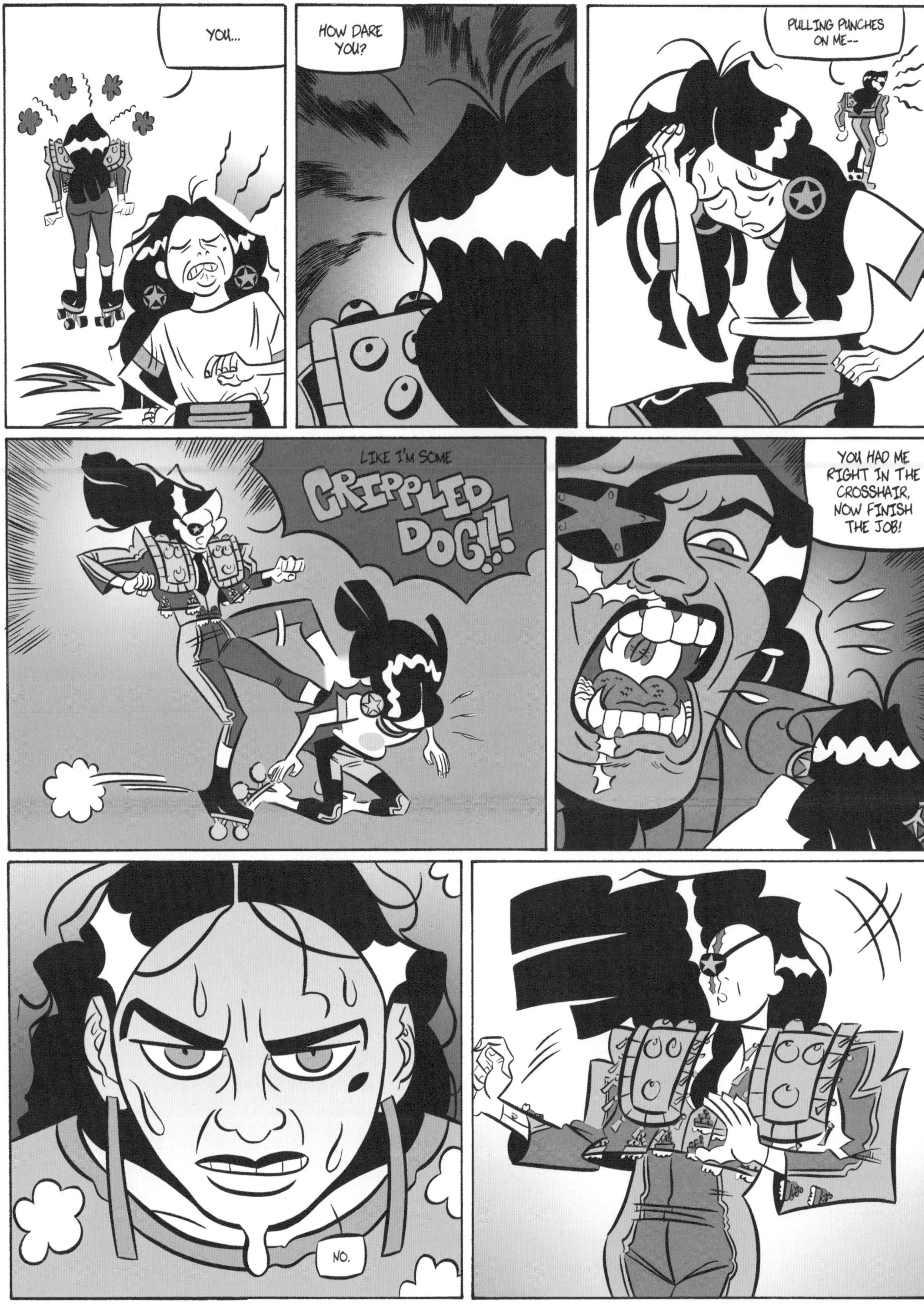
YOU...
HOW DARE YOU?
PULLING PUNCHES ON ME--
LIKE I'M SOME
CRIPPLED DOG!!
YOU HAD ME RIGHT IN THE CROSSHAIR, NOW FINISH THE JOB!
NO.

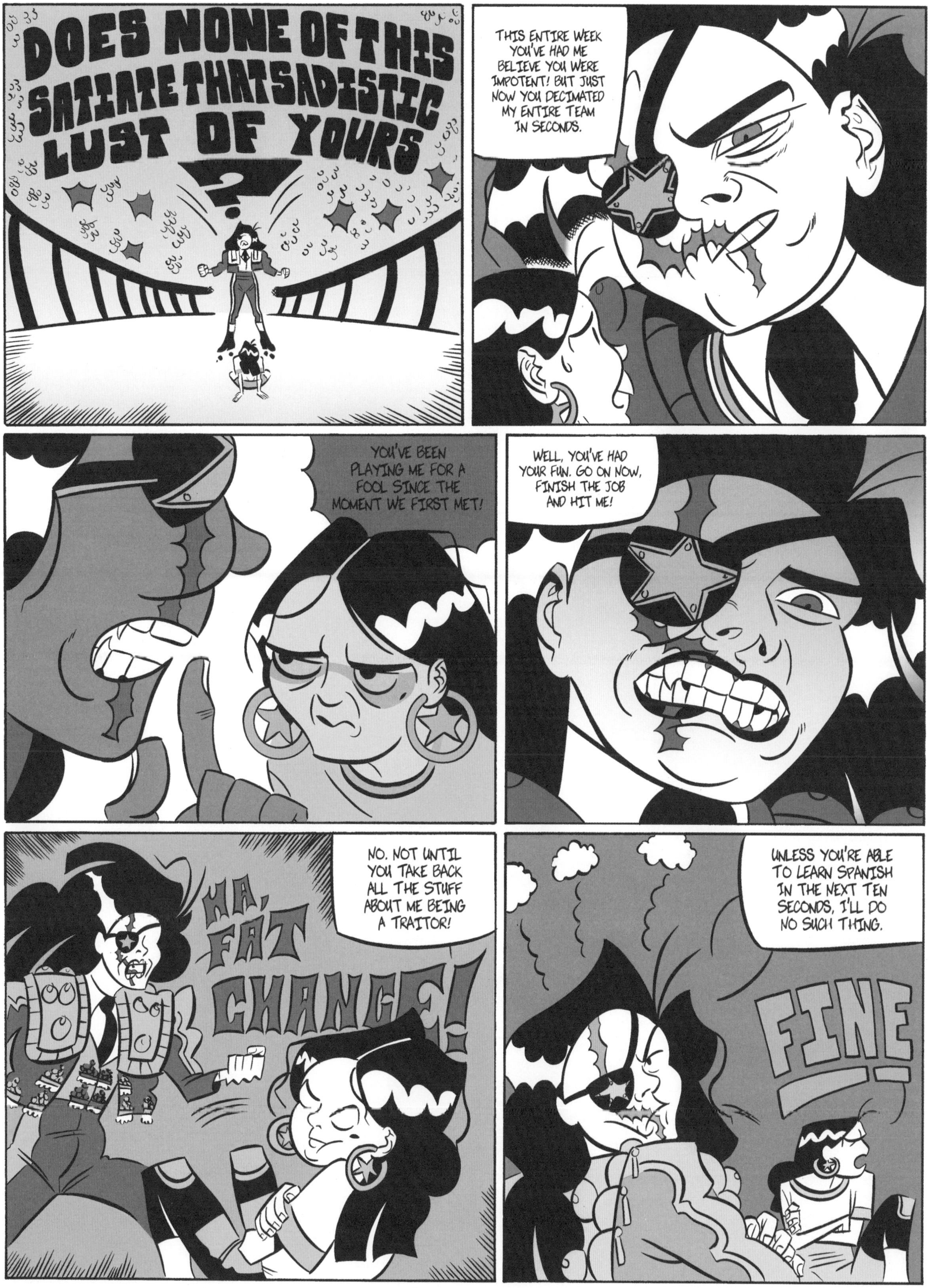
DOES NONE OF THIS SATIATE THAT SADISTIC LUST OF YOURS?
THIS ENTIRE WEEK YOU'VE HAD ME BELIEVE YOU WERE IMPOTENT! BUT JUST NOW YOU DECIMATED MY ENTIRE TEAM IN SECONDS.
YOU'VE BEEN PLAYING ME FOR A FOOL SINCE THE MOMENT WE FIRST MET!
WELL, YOU'VE HAD YOUR FUN. GO ON NOW, FINISH THE JOB AND HIT ME!
NO. NOT UNTIL YOU TAKE BACK ALL THE STUFF ABOUT ME BEING A TRAITOR!
HA, FAT CHANCE!
UNLESS YOU'RE ABLE TO LEARN SPANISH IN THE NEXT TEN SECONDS, I'LL DO NO SUCH THING.
FINE

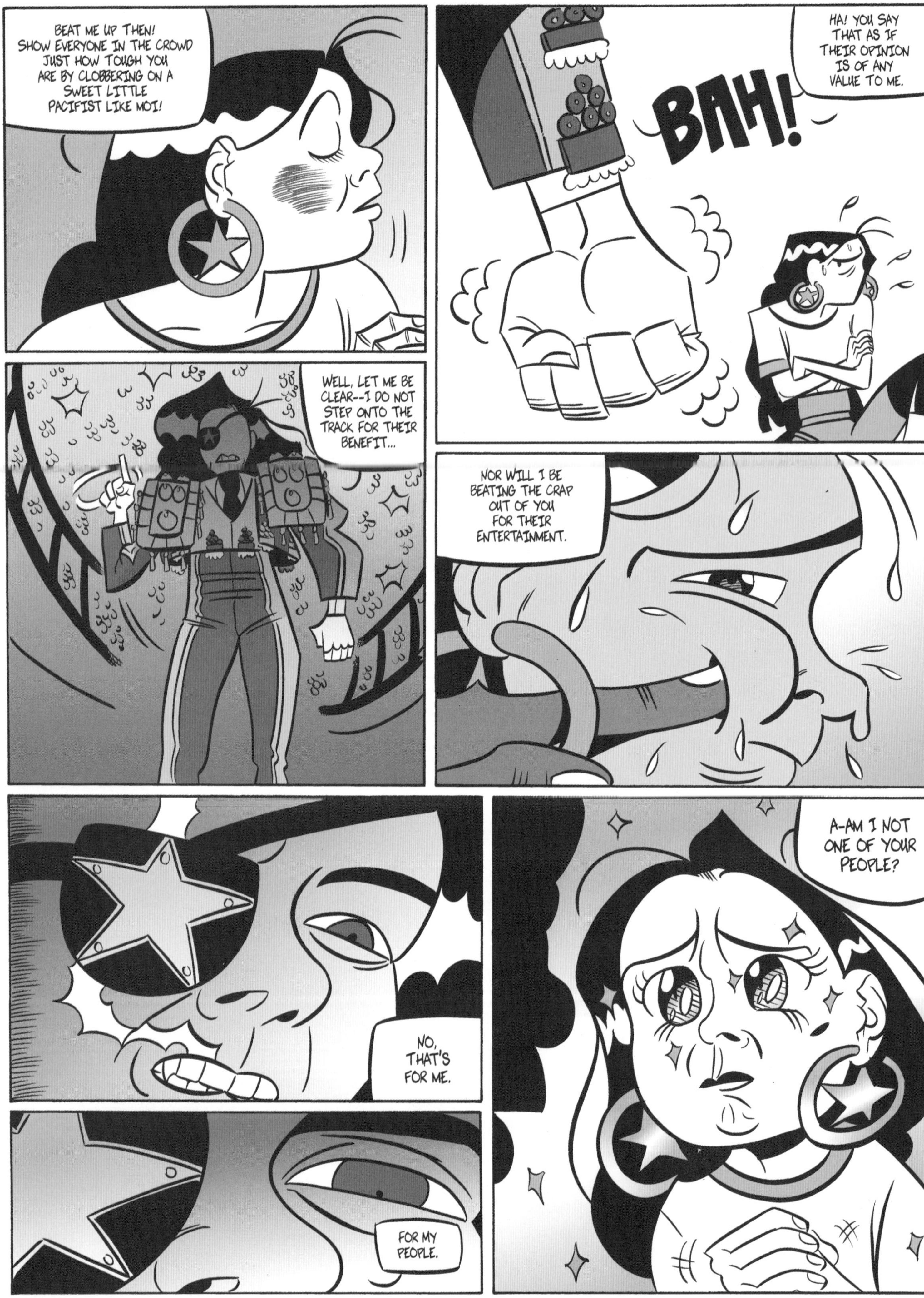
BEAT ME UP THEN! SHOW EVERYONE IN THE CROWD JUST HOW TOUGH YOU ARE BY CLOBBERING ON A SWEET LITTLE PACIFIST LIKE MOI!
BAH!
HA! YOU SAY THAT AS IF THEIR OPINION IS OF ANY VALUE TO ME.
WELL, LET ME BE CLEAR--I DO NOT STEP ONTO THE TRACK FOR THEIR BENEFIT...
NOR WILL I BE BEATING THE CRAP OUT OF YOU FOR THEIR ENTERTAINMENT.
NO, THAT'S FOR ME.
FOR MY PEOPLE.
A-AM I NOT ONE OF YOUR PEOPLE?

...
YOU ARE A...
A..
FLUNKIE
A...
FAILURE
YOU! ARE THE ANTITHESIS OF MY PEOPLE!
DING
YOU...
ARE NOTHING BUT A...
SNAKEY SNEAKY SAD
IMITATION OF MY PEOPLE!

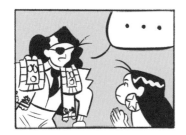

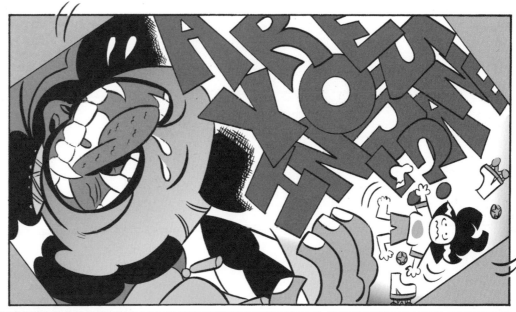

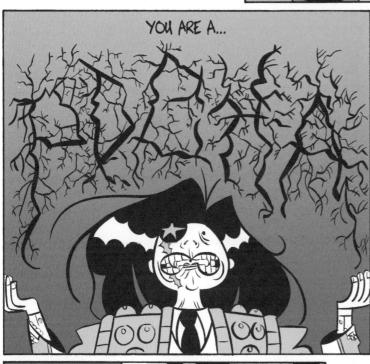

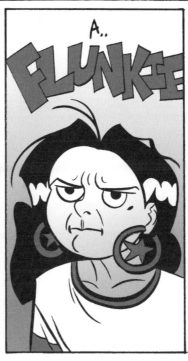

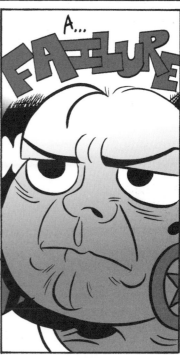

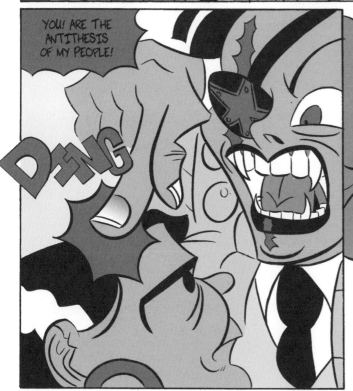

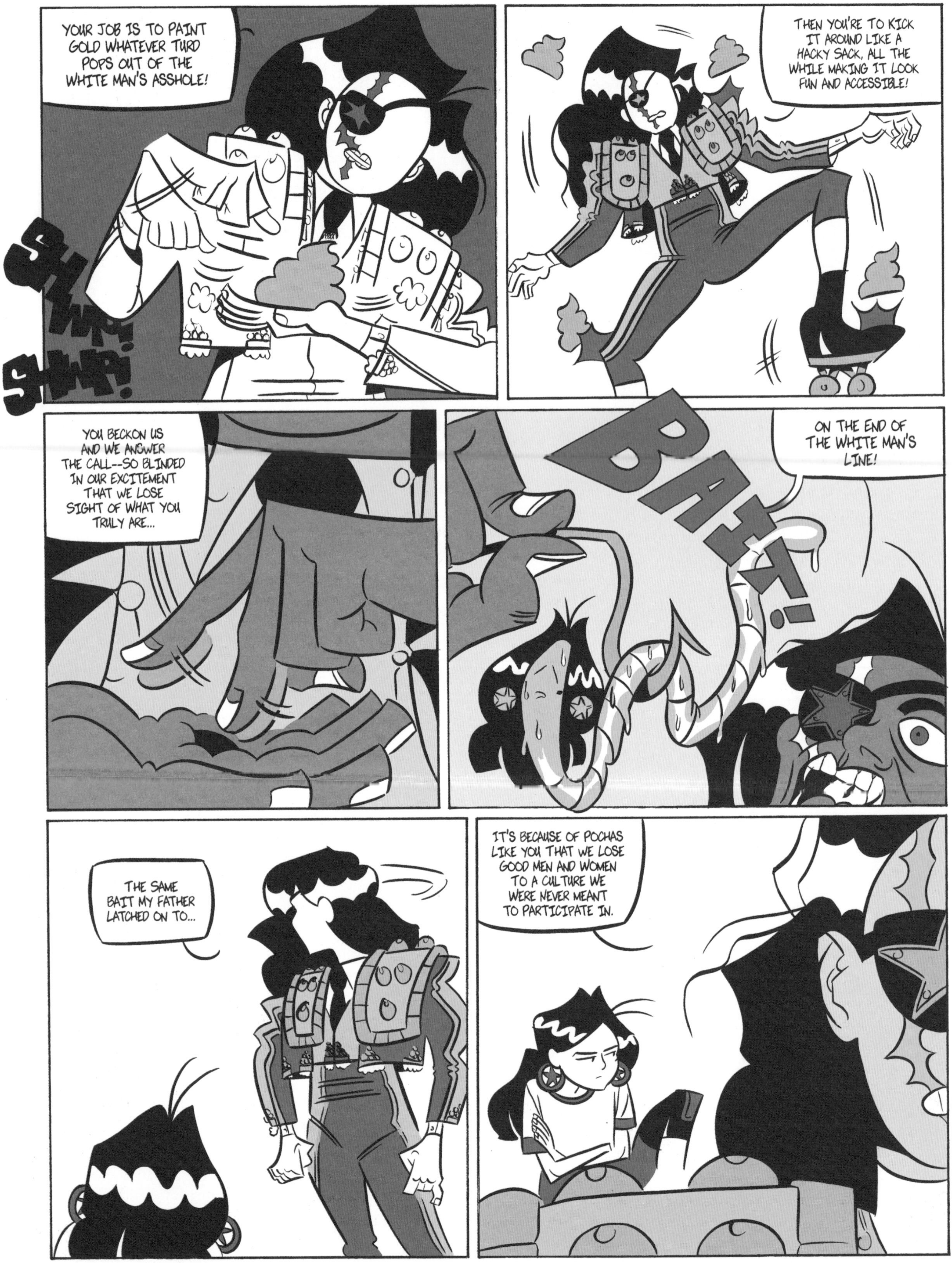
YOUR JOB IS TO PAINT GOLD WHATEVER TURD POPS OUT OF THE WHITE MAN'S ASSHOLE!
SHWP! SHWP!
THEN YOU'RE TO KICK IT AROUND LIKE A HACKY SACK, ALL THE WHILE MAKING IT LOOK FUN AND ACCESSIBLE!
YOU BECKON US AND WE ANSWER THE CALL--SO BLINDED IN OUR EXCITEMENT THAT WE LOSE SIGHT OF WHAT YOU TRULY ARE...
BAIT!
ON THE END OF THE WHITE MAN'S LINE!
THE SAME BAIT MY FATHER LATCHED ON TO...
IT'S BECAUSE OF POCHAS LIKE YOU THAT WE LOSE GOOD MEN AND WOMEN TO A CULTURE WE WERE NEVER MEANT TO PARTICIPATE IN.

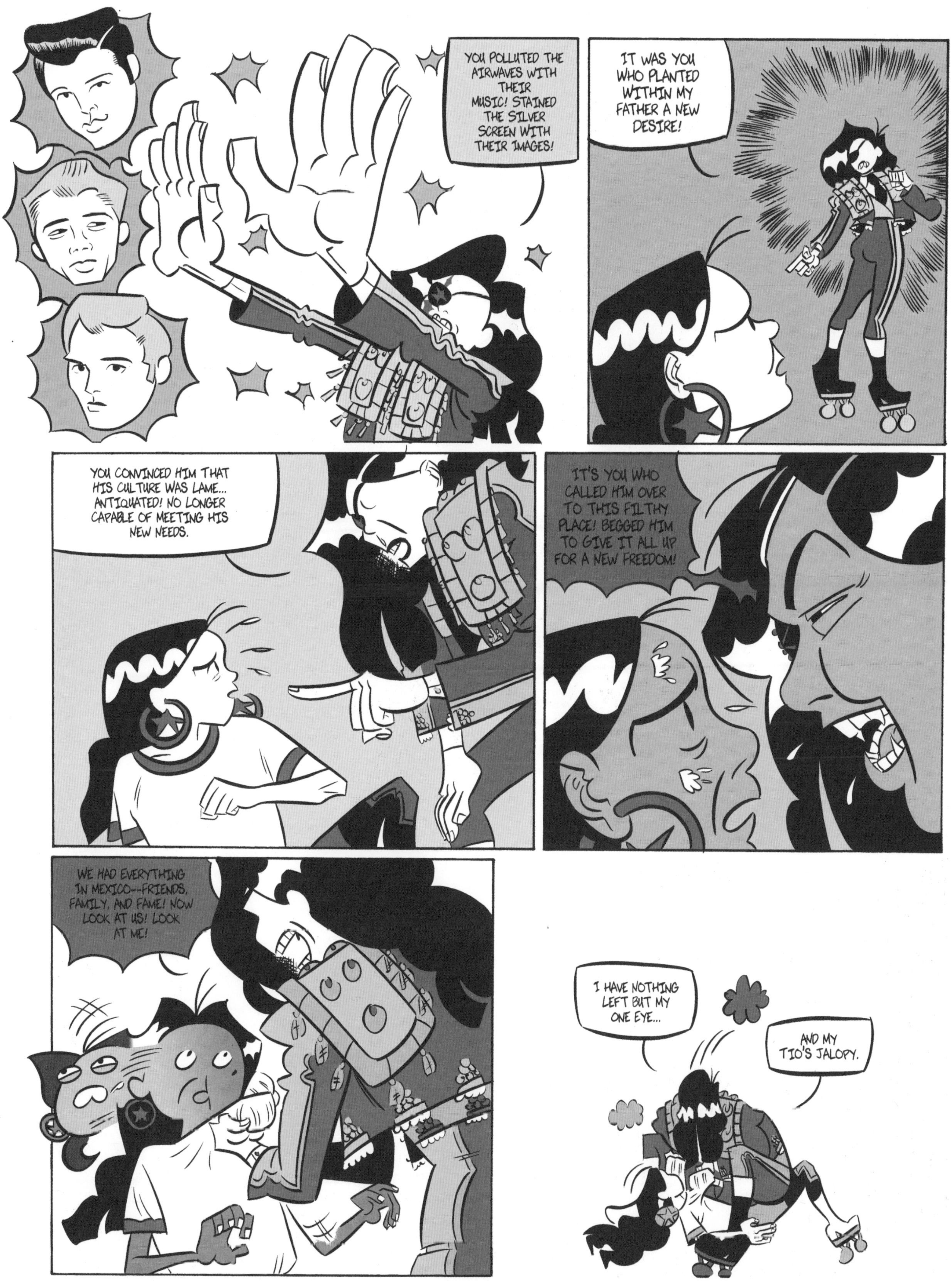
YOU POLLUTED THE AIRWAVES WITH THEIR MUSIC! STAINED THE SILVER SCREEN WITH THEIR IMAGES!
IT WAS YOU WHO PLANTED WITHIN MY FATHER A NEW DESIRE!
YOU CONVINCED HIM THAT HIS CULTURE WAS LAME... ANTIQUATED! NO LONGER CAPABLE OF MEETING HIS NEW NEEDS.
IT'S YOU WHO CALLED HIM OVER TO THIS FILTHY PLACE! BEGGED HIM TO GIVE IT ALL UP FOR A NEW FREEDOM!
WE HAD EVERYTHING IN MEXICO--FRIENDS, FAMILY, AND FAME! NOW LOOK AT US! LOOK AT ME!
I HAVE NOTHING LEFT BUT MY ONE EYE...
AND MY TIO'S JALOPY.

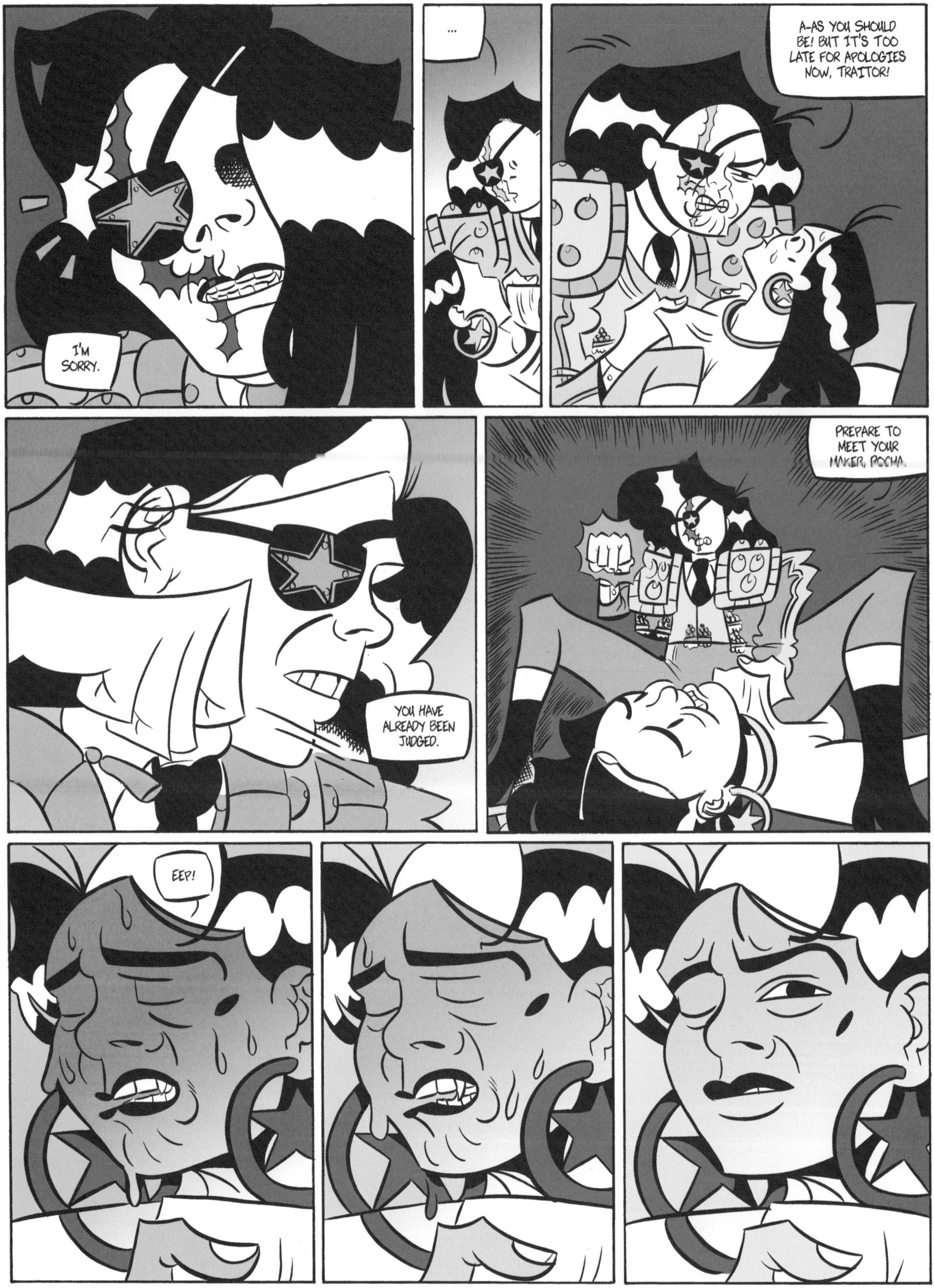
I'M SORRY.
...
A-AS YOU SHOULD BE! BUT IT'S TOO LATE FOR APOLOGIES NOW, TRAITOR!
YOU HAVE ALREADY BEEN JUDGED.
PREPARE TO MEET YOUR MAKER, POCHA.
EEP!

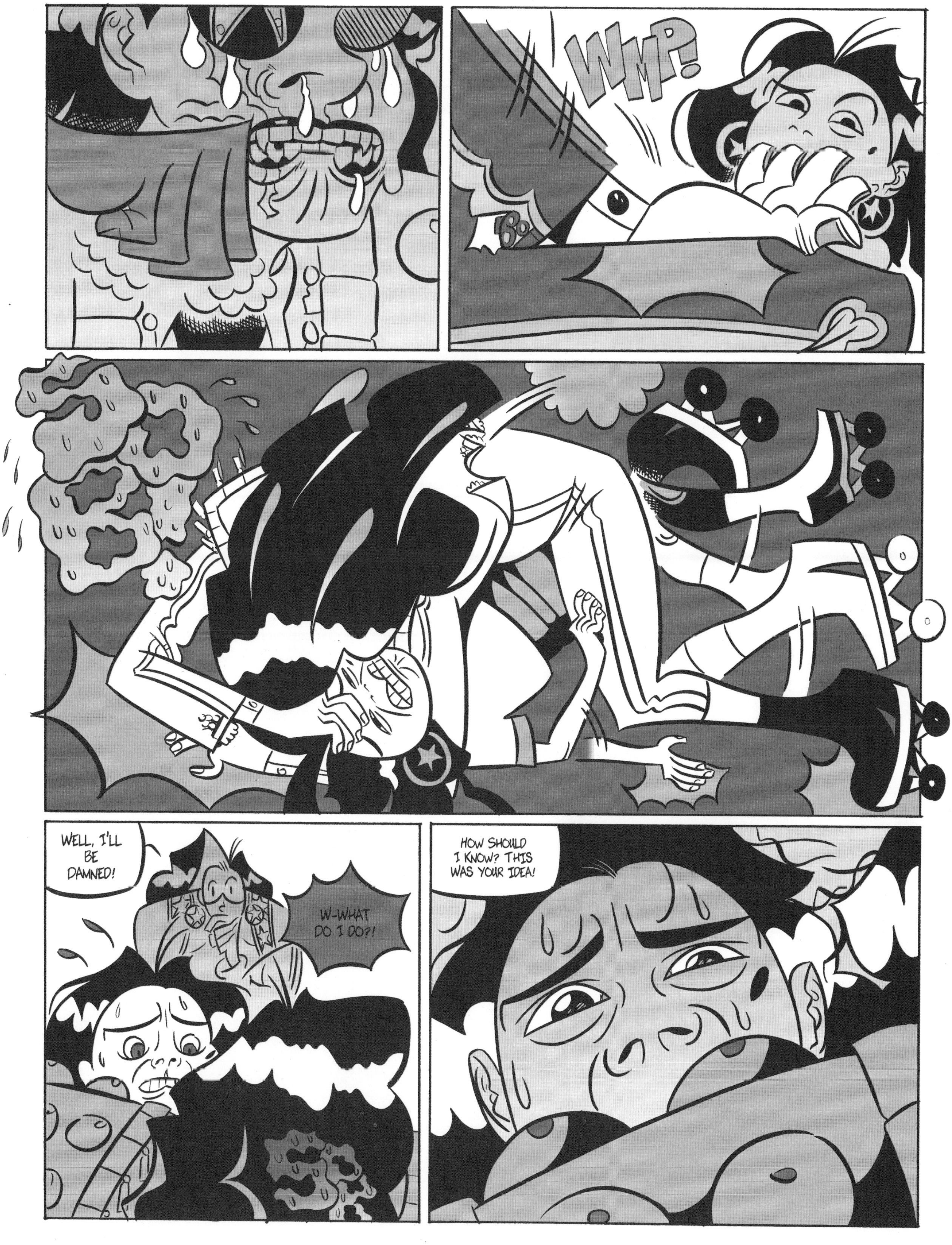
WMP!
WELL, I'LL BE DAMNED!
W-WHAT DO I DO?!
HOW SHOULD I KNOW? THIS WAS YOUR IDEA!

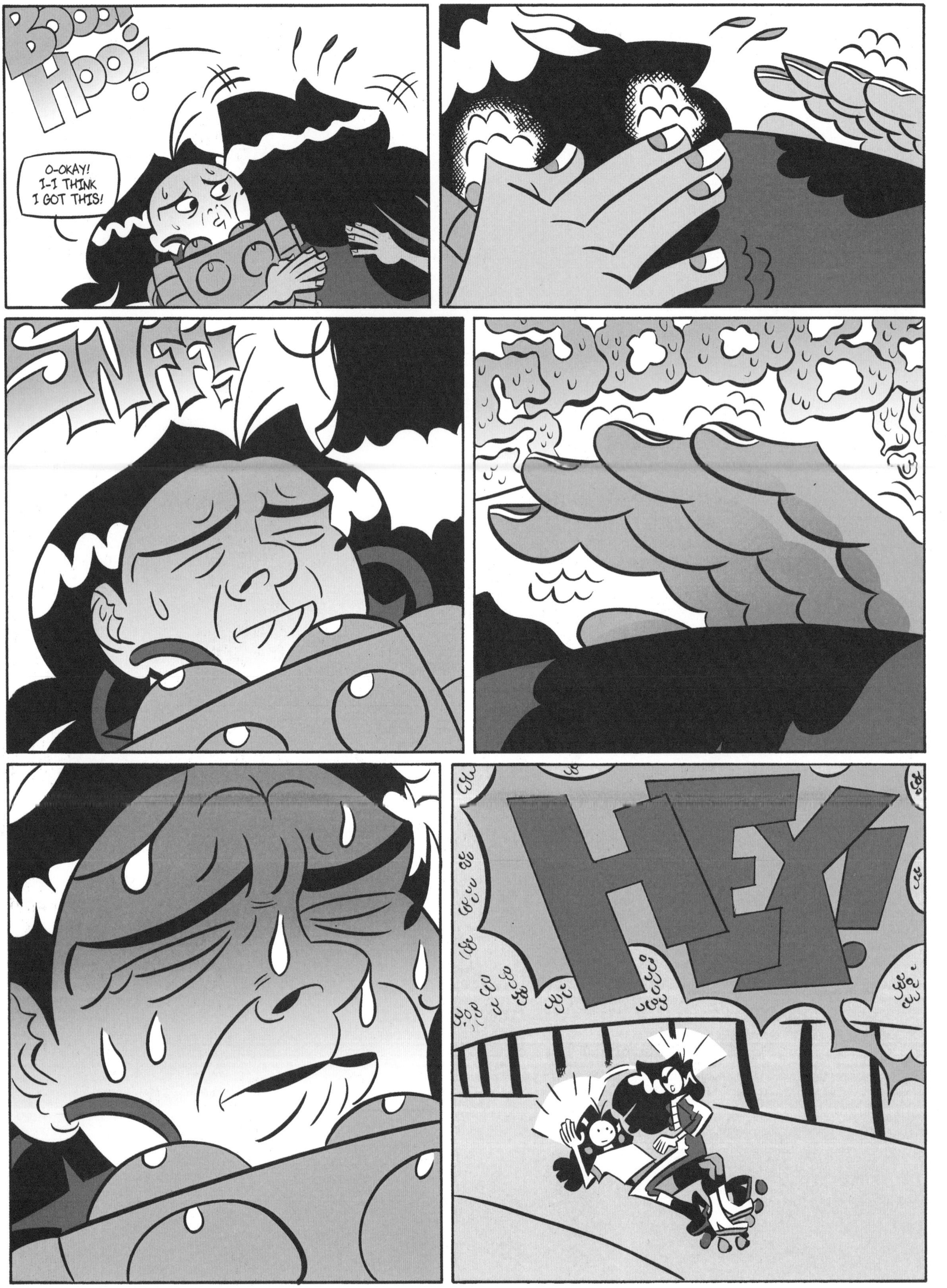
BOOO! HOO!
O-OKAY! I-I THINK I GOT THIS!
SNFF!
HEY!

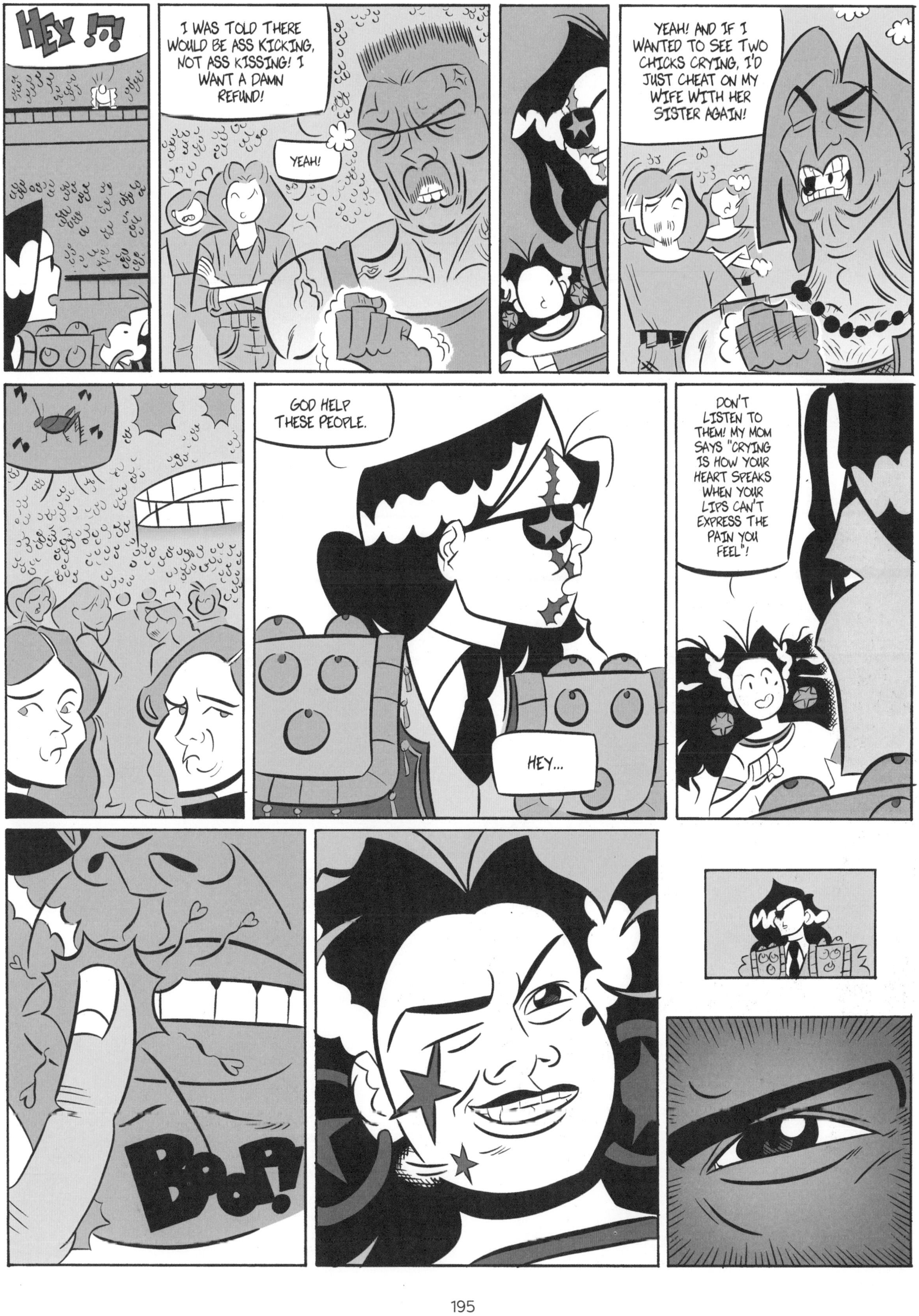
HEY !?!
I WAS TOLD THERE WOULD BE ASS KICKING, NOT ASS KISSING! I WANT A DAMN REFUND!
YEAH!
YEAH! AND IF I WANTED TO SEE TWO CHICKS CRYING, I'D JUST CHEAT ON MY WIFE WITH HER SISTER AGAIN!
GOD HELP THESE PEOPLE.
HEY...
DON'T LISTEN TO THEM! MY MOM SAYS "CRYING IS HOW YOUR HEART SPEAKS WHEN YOUR LIPS CAN'T EXPRESS THE PAIN YOU FEEL"!
BOOP!

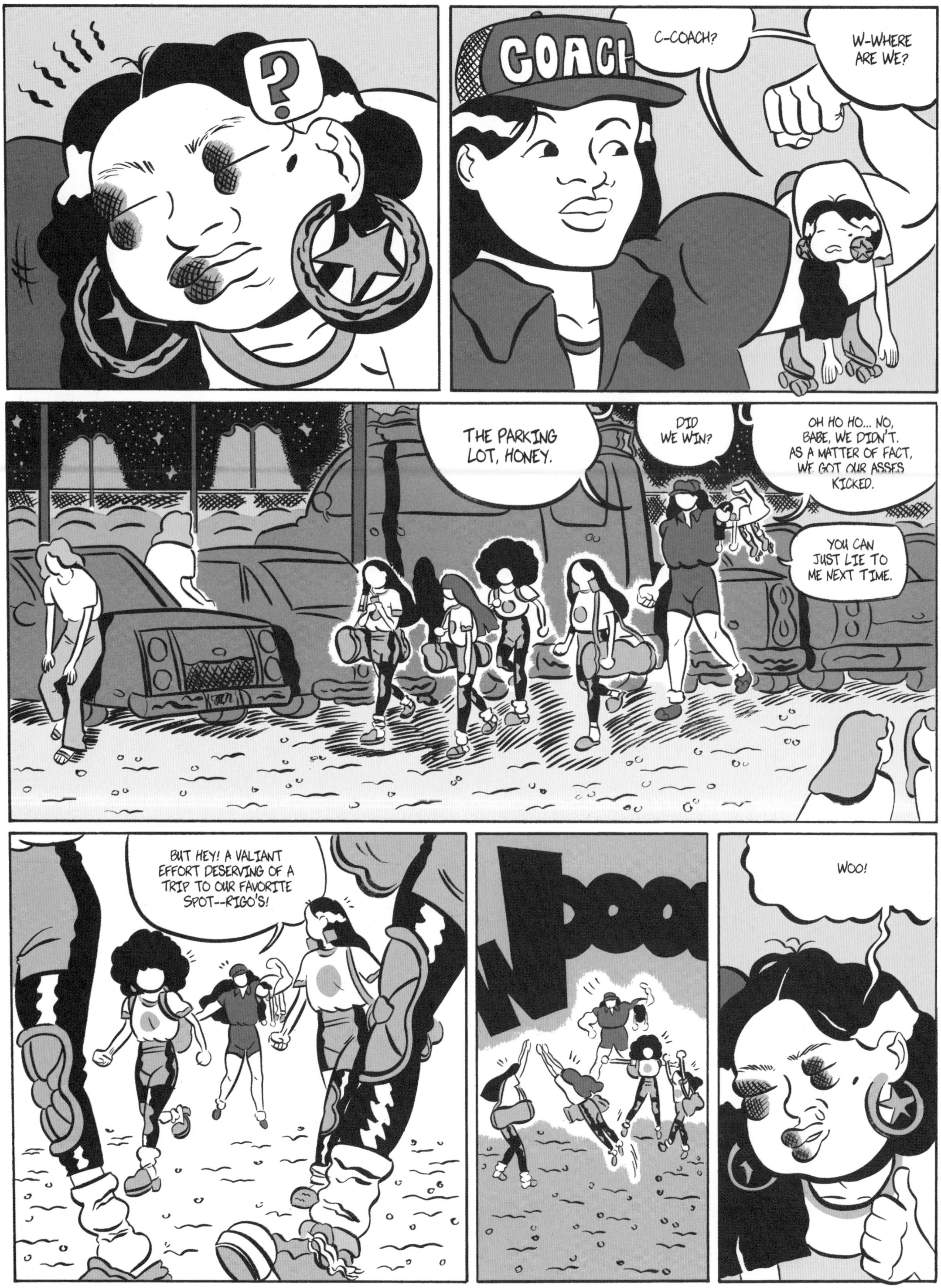
?
COACH
C-COACH?
W-WHERE ARE WE?
THE PARKING LOT, HONEY.
DID WE WIN?
OH HO HO... NO, BABE, WE DIDN'T. AS A MATTER OF FACT, WE GOT OUR ASSES KICKED.
YOU CAN JUST LIE TO ME NEXT TIME.
BUT HEY! A VALIANT EFFORT DESERVING OF A TRIP TO OUR FAVORITE SPOT--RIGO'S!
WOO!

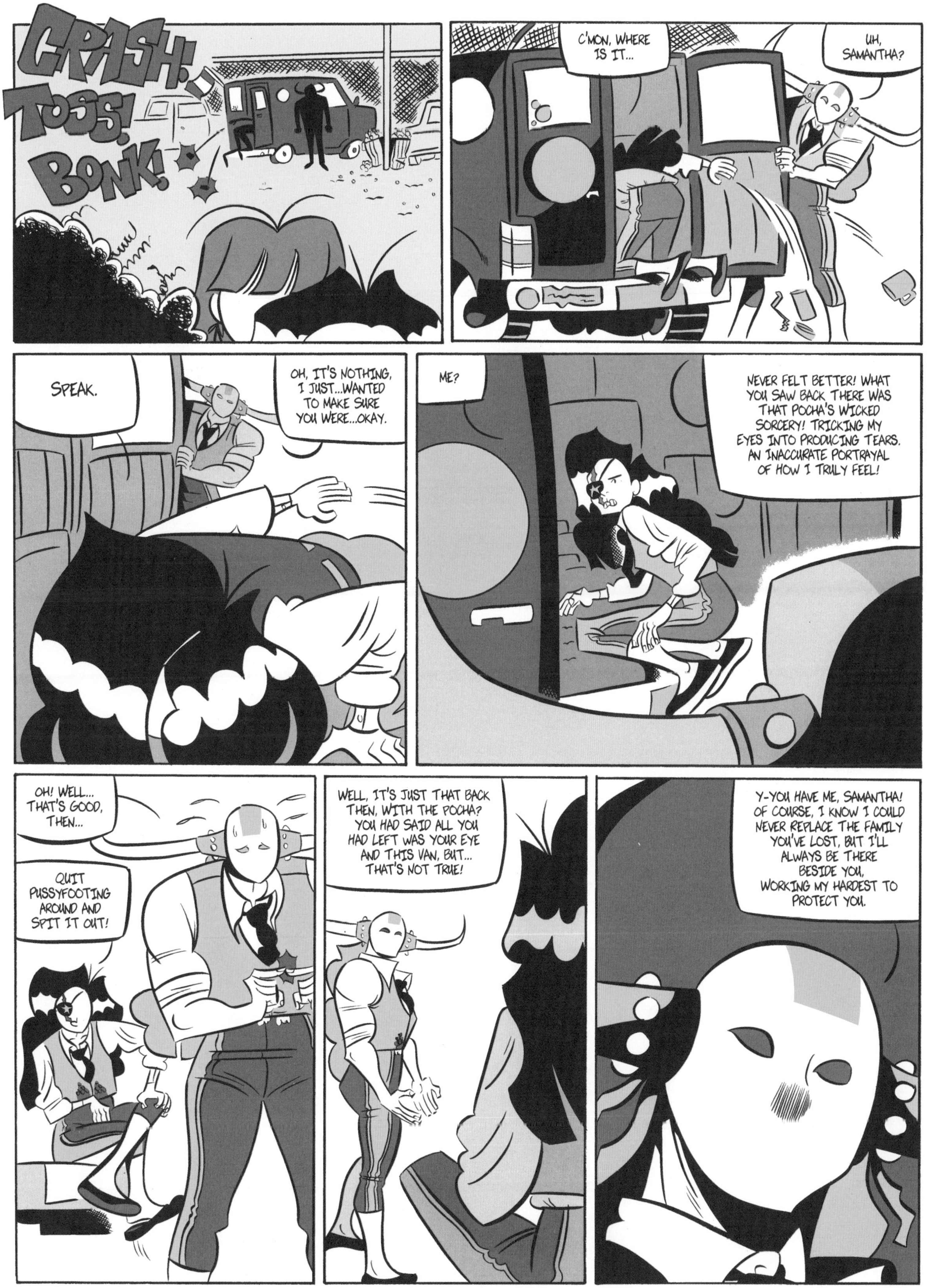
CRASH! TOSS! BONK!
C'MON, WHERE IS IT...
UH, SAMANTHA?
SPEAK.
OH, IT'S NOTHING, I JUST...WANTED TO MAKE SURE YOU WERE...OKAY.
ME?
NEVER FELT BETTER! WHAT YOU SAW BACK THERE WAS THAT POCHA'S WICKED SORCERY! TRICKING MY EYES INTO PRODUCING TEARS. AN INACCURATE PORTRAYAL OF HOW I TRULY FEEL!
OH! WELL... THAT'S GOOD, THEN...
QUIT PUSSYFOOTING AROUND AND SPIT IT OUT!
WELL, IT'S JUST THAT BACK THEN, WITH THE POCHA? YOU HAD SAID ALL YOU HAD LEFT WAS YOUR EYE AND THIS VAN, BUT... THAT'S NOT TRUE!
Y-YOU HAVE ME, SAMANTHA! OF COURSE, I KNOW I COULD NEVER REPLACE THE FAMILY YOU'VE LOST, BUT I'LL ALWAYS BE THERE BESIDE YOU, WORKING MY HARDEST TO PROTECT YOU.

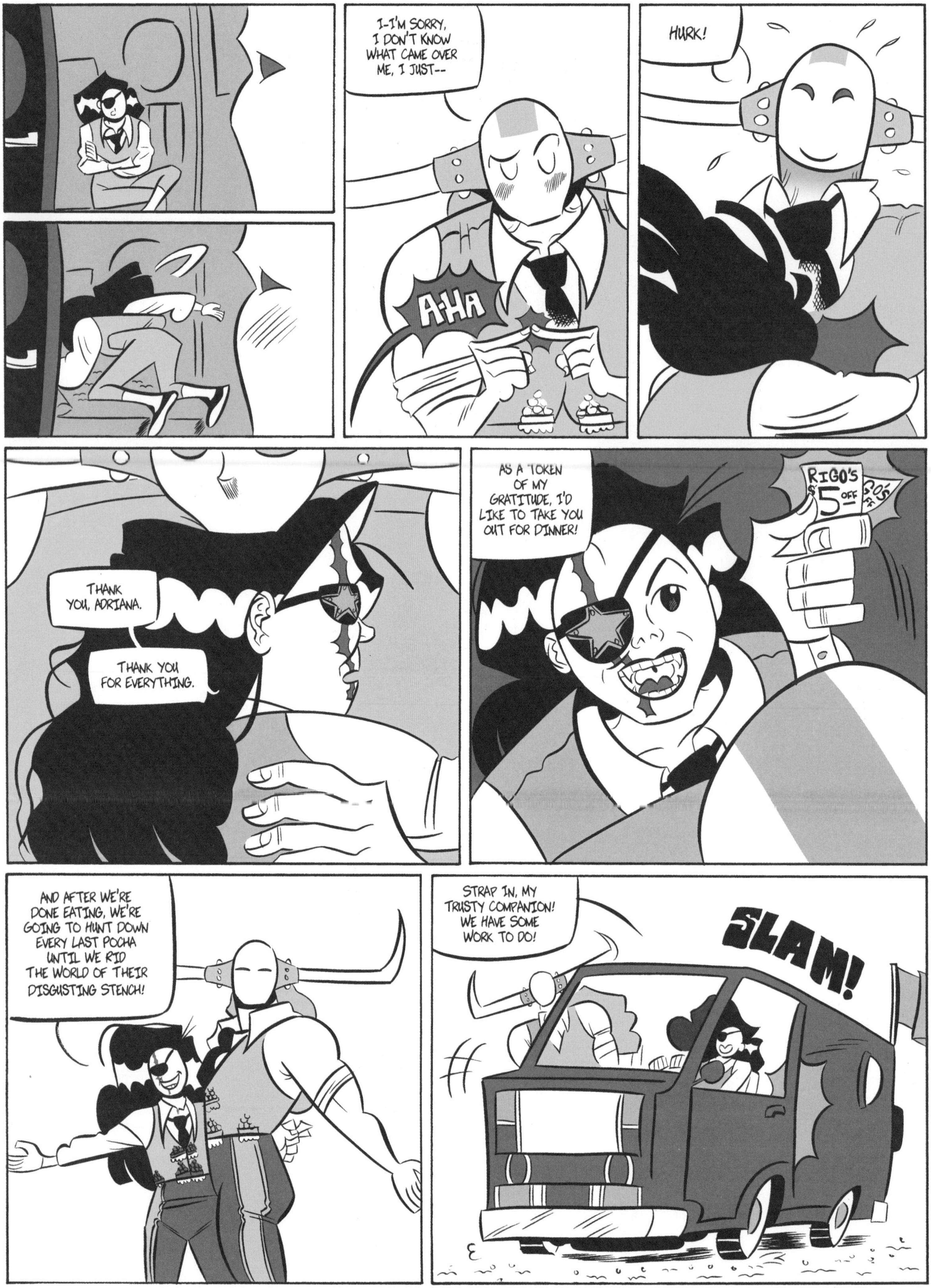
I-I'M SORRY, I DON'T KNOW WHAT CAME OVER ME, I JUST--
A-HA
HURK!
THANK YOU, ADRIANA.
THANK YOU FOR EVERYTHING.
AS A TOKEN OF MY GRATITUDE, I'D LIKE TO TAKE YOU OUT FOR DINNER!
RIGO'S $5 OFF
AND AFTER WE'RE DONE EATING, WE'RE GOING TO HUNT DOWN EVERY LAST POCHA UNTIL WE RID THE WORLD OF THEIR DISGUSTING STENCH!
STRAP IN, MY TRUSTY COMPANION! WE HAVE SOME WORK TO DO!
SLAM!

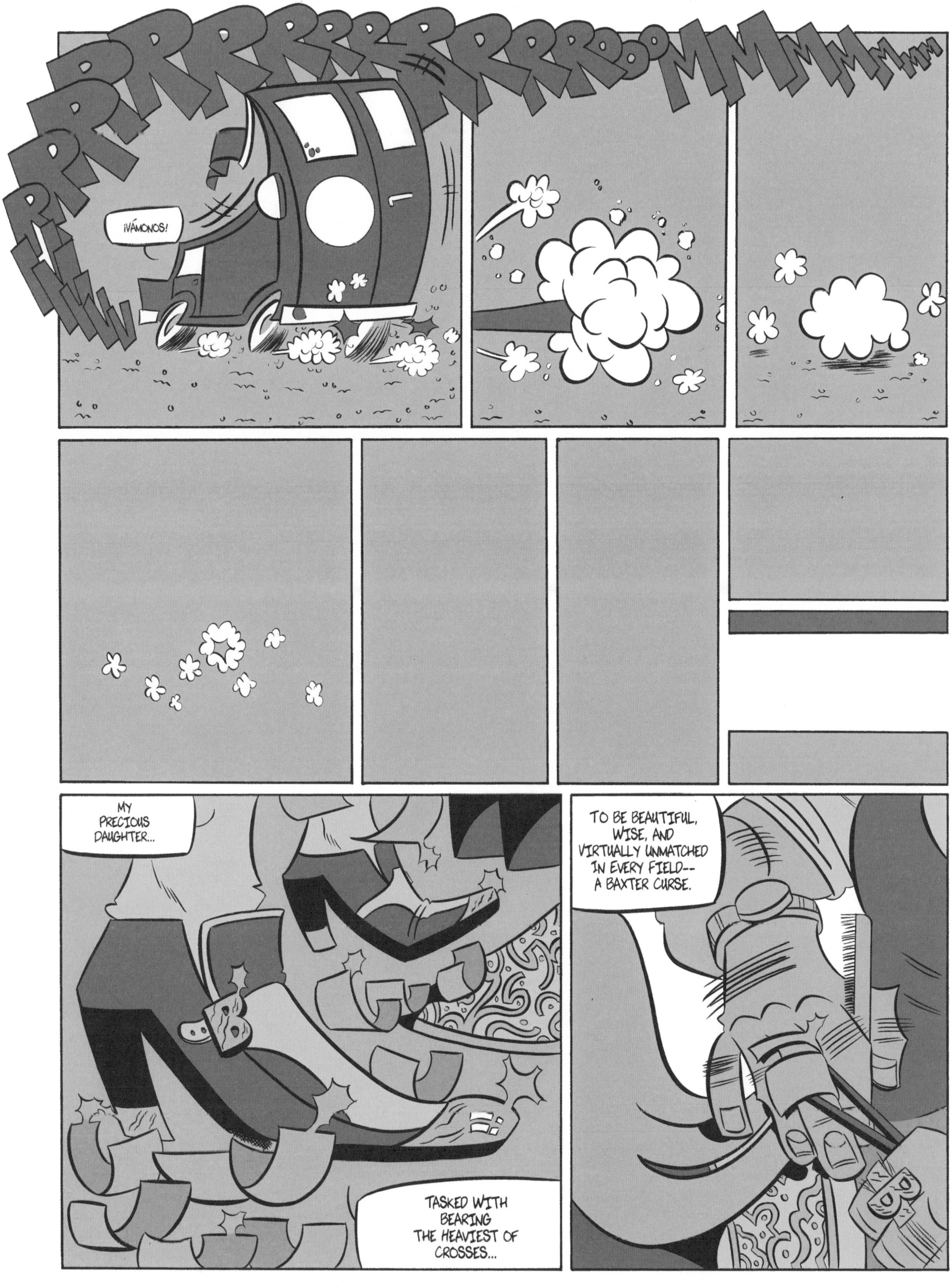
RRRRRRRRRRRRRRRRRROOOMMMMMMM
¡VÁMONOS!
MY PRECIOUS DAUGHTER...
TASKED WITH BEARING THE HEAVIEST OF CROSSES...
TO BE BEAUTIFUL, WISE, AND VIRTUALLY UNMATCHED IN EVERY FIELD-- A BAXTER CURSE.

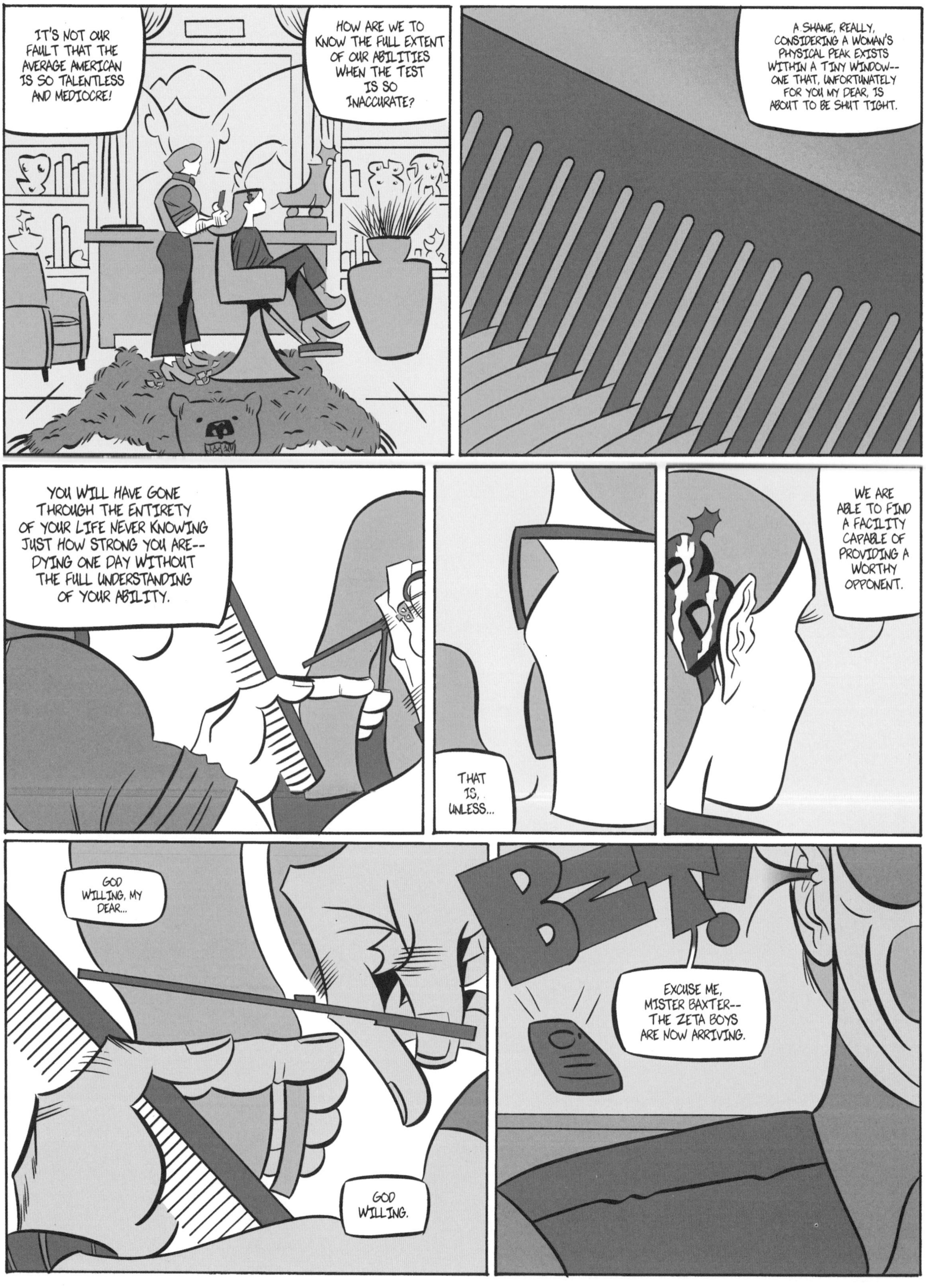
IT'S NOT OUR FAULT THAT THE AVERAGE AMERICAN IS SO TALENTLESS AND MEDIOCRE!
HOW ARE WE TO KNOW THE FULL EXTENT OF OUR ABILITIES WHEN THE TEST IS SO INACCURATE?
A SHAME, REALLY, CONSIDERING A WOMAN'S PHYSICAL PEAK EXISTS WITHIN A TINY WINDOW-- ONE THAT, UNFORTUNATELY FOR YOU MY DEAR, IS ABOUT TO BE SHUT TIGHT.
YOU WILL HAVE GONE THROUGH THE ENTIRETY OF YOUR LIFE NEVER KNOWING JUST HOW STRONG YOU ARE-- DYING ONE DAY WITHOUT THE FULL UNDERSTANDING OF YOUR ABILITY.
THAT IS, UNLESS...
WE ARE ABLE TO FIND A FACILITY CAPABLE OF PROVIDING A WORTHY OPPONENT.
GOD WILLING, MY DEAR...
GOD WILLING.
BZT!
EXCUSE ME, MISTER BAXTER-- THE ZETA BOYS ARE NOW ARRIVING.

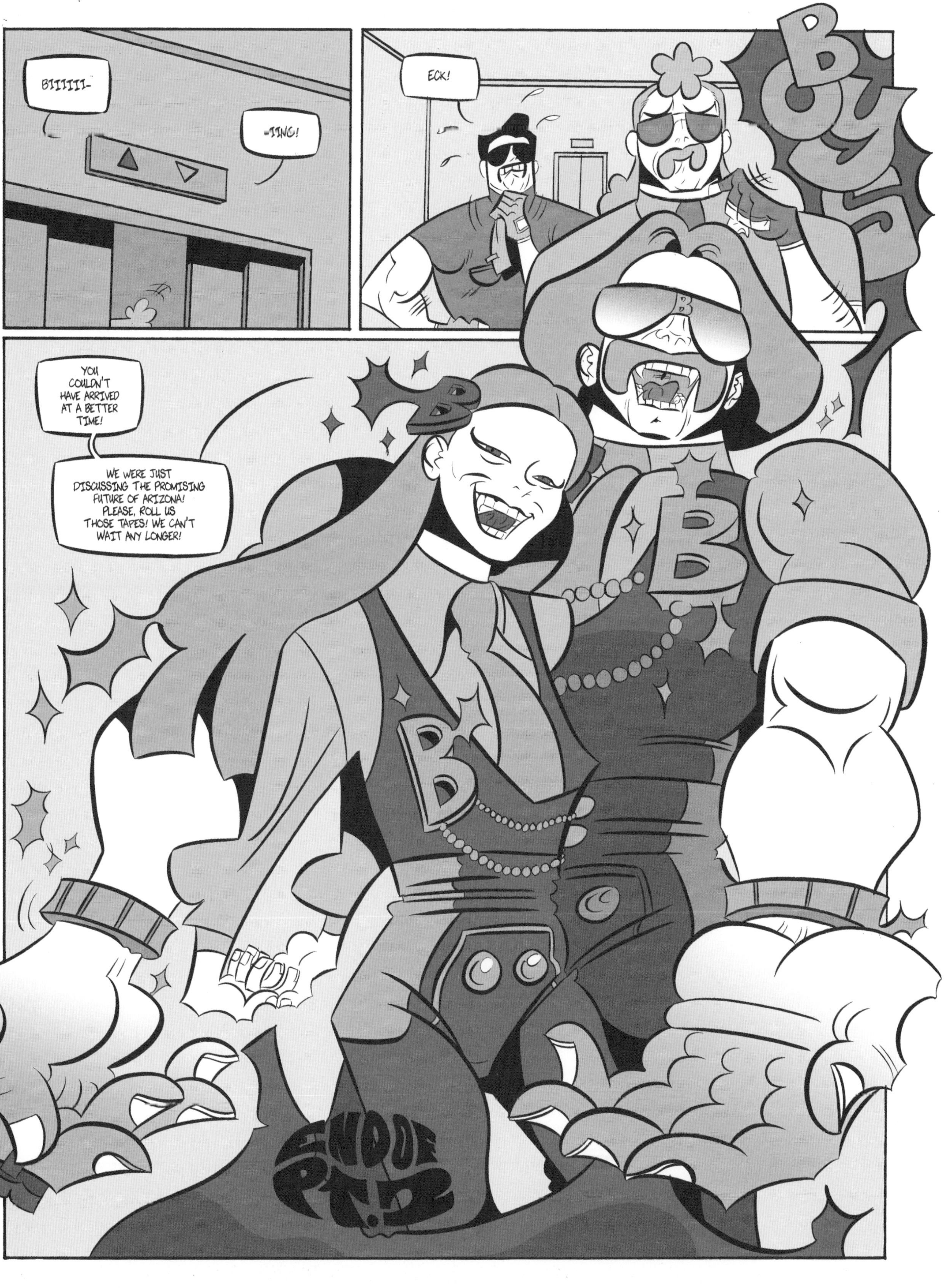
BIIIIII-
-TING!
ECK!
BOYS
YOU COULDN'T HAVE ARRIVED AT A BETTER TIME!
WE WERE JUST DISCUSSING THE PROMISING FUTURE OF ARIZONA! PLEASE, ROLL US THOSE TAPES! WE CAN'T WAIT ANY LONGER!
END OF PT. 2

CONCEPT SKETCHES

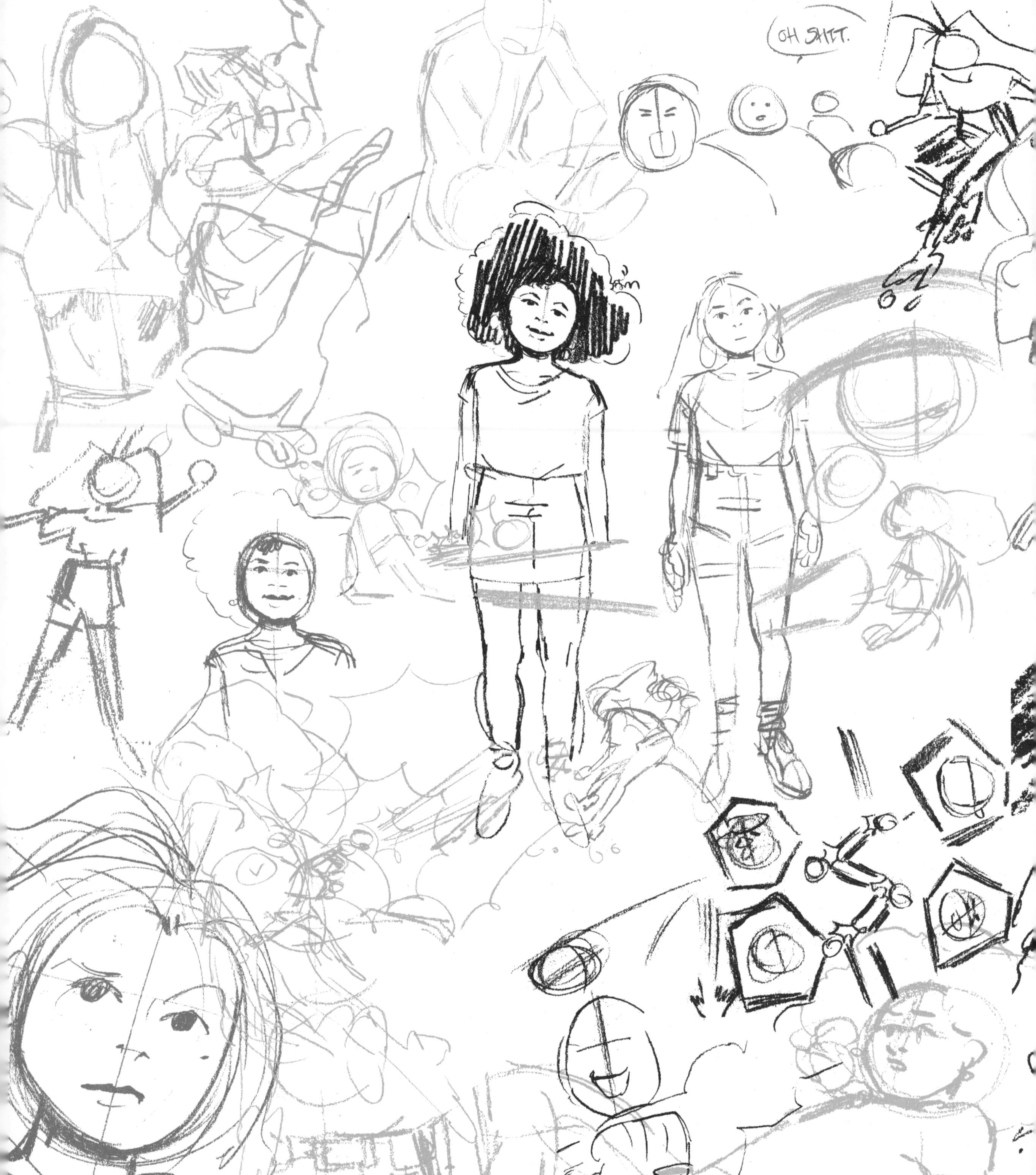
OH SHIT.

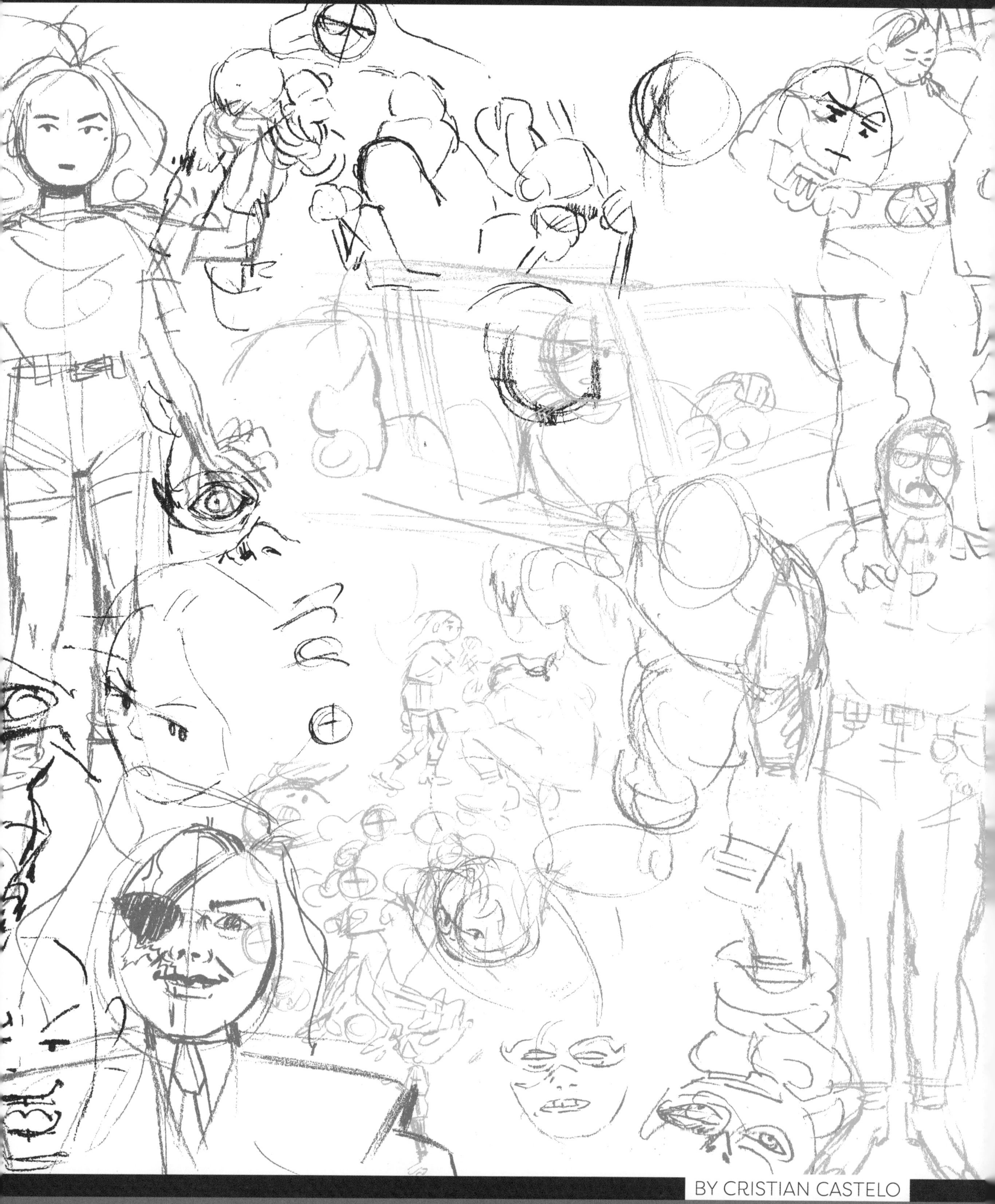

BY CRISTIAN CASTELO

CONTINUED IN **WILD VOL. 2**